POUGHKEEPSIE

DEBRA ANASTASIA

OMNIFIC PUBLISHING
LOS ANGELES

Omnific Publishing
1901 Avenue of the Stars, 2nd floor
Los Angeles, CA 90067
www.omnificpublishing.com

First Omnific eBook edition, November 2011
First Omnific trade paperback edition, November 2011

The characters and events in this book are fictitious.
Any similarity to real persons, living or dead,
is coincidental and not intended by the author.

Library of Congress Cataloguing-in-Publication Data

Anastasia, Debra.
    Poughkeepsie / Debra Anastasia – 1st ed.
    ISBN 978-1-936305-94-0
    1. Contemporary Romance — Fiction. 2. Mental Illness — Fiction.
    3. Homelessness — Fiction. 4. Train Station — Fiction.
    I. Title

                10 9 8 7 6 5 4 3 2 1

Cover Design by Micha Stone and Amy Brokaw
Interior Book Design by Coreen Montagna
Tattoo Design (used on cover and interior) by Shannon Lumetta
Shalumetta.com

Printed in the United States of America

This story is for my daredevil readers.
Its home is in your hands.

1

Green Eyes

Livia parked her aging Escort in one of the last remaining spots on the back row of the Park and Ride. *Crap. Am I running late?* She sprinted for the platform to make the 7:10 train departing from Poughkeepsie.

I am fulfilling my dream, she told herself with every hurried breath. *Dreams hurt. My calves hurt. I hate heels.*

Livia's job as a professor's assistant this semester certainly made grad school more affordable, but every fiber of her being longed for the sweatpants and baggy jeans most of the other students wore to class. By the time she got to the platform, there was much outfit readjustment necessary.

After making herself presentable again, Livia looked up to find the usual suspects waiting in the crisp, fall-morning air — mostly businesspeople headed to work, it seemed. Livia nodded and smiled to each person. It seemed everyone had a return smile for Livia. It was a simple human action she provided like clockwork, even to the homeless man always slumped under the overhang in the shade.

His green eyes seemed to wait for hers without fail, but as soon as the smile reached her lips, his gaze scurried away like a frightened mouse. He hardly looked at anyone, and never asked for money. Livia had come to the train station each weekday morning since she started studying clinical psychology in the city last summer, and she'd spent quite a few mornings "diagnosing" the homeless gentleman.

She always found him in the same spot when she got off the return train at night, and again she'd find his eyes and smile into them. She wondered what could have happened to a seemingly healthy man in his twenties that would leave him on the streets.

Crazy.

The nickname the waiting passengers had given him was grating and harsh to her ears. Granted, the man did spend a good amount of time running his fingers over a flat piece of cardboard, as if he were typing or playing the piano. But calling him Crazy seemed to dehumanize the man in the onlookers' eyes. Livia's nickname for him was Green Eyes, as his were spectacular — the clearest jade and almost glowing.

Livia put in her ear buds and plugged the cord into her iPod.

Wrong song.

She stabbed quickly at the buttons, and in the unintentional silence that ensued, she heard the conversation of a group of teens next to her.

"How about we give that homeless ass a wedgie he won't forget?"

Sneaking a peek out of the corner of her eye, she noticed there were three burly boys. She curled her lip in disdain at their snickering.

"Better yet, let's strip him naked and throw him on the train."

Enthusiastic backslapping rewarded this novel idea. The boys seemed quite proud of themselves.

What the hell are they even doing up this early?

One of the thugs answered Livia's internal question. "Danny, going sightseeing with your aunt's going to be boring as piss. Let's have some fun."

The group headed in Green Eyes' direction. Livia slid the ear buds into her pocket and looked around. The other people waiting for the train seemed oblivious, their backs turned to the teens.

Didn't they just hear what I heard?

In the next beat she got it. *They don't care if Crazy gets a thrashing.*

The teens now stood in front of Green Eyes, taunting him.

"Hey, stinky bastard!" The tallest teen kicked Green Eyes' shoe lightly, then harder. "You're making our wait unsanitary. You're going to pay for that."

The smallest teen grabbed Green Eyes' ever-present cardboard and began flinging it back and forth with the middle-sized idiot like a Frisbee. Livia looked desperately at the men in suits scattered along the platform.

They're dressed the part, but not one of them is a gentleman.

Decision made, Livia strode over to the jerk holding the cardboard above his head and jabbed him in the armpit, stealing it back when he flinched. She put her heels right in front of Green Eyes' legs and faced his attackers.

"You'll leave right now." She tried to infuse as much venom she could into the words.

"Lady, we're just having some fun with our friend here."

Standing close to the tallest one, she could see he would make a handsome man someday. *With a heart as black as hell.*

Livia could feel Green Eyes standing up behind her. Then she caught his reflection in the shortest attacker's sunglasses. He was easily six feet tall. The teens' faces registered shock as he unfurled himself. But instead of trying put the fear of God in the bullies, he whispered in her ear.

"You're going to miss your train."

Livia turned her face slightly but kept her eyes on the tall teen. "I'm good right here. Thanks, though." She put the cardboard behind her back to keep it safe.

"Oh, I didn't realize this fart was your boyfriend," the tallest teen taunted. "You should tell his lazy ass to get a job and stop living off the taxpayers' money."

Livia snorted. "Do *you* even have a job? You're like, twelve."

She didn't get to hear his retort because Green Eyes murmured in her ear again.

"Please, miss, don't get hurt on my account."

"I wasn't planning on it." As she spoke, Livia pulled out her pepper spray. The teens took a step back, just as the train pulled up with a huge clatter. "Get on the train and I'll forget this ever happened." She licked her lips and wiggled her trigger finger.

The authority she pretended to have seemed to finally reach them. They backed away to join the crowd boarding the train, still throwing insults and trying to save face as the doors closed on them and the train pulled away and disappeared.

Now that Livia was alone with Green Eyes, uneasiness pooled in her stomach. Nothing was as desolate as a train platform just after the train left.

She heard him in her ear again. "You didn't have to do that."

When Livia turned, she had to tip her head back to see his face as she handed him his cardboard. *He's beautiful.*

The training she'd received from her father about being alone with a strange man tickled the edges of her brain, but she refused to acknowledge it.

"If they'd caused you pain, I'd never have been able to live with myself," he said as he backed up a step.

"Watching you get attacked would have been more painful than taking a slug to the face," Livia said. "You might want to find another place to sit. Those idiots could cook up a plan for revenge."

Instead of being the friendly advice Livia intended, her words seem to slice into him.

Why is he in such pain?

"I can't leave." Green Eyes took a huge breath. "This is the only place where I get to see you."

He looked like a man who'd just bet his entire fortune and laid his cards on the table.

Livia considered him again. *I should be thinking "stalker" or "freak" or "Run!" But he looks so hopeful.*

Livia took a deep breath and held out her hand. "I'm Livia McHugh. It's nice to meet you."

His green eyes sparkled. "Blake Hartt. It's a pleasure to make your acquaintance."

When his long, slim fingers engulfed Livia's hand, she bit her lip to hold in the wash of tender emotion.

They stood in the silence of new greetings. Livia could scarcely believe the tingling she felt in her hand. She rubbed her palm on her skirt to get the feeling to stop. Blake's eyes followed her hand, and his face registered shame.

Oh no! He thinks I think his hand's dirty.

Livia quickly put her hand on her face, close to her mouth. She was rewarded with an almost-smile from Blake. At a loss for what to say, she watched him shuffle his feet and peek at her from under his long lashes.

Livia took a chance. "It's nice to know your name. I always called you—"

"Crazy. I know what they call me." Blake shifted his gaze to the empty platform, brazenly glowering at the people who weren't there anymore.

"No. I called you Green Eyes in my head, but Blake fits you nicely." Livia watched the understanding reach his face.

"Oh. I like that better." His voice was so quiet and grateful. Livia found herself glaring at the invisible people as well.

The morning sun broke through on its daily climb up the trees, and Blake shuffled backward, deeper into his shade.

"Are you okay?" Livia asked. He reacted as if the sunlight was lava.

"Yes. I'll be fine. I just need to stay in the shade. I'm sort of…allergic to the sun." He shrugged and looked sheepish. "The next train is at seven twenty-six. Will that be satisfactory in getting you where you need to go?"

Livia noticed they were not alone anymore. "I'll be a little late for class—I go to school in the city—but it'll be fine."

Blake nodded and motioned toward the front of the platform. "You better get up there. I'd like to see you get a seat for once." He ran a hand through his dark blond hair.

Livia never even attempted to find a seat—it just wasn't worth the effort. Despite their refined clothes, people fought like wild animals to make sure their rumps were comfortable.

"I'd feel better if you'd go somewhere else for today. I'm going to worry about those idiots coming back."

"Okay. If it'll make you feel better, I'll do it. Have a good day at school, Livia." Blake slouched down again and sat on the ground, his hands resting on the flat cardboard in front him of like a touchstone.

"Have a great day, Blake." Livia continued to linger. She hated leaving him here, defenseless.

"I've already had the most amazing day." He glanced at Livia's eyes, and she could see victory in his. She had a feeling that that they had both felt the same intense pull.

As she got on the train, Livia felt her cell phone vibrate. She pulled it out, but when she saw it was Chris, her boyfriend, she put it back in her bag. She wondered about herself as she sent him yet again to voicemail.

Unbelievably, Livia found an open window seat. She turned toward Blake and found him giving her a casual salute. She waved, but instead of waving back he just smiled like a man who'd won the Lotto.

Livia was relieved to see Blake's usual spot empty when she got off the train that evening. He'd listened to her suggestion. Then as she stepped over the gap between the train and the concrete platform, she felt a shiver all the way up her spine. She gasped as she spotted his tall, lanky frame waiting just outside the train's doors.

He looked instantly regretful when he realized he'd startled her and took a step back.

Another commuter stepped out from behind Livia and asked, "Is this piece of trash bothering you, lady?"

Livia suppressed the need to punch the guy in the stomach. "No, he's a friend of mine," she said. "I'm just surprised to see him." She made a point of reaching out and grabbing Blake's hand.

The tingling started again. Blake looked down at their clasped hands like he'd found a leprechaun in the wild. The commuter shook his head and went on. Livia dragged Blake away from the emptying train.

"I thought you were going to be somewhere else." She used her sternest voice.

An assortment of feelings flashed through his eyes, but his smile remained in place. He glanced again at their hands twirled together. "I *was* somewhere else," he finally said, pointing to the woods. "But I wanted to escort you to your car, to make sure you're safe."

Livia could hear her father freaking out in her mind. He would hate the idea of Livia's brand-new homeless stalker walking her to her isolated car.

Blake let go of her hand to hold his up in a non-threatening manner. "Unless you're afraid of me."

His face looked as though the mere thought poisoned him. Livia couldn't help but admire his full lips and strong jaw.

"No, Blake, I trust you. I'd be honored to have an escort to my Escort. I'm a little afraid of the dark." Livia tucked a lock of brown hair behind her ear.

"I'm not afraid of the dark at all, so this way, milady, to your chariot." Blake held out an elbow, formally.

He looked so debonair in his worn jeans. His hair was unruly, but looked clean and shiny. This man was a contradiction.

"Thank you, kind sir." She took his arm, and they began to ascend the ridiculously steep stairs to the parking lot. "I'm grateful for the company, but why me, Blake?" She looked at her feet as they walked.

"Livia." He seemed thrilled to let the word roll off his tongue. "Do you know that I'm invisible?"

Now I'll find out why this achingly beautiful man spends his time lumped in front of a piece of cardboard.

"No one has really seen me in years." Blake looked at the sky. "Sometimes I wonder how they know I don't have a home. I try to dress decently." He waved a hand at his jeans and army jacket. "I think it just seeps out of me. I'm not the same as everyone else." He shook his head, his eyes reflecting a weary despair. As he looked at Livia again, the despair was chased away with a grin. "But when you saw me for the first time, you actually saw me. You *saw* me, and then you smiled like I was just the same as everyone else on that platform."

Livia's eyes filled with tears. Blake was right. No one saw the homeless — even if they had to step around someone whose bed was the sidewalk.

Blake waited as she dug for her keys in her purse. "You should have those out and ready to go when you're alone." He motioned for the keys when she found them. "May I?"

Livia weighed the options. She hated the thought of mistrusting Blake, but handing him her keys would seem so dangerous in any other setting.

The air thick as he waited for her decision, hand extended.

I can't make him feel like less. I have to treat him like I would a date dropping me off at the door.

She handed him the keys. Blake unlocked her door and held it open. Livia settled inside, and Blake handed the keys back to her.

"Drive safely, brave Livia." Blake closed the door and waited until her vehicle purred to life. Then he turned and walked back the way they'd come. Livia nodded with her decision to trust him. It had somehow created a bridge, giving him a gentleman's job.

Livia's cell phone rang, and she answered it distractedly. "Hey, Kyle. What's up?"

Her super-excited sister could hardly breathe. "Oh my God, Livia! Chris was just here to ask Dad for your hand in marriage!" she gasped. Then a moment later she added, "I wonder if I was supposed to tell you that. Oops."

"Wow. That's really great." Livia could not make her voice match her sister's enthusiasm. *Why?*

Just then, Blake turned around in the poured-silver light of her headlights and gave her a sparkling smile.

2

COOLER OF DEBRIS

In the weeks that followed, Livia played a new game every day. It was always some version of "Ignore Chris and Pretend Nothing's Wrong With That." She was getting quite good at it, and so far it had prevented him from actually proposing.

In her heart she knew she was being very disloyal to their long courtship, but for whatever reason, the idea of engagement was mixed with a heavy dose of dread anytime it bubbled to the surface. And when she wasn't with Blake each morning and evening, she was thinking about him. Chris had slipped way down the list to somewhere between laundry and the Escort's overdue oil change.

Not helping was Kyle, who had gone into hyper-drive and purchased ten different bridal magazines, even though there'd been no proposal. The sight of them on Livia's dresser unsettled her. She kept moving them from place to place around the house and finding things to do besides flip through them. *Of course I love Chris. I must. We've been dating since we started college. Marriage is the next logical step.* Still, Livia ignored the magazines, and as much as possible, she ignored Chris. "It's just very busy these days," she told him. "School is really kicking my butt right now. I have to focus."

Livia had trouble concentrating in the mornings as she anticipated Blake looking for her as she came down the steps at the station. She began arriving earlier and earlier, blaming her change in scheduling on wanting a better parking spot when her family asked.

But it was a lie. She just craved more time with Blake. During those minutes each morning and evening, she felt herself becoming someone she'd never been before. Not someone else, really, but fully herself. She basked in Blake's attention.

Depending on the sun, he sometimes now met her as she pulled in. Her heart would pound as she glimpsed his familiar form from the top of the stairs. Twice she almost wrecked her car because he was staring at her.

When the sun was out, she would walk to find him in his shade. He always stood as she approached. They'd fill the minutes before the train with happy banter and always had so much to tell each other. Blake had inquired politely about Livia's schoolwork and what she studied, but she quickly changed the subject. She was proud to be going to grad school, but Chris had made enough comments condemning her field of study that she was shy about it now. During their last phone conversation he'd reminded her that psychology was the study of psychos. He didn't understand her need to listen to those who might not have anyone else to confide in.

Instead of sharing insights from her studies, Livia made mental notes whenever something amusing happened so she could share it with Blake. Sometimes her cheeks hurt from laughing when he finally held her car door open for her in the evening. He was there every day and every night. For her.

One morning she arrived with her breakfast in her hands, trying to buy even more train-station time. He seemed so distracted by her simple bagel with egg. She wanted to beat herself over the head with it. He was hungry.

I'm a dumbass. Of course. She'd been so selfish—just pleased to be adored and never once thinking, let alone asking, about how he got to her, how he survived. He wasn't an angel, but a live person who needed sustenance and shelter to survive.

The next morning, determined to do better, she arrived with a beautiful breakfast sandwich tucked into her bag. *How many mornings have I smiled at him?* She grinned as she got out of the car and on the entire walk to the platform. As she started down the large staircase, she saw him. The desire to be near him suddenly became a physical presence. *Whoa.*

Today Blake stood in his shady spot with Livia's smile echoed on his face. She had to force herself not to run to him.

"You're early." His eyes stayed on her face.

"I made you a sandwich," she announced, presenting it proudly.

Instead of more smiling, Blake's whole face disengaged. He put his now lifeless gaze on the ground and nodded with grave seriousness.

"I'm not a charity case." His words had sharp edges.

Livia bit her lip. "I make a really great breakfast. I just wanted to share."

Embarrassment crawled up her throat like heartburn. She'd obviously crossed a very prominent line in the sand.

"I didn't earn that sandwich." He stared at it like it might come alive.

"Well, from my point of view you did. You've escorted me to my car, and you've entertained me for weeks. I appreciate it." She watched his eyes for a sign of life.

"Any man should be expected to shepherd an unattended lady to her car." Blake now moved his gaze to her feet.

Of course, he wants to be a thoughtful gentleman, not a trained seal getting food for tricks.

"Are you saying I'm too delicate to walk myself to my car? I shared my fear of the dark with you, and now here you are throwing it in my face." Livia squinted at him and peeked through the lashes of one eye. *Please let this work.*

His eyes flashed to her face. "No, of *course* not. I have no desire to hurt your feelings."

"Well, as an empowered woman, I've decided to repay your kindness. I have no intention of putting a gentleman to a task and not reciprocating in some way." Livia held her nose up with mock-exaggerated dignity.

His tone became a bit more playful. "Like I said, that wasn't a task, it's what manners require. Now, I might be able to take that sandwich if you were also giving these other fifty people on the platform a nice bagel, but I only see the one."

"You're really not going to eat it?"

He shook his head, his hair falling into his bashful eyes.

Fine. Livia changed the subject and chatted politely with Blake about the weather until the train arrived. She didn't mention the breakfast when she saw him in the evening, and left him a bit more quickly than usual. She had to stop at the store.

I'll feed fifty goddamn people every freaking morning if I have to. Just so he can eat one sandwich.

She woke before dawn the next morning and was a whirling dervish in the kitchen by five o'clock. Cracked eggshells covered the counter around the sink, and foil-wrapped circles were stacked on every available square inch of table — and some of the chairs.

About an hour in, Kyle stumbled onto the scene through the back door. "What the hell?" she grumbled. She pulled her messy hair out of her face to better examine the ridiculous preparations. "Are you having, like, one of those sleep-drug-induced wakemares?"

"You're up already? Wait — are you just getting home? That's what you were wearing yesterday," Livia said, eyebrows arched. "And I don't take sleep drugs. What's a wakemare?" She held her dripping hands over the sink.

Kyle opened the fridge and grabbed the OJ. She chugged it like she was in a Tropicana commercial and burped loudly when she was done.

Livia wrinkled her nose. "You're disgusting."

Kyle gave her sister the finger. "You're a pecker sniffer." Kyle lived to shock Livia any chance she got. "A wakemare—I don't know, people take sleep meds and think they're sleeping but really they're up ordering pizza and then doing the delivery guy."

Livia rolled her eyes. "Are you going to tell me where you've been?" She cracked more eggs into a huge bowl.

"Are you going to tell me why you're the scourge of every chicken in Poughkeepsie?" Kyle sniffed her armpit and made a face.

After a moment of silent impasse, the sisters concluded their discussion by sticking their tongues out at each other.

Forty-five minutes later, Livia raced the clock as she packed the sandwiches into grocery bags, with one very special bagel in a cooler. If she missed the train, this whole rigmarole would be for nothing.

When she arrived at the station, with a screech, the sun was out, so she knew she'd be carting her bounty down the stairs by herself. After navigating the steep steps, feeling a little like a pack mule in the process, Livia sat demurely on a bench, trying her best to ignore Blake. He watched her from his shady spot with a curious grin. Finally she looked over her shoulder and pulled out the sign she'd made for the occasion:

Breakfast sandwiches for friggin' everybody!!

She held it so Blake could read it. He shook his head and bit his lip. "You're crazy," he mouthed.

She blew him a kiss, and he pretended to catch it. She felt her hot blush travel from her neck to her cheeks. All their previous conversations could be construed as friendly, but this was flat-out flirting. Livia got tingles all over whenever she glanced in his direction.

Her "customers" accepted their usual smile from her, with the added bonus of a sandwich. Some said thank you, and some complained that the eggs were cold. Livia locked eyes with Blake again, and he shook his head while leaning against the station's brick wall.

When she was down to two sandwiches, she closed up shop. The last few arrivals on the platform, who remained sandwich-less, grumbled. But Livia shook her head and clutched the cooler behind her back as she went over to see Blake.

"Now don't let me down," she said as she stepped into his shade. "That was a lot of work to get you to try my cooking."

"You're a stubborn woman," he said appreciatively. He pushed away from the wall and met her in the middle.

Livia couldn't take her eyes off his lips. "So I'm pretty sure we had a deal, right? I get the pleasure of forcing my sandwich on you now."

"When you put it that way, I must accept your kind gift." He nodded formally.

Livia wrinkled her nose and smiled at this triumph over his obviously strict code of standards. She handed him the cooler, and they sat on the ground. He seemed to get lost in the food. He was obviously fighting an eternal battle to avoid sucking it down like a vacuum.

He's so hungry.

Livia was furious with herself all over again for not bringing food before. Lumped in the shadows every morning, he was hungry and she hadn't fed him. It seemed sacrilegious.

Blake wiped his mouth with the napkin she'd provided. "That was exquisite. I humbly thank you."

Livia was quick to respond. "And I you."

She repacked his trash and zippered up the cooler. His eyes followed her hands taking care of him.

"It's a lovely morning," Livia prompted. She just wanted to hear his voice some more.

"It's a lovely morning," he repeated.

Instead of taking in the splendor of the emerging fall colors and the choppy Hudson River, his eyes scanned her face like it was a million miles of heaven.

"Tell me, Livia, what did you do last night?" He cocked his head to the side.

"I did my homework for class, did laundry, planned a ginormous breakfast. Boring stuff." *Ignored a pile of magazines more threatening than an assassin.*

"What's troubled you? Your eyes look stormy right now," he said.

Livia smoothed her forehead with her fingertips. This man, having eaten for the first time in God knows when, made her worries about the upcoming proposal seem petty and foolish.

"Just girl stuff." Her eyes found his green ones again.

"Are you saying I'm too delicate to hear about your girl stuff?" Blake asked in a higher octave voice, his eyes wide.

Livia ran her hand through her hair and grinned. "Touché."

"Tell me." His voice was sexy and intense, like a spy trying to acquire sensitive information.

Livia shook her head as she began to explain. "Well...my boyfriend asked my father if he could marry me a few weeks ago—almost a month now, I think—and he's hasn't actually proposed."

Blake's eyes registered the verbal punch. He seemed to swallow something that wasn't there.

"But I'm okay with that," Livia added quickly. "Actually, I'm glad...I don't know. I can't figure out what's going on with me, but I haven't even wanted to see him."

"Has something happened?" Blake asked. "You seem distressed."

Safe. I can tell him. Livia took a deep breath. "Chris and I have been together forever—we met when I started college. I know marriage is the next step. It's just..." Livia searched for words to explain her dread.

Livia was surprised when Blake didn't fill the silence with a guess, as Chris would have. He let her complete her own thoughts.

"Chris and I just don't see the world the same way. It took me a while to realize that, and then I kept thinking he was going to change—suddenly discover he's not a teenager anymore." She sighed. "You know the best compliment he's ever given me? 'You're pretty enough to get by.' He's said it so many times."

Blake waited until she set her deep gray eyes on him. "He has no idea the beauty in front of him. He's a fool."

His words made her heart glow. She smiled and looked at her hands.

"Ten minutes until your train." Blake nodded at the platform filling with people.

Livia turned to survey the crowd. She wondered how Blake knew the time; he had no watch.

His eyes shifted over the waiting people. "They worry about you because you talk to me."

Livia realized the other commuters were stealing glances at them. She turned back to Blake like a flower seeking sun.

"They can kiss my ass. I'd rather talk to you than stand with those spineless nimrods any day."

Blake looked fretful. "Livia, you're not invisible to them. There's a stigma for talking to me."

"They mean nothing to me."

"Be that as it may, I'd like to see you have a seat again, so you better go stand with the spineless nimrods." He stood. "Would you like me to hold on to your cooler since it's empty now? I'll return it to you tonight."

He motioned to her arm, but Livia had to step back into his self-imposed shade prison to pass the cooler to him.

"That's so thoughtful. Thank you." Livia smiled.

Blake gently traced his fingertips over her hand before he took the strap. The jolt from this touch was more than Livia could ever remember feeling during Chris's sloppy kisses.

Since they seemed to be sharing truths today, Livia decided to take one last leap. "So, Blake, what are the symptoms of your sun allergy?"

She expected a rash, maybe hives. Nothing prepared her for his answer.

Blake looked around the platform covertly before he locked his gaze on hers. "Livia, I'm made of glass, but it only shows in the sun. I can't be caught in sunlight or everyone will know what I am." He looked eager for her to understand.

Now it was Livia's turn to swallow something that wasn't there. She recovered as quickly as Blake had. "I'm sorry to hear that, Blake. But I bet you're very beautiful in the sun." She watched as his face became triumphant.

He thinks I believe him.

Then, with her world radically different than it had been even a few minutes before, Livia walked toward the arriving train in a fog. Onboard, she magically got a seat and a thumbs-up from Blake when she looked back at him on the platform. She waved, and he smiled like she was the eighth wonder of the world. Livia didn't realize she had tears on her cheeks until the train hit the Marble Hill stop.

I'm an idiot—of course he's broken. He must be so very broken.

On the train ride home, Livia tried to stop chastising herself. She'd spent the day avoiding everything she should have been doing. With an entire faculty of psychologists around her, Livia had failed to ask a single one about Blake's particular delusion. She also kept sending Chris to voicemail and ignoring his text messages. She felt another twinge of guilt as she freshened her vanilla lip gloss and fluffed her hair just before the train pulled in to Poughkeepsie. As the car emptied of its weary passengers, Livia looked for Blake's messy hair and lanky frame.

He stood dead center in the midst of the flow of exiting commuters. Livia's anticipatory smile turned into outright giggling when she saw his delighted face. People continued to pour out around them, but Livia and Blake stood fast like two river stones, immovable in the current.

She finally addressed him. "Hi."

"Hello, Livia." His silvery voice surrounded her name like a veil.

One of the commuters shoved Livia from behind. Not hard, just enough to let her know the regularly scheduled traffic pattern had been interrupted. With one hand, Blake steadied Livia and with the other, he prevented the male commuter from passing.

Livia was about to tell Blake to let the man go — *No harm, no foul*—when she caught a glimpse of his face. He looked like an avenging angel.

"Apologize to the lady," Blake's voice was smooth, calm, and deadly. He'd also unleashed his bright green eyes on the poor bastard, who looked like he might wet his pants.

"Sorry." The guy looked relieved when Blake nodded and let him pass.

"Are you okay?" The concern in Blake's voice made Livia laugh again. He was acting like she'd just been in a train wreck.

"I'm perfectly fine. You *do* know I go to the city every day? I get shoved all the time."

Instead of quieting the riot in his eyes, this news made Blake seem even more troubled. The train rumbled off behind Livia, and they were finally alone in the gloriously deserted station.

"Did you have a nice day?" he asked, watching as if her answer was all that mattered in the world.

"It's better now." *Too much, Livia.* She had no idea why her mouth was so free around him. The mere presence of Blake removed some sort of filter in her mind.

He held out her cooler like a prize.

"Thank you very much for taking care of it." Their fingertips grazed again at the exchange. Something inside the cooler rattled around, and Livia arched an eyebrow.

"You could open it," he offered.

He looked in her eyes as she unzipped the cooler. It was chock full of debris. She felt her heart stop beating in despair. She lifted out the pile of leaves and rocks. Blake looked so expectant.

He thinks I understand what this means. Livia let the silence grow, having no idea what would bring the magic between them back. *Maybe he is what they say.* Just thinking that awful thought put a puncture right in the center of Livia's hope.

In the next moment Blake's face fell as he saw her confusion. Embarrassment filled his eyes, and he studied the ground.

"Let me take a good look at this." Livia headed for the closest streetlamp.

It isn't just debris. She almost cried with relief. Blake had picked out the most exquisite of the fall leaves. Each one had exceptional color. Some even had recognizable shapes.

"A cat! This one has orange in the shape of a cat," Livia nearly shouted.

Blake bit his lip as she discovered the sweet secret in every leaf. The stones came next—some had unusual colors and some had a miraculous little stream of crystals dividing them in half. The last two were plain gray.

Livia looked puzzled and whispered, "I have no idea why these are special."

Blake dared to touch her face. "They're the exact color of your eyes."

Livia covered his hand with her own and moved it down to her mouth. She put a sweet kiss in the center of his palm. *His beautiful hands went through all this trouble for me.*

Blake's eyes flared with desire, making them look greener.

Livia had an unbidden thought of the last time Chris had touched her. He'd twirled her in front of his buddies. "*Hey, her face ain't much, but her ass is slammin'.*" Chris had pled "joking around" when she confronted him later, but the whole scene left Livia feeling gloomy.

"It's getting late, Livia. I think I should walk you back to your car," Blake said.

He made no motion to remove his hand. It felt soft and cool on her mouth. Livia felt a rush of panic as she let go of his hand to check her vibrating cell phone.

"I put it on vibrate so I wouldn't have to talk to Chris."

She'd missed five calls from her father. Livia groaned as the phone lit up again in her hand.

"Dad's calling." She pressed the send button. "I'm fine, Dad," she said by way of greeting. "I know, I'm sorry. I ran into a friend at the train station and we got to talking. I'm getting into my car right now." She sent Blake a panicked glance.

He pulled her by the hand in the direction of her car and did the perfect impression of a dinging open-car-door noise. Livia smiled over her father's worried, angry ranting. She'd been with Blake for over an hour. *It felt like minutes.*

Blake took her keys and opened her car door again. Livia promised her father she'd see him soon and disconnected their call. She couldn't help but notice how brisk the night had gotten. Concern must have shown on her face.

As if reading her mind, Blake made a quiet plea. "Please don't think of me that way. Let me be the guy at the train station."

"You're not the guy at the train station. You're my Blake."

Livia gave the Escort a bit of gas as the engine turned over.

She watched as Blake silently mouthed, *my Blake.*

When she glanced in the rearview mirror, he was standing in the middle of the road. Her red taillights blazed over his skin. He looked like he was on fire.

3

SERENDIPITOUS RENDEZVOUS

Livia's father began her evening with the first of two conversations she didn't feel like having. He spent an ungodly amount of time expressing his disdain for vibrating phones, specifically Livia's, which had delayed their contact at the train station.

Then Livia finally talked to Chris. She started by delivering a small white lie about a rundown battery to explain her latest refusal to answer her cell phone.

"Hey, Livia. You had me scared shitless. I thought I was going to have to run all around Manhattan looking for you."

Chris's concern seemed unusual. He hadn't made any effort past his phone to sustain their relationship in weeks. She covered her lips with her hand and remembered Blake's soft touch. *Betrayal.*

Livia prided herself on loyalty, and her heart wasn't feeling loyal to Chris.

"My grandma had a mild stroke last night." Chris's voice cracked on the word "stroke."

Livia groaned internally. *This* was the one time Chris needed her in all the years they'd been dating?

"Chris, I'm so sorry. I know how much you love her."

Everyone loved Chris's Grandma. She insisted on being called Mrs. Grandma, even by people she'd just met.

"What can I do to help?" Livia asked.

Chris hemmed and hawed for a few minutes before he finally got around to his request. "Well, she comes home tomorrow night, and I'd really love for her to have a nice meal. My mom will be cleaning at Grandma's, but her cooking isn't exactly a special treat."

Livia agreed with Chris there. His mother implemented "The Magic Pot"—a plug-in electric fry pan—and an alarming selection of ingredients far too often for anyone else's tastes. They decided to meet at Mrs. Grandma's at six o'clock to make dinner. Then, as if the medical incident had burst the dam of his memories, Chris proceeded to regale Livia with all his favorite stories about his grandmother. It was kind of sweet at first, but then Livia realized the explanations were becoming more and more about him and less about Mrs. Grandma. Her eyes were heavy long before he decided it was time to stop talking.

The moment Livia's eyes opened the next morning, her brain said, *So little train time*, and she sprang into action. She'd wanted to arrive even earlier this morning to make up for the quick exit she'd have to make this evening, but after staying up late listening to Chris, she'd overslept.

Livia had twenty minutes to wait for her train when she arrived at the station, but she still ran all the way to the platform. It was another cloudless day, so Blake was predictably in his self-imposed shadow cave.

He was sitting this time and kept his head tilted down as he peered up at her. It looked just like an image from a fashion magazine. Blake was so handsome—Livia couldn't believe the other women on the platform weren't taking cell phone pictures of him.

He's still invisible.

This time Livia had packed a small picnic blanket. She quickly spread it out and opened the cooler for Blake.

"Good morning, Livia," he said, looking at her oddly.

"Sorry! Hi. Good morning, Blake." She was so rushed she forgot the simple greeting.

"You look tired. Did you sleep well?" Blake ignored his sandwich.

"No, I didn't. I was on the phone with Chris most of last night." Livia was busy fixing Blake's napkin, but when she glanced again at his face she saw such hurt there.

"His grandma had a mild stroke. I won't be able to stay long this evening. I've got to make her welcome-home-from-the-hospital dinner." She motioned to his still-hot breakfast.

"Livia, you're too kind. I'll take this breakfast as a token of our friendship—thank you—but do you ever do anything just for yourself?" Blake lifted the sandwich and waited for her answer.

"Talking to you." She watched him go motionless as her filter yet again refused to engage. "I do that because I'm addicted to the feeling it gives me."

Blake put the sandwich down and watched her like she was a bomb with a lit fuse.

"See, right there? Telling you that was just for me. I should consider other people's feelings," Livia lamented.

Blake smiled at her, finally. "Have you ever seen a shooting star, Livia?"

She nodded, perplexed at the change in conversation.

"It's very beautiful, right?" He nodded with her this time. "It makes you wonder — is that shooting star just a happy accident or has the universe had it planned for a thousand years?" He tilted his face to the sky, his eyes tracking an imaginary star as it screamed to earth. He looked back to her. "Either way, you can't stop it. You can beg it to slow down or you can just enjoy the show."

"Am I the star in this story or you?"

Blake wrinkled his nose and chuckled. "Was that a bad analogy? I meant *we're* the star, Livia. Us. This." He shrugged his shoulders like it was the most obvious thing in the world. "Us being in the same atmosphere is either a great cosmic catastrophe or the most serendipitous *rendezvous*." Blake pronounced the French word like a closeted foreign language teacher.

The pull toward him came from her center. Her eyes never left his face as she moved to her hands and knees. She crawled slowly over the blanket, the breakfast, his legs, until her hands rested on either side of his hips. His smile lifted only on one side. He took care to stay very still, but his mouth opened slightly as she approached. This close to Blake she could smell him. *Fresh, sweet fall leaves and mint.*

He smelled like a dedicated lover of Mother Earth. The mint was his breath. It wasn't a manufactured toothpaste, but a marvelous herb scent. Livia had never wanted anything more than to taste his lips right then.

"Would you mind very much if I kissed you?" she whispered.

Blake shook his head.

Livia leaned in and took a gentle kiss. His lips were soft, and they tasted perfect. The smell of his skin combined with that wonderful taste almost made her collapse.

Blake steadied her by placing his hand against her chest. His splayed fingers must have felt how fast her heart was beating. Livia pulled back just a bit to see his eyes again. They were half closed and shimmering.

It was his turn to whisper. "Would you mind very much if I kissed you?"

She shook her head and waited, very still. Blake lifted his other hand to touch her face. Livia had to work not to press her skin into his fingers.

His touch was light as a breeze. He traced the features of her face. He trailed his fingers down to her throat and up to her earlobe. *He's so gentle.*

As soon as the thought flashed through Livia's mind, Blake grabbed a fistful of her hair, yanking it enough to make her gasp. Then he kissed the living hell out of her.

Oh, oh, OH. Livia felt her arms begin to shake, and Blake took more of her weight onto his forearm. She'd had no idea kissing was an art form. She knew now. Blake had to be the one to end the kiss.

"You better get over there with the passengers." He could only stare at her lips.

The train. Right. Crap.

Livia had forgotten they weren't alone. She tried to ignore the tremors in her hands as she cleaned up his smooshed breakfast.

"I'm so sorry I kneeled on your food." She tried to put it back together.

"Don't worry," he said. "I'm all good right now." And he was. He looked delighted and kept licking his lips, much to Livia's distraction. "May I take your cooler and blanket for you again?" He held out his hand.

"Please. Thank you very much," she replied.

Livia needed to go further onto the platform to catch the train, but a set of handcuffs seemed to bind her wrist to Blake's. He noticed her reluctance and motioned for her to enter his shade again. He bent at the waist and lifted her hand to his lips. Before he released her hand, he looked out at her from his under his eyelashes.

"Have a wonderful day, Livia. I vote for serendipitous *rendezvous.*"

Livia felt her mouth open a little when he added the French accent again. She stole glances at him as she finally moved to wait for the train.

"Homeleth humper."

Livia looked around to see where the weird words had originated. A balding man glared at her from over his smart phone. Livia pointed to her chest and gave the man a confused eyebrow lift.

"Yeth you. You're a homeleth humper." The man slowed his lisped speech so he could pronounce the insult more clearly.

Livia felt her rage ignite. "Well, Oily Comb-Over, looks like I need to buy you a load of Shut Your Mouth for your birthday."

Livia watched the man turn bright red. She heard Blake's words in her mind, *You're not invisible to them.*

Well, screw them. That was the best kiss of my life, and these jerks were lucky to witness it.

Livia now saw clearly what she needed to do. She would break up with Chris this weekend. She sighed with satisfaction and the lingering effects of Blake's kiss, now tattooed on her heart.

Livia spent a ridiculous amount of time deciding whether or not to buy the potato knish at Grand Central Station. She held the white paper bag in her hands. *Will he accept it without being insulted?* She'd crushed his breakfast being so forward this morning. She shook her head at her behavior. *Where does this confidence come from?*

Chris had once told her he was the only man who'd ever really want her. Instead of making her special, he made it sound like she was lucky he was willing to stoop to her level. "Nobody likes a chick reading books all the time," he liked to complain. "Why don't you live a little instead of always being at school?"

The thought of being out of their relationship gave Livia wings. Why had it taken her so long to see this? With the Poughkeepsie station next, she stood by the doors like one of the uptight commuters and was ready to disembark before the train had even stopped. Her eyes scanned the platform, and she almost fell off the train in her rush to find Blake. Finally, she saw him at the very outer edge of cement platform. His face looked different. *Swollen. Hurt.*

Everything Livia carried slid from her arms. She ran straight for him. When she'd closed the distance, her hands hovered just over his beaten face, not wanting to touch, but wishing she could heal. "Blake, what happened?"

He winced in obvious pain, but insisted on their regular greeting. "Hello, Livia. How was your day?"

"Stop. Stop that. Tell me what happened to you." She gently ran her fingers down the length of his chest. He gasped when she reached his ribs. "You're hurt."

Blake shook his head. "My life outside of this train station won't touch you." His green eyes swam with pain and determination.

No. No. "Blake, I'm begging you. I'm right here. Please talk to me," she implored him.

He tried to straighten his posture. "I regret to inform you that I lost your belongings today. I'll do my best to replace them," he tried to bow formally, but pain prevented it.

"Did someone beat you up for my cooler and blanket?" Livia asked.

Blake hung his head. "There were too many of them. I tried my best, but they thought the cooler might have something valuable in it."

His lip was bleeding. Livia's internal rage flared again. The thought of her beautiful Blake defending the honor of her empty cooler brought tears to her eyes, which she quickly blinked back.

He misread her emotions. "Was it terribly special? I'm so very sorry."

Livia put her finger on his lip, trying to stem the bleeding and his ridiculous words. "If you think I give a rat's ass about that cooler, you don't know me at all. Nothing I own is worth your pain."

She began an inventory of his possible injuries. His hands were scraped, his lip swollen, and his rib was obviously the worst of it. They were silent, the moonlight making his eyes luminescent.

Then, quietly, he took down one of his walls for her. "I know you."

"Blake, will you let me take you to the ER?" She already knew his answer.

"No, I can't pay for their services." He was adamant.

Dignified, proud.

"Well, walk me to my car then, please," she asked.

Blake insisted on helping her pick up the things she'd dropped, even though his pain had him breathing through his teeth.

If he doesn't die, I'm going to kill him for being stubborn.

He opened her car door and looked perplexed when she reached in and popped the trunk. Her father, John, never let her drive without a decent first aid kit.

Blake said nothing, but kept his eyes steady on Livia as she cleaned his wounds and covered what she could with bandages. When she'd done all the plastic kit would let her, she handed Blake the two aspirin thoughtfully included by the manufacturer. He swallowed them without the benefit of water.

"Thank you for not complaining about that," Livia said.

Blake nodded in acknowledgment.

"Come home with me. I can't leave you here like this." This time her voice cracked.

"My angel, you forget, you have to go make Mrs. Grandma her meal." Blake ran the back of his bandaged hand down Livia's cheek.

"Please. I won't be able to breathe from worrying about you." Livia didn't care how crazy she sounded.

"I don't think that's prudent. I don't want you bringing me home like a stray cat." His defenses were climbing back up. She'd asked too much.

"Okay. I'll see you Monday then?" The words felt like sandpaper on glass. Rough and unwanted.

"Yes, sweet Livia. I'll be here. Have no worries." He leaned down to press a kiss to her forehead.

He was gone into the darkness before Livia had closed her car door. The dashboard's green clock clocked taunted her. 5:55. She'd have to drive fast to get to Mrs. Grandma's.

Livia could never have imagined how many things would have changed by the time she pulled into the Park and Ride on Monday morning. A huge, glittering engagement ring from Chris kept distracting her from driving, and her concern about Blake's weekend welfare made her an almost speechless basket case.

It took her two tries to shift the car into park, and based on the burning rubber she could now smell, Livia knew she'd left the parking brake on for her commute. She gathered her things, including a delicious breakfast from the town bakery, and took off running.

Blake.

He leaned casually against the brick wall where his protective shade usually formed. The day's thick froth of clouds was a firm barrier from the sun. His swelling was gone, but he still had bruises. He glanced up and smiled like he hadn't seen her in years.

Livia set her bags down and walked right into him, feeling his arms close around her. She found the crook of his neck and placed a kiss there. She ran her hands all over his face and through his hair. *Here. He's here.*

The ring danced gaudily on her left hand. Blake caught it like a wayward butterfly.

"How did he trick you into this?" Blake looked amused instead of angry.

"Chris's a son of a bitch," Livia declared. "Well, that's not true. His mother's a really nice lady. I could throttle him, though."

Livia pushed herself away and started an animated pacing. "So there I am, making dinner for Mrs. Grandma—who is doing great by the way—and his whole family is in the kitchen. Chris drops to one knee and pulls this monstrosity out." Livia held her hand up. "He has the nerve to say 'Grandma wants to see me happy before she dies, so, Livia, will you marry me?' What the hell was I supposed to say? Mrs. Grandma is there with teary eyes, clapping. So I said yes — to her mostly, even though she's far from dying."

Blake had not moved, but he watched her with a grin.

"Come here," he said.

He held his hand out to her. Livia stepped in closer and let him pull her against him again. He lifted her left hand and smiled sadly.

"I'm pretty sure this isn't a real diamond." He searched her eyes for a moment. "Are you disappointed?"

"You know, I thought it was a little glassy looking. There's really no way he could afford a ring this big."

Blake shook his head along with her.

Livia took her hand from his and yanked at the metal band, but it wouldn't budge.

Tisking, Blake stilled her movements. "May I have a try?"

She nodded.

He placed his hand under hers gently and straightened her fingers. His touch felt like fire and ice and commanded her complete attention.

"Be gentle with yourself." Slowly, tenderly, he eased the ring from her finger, staring into her eyes. He placed the faux gem in her palm.

"Thanks. I know exactly what to do with this." Livia walked off the platform, into the grassy park, and down to the Hudson River. She flung the ring into the water with a satisfying splash. When she heard it, all of the feelings that bound her to Chris snapped like an overtaxed fishing line. In the wake was only relief.

Blake clapped as she returned to him. "Good show."

"I'm more than done with Chris." Livia picked up the large bakery bag.

"The spineless nimrods are going to get all the good seats," Blake warned.

"I was actually planning on playing hooky with you today, if you're comfortable with that." Livia had dressed in jeans and a fleece, rather than her teaching garb.

He put a stern look on his face that didn't quite reach his eyes. "Livia, I can't promote delinquent behavior."

"I want to see what a day is like for you, but we could just stay here." Livia crossed her fingers and peeked at him.

Blake hugged her hard and sucked in a hiss of air as she squeezed back. *The rib is still healing.*

When he'd composed himself, Blake kissed the top of her head. "Like I could ever say no to you."

4

İnto His World

Livia felt the thrill of a victory. "Considering we're erecting a gravestone to the dead relationship of Chris and Livia, we deserve to celebrate."

Blake sat, and Livia spread out the baked goods she'd brought with her, ignoring the curious looks of those still waiting for the train. She passed Blake two more aspirin without a word, and he took them with a swig of orange juice.

"A day in the life of Blake Hartt? Are you sure you're up for this?" He rubbed a hand along his jaw, and his eyes looked devilish.

"I brought my boots." Livia gestured to her thick, serious hiking boots.

"Where to take you? Now that's the question." Blake looked thoughtful as he ate the rest of the breakfast.

Livia cleaned up their trash, and when she returned, Blake had smoothed his piece of cardboard on the cement before him. He placed his hands just over it like a Ouija board. The sight of it jolted Livia with a reminder of why he was here this morning. Not just because he wanted to see her. He was homeless. Different.

Up close, Livia could see well-worn spots from his repetitive touch. The length of cardboard had obviously been rolled up for storage often. Blake smiled at her and began to run his graceful fingers over it.

"What does that do for you?" Livia had to ask.

"I'm practicing piano. I can't travel with a baby grand." He let his fingers dance over keys only he could see. Livia nodded, mesmerized by his behavior. "I'll play you a song." Blake flexed his fingers and concentrated harder on the cardboard, moving his hands methodically over its surface.

What do you say after an imaginary concert? Livia watched as the song came to a close with his careful plucking of certain keys on the cardboard. She couldn't help but glance to see if the commuters were staring.

"I couldn't hear that, but your hands looked beautiful." *The only way I can do this is if I don't lie.*

"Of course not. It's not plugged in." Blake smiled, then watched as she didn't get his joke. "I know it doesn't make noise," he explained. "Going through the motions is comforting to me. I wish I had a real piano."

The wistfulness in his tone was aching to hear. "Did it used to have keys on it?" Livia asked.

"I did draw them once, but it was in pencil. No matter. My heart knows right where they are." He watched her as he tickled the pretend keys again.

"Is the cardboard itself special?" she asked. It seemed like a good question. Cardboard was easily replaceable, but this piece was so old.

Blake smoothed it with both hands in a practiced gesture. "When I went into foster care, I had what I could carry in a box. Although the contents changed over the years, I managed to hang on to the box. It fell apart soon after I aged out of the system, but I kept this one piece."

Livia reached out and stroked the cardboard tenderly. *This is all he has.*

Blake snatched up her hand, and for a second Livia thought he was angry. He pulled her fingers to his mouth and kissed each one of her fingertips.

"Tell me what 'aged out' means," Livia said.

Blake let her have her hand back and continued his silent concert. "I entered foster care at twelve. When I reached eighteen, the state was no longer responsible for my care. I had my box and thirty-two dollars to my name." He shrugged.

"How old are you now, Blake?" Livia hated this story more and more.

"I'm twenty-five."

Livia had a feeling if she could hear his music, this song would be slow and sad.

"You've been living out here on your own for seven years?" Livia tried to imagine a typical day for him, multiplied by hundreds.

"You've been dating Chris the Hump for how long?" Blake countered.

Livia wrinkled her nose. "Five years."

"Between us we have twelve years of waiting..." He stopped playing to look at her again.

"For each other." Livia finished the thought.

Blake rolled up the cardboard and tucked it in his back pocket. "This is the one thing the thieves didn't want."

"I'm glad."

Blake stood and held a hand out to her. Livia could do nothing but rise and press a quick kiss to his lips.

"Get a room, you homeleth bastardth." Homeleth Humper had decided to weigh in. Again.

Livia sighed and whispered to Blake, "That's Homeleth Humper. He hath voithed hith dithpleathure at our happineth in the patht." Livia looked over her shoulder and stuck her tongue out at the man. "I guess I shouldn't make fun of his lisp. That's not very kind."

Blake rubbed her arms in a comforting gesture. "On the contrary. I think he wants you to make fun of him. Otherwise he would mind his own business."

Homeleth Humper spoke up again, throwing his hand in the air for emphasis. "Well, I hope you're at leatht uthing birth control. I don't want to thupport your mistaketh." He spoke to the fellow spineless nimrods, who looked at him like he was out of his mind. He'd gone too far, even for them.

"Oops. Now he's going to wish he hadn't said that." Blake's green eyes narrowed.

"Please, let me," Livia insisted.

Blake motioned for her to go first with an open palm, but he stayed just behind her. Livia watched as the loud mouth put his phone in front of his face like a shield. She plucked it out of his hand like a wildflower in a meadow and let it fall to the cement.

"Looks like you dropped your phone," Livia challenged. As soon as it skittered to a stop, Livia brought one of her sturdy boots down on top of it with a satisfying crunch. "And lookie there. It broke. If you ever talk about my future children again, I'll feed you your own balls, assuming you have any."

Homeleth Humper looked amazed and mortified. He began sputtering to the other train passengers "Ugh. Did you thee what the did? Thomeone call the copth. That wath athault!"

Just then, Livia's countless morning smiles paid off. All the spineless nimrods started clapping, one by one. The clapping became whistling and happy shouts. "Atta girl!"

Livia laughed as Blake twirled her in a quick circle and dipped her, giving her a kiss that made the crowd clap even louder. Blake and Livia grinned as he bowed and she curtseyed to the spineless nimrods. *I'm upgrading them back to usual suspects.*

Blake grabbed her hand, and they hopped off the platform and into his world as the train pulled into the station, drowning out the last of the applause. Blake and Livia ran for a hundred yards, into the adjoining park, before slowing down to hug and laugh.

"I think I need to introduce you to my brother Beckett. He could use some of your lines." This was the first Blake had mentioned of his family.

"Is he older or younger?" *Why is he not helping you?*

"Well, he's actually a foster brother. Cole, Beckett, and I were in the last house together. We really needed each other to survive that year and a half." Blake's jaw tightened, and his eyes clouded over.

Livia touched his jaw until it was smooth again. "How many foster homes did you have?"

"Ten."

Oh my God. "In six years?"

Blake looked off in the distance, embarrassed.

"You do know that's not your fault, right?"

Her question was met with silence.

He blames himself.

He sighed and relayed the bad news. "Livia, I have problems—things that make me undesirable, not viable, dangerous, unlovable."

"Who *told* you those ugly words? I can't...you can't believe that." She reached for his hand. *Who would say those things to a child?*

"If you hear it enough, and people's actions support those words..." Blake shrugged.

Livia pulled Blake to a nearby park bench. "I wish I'd known you. I would've smuggled you into my room. You could've lived with me. I even had a keyboard for you." She cradled this face that was suddenly so dear to her.

"You would've too," he said. "You remind me of a fairy tale princess. You're so kind."

"Did you not see me smash that guy's phone? I never saw Cinderella attack a lisping dude." Livia closed one eye while reliving her actions.

"No, I guess not. You're my kind of princess, then." Blake ran his hands through her hair.

"Hey, maybe I can get that guy a piece of cardboard he can pretend is his phone." Livia held her breath. *Too much?*

"Are you making fun of my piano?" Blake said with mock horror.

"Yeth, yeth I am," she said.

Blake tickled her mercilessly. "You *will* respect the piano." Soon Blake had Livia laughing so hard he had to stop so she could breathe. "We better get over to Beckett's if you want to see how my day goes—before his crowd gets too raunchy." Blake stood up and held out his hand.

"It's eight-thirty in the morning. How raunchy could they be?"

Livia wondered what, exactly, Beckett did for a living. Her question was soon answered. *Everything bad.*

Livia hadn't even known this part of town existed. As they walked, the stores and houses became shabbier and shabbier until they were nothing more than boards nailed to crumbling foundations. Beckett's seedy place of business was within a set of storefronts that probably hadn't been in good working order since before Livia was born.

The parking lot looked like a casting call for a horror movie. The cars that did have tires had their engines rumbling at top volume. Those without tires had various shady characters lolling inside them. Drunken men wandered, people passed out, and in the far corner of the parking lot, someone threw up in a burned-out trashcan.

"This is a great first date." Livia huddled closer to Blake.

"This isn't our first date. I count all the breakfasts. Don't worry, Livia, none of these people will harm us." He seemed confident.

"You're that scary?" Livia whispered.

"No, but Beckett is," Blake said.

Blake and Livia entered a storefront and emerged in an abandoned mall. Blake headed for a door that seemed the entrance to some sort of office. He nodded to a huge, imposing man. The bodyguard stood and knocked on the door.

"Go away. Piss off. Up yours," a booming voice bellowed.

The large bodyguard spoke in an alarmingly high, squeaky voice. "Blake's here. He has a girl with 'im."

The door flew open to reveal a huge, handsome, muscle-bound man in a tight black T-shirt and jeans.

"Blake! What the hell?" The man dragged them into the office and slammed the door.

Blake pulled away and insisted on formal introductions. "Beckett Taylor, this is Livia McHugh."

Beckett held out his giant hand to her, respectful of Blake's formal ways.

Livia tried to focus on his face, but her gaze kept drifting to the surrounding office. It was downright luxurious. Leather, cherry wood, and expensive knick-knacks were overpowered by Beckett's choice of artwork. Almost every square foot of wall had some sort of firearm on it.

"Your lady likes the guns, bro." Beckett's voice was grumbly and dominant.

"Just surprised," Livia answered. "I'm pleased to meet you, Beckett."

As she retracted her hand, Livia noticed the tattoo inside Beckett's forearm: a knife, a music clef, and a cross intertwined.

Beckett followed her eyes. "You like that? What, your boyfriend didn't show you his?"

Despite what was probably going on around here, Beckett's personality was magnetic, and when he focused on Livia, she felt herself blush. Beckett turned to Blake, held his arm up, and made a fist. As if it were a nonverbal command, Blake immediately wrapped his arm around Beckett's. They stood in this pre-arm-wrestling stance for a second and let their matching tattoos touch. It was not an elaborate "man shake," but more a sacred vow.

Beckett took a step back. "First things first, you weren't lying. She's absolutely gorgeous." Beckett let his gaze roam from Livia's boots to the top of her head. "And you know I'm an expert." Beckett smirked like a sleazeball, but somehow, it wasn't offensive. "Second, bro, you'll tell me who messed your shit up. Right fucking now." Beckett went from charming to deadly in an instant.

"Really, it's no big deal."

Beckett shrugged. "Either you tell me who they are and I teach them a lesson about respect, or you don't tell me and I find out anyway and kill the fuck out of them. Your choice." Beckett looked in Livia's direction. "Pardon my French, little lady."

"What part of that was French — the murders?" Livia felt the words slip out before she could snatch them back.

Beckett looked back to Blake. "I like the shit out of this spicy little number. Either I bring the Uzi or the brass knuckles to find these bastards."

Blake blew his hair out of his eyes with a frustrated breath. "I totally forgot I was still bruised or I wouldn't have come here today. I just wanted you to meet Livia, not scare the life out of her."

Beckett was unmoved. "Tell me."

"It was the new group of guys up from the city. There were eight of them." Blake motioned for Livia to sit with him on a lush leather loveseat.

Beckett didn't grab a gun or the knuckle rings. He opened his office door and flung a command. "Mouse, go get the Hummer. I have some heads to bust as soon as my brother leaves."

Mouse, the giant bodyguard, squeaked, "Sure, boss."

Blake and Livia turned to watch out the window as Mouse pulled the hugest Hummer known to man out front. The thick black glass they peered through had blended in with the rundown building's exterior, but now Livia realized it was a portal from Beckett's special hell. Like a swarm of bees, the other working vehicles in the lot fell in place behind the Hummer.

Livia turned to stare at Blake. "I can't believe you faced off against eight guys. Why would you do that?"

"The cooler was yours. When they dragged me into the sun…" Blake's explanation stopped there.

Blake and Livia held hands on the loveseat, surrounded by the overwhelming artillery. Livia watched as Beckett's hand curled into a tight ball. "So, Livia, you date outside your tax bracket?" Beckett settled his bright blue eyes on her.

"I guess I do." Livia's answer was quiet.

"You know, the first time I met Beckett, he was saving the ugliest kitten from a tree," Blake interjected.

"Not that story, man, you're killing me." Beckett hid his face in his massive hands.

"It had these huge ears and giant paws, and it was so skinny it should have been dead two days already," Blake continued. "Beckett was halfway up the tree in our foster parents' yard, and there was this little eight-year-old neighbor girl crying her eyes out."

Beckett banged his head softly on the desk.

Blake's eyes sparkled. "So I get the bright idea to help out. I set down my box of worldly goods and drag out the garden hose. Cats hate water, right? I'll just soak it down a little, and it'll climb out."

"You were a stupid motherfucker," Beckett said into his desk.

Blake started laughing and talking at the same time. "I turned on the hose and squirted the cat, which then jumped like a flying squirrel onto Beckett's back and clung there for dear life."

Blake took a moment to get all of his chuckles out. Even Livia laughed at the image.

"So I start hitting him in the back with the water, to try to get the cat to let go, right? Well, then it uses Beckett like a scratching post and climbs over his shoulder and onto his chest. It's hanging there like a baby monkey, and the little girl is crying, and I'm laughing too hard to stop the hose, so Beckett climbs all the way back down screaming like a woman."

Beckett was now laughing silently, his whole body shaking. "I…was… screaming like a man…with a cat on his nipple." Beckett slapped his hand on his desk.

"Of course he has a filthy mouth, but he would never curse in front of a kid, so he's making up curses as he goes." Blake took a break to laugh again.

"Hot baskets of butt!" Beckett burst out, and judging from the belly-rumbling laughter, that had been the best of the made-up curses.

"When he gets to the ground, the little girl rips the kitten off his chest and doesn't even say thank you." Blake shook his head. "Then Beckett beat the ever-living tar out of me." He smiled at his brother like it was a beautiful memory.

Beckett glared back at him. "Of course the bastard had that whole thing to hold over my head, so I had to be nice to him from then on."

All three of them made slow, wheezing, winding-down noises.

Beckett stood up. "Well, kids, reliving my pain has been fun, but I have some unfinished business to attend to."

Blake and Beckett gave each other a shake and a half man-slap hug. Livia ignored Beckett's hand to give him a hug and kiss on the cheek. "Thank you for watching over him before I knew him," she whispered.

Mouse was at the door again. "Sorry, boss. The whores are here for their test ride. You want them now or later?"

Sure enough, three women stood outside the door looking every inch ladies of the night. As Blake emerged, they surrounded him, talking seductively.

Beckett pulled Livia back into the room by her belt. "Loving that guy is the only thing I've ever done right," he said. "Please don't break his heart."

Livia nodded, eyes wide. Beckett's soul was talking to her, not the tough bad boy he seemed to pretend to be.

As Beckett walked Livia out the door, Blake untangled himself and grabbed her hand. "Well, it was nice meeting you all," he said to the very friendly ladies. "Have great day, Eve, Vikki, and Sweetie."

Beckett walked out with Livia and Blake, issuing orders to Mouse. "Have the chicks do some stretches, and get some Viagra out. I'll be back soon."

Blake shook his head. Livia waved goodbye as the posse rolled out with Beckett driving lead in his Hummer, his face an eerie mask.

Blake leaned close to her. "That's his game face."

A shiver passed through Livia. "So you're the music clef, Beckett's obviously the knife, who's the cross?" She stroked Blake's tattoo.

"You're about to find out. We're headed to church." Blake leaned in to kiss her forehead.

"Of course we are. That makes perfect sense." *From hell to heaven.*

5

446

Blake and Livia walked to their next destination with slow, meandering steps. They kept getting lost in their conversation, each watching the other's mouth carefully like the words were so very important. The town rebuilt its buildings and reputation a little more with every crunch of the fall leaves under their shoes as they headed back the direction they came from. They soon left the paved road to turn down a wooded path, and after a few more minutes, they emerged from the trees to find a very old-fashioned church. Here the fall leaves were swept clean, inviting guests in. Livia studied the sign as Blake opened the door to Our Lady of the River. As they entered, Livia was immersed in the scents of warm wax, incense, and wood polish. The contrast with where they'd just been left her head spinning.

"Father Cole." Blake's voice broke the sanctity of the space.

"Don't call me that, Blake." A man dressed in black came from a door on the left side of the altar.

Livia had been busy admiring the intricate stained glass windows and had to refocus her eyes on the man. Blake dropped Livia's hand to embrace Cole. He whispered something as he wrapped his tattooed arm with Cole's, the same way he had with Beckett. But this greeting seemed comforting, healing—full of forgiveness, not promises.

"Cole Bridge, this is Livia McHugh. Livia, this is my brother Cole. He's not actually a priest, but he's sort of Father Callahan's assistant."

Cole was not as tall as Blake, and he was mysterious and sad at the same time. His features were classic and handsome, his skin the precise shade of mocha. He had yet to smile at Livia, but he nodded cautiously.

Blake shyly touched Livia's shoulder. "Do you mind if I leave you with Cole for a bit? He's kind enough to offer me use of the shower in his quarters."

"No problem." Livia watched as Blake exited through the door Cole had used to enter.

Livia and Cole stood in the thick quiet that enveloped a person in a silent church. Cole motioned to the closest pew, and Livia stepped in and sat on the hard, curved wood. Cole hooked the kneeler with his foot and brought it down with a practiced bang. He knelt and let his fingers weave into a knot. Livia wasn't exactly sure what was polite—to join this priest's assistant, or let him have his moment on his knees.

After a pause, she found herself mimicking his position. In the silence, Livia examined the church. It wasn't filled with horrific statues with faces frozen in pain, like some churches she'd seen. The most prominent decorations were the stained glass windows. The architect of this little church had defied some basic laws of physics. It seemed the glass supported the brick, not the other way around.

"Four hundred forty-six," Cole whispered.

She'd almost forgotten he was there as she tried to make out the scenes in the windows. "What?" she asked.

He kept his head down in what seemed to be a prayer. "He counts. You've smiled at him four hundred and forty-six times as of a few minutes ago. He announces the number every time I see him."

Livia stared at the white-cloth-covered altar and listened to the confessing man.

"I'm ashamed to admit that I didn't think you were real. Considering my line of work, I should have more faith in humanity." Cole shook his head. "I think it was smile two hundred eighty-six that drove me the most crazy. It was the night train. Blake was so sick, feverish. Honestly, I was considering taking him to the hospital. But no. He didn't want to miss a smile. He wouldn't even let me drive him. Blake walked the whole way in the pouring rain for number two eighty-six."

When she glanced over at his rigid jaw, Livia realized Cole wasn't relating a tale of deep romance. He was angry.

"You smiled that night. He was adamant that it had lasted longer than the others." Cole looked at her with troubled brown eyes. "Livia, if I may be so bold, he's going to take your kindness very seriously. If you're playing a game, or trying to get even with a boyfriend by dating the worst thing you could find—"

Livia held up one hand to stop him. "With all due respect, never, *ever* refer to Blake as 'the worst thing' in my presence again."

To Livia's surprise, Cole almost smiled.

"It's been such a short time—I don't even know if I can explain it," she began. "Imagine you were walking in a desert, and you were so hot and very thirsty. The sun won't quit, but you finally come upon the clearest, coolest pond. You jump in, even in your best clothes. You jump in and drink because you absolutely have to. You *have* to. Am I making any sense?"

Livia took in Cole's face. His eyes remained sad as he nodded.

Livia looked back at the stained glass. She took a deep breath before speaking again. "Why aren't you and Beckett taking better care of him?" She watched as Cole's face turned hard.

"Blake's an easy soul to love, but a difficult man to hold on to. He has a tremendous sense of pride, which he will *not* see compromised. He finds no glory in accepting help. If he hasn't earned it, he wants no part of it." Cole rose from the kneeler to stand in the aisle. "It's easy to stand in judgment after knowing my brother only a few weeks. You have some nerve."

Livia sat back in the hard pew. "I'm sorry my question insulted you, but I do have nerve. I'm just trying to fit the pieces together." Livia stood to give herself more confidence.

"You've no idea what you're getting involved with." Cole closed his eyes. He seemed to be reaching inside to calm himself.

Livia took a step out of the pew. "Cole, I can't turn back now. My life leads to his. It's as simple as that."

"Two months." Cole looked doubtful.

"Four hundred forty-six smiles, plus two months of talking twice a day, five times a week," Livia corrected. She smiled cautiously and reached over to take Cole's hand. He pulled it away, but not before she noticed an ugly scar.

Her face warm with embarrassment, Livia forged ahead. "Tell me about Blake and the sun."

"Why don't you talk to him?" Cole snapped. But after a moment he spoke again.

"It's his story to tell—or not tell," he said, not meeting her eyes. "Do you see those stained glass windows? They're beautiful, but you can't see their true magnificence until sunlight touches them. I believe Blake's the same way."

Cole's eyes darted to Livia's, but then he turned to look at the altar door. Within a moment Blake walked through in fresh clothes, his hair still damp.

The church had cleansed Blake. He was fresh and ready to face the rest of the day. Livia smiled back at him. *Four hundred forty-seven,* her mind noted.

Cole leaned closer to Livia as Blake came toward them. "That pond, Livia? The coolest pond? It has many, many undercurrents."

Cole stepped back as Blake joined them and put a possessive arm around Livia's shoulders.

"Thanks for the shower, Cole. I appreciate it."

"Anytime, brother. Anytime." Cole shook hands with Blake as they said goodbye.

"I'm taking Livia to some of my favorite spots," Blake said proudly.

Cole just nodded, saying nothing.

Livia took one last look at the stained glass windows as they left the church and tried to ignore the dread that crept, like a stalking cat, into her chest.

"Where to now?" Livia forced the feeling away and looked expectantly at Blake's green eyes.

"You'll see."

They headed back to their wooded path. Blake seemed to prefer a wandering trail through the trees to walking along any sort of road, so Livia had trouble figuring out where they were—or how far they'd come. Just when she was convinced they were in the middle of nowhere, they arrived at the Hudson River, within view of the train station where they'd met that morning.

"Firefly Park is your super-secret place?" Livia raised an eyebrow at the well-populated leisure spot. Industrial-strength grills and picnic tables dotted the rolling hills.

"No, I'm not Captain Completely Obvious. Come this way."

Blake went straight for the tall chain-link fence that separated mani-cured public areas from the woods. He peeled back a corner of the fence and held it for Livia as she ducked under. After following a footpath for a while, Blake branched off, taking an unmarked trail.

"You walk through here like a herd of buffalo," he teased, looking over his shoulder.

"Well, thanks a lot!" Livia gave him a pout.

"Stop for a second and listen."

Livia stood still as Blake demonstrated his almost soundless gait.

"Now you," he said.

She slapped her feet down in exaggerated stomps.

He hugged her close when she drew near and kissed her nose. "We're almost there, Sasquatch."

Soon they entered a break in the woods—a perfect square with tall trees standing guard. In the center were two curved saplings.

Blake rubbed a hand on his face. "This is mine," he announced.

"It's lovely," Livia said.

Blake walked to the center of the clearing and spread out his army jacket. He took her hand and lowered her to the jacket. "Lay back."

Blake soon joined her, but kept most of his body on the leaf-covered ground. He put his arm under her neck to give her a pillow, and they watched the thick clouds roll through the sky. Blake reached to his side and ripped a leaf off of a droopy plant. He put half the leaf on his tongue and started to chew. He offered the other piece to Livia.

"Seriously? We're munching on plants like cattle now?" Livia eyed the leaf uncertainly.

"Aren't you funny? It's a mint leaf. It tastes good. Try it."

Livia could smell the scent in the air and tried a tiny nibble. "Wow, Daniel Boone, this is mighty tasty."

Blake growled and began his extremely effective tickling. But a twinge in his sore ribs cut the torture short. Wincing, he leaned carefully on his elbow. Soon they were looking at the clouds again.

"Why were you with him for five years?" Blake asked, breaking the silence.

The last thing Livia wanted to talk about was Chris. But she couldn't help being honest. "I'm not sure. It was easier than not being with him, I guess. I liked having a boyfriend. Isn't that shallow?" Livia paused, gazing at the sky. "He wasn't all bad all the time. He fussed over the little stuff, like making sure I paid my bills and registering to vote. That made me feel special. We had fun in the beginning…And sometimes I think I stayed with him because I'd put in so much time already."

"Yeah, you're a real old timer," Blake teased as he traced her face with his finger.

"But the things that were right about him I sort have been able to do for myself for a while now. His constant reminders used to feel like love, but now they feel like he wanted to take control of my life so I couldn't. It hasn't been right for me and I've been ignoring that. And now I think I was waiting for you. I *know* I was waiting for you," Livia said as she trapped his hand against her cheek.

He smiled broadly, and Livia took a chance.

"Blake, why were you in foster care?"

He removed his hand and flipped carefully onto his stomach.

"Really? You want to know?" He seemed surprised.

Livia could only knit her eyebrows in concern. Blake spoke, but in a dull, flat tone she hated very much.

"My mom didn't know who my dad was," he began. "I think she tried taking care of me at first. But by the time I was seven, I was taking care of her. She was an alcoholic—not that she would ever admit it." His fingers played with the grass. "When I was twelve, the state took me away. Four years later, my mother was in a fatal drunk driving accident. She killed herself and the two little girls riding to school in the minivan she hit." The words were like poison leaking from his soul.

Livia rubbed his back, and he gave a toneless laugh. "Feeling sorry for me? Do the math, Livia. I would have been sixteen that year. If I hadn't gotten myself taken away, I'd have been driving. Those girls would be alive." Blake stood awkwardly, trying not to favor his ribs, and ran his hands through his hair.

Livia sat up but stayed on his jacket. "That's a lot of guilt for one person."

"I don't want to wreck this moment with everything I've done wrong. I want to be right for a little while. I was right about you." Blake returned to the ground and touched Livia's hair reverently, as if it were spun crystal.

She kissed his lips and felt his smile form. Alone in this beautiful space, Blake and Livia made things right. Blake kissed her slowly and patiently, like he had all the time in the world. Carefully, they eased back to lie down, and Blake braced himself above her.

He smelled of mint and fresh soap. Livia put her hands on his chest and felt the densely packed muscles there.

Empowered by his adoration, she shrugged off her fleece shirt, enjoying the feeling of being trapped between his arms.

Blake's eyes became stormy seas. "Damn it all to hell," he cursed.

Despite his words, Livia believed she was winning this battle of seduction. Blake kissed her mouth and sucked on her bottom lip. He moved to her earlobe and breathed, "First, I will blow, then I will lick, last I will bite."

Holy crap.

Blake blew a gentle stream of minty breath along the outside of Livia's ear, down to her neck, and along the edge of her breasts where they peeked out of her bright blue bra. Blake took his time creating an elaborate pattern on her stomach, and Livia was pretty sure he'd spelled the word *torture*. He increased the pressure of his breath as he grazed below her belly button to the top of her jeans. He skipped back to her mouth and gave her another long, slow kiss.

"And now I lick," he murmured.

Livia bit back the embarrassingly loud moan she felt building. He gently traced the same trail his breath had left, this time with his tongue. When he reached her breast, she lost control and grabbed his hair, intent on kissing him.

"No. No." Blake held her wrists above her head. "I've done this to you so many times in my mind. I won't have you rush me."

Livia groaned and arched her back in an effort to change his mind. But his slow, sexy smile told her he was doing it his way.

"Fine." Livia dutifully kept her hands above her head as he picked up where he'd left off.

His tongue had her making noises that surely scared the wildlife. He spent an inordinate amount of time licking just above her belt buckle. Then again he was back to her mouth.

He spoke through his kiss. "I'm going to bite you now."

Blake began down the same flaming path on Livia's body with his teeth, nibbling in time with her heartbeat. When it speeded up, he bit slightly harder.

After what seemed to be sixteen million glorious years, Blake was at the top of her jeans again. A light, almost invisible, mist from the gray clouds now gave the clearing a slick sheen. The cool rain and his hot mouth were ecstasy.

Blake unbuckled her belt and used his tongue and teeth to unbutton her jeans. He chuckled as he flipped her zipper with his teeth. Each pop of the releasing zipper filled the woods as he blew again on the newly revealed skin.

Livia knew what to expect this time: blow, lick, bite. *Oh, sweet God! This is heaven.* At last, Livia could no longer obey and reached her hands down to his angelic face.

Blake glanced up as if to rebuke her, but quickly smiled and let her sit up to meet his lips.

Love. Crazy, soon, ever. Love, Livia's mind raged. She tried to tell him with kisses, but it wasn't enough. Blake knelt before her, and Livia straddled his thighs. She pulled back to try putting it into words and noticed how Blake glistened, covered in tiny raindrops. The clear, cool pond she'd described to Cole had just exploded over them. But instead of drowning, they wore it like a cloak.

In her pleasure, Livia didn't notice the slow arrival of the sun until the clouds shifted and shafts of light filled the woods. They combined with the mist to make blurry rainbows all around. For a moment Blake's rumpled hair was lit from behind, and then everything changed.

Nothing warned her before his face contorted with sheer terror and madness. Livia fell from his lap as he stood in panic. Her back hit his army jacket with a vicious thud that echoed against the trees. Blake's running was as silent as his walking.

Livia struggled to take a breath, but her lungs refused. She felt like a fish tossed out of the only watery world it had ever known. She gasped and closed her eyes, unable to speak or move.

"Livia! Livia, please...*Livia!*"

Livia's head lolled toward Blake's voice. He crouched in the shade just a few yards from her sunlit form. She gave him a thumbs up. Getting the wind knocked out of her reminded Livia of the second-grade playground. Finally her body let her draw a deep breath of sunshine-warmed air.

Blake paced the shadows like a claustrophobic man in an elevator. Her thumbs up had done nothing to stem his panic. Livia pulled herself to her knees and crawled a few feet until she could get her legs under her. She staggered and half-ran, half-wobbled to the safe shade.

Blake continued pacing and glaring at the edge of the shade. He seemed not to have noticed her presence.

"Hey. I'm right here," she murmured as he passed by.

Startled, Blake turned and took in the sight of her. He collapsed to his knees, and Livia hugged his face to her belly. She felt his hot, ragged breath in the same place that had driven her wild just minutes before.

He looked up at her, his face stricken. "Did you see? Did you see through me? Was it awful?" His voice was an octave above its usual register.

Livia smoothed his hair back and looked into his eyes. Cole's words echoed in her head. *That pond Livia? The coolest pond? It has many, many undercurrents.*

"No, my eyes were blurry from the mist. I couldn't see," she assured him.

Livia remembered the thoughts of love that had almost burst from her lips before the sun arrived. She hated it for cracking the center of their connection. But maybe she should be thankful. He needed so much more than kisses.

Blake jumped up again, clenching and unclenching his fists. "I hurt you. I'm useless," he whispered harshly.

He stalked to the nearest tree and shouted in frustration, punching as if it was an attacker. Livia was horrified to see an arc of blood leave his fist.

"Stop. Stop, Blake." She tried to speak calmly. Livia moved to stand next to him and reached out, but his fists were flying harder now. She had no idea where to grab him. Finally, she just closed her eyes and stepped between him and the tree. When no punch came to meet her face, Livia opened one eye. Blake stared at a spot just above her head.

"When you hurt yourself, it hurts me." She reached out to take one of his bloody, torn hands.

He flinched and pulled away. "Livia, I'm not even man enough to go into the sun to help you up. Don't spare me a moment of your concern."

"I wasn't hurt. And I believe if I had been you would've come." Livia watched as blood from his knuckles dropped onto the leaves.

"No. I wouldn't come, Livia. I would stand here like a stone. Because *I* am the most important to me. *I* am." Blake barely moved his lips as he spoke.

Livia covered her face with her hands and pressed on her eyes. She had no idea what to say.

"That moment…that moment out there?" Blake pointed at the bed of army jacket, grass, and mint. "I've pictured it in my head for months. Months! I knew it would never really happen, but it kept me going. The beautiful, smiling girl would look at me like a man—a man worthy of her body, worthy of her kiss. Do you realize what a fool I am for hoping?"

Blake took her face in his hands. "You let me touch you. Kiss you. Your skin? It feels like piano keys. My hands know just where to go." He proved it by sliding one hand behind her neck and settling the other just over her heart.

Livia smiled, wondering if he was covering her in blood. It was worth it.

"Four hundred sixty-seven," he whispered. The number seemed to deflate him.

He's still counting. She couldn't give up.

Blake removed his hands carefully and shook his head. "But it never ended like that, Livia. It never ended with me throwing you to the ground. But that's what I do. I knock the breath out of anyone who dares take a chance on me." He rubbed two fingers over his tattoo.

"Show me."

He looked at her and Livia raised her eyebrows in expectation.

"Does it hurt when the sun touches you?"

"No. It doesn't hurt. But you'll never want to be near me again."

"Blake, if I see what the sun does to you, the shock will be over. Then we can be together in the sun—in your favorite spot." Livia looked back at the ground where her shirt and his jacket still remained. "Or anywhere."

Blake ran both hands through his hair, smearing it with bloody highlights. Livia tried to ignore the impulse to care for his wounds as he debated with himself.

"Fine. Okay. It can't make things any worse, right? I've already thrown you on the ground…" Blake came close to her again.

He took her face in his bloody hands and kissed her chastely on her lips. Her body surged with the memory of pleasure.

He geared himself up at the edge of the shade. Livia held her breath as she waited. She begged silently for his skin be different, to be something that could reasonably cause fear in a man.

Blake faced her in the shade, then looked at his feet and stepped backward until he was encased in the full golden glow of the sun. He lifted his face with his eyes closed, and after a moment opened them and focused on Livia.

Livia saw then what Cole meant about stained glass windows. She'd had no idea the true depth of Blake's beauty. His hair glowed with an array of rich bourbon shades, and his green eyes blazed tropical perfection. He tore his shirt open to reveal his chest, giving her more skin to see.

"Well?" Blake waited for her reaction, eyes wide.

Lie to him. Tell him what he wants to hear. Right now is the moment that matters. But Livia couldn't lie. This was too important. "No, sweet Blake. Your skin isn't glass. It's just regular, beautiful skin." Her voice was warm and comforting, but her tears betrayed her.

"What? You can't see this?" Blake pinched his arm and slapped his face.

Livia shook her head.

Blake's scream didn't sound like something a human could produce. He dragged his fingers over his chest, leaving claw marks in their wake. Then he ran right for her at top speed. Livia refused to move and braced herself for the blow. He passed so close to her that her hair lifted in the rush of air. He disappeared into the trees.

Livia was alone, standing in her bright blue bra and unbuttoned jeans. She waited, sure he would return. After a few minutes she left his beloved shade and got dressed. The sun had warmed the day almost to seem like summer again.

Livia continued to wait as the sun ticked off devastating minutes in the sky. *He* will *come back.* When the sun began to fall behind the trees, Livia had her first rational thought in hours: *I need the sunlight to get out of here.*

She gave the sun the finger and tied Blake's jacket around her waist, trying to ignore how heavy her hope had gotten. She was lucky to find the footpath and hazarded a guess at the direction of the park. It was dusk when she realized she'd picked the wrong way. She shivered as the fall now reminded her it was in charge, despite summer's momentary fake smile.

She slid on Blake's army jacket, and her hands found the pockets. When her left hand encountered something hard and smooth, curiosity got the best of her. She pulled it out. The evening granted her eyes enough light to see the pink, heart-shaped stone. Blake had carved the initials "L+B" in its face. The unconventional medium rendered the letters childlike.

Livia and Blake.

She put the stone back in the pocket. Did their connection still exist? Had she broken it? Broken *him* when she entered his carefully constructed walls? *God, please don't let this be a mistake.*

Livia could see a chain-link fence in the distance. She hesitated, wondering if Blake was somewhere close in the woods, following her in his silent way. But sensing nothing, she willed her feet forward.

By the time Livia got back to her Escort at the Park and Ride, the dark had descended, her feet ached from dragging the heavy hiking boots around, and she was screamingly hungry. As Livia dug her keys out of her pocket, she saw that Blake had been to her car.

It was covered with little bits of nature: long blades of grass, twigs, and stones. When she got closer she saw more. Blake had used the flora to spell *sorry* over and over on the hood. And the roof. And the trunk.

She felt touched and angry in the same instant. He'd come here to construct this apology instead of helping her out of the woods. Livia punched the hood, but was unable to inflict damage the way Blake had. *It hurts too damn much.*

Livia tossed herself into the driver's seat. She started her car and drove off a little too quickly. As she pulled away, Livia watched the instruments of Blake's message flutter into the night.

6

WHORE

Livia got home because her car took her there. Driving shouldn't have been a reflex act, but she was thankful for the latent ability she now knew she had.

He left me alone. Livia wanted to be tougher about it; she'd gotten out of the woods just fine. But her sure, true faith had holes now. She didn't want to doubt him, but she couldn't stop. Livia sat in the driveway with the Escort in park. Sobs took her vision in a river of tears.

"Son of a bitch!" Livia slammed the steering wheel over and over.

Then headlights in her rear view mirror gave her a whole new reason to curse. Chris's truck pulled in behind her. Livia wanted to deal with him about as much as she wanted a root canal. She pointed her rear view mirror to the floor to get the reflection out of her eyes. Chris always left his brights on so people could be "blinded by his awesomeness," he liked to say. Livia tried to compose herself before Chris opened her door.

"There the hell you are!" he shrieked as it opened. "For crap's sake, where the fuck have you been?" He stepped back as Livia climbed slowly out. Her long hike had taken a toll on her muscles. *Even blockheaded Chris has the decency to look for me.*

"I've been calling your cell phone for hours." Chris stood waiting for an explanation like a Ken doll with all the right accessories. Livia couldn't find the energy or inclination to describe her afternoon.

He grabbed her blank left hand. "Where's your ring?"

Livia could see more than concern in his eyes—some anger as well. "It's at the appraisers. I wanted to insure it." Livia almost smiled as he blanched.

He avoided an unflattering conversation with an accusation. "Do you want to explain why Dave saw my fiancée sucking face with a homeless man today?"

"No, I don't. I want to go inside and go to bed, if I'm being honest."

"Oh, *now* you're being honest. Where's your ring, Livia?" Chris stepped closer, trapping her against the car with his arms.

"Hey, Chris, you can back up off my sister right about now."

Kyle had come silently from the front porch to stand behind him. Her soft voice had barbed wire wrapped around it.

Chris dropped one arm to placate Kyle. She stepped into Livia's line of sight and bit her lip in concern.

"Did you know your sister's screwing a homeless man?" Chris taunted. "A freaking crazy-ass bastard? She has the nerve to do it in plain sight of my friend, who I'd just told my *great* news." Chris's eyes bore into Livia as he spoke to Kyle.

Livia felt her nerves fray at the insults. Chris wasn't wrong for being mad. She hadn't told him they'd broken up, but she'd certainly moved forward as if she had. Livia rubbed her temples in an effort to make thinking easier.

"Chris, we're over. I don't want to even *date* you anymore, never mind marry you. I'd give your crappy-ass ring back, but I threw it in the Hudson when I realized the underwear I'm wearing is worth more than it was." Livia stared blankly at his familiar face.

"That's it?" Chris tossed his hands in the air.

Kyle took a step closer and stood shoulder to shoulder with Livia. It was comforting.

"Nope. Dave's right. I kissed another man. And he kissed the hell out of me. I think I'm still aroused from the whole incident." Livia watched rage crawl up Chris's arms and tense his face.

He looked at Kyle. "Can you believe this shit?"

Kyle smiled. "Yes. I *so* can believe it. You've never deserved her." Kyle put her tall dancer's body between Livia and Chris. "And you're going to leave right now, or I'll wake up my dad."

Chris inflated himself like a balloon. "You do that, Kyle. I'd love to see his reaction to Livia's homeless boyfriend." Chris turned his rage back on Livia. "Did you sell the ring to buy him a new cardboard box to live in?"

At that, Kyle put her hand in the middle of Chris's chest. "You're done here. Leave."

Livia stood quietly, waiting for righteous indignation to find her and spur a clever retort. Instead she closed her eyes and pictured Blake as he stood in the sun, waiting for judgment. *Have I ruined him? Why did he leave me alone?*

She opened her eyes as Chris walked away with elaborate pointing. Livia knew she should pay attention to his threats. Should she try to comfort him? This news had been a shock. Kyle was like a guard dog, jumping in her anger as he spoke.

"Whore!" The faded insult hit Livia's ears just as her father slapped on the porch light and walked toward the ruckus, clicking his shotgun into position with one hand. The neighbors' porch lights twinkled on like fireflies.

Livia shook herself out of her numbness. "Kyle, go in the house before you hurt him. Chris, quit acting like a Neanderthal and go home. We'll talk about this later. Dad, please disengage the shotgun."

The tone of her voice touched something in each person. Chris climbed into his truck, mumbling under his breath, and John broke the smooth, straight line of his weapon with one practiced motion. Only Kyle refused to move, still using her body as a barrier between Chris and Livia. But she did stop launching insults about his penis. Chris tore out of the driveway, tires squealing.

Livia slammed her car door shut. "I owe you an explanation, but for now let's leave it at this: Chris and I broke up."

Livia turned, passed her family, and went up to the shower. She turned the water handle to red hot as she undressed. The showerhead had one wild stream that created a gentle spray apart from the regular flow of water. Livia reached up and twirled her hand through it as she stepped in. The bathroom light caught little drops of water and made them prisms.

She remembered the forest's rainbow mist. *He left me alone. I could still be out there. Where is he?*

Livia went through all the steps of her bedtime routine, but sleep never came.

Livia hated watching her alarm clock go off. It reminded her of those horrible Jack-in-a-Box toys—shocking, even though she knew it was coming. After she was dressed, she stood in the kitchen chewing on her thumbnail for a while.

Make a breakfast for him or don't make a breakfast for him. That is the question.

But it wasn't really a question. Livia couldn't let Blake go hungry. No matter what kind of mixed bag her emotions were, she wouldn't deny him food. She packed it carefully in disposable plastic containers and a paper bag. She also grabbed some bandages and more first aid supplies. Blake's hands would need attention.

As she backed out of the driveway, Livia noticed the thick, black scars Chris's truck tires had left on the asphalt. His screaming protest was permanent now. *Damn him.* Maybe she did owe him more of an explanation.

Livia shuffled thoughts of Chris to the back of her mind. Her cell phone buzzed like an angry bee in the passenger seat. Livia slid the pink phone open at the stoplight — the way she promised her dad she never did.

Hannah from high school was the most recent text. Livia clicked it suspiciously. Hannah was a screamingly self-centered gossip who'd always seemed to have a crush on Chris.

Heard ur screwing the homeless. LOL! Hobolicious freak @ train station is ur new STD buffet? ROFLMAO. <3

Livia groaned. Chris was obviously spewing his anger around town. Between him, Hannah, and Dave, she could soon expect a sky writer proclaiming the news. A honk reminded Livia to drive. The phone sang a song as Livia powered it down and pressed on the gas.

Remember two eighty-six. Livia now counted on the same sort of feverish, rain-soaked determination that had driven Blake to the train station for smile number two hundred eighty-six. *Please be there. He has to be there.*

Livia parked quickly and hurried out of the Escort. She dropped her phone twice before she managed to get it into her bag. She stopped when she got to the top of the stairs to the platform and searched. And searched. And searched. Nothing.

Livia waited until the last possible moment, but finally she just set the breakfast down where Blake usually sat. She swore Homeleth Humper looked smug and happy. As she boarded, Livia talked herself out of throwing him in front of the train.

On the ride home after a long day at school, Livia commanded her eyes to look at the floor of the train and not search for him. But they took direct orders from her heart and combed the platform as the train pulled in.

The bag she'd left was still there. Livia's heart cracked like an egg in its delicate shell. It was dusk, but Livia took her sunglasses out of her purse and covered her eyes. That felt better. With sunglasses to shield her eyes, she was nothing more than an impassive, immovable commuter.

That night she took four allergy pills to ensure sleep. They also prevented dreams, and that worked just fine too. This became her routine: home from the train, finish schoolwork as quickly as possible, allergy pills, bed. In the mornings, she took care to leave by the back door so she could avoid the kitchen. She couldn't even face the room where she'd once prepared breakfasts in a cooler.

For several days, she arrived to find the breakfast bag remaining in Blake's spot like a tribute. Then animals strewed the contents all over the platform. Every morning and evening, Livia granted her eyes the only thing they asked for all day: a sweeping, hopeful look at the platform. And every time, her gut registered the punch of his absence.

Livia went to school with a vengeance. She asked questions, offered suggestions, and impressed her professors. Her students were less impressed because she made their lives hell as she experimented with teaching by the Socratic Method. She'd been the new, improved, impermeable Livia for a week before Kyle cornered her in her bedroom.

"Your phone's always off. You sleep like a dead person. You keep those goddamn sunglasses on all the time. What the hell's going on with you?" Kyle tossed her red hair in indignation.

Livia just shook her head. As her foggy thoughts tried to form themselves into a response, Kyle ran out of patience.

Crack! She whacked Livia's sunglasses across the room. Livia was too stunned to slap her back.

When Kyle saw Livia's bloodshot eyes, ringed in black circles, she gasped. "Oh, Livia, you're so sad. Tell me what happened. Please tell me this isn't over Chris the giant pussy?"

Livia managed a smile.

"Is it that skanktastic Hannah? I have some photos from a party that would ruin her if we let them loose." Kyle pushed Livia down on her bed.

Livia shook her head and with a huge sigh, unloaded her story. She began with defending Blake at the train station and ended two months later with the brown bag of uneaten breakfast.

Livia's voice wavered with unshed tears at the end of her tale. "I think his problems might be too big. I can't even find him." Livia waited for Kyle's anger to flare, remembering her reaction to Chris.

"Liv, do you think you love him?" Kyle looked like she already knew the answer.

Taken off guard by Kyle's lack of vengeance, Livia was surprised to hear her soul talking after a week of sulking in silence. "I feel like I've always loved him, and now I just got lucky enough to find him."

This revelation lit a fire in Kyle. She leaped off the bed, pointing at her sister with gusto. "Well, Livia, McHugh women aren't quitters. And we definitely don't quit on love. You better bury all this sorry-ass self-pity and man up. If finding him will bring you back to normal, that's what we're going to do."

After all the times Livia had advised and encouraged Kyle, she now just shook her head, laughing. "You're pretty smart for a bratty little sister."

"I'm only a year and a half younger. It's not like it even counts anymore," Kyle retorted. "We're going to find your hobo. We're going to work hard—work nights. Liv, we're going to put our balls into it." She hugged her tightly.

"When did we get balls?" Livia asked, returning her ridiculous sister's hug.

"Just now. So where to first? Pimps R Us or wrathful priest man?" Kyle walked over to Livia's vanity and selected a few choice items from the makeup she found there.

"Pimps, I guess," Livia said, ignoring the thievery. "It *is* night. What do we wear to a drug den anyway?" Livia opened her closet and looked through her clothes for some prospects.

Kyle smacked her lips after applying gloss. "Definitely no opened-toed shoes."

"What?" Livia said.

"I figure there'll be needles or something. Dress like we're headed to the county fair. Cow poop or syringes full of disease, same difference."

Livia felt the warmth of hope light her from within. If Kyle was on board, maybe this was worth pursuing. *He* was worth pursuing.

7

Pimps R Us

Livia followed as Kyle demonstrated how to pick their way out of the house without being detected by their father. Livia gave her sister as many disapproving facial expressions as she could muster, but she obeyed.

Kyle palmed the keys to her chili pepper red convertible so they wouldn't jingle as the two slipped out the front door. She kept them silent as she unlocked the car.

"Don't shut the car door all the way," she advised as they fastened their seatbelts.

"Shouldn't we put the top on?" Livia asked.

Kyle dismissed her with the briefest of head shakes. The convertible's hardtop had her cursing a blue streak whenever she put it on. She started the car and backed out of the driveway without headlights. They were two blocks away before she nodded and flipped on the lights. They both shut their doors more securely.

"What the hell, Kyle? How many damn times have you snuck out of the house?"

Kyle's laugh filled the small car. "Don't ask questions you don't want the answers to. Now tell me more about this drug den." Kyle cranked the heat up to full blast to counter the night wind as they drove.

"Well, it was scary at eight-thirty in the morning, so at ten o'clock at night, we should crap our pants."

"Ah, good times. This should be fun," Kyle said with a smile.

As Kyle followed Livia's driving directions, the town began to crumple into ruins. Livia looked nervously at her beautiful little sister, whose face flushed pink in the glow of the car's custom-installed interior lights. Kyle implemented her funky fashion sense everywhere she went, including her work as a buyer for the hottest local boutique.

But paired with Kyle's outgoing sense of style was an aversion to long-term commitment. She went out plenty, but she never had a boyfriend. Certainly that must have been her choice. And Kyle had passed on college, preferring to learn via a series of jobs and employers until the found her niche. Despite her offbeat way of getting there, Livia believed Kyle had exactly the life she wanted. She exuded a quiet confidence. Well, not so quiet at times too.

"What if he's not okay?" Livia blurted. She felt relieved to finally share her concerns with someone.

Kyle shook her head. "He'll be okay."

"Right up ahead, to your left."

But the directions were unnecessary now; Kyle just followed the explosions of illegal fireworks above Beckett's parking lot. As they turned in, Kyle hit the button for the automatic locks. Livia looked up at the stars.

"That'll keep 'em out. Good thinking, Ky." Livia's stomach bubbled like a pot of boiling water. "Maybe the top would've been a good plan."

"How well do you know this Beckett guy again?" Kyle pulled as close to the building as she could and put the car in park.

"Not well. I'm pretty sure he threatened me the only time I met him." Livia took in the sights around her.

"Great." Kyle's eyes widened as she surveyed Beckett's place of business.

The parking lot was a kaleidoscope of wrong. Wrong people doing wrong things for wrong reasons. Smoke and music filled the air, as each working vehicle seemed to have its radio tuned to a different station. A few bonfires dotted the asphalt, and almost every person held a brown paper bag molded into the shape of a bottle.

A tall, greasy man, clad in a cliché trench coat, flashed his long, white, naked body at anyone who looked his direction. Once he spotted Kyle and Livia, he made a beeline for their car. He flashed his coat open with great flourish in front of them as if on his own personal stage. He wiggled his meager offerings while the sisters watched, their noses wrinkled in distaste. Trench Coat then added a song to his pitiful dance: "Lulooly, Lulooly, Lulooly!"

Kyle pointed right at him and with great seriousness confronted Livia. "Please tell me Mr. Frank n' Beans isn't Blake *or* Beckett."

"No, Cocktail Weenie has nothing to do with why we're here."

"That's one pale, hairless nightmare," Kyle said, still pointing.

"I think I can smell his ass from here." Livia had to work not to smile.

The McHugh girls could do this for hours. The flasher seemed offended by their repartee and closed his coat.

"Let's get out," Kyle suggested, already exiting the vehicle. Livia took a deep breath and joined her. As if the closing car door was some sort of signal, the parking lot's inhabitants began slinking toward them. Weapons gleamed on each person in the gathering crowd. In a group, the derelicts concentrated the smells of the evening into an overwhelming wave.

Livia grabbed Kyle's hand as the shortest, meanest-looking man approached.

"Well, boys, what have we here?" He came closer.

"You tell us, Dentist," slurred a bystander.

Dentist was likely not certified to practice, but he wore a necklace made of what looked like human molars. Livia's breaths came in quick, short gasps.

Dentist licked his lips and put one foot between Livia's legs and the other between Kyle's.

Livia could smell the rot in his mouth when he spoke in a slow drawl. "Too clean to be whores, too fancy to be meth heads." Dentist put a gentle finger on Livia and Kyle's clasped hands. "So either they're here to walk on the wild side or they want to score some blow."

Dentist leaned in and licked Kyle's face. In the same movement, he pulled a switchblade from his belt and held it to Livia's throat. Livia could feel her pulse beating against the knife.

"Ladies, I have a wild side. Do ya want to touch it?" He spoke mostly to the crowd behind him. There was no one home behind his dark, black eyes.

The crowd started a chant. "Teeth! Teeth! Teeth!"

"Open your mouth, rich girl." Dentist addressed Kyle, but pressed the blade deeper into Livia's neck.

Livia felt a warm tickle of blood on the base of her throat as her sister opened her mouth. Suddenly she found her voice. "I'm Beckett's sister."

Dentist caressed one of Kyle's back left molars. He seemed unmoved by Livia's declaration.

"Beckett doesn't have a sister, sweetie."

Kyle chose that moment to chomp down on Dentist's finger.

"Aaahhh!" He pulled it out of Kyle's mouth, and she spit in his face.

Crap. Livia watched rage take the steering wheel from any common sense Dentist might have had. He pulled a pistol from the back of his jeans and opened his dark eyes to reveal whites laced with thick, red veins. His lip beaded with sweat. Livia knew she was taking her last breaths.

"She's his sister." The calm, authoritative voice was female. "Kill her and you'll never see the light of day."

One of the hookers Blake had met the other day now parted the crowd with either her beauty or her ferocious artillery. Gone was the garish makeup Livia had seen on her last time. She was fresh-faced with her long blond hair in a high ponytail.

"Eve," she stated, giving Livia and Kyle a nod. She wore leather poured on like hot wax and accessorized with an automatic weapon across her chest and a fierce knife strapped to her thigh. Boots heeled with metal spikes put the icing on the cake.

"He's expecting these ladies. If I drag them in there dead, he won't like it." She showed no fear.

Dentist took a step back. "Listen, you upgraded whore, I don't take orders from you."

A mumbling ripple raced through the crowd.

Eve stepped forward and smiled. With three effortless movements she disarmed Dentist and kicked him in the crotch with one of those fascinating boots. The sharp heel stuck there for a sickening moment before she pulled it free with a jerk. Livia gathered Kyle in her arms.

Eve pivoted to step between the crowd and the sisters. She pointed at a man in the crowd, but when Eve lowered her hand, Livia realized the knife that had been at her thigh was missing. Following a horrific yelp of pain with her eyes, Livia saw the man singled out by Eve slump to the ground clutching his leg. Eve now scanned the crowd like a robot.

No one else moved.

She returned to the writhing man at Kyle's feet. "These women are with me. If you even look at them again, I'll turn your balls into Swiss cheese."

Dentist's eyes rolled in his head, and they unfortunately landed on Livia's face. There was still no one home.

Quick as a rattlesnake, Eve stomped on Dentist's testicles again. "What did I just say?" she snarled.

The crunch was audible, and the crowd dispersed as Dentist wailed loudly. Eve turned to face Livia and Kyle.

"Stay in front of me and say nothing." Eve had to give Kyle a shove to get her moving.

With the sisters' hands still firmly clasped, the trio marched toward the storefronts. Livia fully expected a shot to the head.

But they made it. Livia opened the glass door and all but threw her sister into the building. Mouse sat in his accustomed spot, flipping through a knitting magazine.

Knitting?

He didn't move as Eve strode forward to open Beckett's office door, not bothering to knock. Livia and Kyle followed her inside.

"Mouse, can you go watch these girls' car before the assholes light it on fire?" she called back over her shoulder.

Mouse looked annoyed. "You're lucky I have internet access on this phone." He set down his magazine and called up a website instead. He disappeared out the door.

Beckett lounged shirtless on his love seat, wearing camouflage pants and combat boots. Livia couldn't help but notice at least three small, circular scars. Beckett didn't acknowledge the women as they entered. He swirled clear liquid in a rocks glass. Frank Sinatra crooned from unseen speakers.

"I found these chicks outside," Eve said disinterestedly. "You know 'em?"

Beckett regarded Livia and Kyle with blurry eyes.

Livia silently begged him to remember her. She bore her eyes into his tattoo in an effort to ignite a memory.

"Maybe." Beckett took a long, gulping swallow of his drink. "But I'm not in the mood. Kill 'em."

Eve sighed and responded calmly. "Quit being an ass. Girls like this don't come here. I bet they have a reason."

She boldly took his glass. Eve gave him a half smirk and drained it, then threw it against the wall where it shattered between two mounted guns.

"I wounded a piece of trash and popped Dentist in the nuts a few times," she informed him. "At least hear these two out." She grabbed a bar towel, threw another one to Livia, and hiked her leg up on Beckett's desk. Livia swabbed gingerly at the cut on her neck, which was mercifully superficial, as Eve wiped the blood off her spike heel.

Beckett slowly extracted himself from the couch. He looked like a life-size GI Joe doll with his rippling chest and army pants. He rubbed the back of his hand across his lips. "All right, what the hell are you doing here, Whitebread? And why did you bring Fairy Princess with you?"

"I want to talk about Blake," Livia said.

Beckett rolled his eyes and let out a mighty sigh. "Hey, killer, take Fairy Princess to the waiting area."

Eve gave him the finger and motioned for Kyle with her head. Livia's hand remained clamped around Kyle's.

Beckett raised his eyebrow. "She'll be safe. I promise."

Livia released her grip, and Kyle followed Eve out. Eve closed the office door, sealing Livia in.

"If I remember correctly, I asked you very nicely not to break his heart," Beckett said, taking a seat behind his desk.

Livia couldn't sit. Her limbs twitched with adrenaline. "Have you seen him?" she bounced on her toes, wringing the bar towel in her hands.

"No, miss. I have not. Looks like you put yourself through this exciting evening for no reason whatsoever." Beckett dug through the top drawer of his desk. From the place where most people keep pens, Beckett withdrew rolling papers and a plastic bag.

Livia covered her face with her hands. "Damn it. What was I supposed to do? Tell him he was made of glass? I couldn't look him in the eye and lie. Maybe that was a stupid mistake." Beckett's jaw tightened as Livia continued her tirade. "And you're no freaking help at all—with your whores and your drugs and your evil goddamn lifestyle."

Beckett looked down for a moment, then eyed her with absolute fury. He gripped the edge of the desk. "I've done my best to make sure my brothers have no blood on their hands," he said with menacing quiet. "Do you know what it's like to age out of the foster care system? I had no one. No one except Cole and Blake." He stood and angrily swiped everything off his desk into a heap on the floor. He rushed to grab her by the arms. The bar towel fell to the ground. "Pretty, pampered Livia wants to lie with the dogs. I take it you're some sort of expert? I'm going to tell you something I've never told a soul."

Livia felt oddly calm. She recognized this Beckett—the one who'd begged her to protect Blake's heart.

"I hit the streets first. So I knew what we were in for. I'm not a smart guy, but I can read a situation. To live in this world without a dime or a pot to piss in, you have to sell your soul or your body."

He let go of her and took a step back, but Livia refused to let him get away. She took one of his big, rough hands in both of hers. He didn't pull it back, but looked at the ceiling, rather than her.

"I wouldn't let them face that choice. I had six months to become the baddest motherfucker who ever lived. So I fucked up piles of people. I sold my soul, Livia, and I sold other people's bodies. But when my brothers stepped out of our foster home for the last time, I had respect. Respect enough to keep *their* souls clean. I'm going to hell, Livia," he said.

He looked at her now, his eyes glassy with tears, and Livia knew she was one of very, very few to ever see him in this state.

"I'm going to hell for all three of us," Beckett said defiantly. Only now did he pull his hand away.

"I think you might be a better man than you give yourself credit for," Livia said, trying to catch his eye again.

Beckett seemed embarrassed. Livia let the emotion ease and stepped back. She finally felt able to sit and collapsed on the loveseat. After a moment Beckett settled on top of his desk.

"So what's up with Eve?" Livia asked. "She can kick ass."

"She's hot shit, right?" Beckett looked at the closed office door as if he could see right through it.

"When I was here before wasn't she a…um…" Livia didn't know how to make the word *hooker* politically correct.

Beckett laughed. "So, yeah, I had to bang the whores that day. I always make sure the merchandise is quality, right? Well, the other two were these lifeless bitches that only moved when they freaking sneezed or coughed, so they were out." Beckett shook his head. "Then Eve walks in, strips naked, and starts dancing like a goddamn showgirl. So I'm here, drooling, when she comes up behind me with a knife she pulled out of her fucking hair. It was insanely hot."

Livia looked doubtful.

"So I'm sitting in that damn chair, ready to die, and I say to her, 'You're the most beautiful thing I've ever seen. I'm so damn glad you're going to kill me instead of some brainless, toothless druggie.'" Beckett smiled again at the memory of his almost-murder. "Then she traded the knife for her lips, and now she works for me." Beckett put his hands behind his head and flexed his giant biceps. "She won't tell me who hired her to come here. She's the deadliest person I've ever encountered. I still think she might kill me, but I can't stop looking at her."

"Well, good luck with that," Livia said. "I wouldn't want her pissed at me. She saved us tonight, no thanks to you."

"You're lucky Eve has a kind heart. I would've just watched the show out there."

"A kind heart, eh? And you would've just watched them do whatever it is they do to me and my sister?" Livia didn't buy it.

"Before, maybe. Now, no," he said.

In light of her new status, Livia tried again. "Where can I find him?"

"Whitebread, you won't find him until he wants to be found. He's the best in the woods—silent, quiet, and patient. No one can find Blake." Beckett nodded, seeming to agree with his own words. Then he stood. "I can tell you no one will touch him. Not now. The only person who's a danger to Blake is *Blake*. And maybe you." Beckett headed to the office door, a signal that the conversation was over.

Livia stopped the door with her hand and insisted on hugging Beckett. He hesitated, but hugged her back. "An anonymous donor recently funded the purchase of an organ for Our Lady of the River," he told her softly. "I'd find out when that's going to be delivered."

He stepped back to open the door, and Livia had to remind her feet to move. She was captivated again by this complicated man.

Perhaps he took her reluctance to leave as fear, but Beckett surprised Livia by walking her and Kyle to the car. Mouse closed his phone and stepped out of the way as Beckett opened Kyle's door for her.

"Don't come here again. Ever," he said, but instead of a threat, this sounded like a declaration of affection.

As Livia looked up at him, she saw Eve literally watching his back. Her hard stare held a tiny layer of concern.

"Beckett, you can kiss my ass," Livia countered. "I'll be here if you need me—or if I need you."

Beckett winked before growling angrily, surveying the parking lot, and turning to go back inside.

8

Midnight Mass

Kyle finally looked at Livia when they'd driven a respectable distance from Beckett's pulsating black hole of evil.

"Um…" Kyle looked pale.

"Yeah." Residual fear backed up on Livia like a clogged sink.

"Okay." Kyle put her eyes back on the road. "I feel like I want to puke. You?"

"I think I've tamped it down. Did we just witness something awful?" Livia rubbed the back of her neck.

"I don't know what that was." Kyle gripped the wheel and appeared to shrug it off.

"What did RoboBlonde say while I was in talking to Beckett?" Livia couldn't imagine what Kyle had been thinking.

"I think she was practicing her cursing in Russian while she sharpened her throwing stars." Kyle raised her eyebrows and shook her head. "I'm not kidding. What did the human steroid have to say? Has he seen your man?"

"You think Beckett's on steroids?" Livia asked.

"I didn't see a World Gym in there, did you?" Kyle answered.

Livia sighed. "Blake hasn't been there and, according to Beckett, I won't be able to find him," Livia said.

"Well, great. I'm glad we dangled our asses over the jaws of death to earn that little nugget. You didn't perhaps get Beckett's cell number so we can avoid this in the future?" Kyle gripped the steering wheel again.

"Wait, I also found out Beckett donated an organ to Cole's church." Livia felt hope caress the sides of her heart.

"Yuck. Which organ?" Kyle looked horrified.

"A *pipe* organ. A musical instrument, dumbass." Livia smiled, and her body considered relaxing a bit.

"Oh. *Oh!* Cardboard piano man gets a crack at a real keyboard. I get it now. You're the dumbass," Kyle said as she dug her cell phone out of her pocket.

"I guess it still has to be delivered," Livia continued. "Hang a right here. I want to drive by the church and see if I can wake up Cole." Livia barely finished the sentence.

"You sound more scared of Cole than you did of the drug den." Kyle flipped open her phone and began texting with one hand.

"His boss *is* powerful." Livia took a deep breath and tried to make herself feel lighter after the darkness that she and her sister had just experienced. It was 11:15. *What does a sort-of priest do at this hour?*

Kyle's texting consumed her as she pulled into the empty parking lot.

"What are you typing?" Livia did not share Kyle's obsession with electronic contraptions.

"Currently, I'm texting Debbi, Michelle, Karen, and Sam. This incident boosts my street cred." Kyle's text was in all caps.

"Oh, pardon me. I didn't realize you were straight-up gangsta," Livia mocked.

"Whatever. I had some bastard's finger in my mouth tonight. I'm milking this story for all it's worth." Kyle hit send.

"Don't tell anyone about Blake, please." Livia covered Kyle's phone so her sister would look her in the face.

"I won't. Listen, can I stay here while you frisk the Pope?" Kyle's cell phone vibrated with replies beneath their hands like an anxious puppy.

"Fine, but we're putting the top on the car." Livia reached over Kyle to pop the rear hatch.

After much grumbling and some heavy lifting, Kyle was back in the covered car with her fingers flying over the minuscule keyboard again. Livia took a gulp of night air, and thoughts of Blake flooded her mind. *Is he cold? How are his hands? Where* is *he?*

Livia put her concern for Blake on hold. *To help him I have to find him.*

Visiting Beckett had been a physical challenge; seeing Cole would be a mental one. As Livia headed to the church, she noticed the stained glass windows were hardly visible in the dark. She studied them for a moment.

The windows had so many fragile pieces, yet fused together they were strong enough to keep the sacred things inside the church safe. As she contemplated, she saw a small glow light up the corner of the window directly in front of her. *Blake.*

She had no idea why one illumination in the dark night filled her mind with his name, but she ran to the front doors. Another light flickered inside. *The church is on fire. Blake!*

Livia burst through the huge, creaky doors and grabbed the bowl of holy water off of the font in the foyer. Livia's heart raced as she turned to see a man with his hands full of flames.

Livia threw the holy water on him and extinguished the candles he held. Cole looked curiously calm in the remaining light from the wall sconces.

"Welcome to midnight mass, Livia." Cole's words were appropriate, but his tone held enormous frustration.

"Damn it. I mean, darn it. I thought the church was on fire. I'm so sorry. How do you clean up holy water? Is it like communion? Do you have to lick it off the floor? Can I help you?"

Why can I not stop talking? Livia watched as Cole set the dripping candles on a small table. *If I die of embarrassment, they can have my funeral right here.*

"I'll just wipe it up with towels," he said.

Cole left her, but soon returned with some very regular-looking bath towels. Livia took the one he offered and apologized again for her gaffe. After they blotted for a few moments, Cole took sat back on his heels. Livia wiped up the last drops and copied his motion.

"You're here about him," Cole stated.

Livia nodded and tried not to let her cracked heart show in her eyes.

"I prayed for you. Did you know that? Of course not. I've prayed for him to have someone like you since before we left foster care. Maybe it was a selfish prayer. I didn't want to have to worry about Blake out here. And now you *are* here—an answer to prayer—and I resent you," he said. His eyes held an ominous contempt that eerily reminded Livia of Eve the RoboBlonde.

"I don't trust you with him," Cole continued. "I'm certain you'll ruin him. You'll want to make him be something other than what he is. He can't change, Livia. He can't be a normal husband or father—or man. He'll never hold a job. He won't provide you with a cushy house and a decent medical plan." Cole's anger was at odds with the peace of the darkened church. The wall candles flickered as if the change in energy had moved the air.

"How dare you? How dare *you,* of all people, not have faith in him?" Livia shot back. "All that negativity? You *believe* it. That's what he is to you? A burden?" Livia's mouth stayed open with the shock of his words and her bravery.

Cole stood and jerked the holy-water-soaked towel from her hands. He covered his mouth with a shaking fist, seeming to search for the right words in a trunk filled with wrong ones.

"I'm sure the *weeks* you spent with him gave you an endless wealth of knowledge, but when you've gotten him out of your system and moved on, I'll still be here. I'll still toss and turn if he hasn't turned up. I'll still care if he eats. So wallow in all the self-righteousness you feel is necessary, Livia. He's homeless. Homeless," Cole said.

Her name sounded like a curse coming from his tight lips, and the word *homeless* could have passed for a terminal illness.

Livia hated her stupid tendency to cry when she was angry, and she tried not to let the tears make her incoherent as she spoke. "He *has* a home, Cole. He has a permanent home in my heart."

"Take your melodramatics and leave." Cole bristled. "My congregation should be here any minute. I have to change."

As she turned to leave, silently cursing Cole, Livia noticed the loft overhead. Livia walked slowly up a twisting spiral staircase. The loft was about the size of a small kitchen and opened to the church below. *Just enough room for an organ.* Fresh boards revealed how the floor had been reinforced. Livia wanted to feel a connection to Blake here, but it was just an empty space. She glanced out the small window that would give the future organist a peek outside—to see when the bride or the coffin arrived.

Tonight the parking lot still held only Kyle's car. Cole's congregation had about fourteen minutes to assemble. Either he preached to a group of faithful Indy car drivers, or he hoped to save the souls of the candles.

Livia was about to descend the narrow stairs when she saw a snaking, slow-moving column of people walking down the sidewalk. The column originated in the building next door.

Livia took the steep stairs carefully. Even so, the quick descent made her a little dizzy. As she returned to the foyer, she found Cole dressed in a fresh, dry shirt. He scowled when he saw Livia still there.

All these people are coming to church. They'll want holy water when they enter. "Cole, the holy water!" Livia stage-whispered.

He snapped to attention. "You get the bowl. Quick."

He leapt over three pews in a row and slid into a carefully concealed supply closet. Livia clambered up the aisle and found the overturned bowl.

They met at the font. Livia settled the bowl where it belonged as Cole poured in new water from a plastic bottle.

"You'd think that stuff came in something fancier," Livia commented, forgetting his anger in the rush of a common goal.

"You'd be surprised what's in the containers around here," Cole responded, seeming to forget his anger as well.

Their eyes met and Livia watched as the anger reappeared to make them hard. But the anger melted again almost instantly when an older man eagerly pushed open the church's front door.

"My congregation is from the retirement community apartment building next door," Cole explained. "We do a midnight mass every Wednesday for them. I'm sort of practicing being a priest. I know that's not how it is done, but Father Callahan is very unconventional. He wants me to experience the whole process before making a lifetime commitment. I guess I'm young blood for the retirement community who support me very much. They're willing to be my experimental congregation. They enjoy the clandestine meetings that give me a boost in my confidence. Not that this is any of your business."

As his friends entered, he finally went forward like a proud mayor, touching parishioners' shoulders and calling them by name. He teased the men and flirted with the women. A few of the people who entered had some sort of mobility problem. No wonder the column moved slowly. Cole guided wheelchairs and held arms in support.

Unlike a line at an amusement park, these people waited with serene peace. They were used to waiting and obviously loved Cole like he was their own child. Livia made a decision and walked out the door.

"Hi, I'm Livia. Can I help you to your seat?" she asked a woman in a wheelchair.

The lady smiled with her whole, crinkled face. "Yes, dear, aren't you beautiful? I'm Bea, and I park next to the third pew on the left."

Cole froze as Livia pushed Bea into the foyer. After a moment he nodded once in her direction and went back to tending his flock. Livia looked at the long train stretching out into the night and decided her sister needed to pitch in. Livia waved to the waiting parishioners as she headed out to the parking lot. A filthy song bled out from around the windows as she banged loudly on Kyle's roof. Kyle jumped and glared.

Kyle hit the automatic window button and turned down the radio at the same time. "What the hell, Livia? You scared the shit outta me."

Livia's eyes bugged at her sister's comment. "Kyle McHugh, why would you play that horrible song outside a church? Who taught you your manners?"

Kyle closed her phone and gave Livia the finger. "You did. So don't act all high and mighty. And last time I checked this church was empty."

Livia stepped aside so Kyle could see the line of people on the sidewalk behind her.

"Holy crap, what's happening here? An emergency bingo meeting?" Kyle asked loudly.

Livia shushed her. "Just get out and help me. It's midnight mass."

Kyle got out and walked at Livia's side toward the building. "I'm sorry? Midnight mass? Did Christmas Eve just sneak up and bite me on the ass?"

Livia squeezed Kyle's arm in the way she hated. "Just help me get them inside."

To Kyle's credit, she followed Livia's lead and they became mobility's version of a bucket brigade. Kyle was welcoming and friendly from the door of the retirement complex to halfway up the sidewalk where Livia took over. Livia made small talk and introductions until she met Cole at the church door. Cole's eyes grew softer every time he saw Livia with another church member. As the last patron made his way through the church doors, Kyle pulled Livia aside.

"Please don't make me go in the church. I don't want to go to mass." Her eyes were frantic.

"Kyle, we went to eight years of Catholic school. You can handle one little mass." Livia reached for her sister's arm again.

Kyle skittered away. "Livia, I'm positive that church will blow up all action-movie style if I put one toe in the door. I haven't been such a perfect Catholic school girl."

Livia held her palms open in disbelief. "What have you been up to? I swear we're having a long conversation as soon as this night's over."

Kyle continued as if Livia had not spoken. "And also the old people are freaking me out. They smell like moth balls, one guy pinched my ass, and I think that last one…" Kyle peeked around Livia to give last gentleman in line a smile and a little wave. "He just crapped his pants." Kyle's whisper had gotten squeaky.

Livia rolled her eyes. "You're ruining the beauty of the moment. Fine. Go back to the car, but play some less hellish music. No cursing."

Kyle kissed Livia on the cheek and skipped off to her car. Livia closed the church doors and scanned the room for a spot. Bea had a space next to her just Livia's size, so she waved and smiled her way to the seat.

Bea was still in a chatty mood. "Livia, what brings you to our little clandestine service? It's not advertised." Bea had put on pearls and makeup for the occasion.

"I had to give a message to Cole," Livia leaned in to explain. "I had no idea this went on in the middle of the night."

Bea practically glowed as she looked at Cole. "This little church has been so lucky to get Mr. Cole. He's like our adopted son. He has yet to choose a path for certain, but we really like to let him feel how proud we all are of him." Bea nodded in the direction of the altar door. As if on cue, another older man entered, dressed in priest's vestments. "I'm surprised Cole let you stay. What we do here is slightly unconventional." Bea looked suspicious and in-the-know at the same time.

"I'm in love with his brother." Saying this out loud to Bea felt like jumping out of an airplane — thrilling and irreversible. In that instant Livia knew her love for Blake was as real as the church walls around her.

Bea took in Livia's face with wise eyes. "Why, yes. Yes you are."

The old woman patted Livia's hand with her cold, soft one. On impulse Livia grasped Bea's hand to warm it.

Bea smiled again. "You're a nice girl, Livia. Love is sacred. Hold onto it. I know a lot at my age. Everything else fails you — money, possessions, sex. But love never fails." Bea touched a locket around her neck with her free hand. "Would you like to see my Aaron? You'll have to help me. I can't work these hands so well anymore."

Livia reverently opened the locket to reveal the faded image of a handsome man in a military uniform.

"We were married for sixty-two years before he passed," Bea said. "I still can't take a deep breath without smelling his scent." Her face filled with strength, rather than tears. "We had a good life. He always made me laugh. Loving him was a wonderful way to pass my time here. And someday we'll be together again."

Livia closed the locket carefully. "He's a handsome man."

Bea nodded.

Cole began the mass. As the familiar service proceeded, Livia saw that the actual priest did only the most essential of the acts. He let Cole lead prayers and give the sermon. Cole did a magnificent job of speaking to a crowd that had already learned most of life's cruelest lessons.

Cole took his place behind the pulpit, and Livia could almost see him trying to ignore her presence.

"Welcome, friends and visitor."

He was doing a poor job of it.

"Tonight I would like to talk about faith in the unseen. Here, in God's house, we have many physical reminders of our faith — our statues, the pews and stained glass, and the very peace we feel here. We have things we can touch, feel, and see. Faith isn't a surprise here. It's expected. We're covered by faith in our church, like a well-used blanket.

"Faith is much harder to feel when we're far from our rituals and must rely only on what we can fit in our hearts. Trials and tribulations rarely happen in church when we're surrounded by other believers to bolster and encourage us. Sometimes we're in a store, struggling to understand how the checker could be so slow. Sometimes we're in a hospital, grasping the hand of a loved one." Cole looked at Bea, who nodded.

"And sometimes we're just a little child inside when someone in power takes more from us than they ever have a right to." He dropped his eyes for a moment.

Livia watched as Bea shot a look of concern to some of the other ladies present. Cole had revealed a tiny bit of himself on the pulpit, and judging from the reaction, he didn't do it often.

"These are the times when God whispers to us," he continued. "We have to listen carefully to his important guidance. Sometimes that guidance is to just endure. And that's when our faith has to hold us up."

Livia continued to hold Bea's hand as Cole concluded his thoughts. When he prayed for the departed, the length of the list became almost comical, until Livia heard Aaron mentioned and felt a squeeze from Bea. *Each name is attached to a heart here.*

Cole seemed truly holy as he recited the words. "I leave you peace. My peace I give you. Now let us all offer one another the sign of peace."

Livia watched the parishioners greet those next to them, then hold up their hands to wave at others around the room. Livia looked around. Sweet Bea in her wheelchair was one of easily sixty people in the sanctuary. Livia was overwhelmed by their quiet kindness. Cole had a roomful of family now.

Livia stood. Waving the peace was a tradition she had every intention of breaking. Cole looked at her with a suspicious eyebrow cocked.

Livia started with Bea. "Peace be with you."

"And also with you, Livia," Bea said as they shook hands.

Livia walked to the front pew and began methodically offering her hand and words to each person. At the second pew, Livia changed her sign of peace into a hug. In her peripheral vision, Livia could see Cole now going through the pews on the opposite side, hugging these people he loved. When each person had been thoroughly hugged, Cole and Livia met in the middle.

She looked at his face, hoping beyond hope to find softness there. "Peace be with you, Cole," she began. "But I think you already have it. You're covered by the prayers of these wonderful people."

Cole nodded. The softness was still there.

"Peace be with you, Livia," he said. He leaned down to her ear as he hugged her. "Maybe you're more than I thought you were."

Livia hugged him back. It wasn't forgiveness, but it was enough for now.

When mass was over, the congregation socialized for a bit, launching mostly into discussions about what a great job Cole had done. Some of the men offered Cole pointers or suggestions like they were his football coaches.

"I saw some construction going on up there," Livia said to Bea, gesturing up to the loft.

"Oh, that's for our new church organ," Bea said eagerly. "The old one was taken out of here about twenty years ago. Dry rot, you know."

Livia nodded and smiled as Bea continued. "An anonymous donor sent Father Callahan all the money to cover it. We can't wait to let Martha have a chance at it." Bea pointed to a small woman with the thickest glasses Livia had ever seen.

"It'll be here tomorrow morning, but will probably take all day to put together." Bea looked happily at the empty loft.

"How are they going to get it up those tiny, twirly steps?" Livia wondered aloud.

"Just like anything, dear. Piece by piece. The right people get the right tools and turn a jigsaw puzzle into something that makes beautiful music." Bea looked at Livia knowingly.

"The right people with the right tools. Of course." Livia smiled.

She hugged Bea and excused herself. It was time to escort the parishioners back whence they came. Livia walked out to the car to find the driver's seat reclined all the way back and Kyle curled in a happy ball. Livia banged on the window like a landlord looking for rent.

"What!?" Kyle looked disoriented, then really irritated.

"Come help me again."

Livia watched as her sister scowled, then began to move. Kyle slammed the car door shut and unleashed her foul mood. "Oh, for crud's sake. This is the most ridiculous song and dance in the middle of the flipping night. Why can't the priest go to the old folks' home instead of dragging all these wrinkly bags and bats around like a set of droopy balls?"

Livia patted Kyle's shoulder condescendingly. "Look at that! You did all that complaining without cursing. That's a good girl."

Kyle grumbled as she helped with the reverse trip. When they were down to the last lady, she looked over at Kyle and said, "Oh, I forgot my purse. Could you be a little sweetie and go get it for me?"

Kyle smiled, took a deep breath, and stomped back toward the church. "Don't blame me when a giant bolt of lightning torches this place," she announced to Livia as she passed.

When Livia walked in a few minutes later to see what had happened to Kyle, she stopped in her tracks. Kyle and Cole faced each other in the center of the room, staring intently and oblivious to everything else.

"Kyle? Hey, did you find the purse?" When her sister said nothing, Livia approached them and took the purse from Kyle's hand. Still no one said a word, so she left to return it to its owner. When she came back, Livia found her sister and Cole standing the same way, lost in one another.

"Kyle, we've got to get going." Livia felt like an intruder.

Her sister's eyes swam in Cole's. "You go on ahead," she said. "I'll get a ride."

"Ky, this isn't a frat party. It's an empty church. Where's this ride coming from?" Livia asked.

"I'll make sure she gets home," Cole said, his eyes never wavering from Kyle's face.

Livia reached into her unresponsive sister's pocket and retrieved the car keys. As she left the church, shaking her head, she heard Cole saying Kyle's name again and again. It was like he'd just discovered fire, and Kyle was the main ingredient.

9

LIVIA'S STUPID FATHER

*L*ivia's stupid fucking father.

Chris grabbed a piece of gum and slid his beer can behind his right leg. He glared into his side mirror as he saw John McHugh step out of his police car. *This is the last thing I need at one o'clock in the damn morning.*

Chris waited until his electric window was all the way down before he looked at the top of John's head. Chris loved how the truck made him superior to everyone else. Even the soccer moms' Suburbans looked wimpy next to The Beast.

John stepped up onto the truck's running board to be even with Chris's face.

Chris adjusted his leg in a way that he hoped concealed his beer can. He tried to remember where the hell his hunting rifle was. *Did I just throw it in the back or lock it in the truck box?*

"Hi, Mr. McHugh." Chris watched as John shined his flashlight in the truck bed and then carefully took in the contents of his cab.

"It's *Officer* McHugh, Chris."

John's face was alarmingly close, and Chris tried not to breathe. *Fucking pig. What a lame-ass job. Why'd I have to drink beer tonight? Should've gone with vodka, can't smell it on my breath.*

"Sorry, sir." Chris put on his best altar boy face.

"Do you know how fast you were going back there, son?"

Fast enough to get the fuck away from bitchy, skank-ass Hannah.

"I'm sure too fast, Officer McHugh, or you wouldn't have stopped me." Chris spoke into his chest so the beer smell wouldn't get in front of the cinnamon gum. He hoped he seemed remorseful.

"Fifty-six in a thirty-five, Chris. This is a residential area. You need to slow down," John said.

"Sorry, sir. I have a lot on my mind since Livia dumped me." Chris tended to get weepy when he drank, and it had never been useful until this moment. He stifled a smile as his eyes filled with tears.

"All right, Chris. You've had a tough time. I'll let you get by with a warning tonight. But it's the only warning I'll give you."

I should give you a warning. Your freaking daughter's whoring it out to homeless men. "Thank you, Officer McHugh. I'm sorry. I'll drive slower from now on." *Or just buy a fucking radar detector.*

John leaned back a bit and the red and blue lights from the cruiser danced across his face. "Tell Mrs. Grandma and your family I'm wishing them well." He nodded and stepped down from the truck.

"Thank you, sir," Chris said. "Can I ask you a question? How's Livia doing?"

"She seems a little sad, but that was some stunt you pulled in front of my house. Stay away from her, Chris, unless she asks you to come back."

Chris nodded. He knew not to push Livia's dad.

He waited for the excruciating amount of time it took John to get back in his car, pull the cruiser away from the curb, and kill the lights. *I swear they take a long fucking time just to rattle you. Bastards.*

Chris's phone came to life in the console. He instantly hoped it was Livia calling and wanted to kick himself in the nuts when he saw it was Hannah. He sent her to voice mail and grabbed his now disappointingly warm beer. Chris couldn't believe how cocky Hannah had gotten since his breakup with Livia. He scratched his scalp through his crackly, gelled hair and grew angry all over again as he remembered his evening with Hannah.

"Chris, I'm not sure I want to go through with this," she'd pouted.

"Hannah, you and I have been screwing around for four and a half years. You pick now to get shy?" Chris was further frustrated that she'd waited until they were both pants-less to mention her displeasure.

"I don't know. I think maybe you should get tested—for STDs and worms and maybe lice." Hannah reached for her discarded panties.

She had fluttered her eyelashes in a way she seemed to think was coy, but she looked like a cow getting branded. "Since Livia's humping hobos, who knows what you've got." Hannah giggled at her unintentional alliteration.

"Screw you, Hannah." Chris had suddenly felt very naked.

"Livia's like Meals on Wheels, except she's on her feet. And she hands out her pussy instead of meals. She's Pussy on Feet." Hannah had to stop buttoning her jeans to laugh.

Chris had felt revulsion wash over him. Hannah had been so much more desirable when she was his piece on the side. "That's not even funny, you stupid slut." Chris found his tighty-whiteys and put them on.

The word *slut* had sobered Hannah and her face clouded over. "You know what, Chris? You're just not doing it for me anymore. I mean, you lost your fiancée to a homeless man? What kind of catch are you? I wouldn't screw you now without at least three condoms and a bucketful of Lysol."

Chris had left Hannah's apartment through the front door instead of sneaking out the back like he usually did.

And now he sat in the wake of John's departed police car with no fiancée *or* piece of ass on the side. There had been a time when Livia needed him so much. How many times did she thank him for keeping track of her cell phone and the oil changes on her car? And yeah, he was young, he wanted his dick to wander free once in a while, but Livia was his. His responsibility. Christ, she didn't even have a mother—he couldn't dump her in the past even when he had wanted to because he didn't want her to melt down.

The phone in Chris's hand demanded his attention again. Dave.

"Talk at me," he answered.

"Hey, you stupid bastard. How's it hanging? Lonely, I bet. Talk about going from hero to zero, man." Dave delivered his insults under the guise of brotherhood. It was a thin guise. "'Pulling a Chris Simmer' is going to be legend for a long time to come. Losing your chick to a homeless man? I think I'd rather find out my girl was into other girls. What are you up to? Want to hang out?"

"No. I'm busy. Fuck off." Chris seethed. He was about to hang up when Dave said something else.

"So I guess Livia's new boyfriend's dead or something," Dave added.

Chris listened.

"I usually see his crazy ass slumped at the train station on my dinner break."

Chris took a jab of his own. "You paying for a good butt-fucking, Dave?"

Chris heard a nervous laugh that he liked. It reminded him he was still top dog.

"No, dude. I save up my pennies and go down there with a few of my work buddies. We whip the change at him. Ten points for a headshot and five points for limbs. I'm up to one-eighty. He never even flinches or looks up. I bet he could take a hell of a beating. Anyhow, he hasn't been there in a while."

Chris ended the call with Dave still yammering. He liked the idea of a good beating. Why hadn't he thought of it himself? If any other dude had moved in on Livia, he'd have met him in an alley with The Equalizer. Chris reached under his passenger seat to stroke the miniature baseball bat. Maybe if the hobo met The Equalizer, Livia would come back to him. That would fix everything, really.

10

ΠΟΤ SORRY YOU'RE HERE

Livia sensed light on her eyelids. She opened them, blinking and trying to focus. Her neck was creaky and stiff like a dried twig. She seemed to have a bruise on her butt—from the gearshift? As the cramped pain became more pronounced, Livia remembered she'd waited for Kyle in the parking lot. Bad enough she had dragged her sister to a drug den, so she wasn't leaving her in the middle of the night with a pseudo-priest who might or might not be friendly.

As Livia tried to avoid thinking about how her feisty sister was getting along inside a Catholic church, the huge front doors flung open. Kyle rushed out, looking as if she had every intention of stalking home half dressed. Livia tapped the horn. Kyle turned, but didn't even look grateful that Livia was still there with the car.

Kyle got to the car door before Livia could find the automatic lock button, so they played a few cycles of Kyle trying the handle while Livia simultaneously tried to unlock the door. Finally, Livia held up one finger to signal her sister to slow the hell down. Kyle bounced up and down like she was standing in a pile of hot coals. Livia locked, then unlocked the door to allow her incensed sister inside. As she entered, Kyle lashed out at anything and everything she could reach, including Livia.

Livia struggled to grab her sister's flailing arms. "Kyle, whoa. *Ouch!* Damn it, calm down. Your freaking boob is hanging out. Pull yourself together."

Kyle bit her lip and ignored her sister. "Damn him. Damn him to hell," she seethed, glaring at the church.

Just then Cole emerged. He too was half-dressed—barefoot and bare-chested. His eyes found the car and locked on Kyle with a gaze that spoke of tremendous, shattering loss. It was as if she'd been swallowed by a fissure in the earth.

Livia looked back at her sister. "What the hell happened?"

Kyle looked at Cole with a matching desperate stare. She shook her head and finally slid her bra back in place to cover herself. "Leave. Drive."

Livia hesitated. The scene before her seemed so raw. Leaving had to be an insult, a mistake.

Kyle looked at the car floor. "Livia, if you've ever loved me, even a little, you'll take me away from here. Please, I'm begging you."

Livia had never heard Kyle beg for anything. The big sister in her took over. She started the car, slammed it into reverse, and made for the exit. As soon as they no longer faced Cole, sobs wracked Kyle's body. Livia felt reflex tears on her own cheeks, her body's reaction to Kyle's deep pain.

Livia watched in her rear view mirror as Cole punched the Our Lady of the River welcome plaque mounted next to the door. It shattered around his hand like a mirror.

Just as Kyle choked out, "I hate him," Livia saw Cole fall to his knees. He looked like a man kneeling in front of his captor, waiting for the whip.

A few minutes later, Livia stopped for a red light and had a horrible, crawling feeling. "Did he *hurt* you?" she asked.

"No. *No.* Not in the way you're thinking. Far from it." Kyle still breathed in little sobs, but she seemed to be calming.

Livia felt relief in every part of her being. *If I'd been right outside while Kyle was being hurt…*Livia shook her head to clear it. "Are you going to tell me what happened?"

Kyle seemed to start and stop four different sentences before settling on, "No. I think I need to be alone with this."

Livia watched pinks and yellows color the sky. She usually loved being out this ridiculously early in the morning, before the rest of the world. The air smelled different, like morning dew scented with promise. But this morning she could focus only on the knot of concern in her stomach and her silent sister next to her.

Kyle remained quiet all the way home, and when they arrived both girls were too numb to remember they'd snuck out the night before. As they slammed their car doors, both opened their eyes wide with alarm. Wordlessly, they bolted to the side of the house.

Livia rolled her eyes and whispered, "We need an apartment. We're too damn old to be sneaking into the house."

Kyle ignored her and went to work. She found the small, flat piece of metal she'd hidden behind a shrub and popped the lock on the downstairs window like a practiced cat burglar. She carefully replaced the tool where she could get to it again and continued to ignore Livia's bug-eyed stare.

"That's why you never wanted a dog? Because it would bark when you snuck in? I wanted a dog," Livia said, finally connecting the dots.

Kyle shrugged and crawled in the window. Livia followed, her muscles still punishing her for her nap in the car.

Her sister stopped in the kitchen and waited. With predictable regularity, their father's sleep noises came, like a gasping, dying bear's, from his room. Kyle picked out a very specific path up the stairs, avoiding all the squeaks, then opened the door to her room.

"Put pajamas on," she hissed over her shoulder as she went inside.

Livia threw on sweats and a T-shirt and was back at Kyle's door. Finding it unlocked, she entered. Kyle lay on her bed, also in sweats, staring at the ceiling. Kyle's room should have been all simple lines and modern furniture, but before she was born their mother, Margret, had spent ungodly amounts of money to outfit the room in the style of a frilly, lavender picture she'd seen in a magazine about celebrity nurseries. Little was changed over the years.

Livia knelt on the bed next to her sister. "Tell me *something* or I'm going to freak out."

Kyle looked pained. "Livia, you've got it all together. You're smart, pretty, and you have always had Chris—until he recently revealed he was a muff wanker. You have goals. I can't tell you how often I've wished I could be that way."

"But you're so beautiful—" Livia quickly interjected.

"Mom left," Kyle continued. "She didn't leave after you were born. She left after *I* was born. Maybe she knew I'd be a disappointment." Kyle held her finger up, stopping Livia's next instant defense. "You asked. Now listen." She twirled a purple teddy bear in her hands. "When you were busy with Chris, I missed you so much. I couldn't find my place and the emptiness in me got bigger and bigger. Don't blame yourself. You have a life, Livia. That's normal and healthy." Kyle's voice was soft.

Livia pulled the bear out of Kyle's grasp and held her hands. She now despised Chris even more, though this wasn't his fault.

"Do you know how many guys I've been with?" Kyle asked, meeting her eyes for just a moment. "So many. You know why? Because in that moment, just before you let them fuck you, you're the center of their universe. It lasts just seconds, but I like that feeling. I crave that feeling.

"This morning—last night? Whenever it was, standing in that church in front of him? I had that feeling. I was the center of his universe. And we

75

had all our clothes *on*. That feeling lasted for hours." Kyle closed her eyes as if to transport herself back there.

"But Margret had something more important to do, and so does he," she suddenly spat, her voice bitter and poisonous. "Something is always more valuable than me."

Livia had heard enough. "Kyle, you're the most amazing, fearless woman I've ever met, and that includes that RoboBitch from the parking lot." She gathered Kyle in a hug.

"Even though I'm a stone-cold slut?" Kyle relaxed and hugged her sister back.

"Even if you're a dirty skankbag." Livia smoothed Kyle's hair in a supremely motherly gesture.

"You still love me even though I'm a whore pit viper?" Kyle grabbed fistfuls of Livia's shirt, her hands belying her teasing words.

Sensing an oncoming tournament of off-color teasing, Livia shifted gears. She wanted to speak right to the emptiness. "I'd rather have you in my life than Margret. I'm not sorry you're here." Livia hugged Kyle again, trying to seal her love into her broken sister.

Just then their father opened Kyle's door. The sisters looked up from the bed to find him surveying them with alarmed eyes. Emotions were not his strong suit.

"You girls all right in here?" His voice sounded like he was responding to a domestic violence call in the field.

Kyle recovered first and offered the only thing guaranteed to make their father bolt. "Yeah, Dad, we're okay. I was just asking Livia about tampons. I think I keep doing something wrong."

Livia buried her face in Kyle's hair to hide her smile. As predicted, their father backed away, nodding, and hurriedly shut the door. His daughters' silent laughter sent them across the bed together. Livia was thrilled to see her sister smile.

Kyle seemed to rally. "Livia, you better get ready or you'll miss your train."

"What're you doing today?" Livia wasn't quite ready to leave Kyle alone.

"I've got work, and tomorrow night I want to go out. I'm going to party my ass off. There'll be pumpkin pie shooters in honor of Thanksgiving." Kyle wiggled her eyebrows and disappeared into her closet.

"I'll go with you." Livia realized she should spend more time with Kyle, especially if her sister would be vengeance partying.

Kyle looked at her skeptically. "If you're hanging with me, you have to dress hot. Not like a psychologist." Kyle paused, still not seeming satisfied. "Tell you what, I'll lay out your outfit tomorrow. I'll pick you up from the train station, and we'll get your *shitieous* car from the lot on Saturday."

"Okay." Livia knew she was committed now.

Livia dragged herself back to her own room, then took a quick shower, got dressed, and hit the kitchen in record time. She thought of Bea, her recent late-night acquaintance, as she made Blake a breakfast sandwich and put it in a paper bag. *Faith.*

Her father came in, arming himself for his day at the precinct. He looked tremendously uncomfortable when he saw her, and Livia felt terrible about the whole tampon farce. God bless him, he tried to take care of his girls no matter what.

"Livia, did Kyle, um...figure everything out?"

Livia nodded and silently begged him to move on. He didn't.

"Because if she needs to see a doctor — or a nurse if that's better — to help her, with, um, stuff..." He shuffled his feet and looked at the ground.

Livia felt her cheeks pink up like they'd been slapped. "We worked it out. She knows where things, um, go now." *Kill me.*

"Alrighty. If you're sure." John put on his police officer's hat, which made him seem about six inches taller and changed his aura from Dad to Authority.

This reminded Livia of a question. "Hey, Dad, if I needed to check someone's background, would you be able to do that for me?"

"That's a little unethical, Liv." John smoothed his mustache. "Is this about a boy?"

Livia cringed. "Yeah, it is."

"Then absolutely. I'd be happy to." He nodded with conviction.

He turned to head out the door, then seemed to think better of it. "Livia, I stopped Chris Simmer for speeding last night." He paused, seeming to want a response.

None came.

"He seemed pretty torn up," he continued. "He asked how you were. As far as I'm concerned he's nobody until you tell me different. But I just wanted to let you know. Angry guys do stupid things sometimes. Be careful."

"Did you give him a ticket?" Livia asked.

"I gave him a warning. I know Mrs. Grandma's in a fragile state." He turned again to leave.

Livia caught the door before he closed it. "Thanks, Dad." On her tiptoes, she kissed his cheek. "I love you."

"Love ya too, Liv." A smile slipped through his professional façade.

Livia followed him out and got in her Escort. She was careful not to crush the breakfast sandwich filled with sausage, egg, and hope.

11

THE MURDERER AND THE MAN OF GOD

Beckett pulled up to the meeting spot in the Hummer. He emerged from his vehicle in an expensive suit, sans tie, with exquisitely costly Italian shoes cradling his feet. Cole was already there, dressed like he was ready to do yard work. He sat on the hood of the church's boring tan sedan, which Beckett had hated since the first time he saw it.

"Still driving around in the dead man's car?" Beckett said by way of greeting.

Cole hopped off the hood and walked toward Beckett until they could wrap their forearms together. The men stood closely for a moment. Someone watching might have guessed they were going to kiss.

Cole stepped back. "The dead man donated this fabulous piece of machinery with his dying breath. So, yes, I'm still driving it."

"This is probably the only twenty-year-old car in existence with four-teen miles on the odometer. That guy really went nowhere but church. It should be in a fucking museum." Beckett hopped onto the sedan's hood, and the car creaked in protest.

Cole said nothing. The men scanned the woods. Today was cloudy, so they could expect to meet Blake here, where they'd parked, rather than traveling into the cover of trees.

"He ain't comin'," Beckett said. "Not by a long shot."

But neither man moved. They would wait for the hour they promised, just as they had for the past seven years. This wouldn't be the first time Blake hadn't shown up.

Beckett took a closer look at Cole. "You look like crap on a pile of crap. What the hell have you been doing, self-flagellating instead of whacking off?"

"Did someone steal a Word-a-Day calendar recently?" Cole retorted.

Beckett leaned over and gave an exaggerated sniff. "You smell like pussy! Did you get pussy? Are you nailing an old chick?"

"You make me sick." Cole turned, doing his best to ignore Beckett.

But Beckett never gave up. "Did you put on a muumuu, grab some Bengay, and head to that glorified Denny's like Don Juan? You da man!" Beckett pounded Cole on the back.

Cole looked at him, face wreathed in despair, and the pounding stopped.

"What? What happened?" Beckett lost his swagger, and his voice softened.

Cole grabbed a fistful of his own hair. "Beckett, I met the most amazing girl this morning. I can't think straight."

"Now that right there is some soap opera bullshit, and I feel for you, little bro. Aren't you supposed to be Jesus' bitch?" Beckett studied Cole's face.

"I'm not going to let down the people who've fed me and clothed me and gave me a chance when they didn't have to." Cole had actually pulled out some of his hair and now picked it from between his fingers.

"Not to be a bastard, but, dude, aren't all the people who were there when you started dead now?"

Beckett waited for Cole's wrath. He hated when anyone disparaged his congregation.

"It's the spirit of the thing. And no, some of them are still alive. Father Callahan is definitely still alive." Cole scanned the woods again.

"A woman can make you want to change your ways." Beckett touched the small scar Eve's knife had left on his neck. "Speaking of which, did Livia come to see you?"

Cole's eyes shut. "Yes, we've met."

"That's not who you're talking about, is it?" Beckett said, suddenly alarmed. Cole gave him a withering look. "I want her to be right for Blake so bad."

Cole nodded, but then shook his head. "No, it's not her. Beck, Livia's a regular girl. How can a regular girl handle it?"

"I don't know. I think she's braver than most. Did you know she came to see me in the middle of the night? Tssk. I almost watched Dentist kill her and her little sister in my parking lot."

In an instant Cole threw Beckett on his back and squeezed his throat for all he was worth on the hood of the donated car.

Beckett lay quietly and refused to fight back. He'd never lay a hand on Cole in violence, ever.

Cole shook his head, seeming to come back to himself, and released Beckett's neck. "You almost watched Kyle die? What kind of monster are you?"

Beckett absorbed the verbal blow as he sat up. "I'm the worst kind, Cole. The worst kind."

The brothers sat in silence again, scanning the woods for prodigal Blake.

After about ten minutes of awkward silence, Beckett tried again. "So, Fairy Princess is the lady who has you all jacked up. Livia's sister."

Cole nodded.

Beckett resumed telling his story as if Cole had not just tried to choke him. "Livia came to my office and managed to ask me about Blake, even after witnessing some serious shit in the parking lot." Beckett watched as Cole's jaw tightened. "She's braver than she needs to be," he continued. "Maybe, just maybe, she could be the one."

Cole stood and dusted off his pants as if they were as expensive as Beckett's. "I hope he shows up today to check out the organ."

Cole got back in the miraculous tan sedan and started the perfectly maintained engine with Beckett still sitting on the hood. Beckett jumped off and went to the driver's side window. He smirked at the manual crank as Cole rolled down the window.

"Shut it," Cole snarled.

Beckett held up his knuckles for a bump. "If I watched your church burn down, would you kill me?"

Cole looked suspicious. "No, and that's a bizarre question."

Beckett looked toward the woods one more time. "If I watched Kyle die, would you kill me?"

Cole's eyes practically glowed red.

Beckett nodded. "You might already have the answer to what's hurting you."

Cole let out a giant sigh. "I'll text you if he shows up."

Beckett smiled crookedly. "Text me *when* he shows up. I know my boy. He'll be there for a keyboard."

Cole pulled away carefully, but he still left a cloud of dust that covered Beckett.

Beckett wasn't ready to leave. His brothers might never understand how much he hungered for their monthly meetings. He loved feeling like he had a family. He was so used to watching his back and striking first. The easy camaraderie they shared was a balm on his frazzled nerves.

Beckett's cell phone vibrated in his pocket. He pulled it out while he brushed off his clothes. Eve's text gave him peace:

Chaos reported Blake sighting, gave him tat. Meeting go ok?

Eve hated to talk on the phone. Calling her was like conversing with someone who didn't speak his language. Most of the time she just hung up without saying goodbye after she got the information she wanted.

Beckett's huge fingers hated texting, and he sent horribly misspelled messages back to Eve:

GooiD NEWWS. Meeti%ng Fine. Shipment on Tuess.
UR an excellent fuck.

She returned the text so quickly, Beckett laughed out loud:

U will know when u have been fucked.

Beckett put the phone in his pocket. He kept messing with her, trying to get her to sleep with him, but Eve had yet to do anything but tease him. In a world full of whores and junkies, *not* getting laid was a huge turn-on.

Beckett scanned the trees again and felt a twinge of jealousy that Blake had gotten another tat. It was their thing, the brothers. Their matching tattoos had been the only ones any of them had. *Fuck him, it's his body.*

Beckett pulled himself up into the Hummer. He'd wait a little longer, just in case. There were a lot of illegal, deadly things stored in Beckett's car, but the only thing he kept hidden was the CD he now pulled out from under the driver's seat. He slipped it in the player and turned on the power, letting the classical music sweep over him like a cool breeze. It was the soundtrack of his boys. The music that saved them. Blake's music.

Fueled by the melody, Beckett's mind drifted over his past as he waited in the Hummer. After the botched cat rescue, Beckett had had to give Blake a beatdown to get him to stop with the goddamn hose. The cat scratches hurt so fucking much, but he kept hitting the new kid through the sting. Beckett's balls had actually crawled inside his body like fucking ostriches from the pain.

When he had finally seen Blake's passive green eyes, he'd had the sick feeling he was beating on Jesus Fucking Christ. Beckett got up off the new kid and stormed into the house.

New kid had followed him in, carrying a pathetic box of useless crap. He spoke in a ridiculous, cultured voice. "Where do they keep medicines and such in this house?"

Beckett pointed with one of his thick fingers. "Up there, above the stove, so the kids don't fucking eat 'em."

New kid had rooted around in the messy cabinet like a goddamn truffle pig finding mushrooms. He came back holding a tube of cream and stood behind Beckett.

"Listen, I plan on being an ass virgin until prison, so you may back the fuck up. Now." Beckett could feel the blood sticking to his shirt.

"Well, unless you're circus-style double jointed, there's no way you'll be able to reach these scratches on your back," the new kid had astutely observed.

Beckett had grumbled, but pulled off his shirt. In as masculine a way as they could, the two cleaned his back and smeared some salve on the long red scratches. Beckett went to get a clean shirt from his bedroom, and the new kid followed him.

"That's your bed right there," Beckett said, pointing to one of two worn-looking twin beds in the room.

New kid had retrieved his beat-up box from downstairs and hefted it onto his bed.

He'd turned and given Beckett a formal greeting. "I'm pleased to meet you. My name's Blake Hartt."

Beckett had looked for a moment at the outstretched hand and finally accepted it. "I'm Beckett Taylor, and we've already been as fucking intimate as we're ever going to get." He'd put some extra testosterone in his handshake.

"Beckett, I hope I never have to rub you with anything again. It might help if you let ugly kittens get themselves out of trees."

"Have you ever *seen* such an ugly damn cat?" Beckett had said with a wry smile. "Aren't kittens supposed to be all cute and shit?" He liked this kid.

"It was nice of you to help that ungrateful little girl out." Blake unloaded his belongings onto his bed.

"Ah, I've got a soft spot for kids. They're so fucking little."

Beckett had turned to go, but thought better of it. Something in Blake spoke to him, maybe it was the Jesus eyes. "Dude, do yourself a favor and don't go into the woods after dinner—at least until you see me back in this house."

Blake had looked at Beckett suspiciously and nodded.

It wasn't long after that when Beckett had figured out Blake was different. He avoided the sun at all costs and had more pill bottles than an AIDS patient. But Beckett wasn't a bully. He didn't pick on somebody just because he didn't fit the fuck in. He only spoke with his fists when he was attacked, verbally or physically. Granted, the definition of "attacked" had a sliding scale.

By the time they'd finished dinner that first night, Blake had made his formal introduction to his new foster parents and the assortment of other kids who lived in the house. After the meal, Beckett rose and went out the back door. His foster father, Rick, was close on his heels.

Beckett stopped at the oak tree that was their meeting place. He stood, as requested, with his hands clasped in front of him. Each night, Rick geared up and beat Beckett repeatedly. With punches, cracks, slams, and grunts, Rick unleashed a fury he kept hidden just for Beckett.

Beckett had had no idea Blake was as tricky as fog in the woods, and that he watched the scene unfold night after night with his clear green eyes.

"Why aren't you fighting back?" Blake finally asked one night as Beckett lay on his bed.

"I told you not to come the fuck out there, didn't I?" Beckett hissed.

"I like the woods," Blake said. "I don't like knowing what he does to you."

"Rick's a beater. He likes it. When I first got here, he beat all the kids. I told him I wanted to take it for everybody." Beckett had shrugged like he'd just eaten the last cookie. "I'm a big fucking bastard. I can handle it."

"What about letting your social worker know?" Blake countered.

Beckett shook his head. "No, she's cool as hell and all, but I have to get through this on my own. I have this worked out. I have a plan. Don't worry about me. I got this." Beckett sucked at school, but he knew he could take few beatings.

The next evening, Beckett had waited for Rick in his usual spot, head down and hands clasped in front like a condemned army cadet. As Rick approached, the sound of a solid punch suddenly snapped Beckett to attention. Blake stood in front Beckett with his arm in obvious recoil from the blow he'd landed on Rick.

Beckett groaned silently. *Stupid fucker. This'll ruin the plan.*

But instead of starting a brawl, Blake had assumed Beckett's position, hands holding one another in submission. "I'd like to take Beckett's beatings for tonight, if that would be acceptable," he said.

It was obvious Rick agreed when Blake's body buckled with the force of a blow. Beckett knew from experience that the kidney jab Blake had absorbed hurt like a bitch. Rick proceeded with extra vigor, leaving only after he was exhausted. He'd done his typical masterful job, leaving marks only where they could be covered.

"Dude, that's the last fucking time you set foot out here." Beckett was furious.

"Beckett, you're doing this for people who don't even know you're protecting them. We're in the shade here. I can do this. Let me do this. I can't stand by and watch."

Beckett thought for a moment, saying nothing. Blake had taken the beating like a pro. *Too good to be his first time.*

Beckett had had a moment of weakness. He selfishly wanted to take Blake up on his offer, so he did. Every night after that, Blake would show up and stand next to Beckett, head down, hands still.

Beckett now got half the beating he used to get. Rick didn't know that with every punch he was pounding his own coffin closed, but Beckett knew.

Sometime later, Cole entered the situation. The quiet, thoughtful kid came with a rap sheet that belied his peaceful, Bible-carrying persona. Beckett wasn't sure if Blake had confided in Cole or if Cole just stumbled upon the ritual, but one night he joined Blake and Beckett. And then there were three.

Now just one third of the punches fell on Beckett. When Rick's hands began to hurt, he switched to tree branches and his belt. Beckett felt like a big moron taking a beating from this twisted little fucker. He'd stood there motionless with two other guys, when together they could easily take him. But there would be ramifications.

If Beckett had learned anything from his washed-out childhood, he learned he had to pick his battles. Rick was a respected retired music teacher. He'd promised Beckett he'd written down a very believable statement that Beckett had abused the younger kids. If Beckett ratted the beater out, he'd get stuck with a stigma he'd never be able to shake. Wouldn't even matter that it wasn't true.

Beckett couldn't have people think he was what Rick insinuated. Not with little fucking kids.

In the woods the three broken boys had bonded, bound together by punches they could not return. They survived together.

Then one night Blake had saved them all. The evening's beating had been over for about an hour when the three decided to check out their foster parents' cluttered basement. Under an old, dusty sheet, Blake found a Hammond organ. He plugged it in and looked like a kid who found a fucking present under the Christmas tree.

When Blake sat down at the organ, his whole demeanor changed. Cole and Beckett stopped throwing an old baseball to each other so they could listen.

Blake made the old organ into a tool. You could see right into his soul through the notes he played. Beckett knew why Blake had Jesus' eyes. Kindness, hope, and light filled the music he played.

In an instant, Rick came down the stairs like a new husband to his virgin bride. He was drawn to Blake like a moth to flame. Blake stopped playing and looked Rick up and down. The boys recognized an addict when they saw one.

"Play more, Blake. That was wonderful," Rick begged as if he'd never thrown a punch.

So Blake had played, trapping Rick like a geisha with an opium pipe. After a week, he gave Rick an ultimatum. He would only perform after dinner. No beatings bought Rick a ticket to Blake's nightly organ concert. Rick preferred *Ave Maria*, and eventually, as the boys' wounds healed and cracked bones knit, that was the only song Blake played, over and over again.

Beckett's plan had commenced before he left the foster home, and now he had two accomplices. Blake's quick, careful eyes located the key to the safety deposit box that contained the slanderous letter. Cole's relentless patience led to a bank statement that included a yearly payment to the bank for the box. Beckett sold a boatload of pot to a teenaged teller at the bank, while videoing the transaction in secret. Then Beckett aged out first, Cole six months later, and Blake two weeks after that.

The day Blake aged out, his jeans pocket had contained a small manila envelope with a shiny silver key. With the video providing needed motivation, the bank teller helped Beckett enter the vault to extract the miserable letter from Rick's safety deposit box.

The day the three boys met with Chaos—just before his sentencing for yet another felonious journey—they discussed Rick and his current lack of musician. As Chaos and his needles worked, Beckett assured them he'd take care of it as soon as he could. Neither brother asked what he meant, but there were only young children left in Rick's house now.

One sunny Saturday a few months later, almost precisely a year after he'd aged out, Beckett went back to see Rick. He knocked on the door and played the part of a happy-go-lucky friend. As Beckett looked past Rick into the house, he saw one of the foster kids nursing his left side. Just as Beckett had known he would be, Rick was beating again. Hurting helpless children.

When Beckett suggested a trip back to the oak tree, Rick eagerly agreed. When they arrived and Beckett pulled the snub-nosed pistol out of his waistband, Rick began to apologize for everything he'd done, for anything he'd ever do.

Beckett ignored Rick's pleas and pulled out the pathetic, lying letter that had kept him and his brothers still for Rick's fists. Rick paled when he saw his blackmail in Beckett's hand.

"Rick, you sick, ass-sucking fuck, I want you to know I'm not here because you beat *me*. I'm not even here just because you beat *children*. There are lots of ways I could get you for that. But you're going to die like the gasping pussy you are because…" Beckett advanced until he was nose to nose with Rick.

"You." Beckett pushed on Rick's shoulder until he kneeled.

"Touched." Beckett leveled the pistol between Rick's eyes.

"My." Beckett cocked the hammer with a quiet click.

"Brothers." Beckett smiled as he pulled the trigger.

Beckett had rolled his head on his neck. He didn't feel the release he had longed for. Killing this bastard wasn't enough.

So Beckett had beaten Rick's body like he was killing him again. Then, one quick phone call later, Mouse had helped him bury the body. Beckett had set things right. He'd made Rick pay.

Taking a deep breath, remembering how he'd stood up for Blake and Cole, Beckett smiled in satisfaction once again. He opened his eyes to scan the woods for Blake one last time. Nothing. It would be up to the organ to flush this guy out.

Beckett started the Hummer and texted Eve:

Tak4e Ur Cloth3s OFF Im on my qway

Her reply came back quick as lightning:

Take ur clothes off and fuck yourself.

"One way or another, this chick is gonna kill me," Beckett growled as the Hummer roared away.

12

SORRY

Blake waited outside. He'd forgotten the special knock. After a moment he tapped tentatively on the door and hoped that would do the trick.

Almost immediately the man he'd come to see opened the door with a flourish, as if it were the threshold to a palace, not a tiny shack behind someone's trailer. "'Sup," he said in greeting.

Chaos was a small, sinewy man with dark eyes and a fondness for black jeans and concert T-shirt. He'd been in prison more than he'd been out of it. When he was out among the "free" people, he gravitated toward small places. He seemed to seek close quarters like a newborn who wanted to be swaddled.

Blake cleared his throat. He hadn't used his voice in a while. "Chaos, it's nice to see you. Thanks for taking my call."

"Don't pull any bullshit, kid. I know what you came for." Chaos stepped out of the way and motioned for Blake to enter his self-imposed cell. "Lay down there," he said, pointing at an army cot shoved in the corner among gardening tools, old tabletop appliances, and broken toys.

Blake was glad the space was dirty. That was all he deserved.

Chaos centered his attention on the needle he prepared. When the sliver of hard silver took a bite out of his arm, Blake resented the pain. He'd nurtured his numbness like an elaborate garden.

The blood that pooled around the needle's point reminded him of the smears he'd made on his beautiful angel's face. He'd touched Livia with his craziness and left a mark. How could she ever look at him again? By now she'd probably switched to a different train station anyway.

Chaos poked him again, and Blake welcomed the pain this time. *This pain will remind me why I shouldn't find her.*

Blake hated his weakness, but he let the pain transport him back to the clearing, to her face. He vowed it would be the last time, but he wanted to remember her noises and panting as he tasted her soft skin. *She smelled like cinnamon.*

Blake tried to see her face in his memory: trusting Livia, submitting to his hands and tongue. Instead he saw her pain as she told him she didn't see his skin turn to glass in the sun. She'd tried to hide her knowing.

Brave, beautiful Livia. She'd stood there waiting and never even flinched when he ran past. He could have plowed into her. Blake knew what it took to stay still when your mind screamed *Run!* A person had to find a place inside to die while things they didn't want happened to their body.

Chaos inserted the needle again and again with a skilled, practiced motion. The jabs blended together into a type of ecstasy. Blake made a fist with the hand Chaos didn't have trapped, feeling the scabs and scars that had formed there.

How did I do that to her? Her? Punching trees and screaming? She must have been terrified.

Soon his hands would heal, so he might forget the pain he'd caused her. He'd left her in the woods. *Left* her. Watching her find her car and punch it with the same delicate hand she'd put so trustingly in his was too much.

Blake needed something more permanent — a reminder so he'd never forget she was better off in her world, surrounded by food and family and love.

Chaos and his needle droned on.

Blake's weakness disgusted him as he began to remember his favorite smiles. Number 134 was one of the best. Livia had dropped her cell phone and cursed quietly, but creatively: *"Hairy-ass bitch."* She'd felt Blake's watchful eyes on her and given him an embarrassed smile. Number 134 made Blake realize she was a real, live girl.

On that day he'd had hope. Maybe a girl flawed enough to curse would someday say hello out loud. To him.

Number 198 was wonderful too. Blake had watched a good-looking and ridiculously pretentious guy hit on Livia. The fancy man dropped expensive name after name as he showed her all his accessories. When he finally pulled out his wallet to show her a "highly desirable luxury credit card" Livia had rolled her eyes in Blake's direction with smile number 198.

He'd had to swallow a snicker when he heard her tell the fancy man she was debt free and didn't even have credit cards.

Blake knew that was a lie because he'd seen her pay for tickets with a card at the train station. That made number 198 a secret joke between just the two of them.

Chaos wiped blood away with a towel and hummed quietly. He was in his happy place, creating something that would never go away.

Number 1 was the hardest to think about now. *After*. But Blake let himself go there as Chaos pressed into the deepest punctures.

Blake liked the train station because the trains offered reliable percussion for the songs he played in his head. When Livia had first stepped onto the platform, Blake had tried his hardest not to stare. He knew moneyed people didn't like their women getting ogled by the homeless. But she was so friendly, even in this place where people built their own personal bubbles and stayed in them. When she smiled she looked like a walking ray of the sunshine he had to avoid.

Her eyes had found his and shocked him. Blake was used to the blank, anesthetized eyes of those looking everywhere but at him. Her smile was resuscitation for his soul.

Me! She sees *me.*

At first he chalked it up to her mistaking him for normal. But smile after smile came, long after he knew she must have realized the truth.

Finally, Chaos held Blake's wrist up and inspected it carefully. He turned it toward Blake, who nodded his sad approval.

There. Now as long as I have my arm, I'll remember to stay away from Livia McHugh.

"I don't have anything to pay you with now," Blake said, turning toward Chaos. "But just tell me how much, and I'll make sure this debt is paid."

Chaos shrugged. "Dude, I owe Beckett. Just let him know."

Blake nodded and stood. *Of course. Everyone owes Beckett something.*

Chaos' attention drifted from his workstation to the shed's only dingy, dirty window. "Man, don't keep yourself locked up. Or else someday, even when the door's open, you won't want to walk out anymore."

Blake nodded and held out his hand. Chaos stood to shake it.

"Your work is amazing. This is just what I needed." Blake double-checked that the sky was still cloudy before he stepped out of Chaos' shed.

He rolled down the sleeve on his filthy shirt, covering the bloody, freshly tattooed word: **Sorry**.

He looked at the tattoo on his other arm and realized with a devastating thud that he'd missed the meeting. His brothers would be long gone by now.

His hands spread wide in anguish as he stood, unable to move, on the road in this horrible part of town. He'd disappointed the only people that mattered, his mistakes now documented on both his arms.

His only salvation would be in the church, tonight. If Cole would still let him play the organ.

13

Let Him Come to You

Livia approached the platform, specially made sandwich in hand. When she drew close enough, the view from the steep stairs let her head in on the secret her heart already knew. No Blake. Livia set the bag down in his empty spot anyway. *Maybe he's watching.*

Her train ride to the city was full of sleepy commuters and not much else, but when she arrived, she skipped her class and went straight to the library.

Books had always held answers for Livia. She liked their solid feel in her fingers. She looked down the long row of hardback books. Their plain, faux-leather covers had little wrinkles like elephant's skin. She gathered them until they piled high in her arms.

As she sat and read through them, Livia decided that if the covers truly matched the insides of these books, they'd be wreathed in images of people in torment — doctors and patients alike. In short, mental illness was a struggle to understand. Naming and classifying a disorder was like throwing bread to a group of pigeons. The psychologists in these books picked apart each definition or diagnosis until it was riddled with holes. There were twists and turns and contingencies.

Of course Livia already knew this. She knew it from classes and tests and papers. But now the name of the game had changed. *Blake.*

As the hours passed, Livia found a few things she could hold onto. One, delusions arrived for a variety of reasons and in varying intensities. They ranged from realistic nightmares to extreme forms of obsessive-compulsive disorder. Some delusional patients believed doing one task repeatedly would affect the future. But beyond that, not much was clear.

Livia slammed a book shut in frustration. The librarian hissed. She was missing lectures and classes today just to waste time learning things that the peers of the author then tore apart. The pile of photocopied papers and books in front of her had accumulated like a silent snowstorm.

Livia shoveled the blizzard into her messenger bag. Theory was getting her nowhere. She needed specifics—a person, a professor to talk to about Blake's case. As she trudged to the psychology department, Livia knew she was risking rejection. More than one professor had warned students about getting ahead of themselves. *But this is an emergency. I may be the only person who can get to him.*

As she stepped off the elevator, Livia tried to hold onto her urgency, but her hands started to shake. Office door after office door was closed. Nothing the least bit welcoming or inviting. Livia put her hand to her forehead and took some steadying breaths. She was scared that there'd be no good answer for Blake, no way to fix him.

"Why, hello there, young lady. Are you feeling okay?" The woman speaking carried a huge mug of coffee and wore an obscene amount of both jewelry and perfume.

"Hi. I'm fine, thanks. I was just leaving." Livia waved away her own disruption and turned to go.

The lady persisted. "Were you looking for a certain professor? I have paper in my office. You could leave a note." The woman produced a large set of jangly keys.

"Actually, I'm *not* here to see anyone specific. I just wanted to talk to a professional." Something stopped Livia from returning to the elevator.

The woman opened one of the doors and raised her eyebrow. "I'm not sure what you're looking for, but my office hours are now. Would you like to come in? Maybe I can steer you in the right direction. Some of our faculty are screwballs, and I wouldn't want you to get a dud."

Livia's mouth dropped open.

She looked in as the woman entered her office. It was far from what she expected. Actually, it made Livia a little nervous. This woman was not as motherly as she'd seemed. The office furniture looked cozy and soft, but everything else was macabre. Skulls, skeletons, and autopsy photos were the décor of choice. Livia hovered in the doorway as the woman lit a few candles. She finally glanced up to find Livia still standing there.

"Oh, forgive me. I'm Valerie Lavender. I teach the death and dying course. Does that make my office any less of a horrifying sepulcher?"

Of course. Valerie Lavender was a legend. Death and Dying was the toughest class to get in to at registration. Getting a seat was a sign of seniority.

"I'm Livia McHugh, and I'm searching for some advice on a delusional friend of mine. He needs help, and I want to be there for him." *Whoa. Just lay it the hell out there, Livia.*

"That's admirable. Please have a seat. I may not be the person you need, but I'm willing to listen."

Dr. Lavender sat down and looked as if she had all the time in the world. So Livia collapsed in a chair and unloaded her whole story. As she tried to include all the little bits of Blake that floated in pieces around her mind, she found herself going into alarming detail about her time with him in the woods. But she didn't stop talking.

This woman inspired confidence. Dr. Lavender listened with her whole body. Her eyes followed Livia's lips and movements. Every nod and smile urged Livia to continue. Almost an hour ticked by, and finally, Livia's story reached the present. Dr. Lavender asked for a moment and made a phone call from her desk.

"Hey, Lara. Can you do me a favor and tell my class to read chapters fourteen to twenty-five in the text and do the questions after each one?... No, they don't have to stay...Thanks. I'm fine. I have a student who needs a little extra help." She hung up the phone and motioned for Livia to join her on the deep-pillowed couch.

"Dr. Lavender, I feel awful for having you skip your class." Livia couldn't believe the precious time being lavished on her.

"Do you think this is an emergency, Livia? I mean, you might see Blake tonight, right?"

"I think it's an emergency, yes," Livia said. "It feels very urgent."

"Well, I'm going to be honest. Delusions aren't my specialty. I deal in death, and I can only give you advice from *my* experience. But no one else is here, and you seem to need help right now."

Dr. Lavender smiled kindly. "I teach this course here, but one of my other jobs is to go the site of tragedies or soon-to-be tragedies. Companies hire me to provide support for bereaved, shocked families." Dr. Lavender glanced at an exquisite replica of a death pyre on her bookcase. "So I'll take a shot."

Livia nodded.

"I've learned that in the center of someone's mourning, the best you can do for them is listen. That's really what I do. When I arrive at a disaster, I go into a tent full of families who are waiting for, or have just received, the worst news of their lives. I can't make it better, but I can let them talk. It's a gift to hear someone talk — even about a loss — from the depths of their love.

"Your Blake is mourning something. I think that pain is manifesting as his glass-skin delusions. You're going to have to approach him as if he's in one of those tents I walk into. My advice is this: Listen, Livia. Listen to him. Saying words out loud can heal."

Livia was desperate to intervene, to *fix* Blake. But perhaps his past was a plane crash she couldn't change the outcome of.

"And one more thing, Livia. No matter how you treat a corpse, throughout the centuries dead is dead. Death should not be feared; it's the catalyst for some of the greatest living. Make your day count, Livia, because you never know when it's your last one."

Instead of sounding like a Beckett-style threat, Dr. Lavender's observation solidified something. Livia would live for love. *Today will count.*

"Thank you so very much. I'm glad the other doors were closed." Livia stood as Dr. Lavender did the same.

Dr. Lavender took Livia in a perfume-flavored hug. "Thank you for sharing the story of this amazing man. Your soul is very beautiful, and I'm glad to have a peek at it."

As Livia grabbed her overstuffed messenger bag, Dr. Lavender added one more observation. "Livia, just a gut feeling, but let him come to you."

With the information she needed, Livia ditched the rest of her day and took the train back to Poughkeepsie to prepare. After assembling supplies and telling her dad she was off to a study group, Livia drove to Cole's church. She parked in the retirement center parking lot and at the rear of the building. She was dressed in black with her hair in a ponytail. When the night finally rested firmly on the ground, Livia used it as cover and left the car to sneak over to the side of the church.

Blake. He would wait for night, she hoped.

Livia had a backpack full of provisions, and she knew that made her a candy-ass. Blake had waited for her all those times without any luxuries like Tasty Cakes, an iPod, or crackable hand warmers. Still, backpack in tow, Livia worked her way to the spot she knew would be perfect for waiting: just below the window in the organ alcove. By the time she got there, she knew Blake had been right. She sounded like a herd of buffalo in the wild.

Livia slid down and sat with her back against the church's brick wall. It was cold and uncomfortable. She'd been there about three minutes before she opened a cake. The ground was deceiving with its fluffy green grass. It wasn't fluffy at all. It was hard. And she felt a thousand creepy crawly itches. She slapped at any little tickle.

This is going to be a long night. But Livia wasn't leaving. *Tonight he'll be here.*

Blake would play the organ. Livia knew this as surely as she'd ever known anything. So she waited.

Cole waited in the church. The organ was ready. It was bizarre to see it there—settled into the alcove that had been empty and abandoned since before his seven years here. He knelt in a front pew, trying his best to slide his piety back on like a coat. But he kept missing the armholes and turning it upside down as he tried—and failed—to find his entry point. It was no use. She was still here.

In the sanctity of this place, the center of his purpose, Kyle was everywhere he looked. He almost laughed when he remembered how he'd questioned Livia's devotion to Blake after knowing him such a short time, but he didn't make a sound. Even a week with Kyle would feel like forever. Cole looked over at the two pews where they'd stood when he first saw her.

When their eyes locked it had been like a head-on collision—jarring, shocking, and something he wasn't fast enough to stop. When their hands touched, their souls had stepped out of their bodies and joined. But Kyle and Cole could only stand in shocked stillness. Cole knew at some point he'd sent Livia on her way, his eyes never leaving Kyle.

His sole focus had been on keeping her. That was all he knew for sure. He had to keep her there until his soul was done seducing hers. Eventually they'd moved to sit next to each other. His soul had begun an intimate exploration of hers, without asking his permission, and Cole had to talk as if he wasn't affected at all. As he gazed at Kyle, her wide eyes made him believe she felt exactly the same.

They'd sat with their legs barely touching, catching up like long-parted best friends. At times their words overlapped in their hurry to be shared. He told her of his horror, his reason for being alone. She had taken the information like a muse—knowing and comforting, giving every assurance that what he was missing would be his someday.

Then she told him of her mother. Kyle believed her arrival had scared away the woman she desired most in the world. At this Cole had gathered her in his arms, kissing her soft, red hair. Physical touch caused his soul, endlessly intertwined with hers, to sigh with pleasure, and his body began to demand the same connection.

Again he realized Kyle must be feeling exactly the same. Cole remained rooted to the spot as she began a dance as old as time. Woman for man.

Kyle was exceptional. She must have practiced this seduction many times, both alone and with an audience. She shed her clothes patiently and with a playful knowledge of the tease. But her eyes became foggy as the production went on. Something else took over, and she wasn't there with Cole anymore. She was with every man who'd ever touched her, every man destined to touch her—if Cole didn't stop her.

Her soul seemed to push Cole's away, just as his connection to her evaporated as well. The separation was as painful as a burn, and Cole felt his soul assume the fetal position.

But sweet Kyle continued on. Soon she was naked. As she pranced around him, Cole stopped searching her lifeless eyes for the real Kyle. She reminded him of a tiger, trapped for years in a very small cage. He believed she knew there was more out there than this, but she was unable to free herself to find it.

Cole's breathing had quickened again at the memory. He looked down at his hands, fingers now woven into a guilty basket. He couldn't even find solace in the altar. She'd been there too.

He'd stood, knowing he should stop her, as Kyle crawled up on the altar. She grabbed a lit candle and lay on her back. She tilted it just enough that the wax dripped over her right breast. She locked eyes with him then because it was what the performance demanded.

Cole raised a shaking hand to his bottom lip and rubbed it. He took the steps quickly before she could do it again. Up close her skin was fiery red where the wax had hardened on it. She was in pain, and yet still she writhed and gyrated for him. She simply could not stop.

"Stop. Please stop." Cole took the candle carefully out of her hand.

Suddenly Kyle was painfully present again, her eyes confused. A moment later embarrassment touched every inch of her beautiful body. The look on her face was so vivid he could almost hear her thoughts: *I repulse him.* Cole blew out the altar candle and set it on the floor. He gathered the white altar cloth around Kyle to cover her. She had so much shame.

As he tucked the cloth around her shoulders, Kyle tried again to please. She licked his neck.

"Kyle, please. Stop. This isn't you. You aren't even here anymore," Cole said softly with his arms around her.

Kyle blinked and shook her head. *Shame. Again.*

Then she fought him desperately—eyeing her scattered clothes and the door.

"You don't have to do this for me. I don't want a show." Cole put his hands on her face and kissed her lips gently. For the first time.

Their separated souls rejoiced and found each other again. He lifted her off the altar and set her on her feet.

"Be *you* for me, Kyle. Be the Kyle you're so very afraid of being. I'll keep her safe." Cole skimmed his lips along her cheek and looked at her hopefully.

Kyle gazed into his eyes and nodded solemnly. The moment seemed bigger than the two of them.

Cole asked permission. "Kyle McHugh, may I worship you?"

A tear fell from her eye as she whispered, "Yes."

Cole took a step back and whipped the cloth off her shoulders. She was no vixen now. Kyle looked terrified. She clenched her fists, as if willing herself not to run. Cole turned and gathered her scattered clothes. He found her panties and took them to her, kneeling at her feet. Kyle looked puzzled, but as he worked the panties up her legs, she got it. Unlike all the other men, he was *dressing* her.

As Cole continued to adorn her, she made it easier. She moved her arms intuitively to help him as he gently put her bra back on and fumbled with the complicated front closure. He motioned for her to stop when she reached for her pants. He cradled the back of her head as he kissed her.

"I'm doing this," he said.

They tackled her jeans next. They were rather tight, and the two laughed as he bounced her up and down to get her feet to the right places. He buttoned up her shirt, being careful not to touch her breasts. By the time he got to her feet, her toes were cold. Cole rubbed them and slid her socks on. Instead of adding her sneakers, Cole picked Kyle up and brought her to the first pew. He sat her there and lifted her feet to his lap. He rubbed them until they were warm.

That pew became a confessional. There, with a fully clothed, fully present Kyle, he left his plans for lifelong commitment to only the Church in a smoldering pile. This woman, this broken, brave, perfect woman was what he needed. They talked again — about funny parishioners and childhood stories. Anything they thought, they said.

He kissed Kyle, checking to see that her eyes stayed sure and real. They did. Instead of saint and sinner, they were man and woman now. When Cole finally tasted her skin, the flavor was honeysuckle. Heaven was not something he had to die to enjoy. Kyle was here now. She offered him more of her skin to taste as she unbuttoned his shirt, sliding it from his shoulders.

Right after that thought, his cell phone had rung. It was the tone Cole had set for Beckett.

Beckett. As the rising sun began lighting the stained glass, sending shafts of color to dance with specks of dust in the air, the vow Cole had made came back to him. He felt like he was choking. With Kyle still in his arms, Cole was surrounded by the day he'd followed Beckett into the woods seven years ago.

Cole had lived in Beckett's little branch of hell for a few months right after he'd aged out. He hated it, hated all the drugs and stupid, angry people, but he'd had no place to go. No one but Beckett to turn to. Maybe that was why he'd followed.

Hidden in the familiar woods, Cole watched as Beckett swaggered to the oak tree. He could only pray silently because his feet refused to move. He knew what was about to happen. His mind begged and gagged its way through the Our Father.

Our Father, Who art in heaven

Hallowed be Thy Name;

Thy kingdom come,

Thy will be done,

on earth as it is in heaven.

"…You're going to die like the gasping pussy you are because…"

Cole heard Beckett's voice, and his bleary eyes opened for a moment to find Rick kneeling. He squeezed them shut and continued his silent prayer.

Give us this day our daily bread,

and forgive us our trespasses,

"you"

as we forgive those who trespass against us;

"touched"

and lead us not into temptation,

"my"

but deliver us from evil…

"brothers."

Amen.

With his *amen* came a single gunshot. Cole hadn't stayed to see what happened after that.

As he'd fled the scene that day, in a car that smelled like incense and Taco Bell, Cole took his own vow of priesthood. He begged God for a chance to redeem Beckett and himself for Rick's death.

When he'd hit the stoplight in front of the retirement community, Cole's eyes fell on Our Lady of the River. The sun glistened on the stained glass, and he had his answer. He pulled in, went inside, and found Father Callahan. In confession he admitted what he'd just witnessed and asked for guidance. The elderly priest—perhaps because he was afraid to let Cole out of his sight—offered him a volunteer position as a live-in handyman.

Cole accepted on the spot, thrilled to have a new place to live and convinced the church walls were meant to be his home. Over time his handyman's job turned into so much more. Father Callahan saw endless promise in his new apprentice, and after a lifetime in the church he liked to say he consulted the bishop on a "need to know" basis.

Cole had made this commitment to save Beckett from hell. So he had to keep it, no matter how endlessly his soul cried in the corner of the church, begging and reaching for Kyle. At that moment he'd built a wall between her soul and his. Confusion turned to anger, which turned to panic as Kyle tried desperately to bring him back, to reconnect.

"You told me *I* disappeared, now where have you gone?" she shrieked.

She tried to kiss the truth out of him, but he turned his head and held her at bay. She fell to her knees, but he just shook his head. His future was predetermined. Even if banishing this newborn love sliced his heart in half, it had to be done.

Kyle had swallowed her disappointment and, deeply wounded, fled from his sanctuary.

After reliving the memory, Cole found himself once again in the depths of post-Kyle despair when the church door creaked open. He turned to see Blake standing in the foyer. He was filthy, and one of his shirtsleeves seemed to be caked with blood.

Cole stood to go get the first aid kit, but Blake just nodded once in his brother's direction. Then his eyes found the organ.

"Cole, I know I haven't earned it, but would you mind very much if I tried the organ?" Blake's voice filled the empty church.

Cole smiled sadly. "Of course, brother. It would be an honor to hear you play again."

Cole's despair settled into his bones. His crying soul now had the worst kind of company: another soul crying just as loud.

14

TOO MUCH DIRTY IN ME

"You can go on up," Cole said, his eyes following Blake's to the loft. "I'm going to get a bandage for your arm, if that's okay?"

Cole looked pointedly at Blake's bloody shirtsleeve. Blake looked down and seemed surprised by the carnage there. Cole went to get supplies from his sleeping quarters. He texted Beckett as he walked:

He's here. Arm is bleeding.

Beckett's reply came as Cole opened his door:

He got a ta5t. playingh yet? Need me? Can com3e noqw

Cole grabbed a fresh T-shirt in case he could convince Blake to wear it. *If he doesn't run.* He might very well run. Cole heard the organ gasp to life with a jangle of mismatched notes. It sounded like Blake was slapping the keys.

Crap.

Cole updated Beckett:

Stay where u r. Not sure how this will go. He's playing now.

Cole glanced at Beckett's response:

Ave Fuckong Mariea?

Cole wondered how to put it:

No, just noise. Not music.

Beckett's next message had no typos:

Shit

Cole ran until he reached the door to the sanctuary, but as he opened the door he tried to look unhurried. He walked calmly until he was out of sight, then took the spiral steps three at a time. The music sounded crazy. Crazy—as if Blake had never known how to create a coherent song on a musical instrument.

Maybe this Livia thing has finally broken him. A soul like Blake's can't make it in this world.

Cole had long had his doubts, so he also had plans. He was prepared to tell the authorities Blake had attacked him so they'd admit him to a psych ward. Blake had once had an array of medicines and doctor's appointments, but a person needed a schedule for either of those things to do any good. These days Blake went where the wind took him. Cole watched as Blake tried to make his hands move the way they used to. *Maybe it's been too long.*

As Blake reached for one of the highest keys, Cole noticed blood dripping from his arm. He stepped forward and put his hand on Blake's shoulder. The first two manuals on the organ were covered in blood. Blake seemed oblivious. The rows of bloody keys reminded Cole of shark's teeth.

"Brother, please let me dress your wound." Cole tried not to sound angry or upset.

Blake gasped when he saw the mess. "Cole, I apologize." He pulled off his shirt to mop up the offending blood. It had seeped between the keys.

Cole had no idea how to maintain an organ, let alone get blood out of it. He ignored his vibrating cell phone, sure it was Beckett wanting a progress report.

"Please, let me see your arm."

Blake turned and held out his bleeding arm. Cole went to work wiping it clean.

"Chaos' work?" he asked as the tattoo became visible. Cole waited for the answer, wanting to see how bad off Blake was at the moment.

"I left Livia in the woods, Cole. I need to remember that. All the time." Blake finally met Cole's eyes.

Now or never. Tonight's the night. Cole decided to break Blake right now.

He would get Blake the help he needed before he could dig himself in any deeper. He was only destined for more pain.

"Blake, Livia came to see me." Cole smeared antibiotic cream over the tattoo.

Blake just stared with wide eyes. Apparently he'd never considered that Livia would be looking for him.

"Was she angry?"

What will set him off? The truth or a lie? "She was wonderful and caring with my parishioners. She honestly wanted to find you. I'm not sure how angry she was in the woods, but she just seemed determined to locate you when I saw her." Cole unwrapped the largest bandage he had.

Blake began wringing his hands. Cole felt his cell phone vibrate again. If he didn't respond, Beckett would be here soon.

"She went to Beckett as well." Cole started down the path of no return. Surely if Blake knew Livia and her sister had risked their lives to find him, the Sorry tattoo compounded with regret would drive him insane enough to be admitted.

Blake sat back on the organ bench and faced Cole, quiet as he absorbed the information about Livia.

"She went at night with her sister. Dentist had them cornered and was about to do his worst when one of Beckett's employees saved them." Cole added a grim overtone to his voice.

Blake looked like he might throw up. "Are they okay?" he whispered.

"Yes, they're fine. Well, Livia had a little wound on her throat. It had stopped bleeding by the time she came to me." Cole put his hand in his pocket. He texted Beckett without looking:

Stay where u r

Finally all the clandestine mid-mass texting paid off.

"She came to find me. She came to find *me*," Blake said. His voice was a mixture of revelation and revulsion. "Do you think, Cole, that I could love her? Could I have a life with her?"

Cole had not been expecting that question. He'd expected Blake going off the deep end. He weighed his options.

"Blake, I think you two would have a beautiful romance. But long term? I don't know. I'm scared. What if she wants a family? Or a man to sit at the dining room table or run the grill for dinner? Every night, for years? Do you think that's possible for you?"

Blake allowed Cole to cover his wound.

"And what about you?" Cole continued. "What if she was yours and she walked away?" Cole saw Kyle's face as he spoke to Blake.

Blake looked solemnly at Cole. "I would try very hard to be the man she needed. I would try harder at that than anything."

Cole felt a stab in his own chest and wondered if he spoke from his own pain. Was he helping his brother at all?

"I think love would end you, Blake. I think you wouldn't be with us anymore. It requires more common sense than you have."

Cole's words were bitter, and Blake looked quickly away, almost as if he'd been slapped.

Cole turned and went down the stairs to wait for the inevitable. Soon Blake would descend the stairs and into madness.

But Blake had only taken his favorite parts from Cole's little speech. Livia had tried to find him. Livia needed him to keep her safe. Blake turned to face the organ. The keys had danced mockingly like disjointed puzzle pieces before, but now…Now they waited obediently. His hands knew them. His hands could sweep them together and create.

So he did.

He leapt right over the *Ave Maria* as if Livia held his hand to help him jump.

No more Ave Maria.

His hands flew over the organ, composing, painting, revealing all that was within him. Blake would show Livia all he had inside for her. If she was looking for him, she didn't hate him. If she was looking for him, he was allowed to love her.

Even if Cole was right and Blake didn't have the common sense to be with her, he could watch her, like a knight and his queen. He could protect her so she never faced anyone like Dentist again.

Blake was allowed to love Livia. And he did.

Blake loves Livia.

You can play. You can play. You can play! Livia leaned against the wall, her aches and pains and shivering chill melting away now that Blake's playing had become something beautiful. She tilted her head back and opened her mouth, as if to drink the music. She couldn't imagine how he created it—it sounded as if three people must be playing. She heard bells, then the notes sounded like voices. So clearly the music sang to her: *Blake loves Livia. Blake loves Livia.* She stretched her arms out and dug her fingers into the rough, scratchy brick, trying to hug him from the outside of the church. She wiped tears from her cheeks. She wanted to run inside and see him creating. She wanted to see his strong arms and intuitive fingers crafting the notes. Blake's sounds enchanted her.

Livia, just a gut feeling, but let him come to you. Dr. Lavender's words forced themselves through the music to the forefront of her mind.

Blake had to find Livia. And he knew where to find her. He could come to her any day at the Poughkeepsie train station. But it had to be his choice to come back. Suddenly leaving him here to play his exquisite music didn't feel like giving up. It gave Livia hope.

Livia stole quietly away from the scene of the beauty. She left Blake, but she never stopped hearing his music that night.

As the orderly, elegant notes drifted down, Cole returned to his pew and kneeled. Blake's music was back. It was airborne poetry—diving and looping and loudly victorious. Telling Blake about Livia had not broken him. It had given him wings. Cole prayed for forgiveness for the jealousy he felt. He pulled out his phone and texted Beckett:

He's playing! Like an angel. No Ave Maria.

Beckett's reply came from ecstatic fingers:

MdamttohAwebome!!!

A few minutes later Beckett pulled up onto the lawn of the church and hopped out. Cole met him at the door and they locked arms. "Cole, that right there is *not* the *Ave* butt-fucking *Maria*." Beckett raised a fist in the air and pumped it.

"Beckett, could you not?"

"Sorry. No butt-fucking in church. At least that's the party line, right, hot stuff?" Beckett raised his eyebrows.

Cole ignored him. "Do you have to park on the lawn *every* time?"

"I'm telling you, Cole, that's how it all gets started," Beckett began, retreading a familiar argument. "The government's beating us down, and it all begins with those goddamn lines in the parking lot. Set yourself free, my brother. If you see a line, ignore it."

Beckett ran past Cole and up the spiral stairs. No one else would dare interrupt Blake's playing, but Beckett scooped him into a bear hug and pounded him on the back. "Look at fucking you! Playing this fucking multi-tiered nightmare!" Beckett waved his hands over the complicated organ.

Blake laughed as Beckett set him back on the seat and pointed a thick finger at the organ. "You ass-fuck this bitch. Ass-fuck it." Beckett peeked over the balcony at Cole below. "Sorry, baby. I have too much dirty in me."

Cole shook his head and smiled. Blake resumed playing, and Cole and Beckett migrated to different places in the sanctuary. Cole straightened the hymnals in the backs of the pews while he listened, and Beckett slunk to the very center of the magnificent room after daggers from Cole's eyes shooed him away from the altar. He always found very blasphemous places to rest his feet.

When Blake took a break to stretch his back and fingers, his brothers clapped and hollered like they were at a championship baseball game. And Blake smiled, clearly thrilled to be reunited with an instrument. When the sun began to light the window by the organ, Blake came down to the spiral stairs.

"What time is it?" he asked. He stood shirtless, looking from brother to brother.

Beckett glanced at his cell phone. "Seven sixteen a.m. So do you have to be half-naked to play, Liberace? 'Cause you play for the old biddies in this place like that and Cole better pack a defibrillator."

"I missed the train." Blake looked like he'd missed catching a baby bird falling from its nest.

"Blake, why don't you go get cleaned up? Livia always comes home too," Cole said pointedly as he began readying the church for eight o'clock mass.

"Bro, you want me to hang out? I'll drive you to the station." Beckett was laid out in a pew like it was a lawn hammock.

"No, that's fine. Thanks." Blake looked down at the sunlight pooling on the floor in front of the windows. "I need to get going," he said, though he didn't move.

Beckett yawned, stretched, and stood, insisting on their formal good-bye. The three stood with their tattooed arms braided together.

As they stepped away, Beckett nodded toward Blake's bandaged arm. "What'd ya get?"

"It says 'Sorry,'" Blake said as he went out the door to Cole's private quarters, leaving his brothers alone.

Beckett dialed his cell phone and spoke to Cole while it rang. "What time's good for you?"

Cole sighed. "Around one-thirty today would work."

"Chaos!" Beckett yelled into the phone. "Fit me and my brother into your busy fucking schedule of dusting lawn gnomes and staring out that dirty shed window. We'll be there at one-thirty."

15

500

A very bouncy Kyle woke Liva at some ridiculous o'clock on Friday morning.

"Wakey-wakey, you sloppy, old whore. It's time to do you up. You're going out tonight, so you don't get to dress in nursing home casual." Kyle ripped off Livia's covers.

"Kyle, I have school." Livia reached for her blanket again. "We'll do this craziness later." Livia wanted to get back to Blake's music. It had filled her dreams.

Kyle karate-chopped Livia's sleepy hand. "Listen, Liv, you want to come party with me? I get to create your look. And now is the time. Go shower and use *my* conditioner."

Livia wondered if she *was* still dreaming. *The expensive conditioner? This must be big.* So it was a forty-five dollar hair product that shut Livia's complaining mouth after her shower as Kyle hovered and plucked and curled. The outfit Kyle had selected and titled "Check to see if I'm wearing panties, boys" made Livia cringe: a plunging halter-top and a miniskirt with safety pins down the side.

"Just change into this before you get on the train." Kyle handed Livia a black-and-white polka dot bag with a big, red satin bow. She clipped a red umbrella to it and stuck in a pair of ridiculous red heels. "And practice this: '*Yo no soy una puta.*'" Kyle said the words in an angry, accented voice.

Livia raised a sensitive, red, now-thin eyebrow at her sister.

"It means 'I am not a hooker' in Spanish. And you already know it in English, so you should be good." Kyle gathered her torture implements and headed off to the shower herself. "I'll pick you up at the train station. What time do you get in?"

Livia mentally ran through her Friday schedule. "Around seven o'clock tonight."

Kyle dumped all her stuff back into her room and returned to Livia at a full run. Livia caught her launched sister like she was a baby monkey.

"Thanks, Liv," said Kyle, squeezing her. "You have no idea how happy this makes me. I really need this tonight."

Livia set her sister down. She didn't like how determined Kyle sounded. *Sadly determined—like she's planning to punish herself.*

Livia slipped into some jeans and a button-down shirt so she wouldn't mess up Kyle's masterpiece on her face. She made Blake's breakfast with extra care and added a thick slice of crumb cake. When she got to the train station and saw the empty spot again, she had to dig deep to find her faith. *It's sunny. Maybe he can't get here.*

When she heard her name shouted behind her, she recognized the voice before she could hope it was Blake. *Chris.* He hustled down the platform steps holding a bouquet of red roses and a black velvet box. *Oh crap.*

"Livia, I'm glad I caught you. Hey." He stepped into her personal space, breathing hard, and gave her cheek a kiss that she tried to dodge. "Whoa—you're looking above average today," he noted, appraising Kyle's makeup job. "I just wanted to let you know I miss you. I miss us."

He stepped even closer. His cologne now seemed chokingly strong. He started in with the crude baby talk he considered suave. "Come on, sweet baby, let me into your silky hole again. You know you want me."

I can't believe I ever put up with this shit. "Chris, I don't have place in my life for you anymore. We just don't look at the world the same way—or want any of the same things. I'm sorry if that hurts you, but it's the truth." Livia took a step back.

Chris's jaw tightened. "Is it the bum? The fucking bum that lays there?" He pointed at the place. "You know, we think he's dead. So you might not hold out hope for his crazy ass."

Livia shut her eyes. His voice had morphed into that of typical, spoiled Chris. He hated not getting what he wanted.

"That's right. Dave and his buddies throw pennies at him, and they've been missing their target practice."

Livia shook her head and glared at him. Chris lifted his chin defiantly. *Is this really who he is?* "You think that's okay?" Livia made a mental promise to mess up slimy Dave in a serious way.

"Ah, Dave's a big, banging nerd. I think it's a stupid hobby." Chris looked forlornly at his batch of roses, as if suddenly remembering his mission. "Listen, really Livia. I got you a real ring. I'll forgive you for being with this fruitcake. We'll chalk it up to experimenting."

Chris went down on one knee. Livia felt the stares of the other commuters.

"Chris, stand up. Please. Don't do this," Livia demanded quietly.

Chris stood up, his face shading red. "This is because of that guy? Really?"

"No, Chris. This is because you cheated on tests in school. This is because I don't trust you and Hannah. This is because your job in the summer is killing defenseless deer." The list she'd spent so long carefully ignoring now blared in her head.

"I work on a deer farm," Chris said, selecting only this for response. "It's a legitimate business."

Livia nodded. "Yes, I know. But there's something wrong with walking out to a paddock full of deer and shooting one. I mean, shouldn't they at least get to run?"

"I only shoot the ones that *don't* run."

Chris seemed to think this made it better, but it only made it worse. The train approached, and Livia willed Chris to leave so she could drop Blake's breakfast safely.

"Go home, Chris. Return the ring and get your money back. I'm not dating you anymore. It's as simple as that." Livia tried to avoid looking at Blake's spot.

"So does he have, like, a really monster dick or something?" Chris still couldn't accept his failure.

Livia didn't want to stoop to his level, but she needed him to leave. "Yeah, it's fantastic—so big it's almost a medical condition."

Chris tossed the roses in the closest garbage can and pocketed the ring box. "You're a filthy, cock-loving whore, Livia McHugh."

She watched him stalk up the stairs. Livia dropped the brown bag where it belonged and shuffle-ran to the train before it closed its doors. Forced to stand, she leaned her head against the smudged silver pole that served as a handhold and thought of...*Chris?* His eyes had shown such hurt. Livia knew he was a narcissistic, small-minded boob, but he'd really seemed to believe she'd say yes if he bought a real ring and forgave her indiscretions. He really thought she'd come back. His hurt look took a while to fade from Livia's memory. She had no idea why a knot of fear had formed in her stomach.

After her day of both teaching and attending classes — all the while feeling a little like a clown in her sister's dramatic makeup — Livia changed into her Kyle-prescribed getup in the ladies' bathroom at school. In spite of it, she spent the whole train ride hoping.

He'll be there in his shade spot, out of the rain, she told herself.

Carefully following Kyle's instructions, Livia waited until the White Plains stop before reapplying her makeup. Kyle had used some serious beauty-pageant-strength stuff, so Livia just followed the lines that still existed. She packed everything back in the polka-dot bag and looked out the window as the train pulled into Poughkeepsie, but the rain prevented a clear view. *No Blake?*

Livia tried to look again, but the lights came on in the train and she could only see her reflection. She knit her eyebrows in frustration. Was the breakfast bag still there? Had he been there today? Livia stood in the doorway of the train and opened the red umbrella Kyle had uncannily predicted she would need. It matched her hooker heels perfectly. She took a few steps forward and stood for a moment, watching the other passengers run like drowning rats from the platform. There was no bag, but there was a man. *Oh dear God. There's a man.*

Livia stepped further forward, and the train pulled away behind her. The rain was ice cold and so loud it sounded like sizzling bacon. It pounded on the umbrella and she couldn't hear anything else, but there he was. He'd come back for her. *Blake.*

His silhouette was blurry through the angry, sheeting rain, but she could see his hands were two fists. Was he angry? Livia walked toward him, leaving her heels behind after two steps. She let the umbrella tumble off her shoulder shortly after that.

The cold rain made her gasp. It poured over all of Kyle's handiwork. Livia kept moving until she stood before him. She closed her eyes against the burning of Kyle's hairspray as it ran down her face.

Livia reached out to touch his arms. She felt her way down to his fists and gently unfurled them with her fingers. She leaned forward on her tiptoes until her cheek touched his jaw. She sighed as his ice-cold face met her still-warm one.

Livia's hands followed his arms back up to his chest. She frowned at the bandage on his forearm. When she found his chest, she used it as an anchor as she walked carefully around him. She settled her face on his broad back and hugged him.

She felt and heard him breathe. "Livia." But he did not move.

She rubbed her face on the back of his wet black T-shirt to wipe her eyes. When she could see clearly again, she peeked over his shoulder and saw the red heels waiting patiently. The rain had filled them like little ponds. The umbrella lay on its side, catching water like a bucket.

Livia leaned up to his ear and said, "Face me," in a husky voice she'd never used before.

Blake turned achingly slowly until the platform light finally revealed his face. Despite the rain everywhere, Livia knew she'd been dying of thirst, and the sight of him was water.

He finally reached for her with his cold fingers and tilted her face to the emptying sky. "Were you meeting someone?" he asked as the rain and his fingers wiped the last of the makeup from her skin. "You're all dressed up. You're dressed...differently." Finally, his hands were still, and the rain slowed, as if its job was completed.

Livia blinked her now clean eyes open and was relieved to see him again. "No, of course not! Why would you—oh! This crazy outfit. I'm supposed to go out with my sister. She picked this for me."

Something flickered in Blake's eyes for a moment—relief?—but then he charged forward, his words tumbling out. "Livia, I'm here to say it's okay. It's okay if you want to leave, live a normal life, have a husband with a great job and beautiful children with your gray eyes." His breath caught a little as he finished.

Livia, just a gut feeling, but let him come to you...Listen to him. Livia stayed silent instead of rushing in with words.

"I'm asking permission to watch you from a distance, just to make sure you're safe," Blake continued. "You won't even know I'm there. I promise." Blake removed his hands from her face.

"Are you done?" Livia wanted to make sure.

Blake stepped back and nodded as if they'd just completed a painful business transaction, like buying a coffin. Livia shook her head and launched herself at him. He caught her as she wrapped her legs around his waist. She held his face like he'd just held hers. His green eyes were unsure, but a tiny spark danced within them.

"Blake Hartt, I choose you. I *deserve* you. I want you." Livia proved it by kissing his cold lips until they were warm.

Blake laughed and pulled away to look at her with tears and rain in his eyes. "Really? Really. Really!"

Livia nodded. "Absolutely."

Blake kissed Livia this time. He started out gently and then became more serious. He carried her over to the station's brick wall and pressed her back against it. He put her feet on the ground as he grabbed a fistful of her soaking wet hair. Livia reached under his T-shirt to feel his stomach and then his chest. Blake moaned and pushed her harder against the building. But again he pulled back to look at her.

"Me? I want you to be sure," he said.

"You," Livia whispered.

"Me." His eyes were full of intent.

"Always you." Livia gave him her biggest, heartfelt smile.

"Five hundred." Blake touched her face as if she might be a mirage and smiled back only when she didn't disappear.

Livia was content to prove right here how much she'd missed him. She was finally grateful there was so little of her outfit to get in the way. Blake leaned in for another kiss, but he stopped. His eyes cut to the parking lot. Livia followed his gaze to a set of headlights pointed straight at them.

"Oh, that must be Kyle—my sister. She's picking me up." Livia tried not to feel annoyed about this.

Blake kept his eyes on the headlights. "What does she drive?"

"A sporty little convertible." Livia arranged her skirt to be as presentable as it was going to get.

"That's a truck. Maybe an F-250 from the size of it." Blake's whole body tensed.

"Chris drives that kind of truck—"

Before the words were completely out of Livia's mouth, Blake had pushed her around the corner of the building.

He kept her pressed against the wall, his eyes scanning their surroundings. Livia and Blake hugged in the cold and wet. Their clothes felt like they weighed a thousand pounds. She opened her mouth to ask a question, and Blake put his finger on her lips, shaking his head no.

He seemed to brace for something and pulled Livia closer to his chest. An instant later, she heard the very definite sound of one car smashing into another.

Blake peeked around the corner of the building. "Someone just crashed into that truck. Looks like a little car."

Kyle's angry words echoed in the little valley of the platform. "Chris Simmer, you stupid fuck!"

"Kyle!" Livia screamed.

Blake took off running toward the accident. Livia followed, but he was much faster than she was in her bare feet and restrictive skirt. By the time she got there, Blake had planted himself next to Kyle's convertible, the front of which was lodged underneath the running board on Chris's truck. Kyle stood on her car's now slightly bowed hood and whacked the truck with the Mag light their father insisted both girls keep in their cars.

Chris keeps his guns in the truck bed. Livia knew he was fastidious about keeping his guns protected. She prayed they were *locked* in the truck box.

Blake tried to reason Kyle down. "Ms. McHugh, I'm afraid you'll need to remove yourself from this situation."

Kyle ignored him and started whaling on Chris's window with the flashlight. "You stalking, drooling dickhead! I will cut you. Leave my sister alone!"

Chris's driver's side window was beginning to crack under the pressure. Chris looked right at Blake, who returned the gaze with terrifying calm. Blake did not seem afraid of Chris or his truck.

Livia tried to reach her sister over the twisted metal of the convertible's bumper. "Are you hurt? Get the hell down here!"

Chris broke eye contact with Blake and turned to sneer at Kyle, his mean smile echoed in his eyes. Chris put the truck in reverse and turned the wheel hard. Blake sprang into action. He grasped Kyle around the waist and lifted her like a child throwing a tantrum. He grabbed Livia's hand and put the girls behind the cement road divider that kept cars from overshooting the parking spot. Livia held her sister in place as Kyle strained to go after Chris and his truck again. Blake climbed up and stood on the divider to get a better look.

"Blake, please get down," Livia urged. "Chris's not right tonight. Something's off in him." Livia grabbed the back of Blake's t-shirt.

Chris reversed with such force that he actually repositioned Kyle's whole car. The harsh sound of moving-but-unwilling metal filled the parking lot. Chris rocked and swerved until his truck was free, then he stopped. Blake remained where he stood, eyes locked on Chris. Livia tugged harder on his shirt.

"Could we please just go?" Livia asked, swallowing back her panic. She had no idea what Chris might do — or Kyle, for that matter.

Blake hopped down without turning around and helped Livia corral Kyle, who seemed to be made of dynamite and forty arms. Together they got her down the stairs and behind the train station building.

"What the hell were you doing?" Livia grabbed Kyle's angry little face.

"I was killing Chris Simmer until you friggin' stopped me!"

"You were going to kill Chris with a flashlight? Did you think he was going to hold still for that?"

Livia watched Blake's face as he kept his eyes on the threat.

"No. I was going to rip his tiny little sack off and choke him with his pathetic-ass undescended balls. *Then* I was going to brain him with Dad's flashlight." Kyle seemed to be calming, but Livia kept one hand on her arm.

"He's pulling out of the lot," Blake said, speaking for the first time since the altercation began. His eyes squinted. "Is he possessive about that truck?"

Livia ran a hand through her wet hair. "Yes, he's insane about it. He calls it The Beast." She thought of the time Chris had lost his shit when she'd let the passenger door touch the side of a shopping cart.

Blake took the information with a nod.

"Oh, look at you," Kyle said, really looking at Livia for the first time. "You ruined yourself. Damn it, Livia. Couldn't you just leave it on?"

Blake stepped forward and introduced himself. "Ms. Kyle McHugh, I assume. It's my pleasure to make your acquaintance. My name is Blake Hartt, and I'm entirely to blame for Livia's clean face. I let the rain wash everything away. Please accept my apology."

Kyle looked at Blake as if he was a tap-dancing cricket. She held one pointy finger close to his nose. "You grabbed my tit a little, Mr. Old Timey Talker."

Blake seemed to swallow a smile. "Manhandling a lady is inexcusable. I would only do so if said woman was too stubborn to remove herself from a dangerous situation." He took Kyle's hand and kissed the top of it lightly.

"Aw, crap. Well, aren't you too fucking charming for words?" Kyle smiled despite her best efforts to look tough. "All right, Mr. Old Timey, I'll let you get away with the boob palming this time."

"That's fortunate because I hate ingesting my own testicles." He gave her a devilish grin with naughty eyes to match.

Kyle looked at Livia. "He's adorable."

Livia saw happiness on Kyle's face and sadness in her eyes. "Hey, let's get you to the ER. You were just in a car accident." Livia tried to feel Kyle for any injuries.

"That wasn't an accident. I did it on purpose. I saw fuck-knob Chris staring at you two like it was a peep show. I don't put up with that shit. You two are over, and he needs to move the fuck on. I was braced for it. I feel fine. The airbag didn't even deploy. We're going out. I have to get some party on."

Kyle stopped her monologue abruptly and looked from Livia to Blake. "If you still want to, that is. I mean it's fine if you don't."

Livia nodded to assure her sister. "Kyle, I'm still coming. We'll both come!"

Blake nodded and smiled, although his eyes darted around a bit anxiously.

"All right, then," Kyle announced. "We've got to get home to change into some fuck-awesomely hot outfits."

Livia took Blake's arm. She doubted any amount of partying could erase the sadness from Kyle's eyes.

16

THE BLUE DRESS

Blake was the first to remember Livia's borrowed shoes, and he led her back to where she'd discarded them. He knelt as he poured the water out of the right one and held out a hand for her foot. He slid the shoe on, careful to let his hand brush over her whole foot. He repeated the motion with the left high heel and kept his eyes on hers as he ran his hand up her leg. Then he poured the rain out of the waterlogged umbrella, which swelled the tiny rivers the shoe runoff had created. He held out his elbow and led Livia up the stairs to Kyle's car.

Getting home was going to be a challenge. Kyle's zippy pride and joy was a little mangled. While Kyle and Livia discussed their options, which did not include calling the police because of the instant alert it would give their father, Blake circled the car with a slow saunter. Just when Livia had decided to investigate whether or not her cell phone still had a roadside emergency plan, Blake gave the convertible a swift kick in the bumper, which clattered to the ground.

"The fuck?" Kyle spun around, eyes wide at the sound of the latest injustice to her vehicle.

Blake nodded politely and used the disembodied fender like a baseball bat to smack a piece of wayward metal out of the wheel well.

"Don't you think it's been through enough?" Kyle looked ready to go ballistic, alternately wringing her hands and clenching them into fists.

Blake got down on all fours and peeked at the undercarriage. "May I borrow the Chris-basher for a moment, please?"

Kyle took a deep breath and put the Maglite in Blake's extended hand, seeming to trust his new stance as a knowledgeable one.

He rose to deliver a diagnosis. "It looks like the headlights are gone, but I might be able to drive it to your house if I follow Livia's car closely. It will save you the towing cost."

Kyle looked less pissed off now, but still unsure. "I don't know. Pretty much I'm the only authorized driver of the convertible — except Livia when absolutely necessary."

"I would feel quite uncomfortable allowing either of you lovely ladies to handle this unfortunate task," Blake explained. "Are you afraid I'll dent it?" He grinned.

Kyle tossed Blake the keys a little too hard, but he caught them deftly. He put what was left of the convertible's bumper in the Escort's trunk and took his place behind the convertible's wheel. Livia had to push on the driver's side door to get it closed behind him.

He got the vehicle started and rolling slowly, without any parts dragging on the ground. So began the sluggish, steady funeral procession for Kyle's favorite car.

Chris pulled into a gas station to assess the damage from Kyle's unprovoked attack: a bunch of scratches on the bumper, a few dings, a sizable dent in his driver's side door, and a tiny crack forming on the window. He tried to look underneath without getting himself dirty. Her pansy-ass sports car had better not have bent The Beast's frame. *Stupid slut Kyle. Fuck her shitty bitchiness.*

Chris didn't want to admit to anyone why he'd wanted to see Livia at the train, least of all himself. But Kyle had known. It must have been obvious in his face. Now that Livia wasn't looking to him as savior, Chris felt like less. His friends looked at him like he was less. *And I don't fucking like it.* He had to get her back.

Practically his whole family had made little remarks about how much they missed her. Now that he couldn't touch her any more, he was obsessed with her. More than that, he wanted to make her stop looking at him the way she had at the station that morning — like he was a worthless piece of trash. *I have a job, a fucking pussy-magnet truck, and awesome hair.*

Chris checked himself in the rearview mirror as he climbed back in. His reflection captured him for a few moments, like it always did. When he finally looked away, he knew what needed to be done.

Livia needed to see that homeless bastard shamed. Shamed in front of her. *A good beating—and then just when he's begging for mercy, I'll be the big man and let him go.*

That would be perfect. Livia would see that Chris really was a thoughtful guy. But first he had to find this fucker and Livia.

Chris texted Dave:

Do u still have the pic of Livia w. the photoshopped hoots?

Dave texted back so quickly, Chris gave him the finger through the phone. Stupid nerd kept his phone attached to his hand. Chris suspected that Dave texted himself just to look popular.

Dude, Hell yeah - that pic is EPIC.

Chris responded:

I wish I had a pic of the homeless bastard.

Dave's excitement seemed to buzz the phone with extra force:

*I got 1! Holy Shit! I took a pic 2 prove I hit him in the face
with a penny! 10 points u know.*

Chris felt a smile form on his lips as the two requested pictures beeped through on his screen: a decent headshot of Homeless and a sweet picture of a "topless" Livia with a set of gigantic fake tits.

Dave was a waste of skin, but at least his affinity for creating porn with pictures of girls he knew was coming in handy. Chris had to give him props.

*Sweet. You sick fucker. I should kick ur ass. Send those pics 2 everyone
u know. Tell em I'm looking for those 2. Tweet me if u c them out.*

Dave's response was just what Chris hoped for:

*R U going to beat the fuck outta that guy? For taking ur girl?
Everyone will b all over this shit!*

Chris didn't respond. Not knowing would get more of a response from all his so-called friends. They loved to watch an ass kicking. And a Homeless ass kicking would make them go ape shit. The only person he could think of who might stand up for that dirty bastard would be with him already. Livia.

Chris composed a Tweet and set it to repeat. Everyone would see it eventually:

Looking for McHugh and new boyfriend. Hit me here if u c them.
Dave will send a pic if U want.

Let it begin. Chris started The Beast and let the vibration from the motor tickle his balls.

Livia kept glancing back, trying to get a glimpse of Blake as she drove, but the lack of lighting denied her the pleasure.

"Do you know he squeezed my ass? And not just once either." Kyle pulled out her phone and started texting.

Livia let the statement hang for a moment, but Kyle was already way past the words she'd just uttered.

"Chris?" Livia tried to spur more information out of her sister.

"Of course Chris. Please. Captain Romance back there wants to inject himself into you like a vaccine." Kyle's fingers flew over the tiny keys.

"Why didn't you tell me?" Livia asked.

"Agh. I dunno. I didn't want to break your happy." Kyle began composing another text.

Livia was overcome for a moment. Between Blake's return and Kyle's unwavering devotion…*It's too much.*

They pulled up in front of their house, and the convertible wheezed in behind them.

"Kyle?" Livia watched her sister's face, illuminated by the phone's screen.

"Mmm?" Kyle was completely absorbed by her little keyboard.

Livia covered the phone until Kyle looked at her. "You're simply the best lady I know. I promise not to be oblivious anymore."

Kyle nodded. "I love you too. Want to make out?" Despite her mocking tone, Kyle squeezed Livia's hand before getting out of the car.

"Well, that drives like crap." Blake smiled as he dangled the keys in front of Kyle.

"Just for that, Mr. Pompous Fancy Man, I get to dress you for the evening." Kyle claimed her keys and ran for the house. "Dibs on the shower!"

Blake held a hand out to Livia. She grabbed it and hugged his arm. As they entered the house and dripped their way, soaking wet and freezing, into the kitchen, Livia had panicky thought. *Will this be like bringing a feral cat inside?*

She watched his face as he took in their surroundings. The warm, small room was by no means a palace, but it was a home. Blake looked a bit shy, but not alarmed as Livia directed him to sit at the kitchen table. The dishwasher suddenly looked obscenely luxurious, and the piles of shoes by the door seemed ridiculous. *So many shoes for just three sets of feet? All he has is what he's wearing and a cardboard piano.*

Blake's lips were still tinged blue from the time he'd spent waiting for Livia in the rain. Livia decided to change that. She sat in his lap and pushed the hair out of his eyes. His hands found a sliver of bare skin at the small of her back. Livia knew his touch registered on her face when his lip lifted in a snarl. She let her head fall back so her hair would skim his hands.

Blake blew on her neck. She knew what was next. She'd been picturing it since the meadow. His tongue was slow and meandering, and even though she should have been prepared, his teeth still made her gasp. Livia wanted to do so many bad things to him on the kitchen table. She was pretty sure she could actually speak in tongues if she tried right then.

A knock on the front door forced her to give it a shot. "JaPleaseUs!"

Blake stood and moved Livia behind him in one movement. He hit the light switch and plunged the whole first floor into darkness.

"Stay here," Blake whispered.

"Hell no," Livia whispered back.

They went to the bay window and peeked out.

"That's Kevin. He's a friend." Livia flipped the light back on and swung open the front door.

Kevin Connell lived two houses down. He was endlessly fashionable and easy going, which had made him and Kyle lifelong buddies. He held out a garment bag and a duffle bag.

"Hey, am I interrupting a surprise party or is your Clapper malfunctioning?" he asked with a smile.

Livia shook her head. "How did she force you into this?"

Kevin held out a hand to Blake. "I'm Kevin. Nice to meet you. Are you the plumber and some pipes busted in there?"

Blake smiled. "No, sir. The soaking clothes are entirely the weather's fault. Blake Hartt." Blake gave Kevin a firm handshake.

Kevin addressed Livia's question. "If you must know, she threatened to blow up my house, and after seeing her car out there, I'm glad I came. What, did she try to parallel park?"

Kyle came stomping down the stairs in her robe with wet hair. "Kevin, you skinny donkey puncher, give me that crap already."

"Here's Miss Bubbly now," Kevin said, eyebrows raised. "Looks like you tried to use your car as a vibrator. Again." He passed his bags to Kyle.

She ignored his insult. "Are you coming out tonight or going home to breastfeed like the mama's boy you are?"

"I might be out. Text me when you know where you're headed."

Kyle nodded and slammed the door in Kevin's face.

"Kyle! That was incredibly rude," Livia shrieked.

But Kyle was busy unpacking the contents of Kevin's bag on the couch. "Eh, he'll be fine," she said. "That's how we relate." She turned her attention back to the array of clothing now making a pile on the floor. "Nope. He's a *girl*. Hell no. Maybe. Holy crap, pink?" Finally, Kyle selected a white long-sleeved shirt, a skinny black tie, and black pants with a hint of a pinstripe.

"What's your shoe size, Lord Fauntleroy?" Kyle held up a pair of funky black Chuck Taylors.

"Eleven and a half," Blake responded with a raised eyebrow.

"Good enough." Kyle passed a bundle of clothes to him. "Go up, shower, and I'll handle the hair," she said, already eyeing his head and looking slightly perplexed. Man hair wasn't her specialty.

Blake winked at Livia and headed up the stairs.

"I'm going to create myself, and I'll redo you after your shower." Kyle skipped upstairs.

Livia went to the fridge and pulled out what she needed to make Blake a plate of leftover meatloaf and green beans. She popped a potato in the microwave. As the food warmed, Livia tried to ignore her cold, wet clothes and the fact that Blake Hartt was naked in the shower directly above her head. She grabbed some silverware and a soda and went to her room to wait for him with the food.

I want to screw him on the table and make him eat in my bed. Livia giggled out loud at her crazy logic. She opened the TV tray she kept in her room for late-night studying snacks and arranged the food. Kyle knocked on the bathroom door and was admitted with a manly murmur—a murmur that made Livia shiver. After some blow dryer noise and cursing (from Kyle), Blake appeared in the doorway to her room polished, shaved, and styled. The Blake Livia had always seen was now revealed in living color for everyone else's eyes as well.

Kyle tromped in behind him with directions. "Livia, you're next. Isn't he creamy? You can thank me later. No schmexing in here! Don't get him dirty or wet. I'm going to put on my shoes."

Kyle was a thin, leather assault on the eyes. Livia couldn't imagine how she'd gotten into her bustier and capri pants. But Livia's gaze quickly found Blake again. He was sigh-worthy. Even if he'd never waited for her in the rain, never counted her smiles, Livia knew her mind would've melted at the sight of him tonight.

His green eyes sparkled as he entered, and Livia kicked her door shut. He caught her hands, and Livia let her lips touch his. They leaned into one another, mindful not to let her still-wet body touch his freshly dried one. It was like their kisses were over an imaginary wishing well.

"I'm sorry I took my shower first," said Blake between kisses. "You must be chilly and uncomfortable."

Livia's mind cried a little. She'd been comfortable for years.

"I'm fine, really." She made no move to get to the shower.

Blake rubbed her arms to warm her. "Honestly, I only went first because I'm a little afraid of her."

"Everyone is." Livia smiled.

"Five hundred twelve." Blake's eyes went from joking to smoldering. He kissed smile 512 right off her lips.

Kyle banged on the door. "I said no sex! So help me God, Livia, I'll come in there and pry you off of him!" Kyle turned the knob Livia hadn't had the foresight to lock.

"Go — the shower will warm you," Blake insisted.

Livia kissed him one more time and went into the hall. Kyle stood on one elaborate high heel that laced up her calf in a criss-cross pattern.

"Where's Dad anyway?" Livia pulled a fresh towel from the hall closet.

"He's twenty-four on." Kyle watched Livia enter the bathroom and only then headed back into her room.

So Dad won't be home until lunch tomorrow. Blake could stay the night.

The hot water turned her skin pink. She loved the idea of Blake in her room.

Blake knocked on the doorframe to Kyle's room. She was finally tying the bow on her elaborate shoe.

"Pardon me, Kyle. Can I have a word with you?" Blake waited just outside her door.

Kyle sat up on her bed and assessed her work on Blake. *I rock. He's scrumptious.*

"'Sup?" Kyle wasn't sure what they had to talk about.

"I know you're designing Livia's look tonight, and I was wondering if I might make a request?" Blake lifted his eyebrows.

"Request away, rock star." *Here it comes. "Can she wear a push-up bra? Leave off the panties?"* Kyle knew what boys liked.

"When my lips touch her face I like to taste her skin, so maybe the makeup could be on the light side?" Blake closed one eye.

Holy fuck, that's sexy. Kyle felt her heart spit on her soul, taunting, *Cole would want you as you are, if you were important enough. But you're not.*

Blake watched Kyle's eyes cloud over. "I'm so sorry. I hope I haven't offended you."

Kyle smiled at the tall piece of perfect tripping over his manners in front of her. "I'm not twisting your nuts, babycakes. I was thinking it was a nice suggestion."

Blake looked into Kyle's eyes. She seemed to be crumbling from the inside out. "Is there something I can help you with?"

She stood on her impossible heels. "Sure. Why don't you tell me why my relationships only last as long as it takes a guy to remove a used condom?"

"You're worth so much more than that," Blake responded immediately.

She was shaken by his quick, sure answer. "Um, hey, can I get some privacy? I need to do some boob wrangling."

Blake didn't move, just looked mystified.

Kyle aided him by pointing to her bosom and shaking like a plate of Jell-O. "Do you think these puppies snap to attention just because I talk nice to 'em? No, I have to drag them into position."

Blake used his hands to wave away the new information. "I'll be going then."

Just loud enough for Blake to hear, Kyle added, "Don't worry. She'll look like Livia." Then the door clicked shut.

Kyle leaned against it, and her smile fell. Her full-length mirror mocked her. She could see all the parts of her that were wrong. She looked at the floor, avoiding her reflection. She knew exactly what Livia should wear tonight. She dug through her closet until she got to three smooshed-up prom gowns. Stuffed between the sequins and satin was a blue cotton dress. Kyle pulled it out and smoothed it with her hands. It was so soft, almost like pajamas. The blue would look stunning next to her sister's skin.

Kyle cut the tags off of the dress with a pair of toenail clippers. *There's no need to save this anymore.*

Kyle had been saving the touchable blue dress for her reunion with her mother. If Mom ever decided to come back, Kyle would wear this dress to show her who she really was, Kyle always told herself. Then her mom would stop hating her.

Kyle stomped into the hallway and hung the blue dress from the bathroom door for Livia. *Fuck this shit. I'm going down in flames tonight.*

When Livia finally entered her bedroom, the beautiful blue dress Kyle had chosen for her was already comfortable. *Why have I never seen Kyle in this before?*

Blake stood at Livia's dresser with a ceramic Cinderella and Prince Charming figurine in his hands. He almost dropped it when he looked at her, dressed for him.

"Thank you, Kyle," he said, not loud enough for Kyle to hear.

She smiled and was pleased when he counted, again.

"Livia, you make the rest of the beautiful things in the world cry for even trying at all. You make it hard for me to breathe." Blake looked reluctant to move.

Livia felt a pedestal forming under her feet.

"Blake, I'm about to kiss the hell out of you for saying that." She scampered around her bed to get to him and pressed her now clean, dry body against his warm chest. Blake refused to drop her keepsake from Disney World and twirled it in her hair as he accepted her kiss. He worked hard to get every bit of vanilla gloss off her lips.

"This lipstick is like icing on the most delicious Livia cupcake," Blake murmured.

Livia wanted to say something equally sexy but could only manage a small moan.

"All right, you two, do I need to put a hose on you or are you going to come willingly?" Kyle stamped one of her pointy heels.

Blake laughed and had to wave Kyle over to help him untangle the figurine from Livia's hair.

"Am I allowed to put shoes on?" Livia asked.

Kyle looked her up and down and declared, "Black flats and your black dress jacket." Then she went off in search of her pinging phone.

Livia dug around in the bottom of her closet while Blake put the figurine back where it belonged. He handled her belongings like he was the curator in a world-renowned museum.

"This bear looks well-loved." He gently lifted the hairless, torn bear that Livia kept in a prominent position on her shelf.

"That's Teddy. He's my favorite." Livia felt herself blush.

"Obviously. What a lucky bear." Blake sniffed the frazzled old toy. "He smells just like you."

Livia located her fancy jacket and stepped out of the closet. Blake took the coat from her and held it out in an old-fashioned ritual only he could get away with. He moved Livia's hair out of the way and kissed her neck as he buttoned each of her buttons from behind her. He skimmed parts of her she wished he would linger on. She turned her head to claim his lips.

They kissed until he stepped back and shook his head, as if to clear it. "I can only take so much of that with your bed so close."

Livia wrinkled her nose. Blake noticed the pile of stuffed bears in the corner of the closet.

"Why are those poor suckers in prison?"

"Ah, they were replacement bears from people who thought Teddy wasn't good anymore." Livia shut the closet on the tokens of misplaced goodwill.

"They didn't know you very well. You're exactly the type of person to love the hair right off of something." Blake gestured to the door.

Livia almost told Blake the bears were mostly from Chris, but she didn't want to bring his name into this beautiful moment.

"Let's get a move on," Kyle yelled from the front door. "The party doesn't start until I get there."

17

THE MAXI PAD

Kyle insisted on sitting in the back of the Escort. Blake held the door for both ladies before taking his spot in the passenger seat. Kyle spent most of the drive leaning up between Livia and Blake to adjust the radio. She cranked it to an ear-splitting level. Like a football team before the big game, Kyle seemed to be psyching herself up. Every once in a while she'd put her hand in front of Livia's face and point the direction she wanted the car to turn. When she finally told Livia to park, they found themselves at The Launch Pad.

The Launch Pad had formerly been a gym called Maximum Exercise, and the new owners had invested precious little of their money in a remodel. The club's flimsy sign was not quite opaque enough to hide that of the previous business behind it, which gave the illusion that the club might actually be called The Maxi Pad.

Blake tried to get to Livia's door before she could open it, but he failed and had to satisfy his gentlemanly urges by holding it ajar and shutting it behind her. Kyle seemed rejuvenated by the ride and bounced out of the car. She'd brought a small duffle bag instead of a purse, which had Livia a little worried.

"We're waiting for Todd, Debbi, Karen, Sam, and fucking Kevin — at least they *said* they might be here," Kyle announced as she began digging in the bag.

She pulled out a small, insulated cooler, and from that emerged the six Tupperware cups, with lids, that Livia and Kyle had used when they were children. She handed a little cup to Blake and offered one to Livia.

Livia looked at Kyle like she was crazy. "We're having a picnic at The Maxi Pad?"

Kyle drained one of the cups as Blake drank deeply from his.

Blake licked his lips. "I love this juice."

"Kyle, is there more than juice in those cups?" Livia watched as her sister and Blake each slugged back another cupful.

Kyle wiped her mouth with her hand. "Of course."

Blake's face blanched. "What else does this contain?"

Kyle gave him the smile that had so often gotten her out of trouble. "It's Hairy Buffalo. I brought some alcohol-soaked fruit too. Would you like some?"

"How dare you give him that without telling him what it was? Are you out of your mind?" Livia snarled.

Kyle took the cup back from Blake and looked guilty. "Sorry, Mr. Mary Poppins. That stuff has a considerable amount of Everclear and a few other things from the liquor cabinet in it."

Blake swallowed, eyes wide.

"If you hurl, it'll hardly affect you." Kyle pulled the fruit out of her bag and began munching on a piece of pineapple.

Blake bit his lip. That didn't seem to be a very appealing option.

Livia smacked the fruit out of Kyle's hands. "You brought us here to watch you get wasted? Is that your idea of a fun night out?"

Kyle shrugged off Livia's words and pulled on a protective attitude. "I thought you might join me. Whatever."

She motioned for Livia to unlock the Escort and tossed her duffle bag inside. She seemed to make an extra effort to appear nonchalant as she turned to go inside. "I'm here to dance. This place has the best music. Leave if you want. I'll get a ride," she tossed over her shoulder.

Livia took a deep breath and tried to forgive, considering the week her sister had just experienced, but looking at Blake going green kept making her angry.

"We'll be inside in a minute. I'll be the one to drive you home tonight," Livia said. She held Blake by the elbow to steady him.

Kyle marched off to the door. She bypassed the small line, and the bouncer waved her in.

"Her Hairy Buffalo is intense. I highly suggest purging." Livia wanted to give Kyle the biggest noogie of her life.

"That's not very romantic, and I had the meal you prepared for me." Blake looked at the ground shyly.

"Sweetheart, I think it's going to happen one way or another. I'm going kill Kyle. A lot." Livia sent her sister the evil eye through the building's walls.

"I'll be okay. I've had alcohol in the past. Let's get inside and see what your sneaky sibling is up to." Blake held out his hand.

As they approached the back of the line, Beckett's Hummer crashed into The Launch Pad's parking lot from the side, pounding the surrounding shrubs into flat testaments to his gigantic tires. His music vibrated the air as he parked in what was clearly the middle of the parking lot, nowhere near an actual space, destined to jam up the lot until he left.

"*There* the fuck you two are." Beckett hopped down from the Hummer as the rest of his posse pulled into the parking lot conventionally. The Launch Pad was about to be busier than it had ever hoped to be.

"Why the hell are you at The Flaming Tampon? Do you have some sort of craptastic death wish?" Beckett trotted up to Blake and pounded him on the back like an exuberant Labrador retriever.

The pounding must have mixed up the meatloaf and Hairy Buffalo, and Blake barely managed to get behind a shrub before losing the contents of his stomach as discreetly as possible.

Beckett looked Livia up and down and planted a kiss on her cheek. "Whitebread's so hot she's smokin' tonight."

Blake peered up from the bushes and looked as if he might die of embarrassment. Beckett laughed out loud, stomped over to the shrub next to Blake's, and pushed his finger down his throat in a well-practiced motion. He stood up smiling. "That's right, bro. Puke and rally, baby. I think there are some pubic hairs in mine." Beckett banged a fist on his own chest.

Blake looked mortified but laughed.

Beckett pointed to his parking lot-jamming Hummer. "I got toothpaste and Listerine in there. You wanna hit that?"

Blake nodded as he followed his brother to the car. Livia tagged along. Mouse had the mouth-cleaning implements at the ready as they arrived. After removing the unpleasant taste from their mouths, Blake and Beckett touched tattoos in greeting. Beckett turned his other arm over to show Blake his bandage. Blake lifted one eyebrow, and Beckett peeled the tape back to reveal his new $orry tattoo, a perfect replica of his brother's.

"Cole got one too," Beckett said.

Blake looked off in the distance as his eyes filled with emotion.

Beckett pulled Blake's face back to look at him and held it in his hand. "Never alone, bro. You're never alone as long as I live."

Blake nodded. "Thanks."

Beckett turned the touch into another pounding-of-Blake session. Then he looked at his crew. "Quit gaping at me fudge-packing my brother. Let's get in this Maxi Pad and knock it the fuck out."

His crew seemed minimally enthusiastic as Beckett pushed past the people waiting in line. The bouncer almost genuflected as he saw Beckett's face.

Beckett turned to the potential customers. "This dump is at capacity now. Go home and whack off."

Beckett lowered his voice. "Mouse, get one of our douchebags to take over here, and I want all the exits covered."

Beckett hustled Blake and Livia into what used to be the fitness center's reception area. The Launch Pad's owners had not done much with the inside either. The immediate view was a cheesy mural of people working out, circa 1980, complete with leg warmers and sweat bands.

"Why for an assfuck's sake are we in this shithole?" Beckett took in the interior like he was a tourist in a confusing foreign city.

Livia sighed and leaned her cheek against Blake's shoulder. "Kyle wanted to do some revenge partying, and I didn't want to leave her alone. She also tricked Blake into drinking some Hairy Buffalo."

Beckett smiled. "Fairy Princess is on a bender, huh? And she manufactures her own Jesus Juice? Sounds like we better keep an eye on her."

Beckett turned to Mouse again. "This place's a festering whore's crotch. Do I own it?"

Mouse spoke up—louder and squeakier as the glass doors to the dancefloor opened and took the music up a notch. "No, boss. You want me to arrange that?"

"We'll see. Remind me tomorrow." Beckett now headed for the glass doors that had just returned to their closed position. With both hands he flung the double doors wide. "You bitches are welcome!" he shouted. "I'm finally here!"

A wave of sweaty air hit Livia in the face as she and Blake followed Beckett's grand entrance through the doors. For a place this horrible, Livia was surprised to find Kyle had been right about one thing: the music was great. As they wove their way through the humid room, Livia recognized Lorraine as the DJ, and it all made sense. Kyle and Lorraine had been in ballet together for years. Music had cemented them together at the beat before Kyle gave up her dream and stopped training. She claimed no one paid her to practice, and anyway it was getting in the way of her social life.

But now Kyle was dead center on the hardwood dancefloor, which had probably been an aerobics room in its former life, lost in herself and her dancing. She was fantastic. Even soused up on Hairy Buffalo, she moved like silk blowing in the wind—smooth and beguiling.

Blake held Livia's hand as Beckett claimed a table in the corner of the room. The poor patrons already sitting in the prime spot watched as Beckett hefted their drinks and slopped them onto a new table. No one had the guts to reprimand him as they slunk away.

Beckett watched as Kyle danced. "Looks like Fairy Princess has wings."

It was as if she were alone in the room. She owned the space as she combined flying jumps with conventional dance club moves. No one could touch her talent, so they stayed on the perimeter as a backdrop to her unchoreographed show.

"She's always been a beautiful dancer." Livia sat down in a chair that faced the dancefloor and Blake.

Blake seemed preoccupied with a pile of pink napkins the table's previous occupants had left behind. Livia smiled at him, trying to gauge how he was feeling in this bizarre setting, which probably bordered on surreal for him. Blake met her eyes and ran one of the napkins through his fingers.

The music was so loud, all Livia could do was mouth, "Are you okay?"

Blake nodded. "You're beautiful," he mouthed in response.

Livia blushed, and when the music cut off abruptly, Livia blushed more deeply. She knew what was next.

Kyle's voice, magnified by a microphone, echoed through the club. "Livia McHugh, get your ass out here and dance with me." Then a speaker-blowing electric guitar riff jumped out of Livia's childhood and into her ears.

"Oh, crap." Livia shook her head.

"Livia, if you love me, you'll dance with me," Kyle taunted.

Blake looked both amused and slightly concerned as the crowd around Kyle began clapping and chanting "Li-vi-a! Li-vi-a!"

Beckett unleashed an ear-piercing whistle, followed by a round of hooting.

"Excuse me," Livia mouthed to Blake and stood up.

Blake rose as well, and it took her a moment to realize he was getting up because she had. When she walked away, he resumed his seat. As Livia reluctantly stepped onto the wood floor, Kyle came at her with a running jump. Her eyes were hooded and glazed, and she hung onto Livia like a leather-clad koala bear.

"Do the routine for me. Please, Livie. I love you. I'm sorry I poisoned your boyfriend. I'm the one who made him so cute, though. You have to forgive me, Livia. I'm so bad." Kyle looked close to tears.

"He barfed and now he's fine," Livia said. "You know I love you, and you're not bad, you just make bad choices. Do I still have to do the routine?"

Kyle smiled and wrinkled her nose. "Oh, yes. The routine must happen. Assume the position."

Kyle bounced out of Livia's arms and gave Lorraine what must have been the universal hand gesture for *I just tricked my sister into humiliating herself. Start the music before she runs.*

The opening bars of the familiar song once again vibrated to life. It was very easy to dance with Kyle; she never forgot a step and could cover for her partner's mistakes. In this case she'd been doing it since the fifth grade, thanks to her odd penchant for classic rock and her ability to get Livia to do whatever she wanted. The audience heckled the very juvenile dance routine, and Livia smiled at her sister while plotting to fill her breakfast orange juice with liquid laxative. The dance ended with three cartwheels in a row from Kyle while the less gymnastically inclined Livia waved frantic jazz hands.

Thankfully the music shifted seamlessly and the dancefloor filled again after the embarrassing routine was over. Livia continued dancing near her sister while stealing looks at Blake, whose attention was either on Livia or the napkin in his hand. Eventually, as always happened, Livia grew tired before Kyle showed any signs of slowing down.

"I'm sitting down," she shouted to Kyle and pointed at the table.

Kyle nodded and danced away, dismissing Livia with a wave of her hand. Livia made her way back to the Beckett-jacked table, and Blake watched her as if she were crossing a tricky, ice-covered river. Livia tried not to trip as he stood when she came to the table. He held her chair as she sat and then resumed his own seat. He leaned toward her, and Livia put her feet on his chair.

"You're beautiful." Blake said hello as he'd said goodbye.

"You said that already," Livia mouthed over the banging music.

Blake just shrugged. He flashed Livia a shy smile and held out the pink napkin to her. He'd turned it into a beautiful, perfect rose bud with a single leaf. Livia took the rose from his hand and turned it over carefully. He'd pinched tiny thorns into the paper stem. Livia put it to her nose as if to smell it. She realized he was waiting.

"You're beautiful," Livia mouthed. She would have hugged the rose if it weren't so delicate. She hugged him instead.

With her ear so close, Blake was able to murmur into it. "May I have this dance?"

Livia giggled as the room vibrated with a rhythm they could feel. Blake stood and very seriously held out his hand. Livia couldn't imagine turning him down, even if she had to figure out how to grind in time with the beat, but Blake had his own idea. He didn't lead her to the dancefloor. Blake took her deeper into the corner behind their table.

With the pink rose cradled carefully in their combined hands, Blake and Livia began a slow dance to music only they could hear. Livia danced to the symphony she heard flowing out of the church window the night she found out he could play. She opened her eyes to see Blake's serene face. She wondered if he danced to music he was composing in his head at this very moment — music that had not yet been played.

Livia and Blake danced like they were alone, not stuck in a blaring, sweaty night club.

Beckett eyed them as he lounged on three chairs he'd shoved together into a hard, uncomfortable couch. *They're so fucking innocent. They don't have a clue why I showed up here tonight.* If there hadn't been an obnoxiously repeating Tweet about them, he certainly wouldn't have come to this crapholc no matter who was here. He scrolled through his text messages and found a new one from Eve.

This ur homeless brother?

She'd attached a picture of Blake slumped in the shade with a fresh red welt on his face. He was not looking at the camera. Some brain-dead mouth-breather had added a point total at the bottom of the pic:

Pennies Thrown: 34 Pennies Landed: 23

Beckett rubbed his hand over his mouth to hold his anger in.

He rarely did the killing himself anymore, but the photographer and the Photoshop artist would feel the full extent of his talent. Pennies would be used in every torture he could imagine, and Beckett had an extremely active imagination. He was currently contemplating how many sizzling-hot pennies could fit on the surface of one human's skin. Branding their eyes shut would be the very last step, and the smell of burning skin would be his reward. Beckett ran a hand through his hair. *Patience.* If he spooked them, he'd never find them.

Beckett surveyed the crowd that had gathered around him. He caused a stir wherever he went nowadays, probably because he provided the resources for lots of experimenting among the poor souls of Poughkeepsie. There wasn't a vice Beckett couldn't supply, and the evils he offered were the highest quality. Beckett smiled at his past and future customers with both his dimples. No need to feel alarmed, his smile told them. The devil always had the biggest welcome mat at his door.

But all the while Beckett smiled and entertained with his filthy mouth and shameless flirting, he kept a watchful eye on Blake and Livia. The other picture Eve had sent to his phone was a doctored picture of Whitebread. She rocked at least double Ds in the picture, uncovered to boot, but Beckett put her at a B+ at best, and she seemed like the least likely girl in any room to pose for a nude photo. He was an expert.

Someone out there was tracking those two, so The Maxi Pad was now on unofficial lockdown, courtesy of his crew, and Eve was doing her best to track where the Tweet with the photos had originated. Beckett found himself grateful that Mouse was woman enough to frequent the ridiculous site. Eve reported that he'd found the picture floating on one of his knitter friend's daughter's page.

Beckett glanced over at the dancefloor. Fairy Princess was whore-bagging it out hard core. She could dance—he'd give her that—but she had the eyes of a veteran prostitute ten minutes before she retired for good.

"Merkin!" Beckett called over one of his minions.

Merkin could melt into any crowd. People never remembered he'd been there. He also had an unfortunate toupee, hence Beckett's loving nickname.

"Boss." Merkin arrived and awaited command.

"See that cute little fucking dancer? Get a shot of her when she's smashed between a few dudes." Beckett flipped his phone in Merkin's direction.

Merkin nodded and slipped away. Beckett watched as he did some extremely white-man dancing to get close to the circle of guys closing in on Kyle. She was grinding against three men while she sucked on her finger seductively. After checking that the shot was clear, Merkin retreated and handed the phone back to Beckett, ensconced in his cluster of hangers-on.

"Thanks, you fucking muffin fluffer." Beckett started his inaccurate texting as Merkin dissolved again into the crowd:

Hey# Cole U stuypid monk ur girll iz going dowen like the Hindenburg. We r at the Maxzi %Pad

Beckett ordered a round of watered-down drinks for the fools around him. He threw in a request for a couple bottled waters for fucking Romeo and Juliet. They might get thirsty, even in their own damn world. His brother was lost in Livia, twirling her hair around his finger like he was making a magic fucking wand out of it.

Beckett watched Livia look up at Blake and realized she was just as lost in him. He decided right then to set the two of them with a beautiful life together. Blake would have to agree. He'd want his woman to have the best, and Beckett could give them that — maybe somewhere far away so none of Beckett's shitload of evil would ever touch them. In his head Beckett put the two of them in a big snow globe with glitter that he could shake when he wanted them to fucking sparkle together. *Perfect in their condo with a dog and a kid and glitter.*

Blake turned to lead Livia back to their chairs, which Beckett had noticed were clogged up now with other people's asses. Beckett nodded to Mouse who carefully put down his fucking knitting, grabbed two poor bastards by the backs of their shirts, and tossed them to the floor. Blake shook his head at Beckett's lack of manners but held the chair out for Livia. She sat and smiled at Beckett like he was a guest at her freaking wedding. *She's so damn happy.*

Blake accepted the two water bottles from a server with a nod of gratitude. He opened his first and handed it to Livia, taking her unopened one as his own. She bit her lip and smiled.

Simple shit makes this chick crap bubbles and rainbows. Beckett shook his head, rattling his mental snow globe again as his phone buzzed. He looked at his phone to find a text from Eve:

I'm here

She was a woman of few words. Beckett gave the club another scan, and Kyle's continued frantic dancing caught his attention. *Fairy Princess-fuckingrella is kicking her slutting up a notch.*

He saw Livia tense out of the corner of his eye. *Shit. Kyle's going to ruin their night together.*

Fairy Princess was flexing like a yoga instructor with an IV drip full of Red Bull and lion piss. There was a circle about two dudes deep around her, all with their cocks pointed like they were water sticks and she was Niagara Falls. Beckett had to put an end to this shit. He stood.

He heard Livia's voice as he waded through the assholes and headed for the gyrating nightmare. "Blake, what's he going to do?"

He faintly heard his brother's reply. "Beckett won't hurt her. Don't worry."

Faith. Blake had all the faith in the world in him. All these new, different people to protect were starting to scare him. *How many fucking people will I have to beat the shit out of to keep them all happy and safe?*

Beckett hit the dance floor just as a brain-melting new song came on. He let out a perfect imitation of a circa-1992 Michael Jackson scream. The people bouncing on the dance floor turned around, even the wall of men surrounding Kyle.

A slow grin spread across his face, and he danced like he was born to do it. He embodied the beat, and the people who had turned for his scream now stayed for the show.

He stopped in the center of the dancefloor and slowly rotated his hips. He pointed at Kyle and called her out. "Dance with me, baby!"

The dancer in Kyle couldn't turn him down, and she sauntered over. He grabbed her by the waist, and Beckett and Kyle made dancing an Olympic sport. She would give and he would take; he would give and she would take. Kyle turned up the heat by adding some ballet leaps, daring Beckett to match her. His smile grew broader as he caught her smoothly, again and again, begging Kyle's body to do the impossible. Whirling as if partners for life, they complemented and contrasted each other like vodka and tonic.

Beckett pounded his chest in a heartbeat rhythm, and Kyle countered with a backbreaking, top-testing stretch. Beckett closed the distance and whispered to her as she threw her arms around his neck. "Hey, Fairy Princess, how fucking wasted are you?"

Kyle's coordination hadn't suffered, but her speech was slurred. "Enough to be numb." She used her hips to rock herself to the floor, then climbed sexily back up Beckett's leg.

Beckett wrapped a huge arm around Kyle's waist and slammed her body into his. "Sometimes when girls advertise, they get what they're asking for."

Kyle twisted so her back was to his chest. "Are you threatening or promising, big daddy?"

Beckett spun her around and held her face to his so their lips almost touched. The crowd went wild with perceived sexual tension.

"If I was threatening you, you'd already be beggin' for your real daddy," Beckett whispered.

Beckett felt Kyle shiver as he held her close, forcing her to stay pressed against him. Then she seemed to power through her fear and ran her hands down his face.

"I have things I need to forget tonight," she told him. "This is how I forget, you big, fucking pimp."

Kyle fluttered her hands like two swirling birds as she slipped into a deep backbend over Beckett's arm. He let her sway upside down from one of his hips to the other as he scanned the room. He saw plenty of ladies who'd realized, deep down in their panties, that he'd be an amazing fuck, but he was looking for someone in particular. He found her in the corner, dressed like a man.

Shit. If Eve was a man, I would gay it up. Hardcore.

He wanted her to see him like this—powerfully sexual and capable. He pulled Kyle up and found Eve over the top of Fairy Princess's hair. He saw Eve smirk as she watched him move with another woman.

Got her. She's jealous.

Eve looked away for a moment, then locked her ridiculous baby blues on him. She whipped a knife out of God knows where and held it in front of her face.

Oh, crap. She's gonna try to kill Cole's girl.

Eve held his eyes and confidently licked the length of the razor-sharp blade with the tip of her tongue. Red blood beaded up on her tongue, and she licked her lips, giving them a fresh coat of color. Eve used the knife to blow a kiss in Beckett's direction and disappeared into the crowd. Beckett forgot to keep dancing. He stood stock still with Kyle still twirling around him.

Eve had just fucked his mind so hard, he wanted to smoke a cigarette and cuddle like some soap-watching woman.

18

I Do Not Want This

Through her wild movements, Kyle saw the sexy blonde in man-drag lick her knife like she was Marilyn Monroe and Freddie Kruger's love child. She felt an immediate reaction in Beckett's pants, and for a moment he stopped dancing completely.

Figures. The minute I think I'm the belle of the ball, he only wants someone else.

When Beckett snapped out of it and grabbed her again, Kyle tried to push him away. She stopped rocking her body to the music.

He looked in her eyes. "You feeling okay?"

Kyle nodded, her knowing now complete. She would not get the release she needed from him. "I need to take a piss. I broke the seal." Kyle pushed harder, and Beckett made his arm a steel barrier around her waist.

He scanned the room again and finally put his mouth close to her ear. "Kyle, I have a lot to do here tonight. I need you to take care of yourself. Don't make me kill anyone."

Kyle felt revulsion roll through her, and she took a deep breath. Hairy Buffalo mixed with the knowledge that he would actually off someone almost ended her night. *I need another drink.*

Beckett pulled his phone out and smiled the most villainous smile Kyle had ever seen. "I have to go," he murmured. "Don't get your wings wet, Fairy Princess. It will be too hard to fly."

Beckett dipped her one last time and twirled her to release his hold. Kyle did her favorite stripper toe-drag walk over to the guys bolstering their courage after Beckett's departure.

Channeling her best Southern belle, Kyle batted her eyelashes and declared, "Holy shit! I feel so thirsty. I wish I had a drink."

In an instant, Kyle had her choice of three different glasses held by spellbound men. She poured the two shots into the beer and chugged the concoction with as few swallows as possible.

She heard a garbled, "See, I told you Kyle swallows," but ignored all it implied. She proceeded to give the men a show so arousing they should have had to pay for it.

As she danced along the bar, Kyle craned her neck and caught glimpses of her sister, who sat almost nose to nose with Mr. Blake Perfection. She tried to shake off the familiar look on his face as he traced Livia's jaw with his finger. *Cole.*

Someone handed Kyle another drink, which she pounded. The liquor in it tasted like gasoline, and she felt the burn in her nose as she handed the glass back. *There. Perfect. Everyone's blurry. Anyone could be him. Everyone will be him tonight.*

Kyle willed herself to believe she was too numb to feel the liberties her multiple dance partners now took with her body. *I don't feel it. I won't feel it.* Over and over she flashed her smile at the nearest guys, letting them grind into her. They were too drunk to be careful, and she knew she'd be bruised in the morning.

Across the room Blake rose and stood behind Livia. Kyle could see him move her hair and plant a kiss on her sister's neck. Livia's happiness rose like smoke from within her.

Kyle turned her back on the lovers and swayed her hips into another sweating man. She wished Beckett would come back. He wasn't sweating and had smelled so good. He would hold her steady. She felt *so* unsteady. Kyle disentangled herself and stumbled on her sharp, elaborate heels. One shoe's laces had come undone and trailed behind her like a deflated scream. *Bathroom.*

With a worried eye, Beckett watched as Kyle headed for the bathroom, but when his phone buzzed he looked down and lost sight of her. One of Beckett's douchebags had texted him. As he read the screen, Beckett felt the joy from the tips of his toes to the top of his head.

Boss, we have a bunch of cars and trucks arriving in the lot.

The sender of the Twitter hit on Blake and Livia must finally have received the Beckett-planted tip to come to the Blazing Crotch Cotton. A different douchebag lit up his phone as Beckett went to meet up with Mouse.

Cole side door. Let him in?

Beckett hit a quick reply: *Y*

Perfect timing, Cole can sop up the mess Fairy Princess is becoming. Beckett liked that all his people were in the club now, and the potential problem was outside it. When Beckett found him, Mouse was knitting an elaborate tube, using at least four damn double pointed needles.

"Mouse, quit finger-fucking that porcupine," Beckett ordered. "I need you on Blake and Whitebread."

Mouse's fingers were like a surgeon's; he brought the piece to a resting point in the pattern with practiced efficiency. He twirled his work of art into a sack and gave his boss a nod. Beckett knew Mouse would be on high alert now. The exemplary planning and foresight that made him a stellar knitter also made him an exquisite bodyguard. Mouse went to make sure Livia and Blake were behind him.

Beckett hit the front doors of the club. His Hummer had caused a ginormous clusterfuck of fake gangstas. Their Volvos, assorted sedans, and pussy little hybrids formed a fateful line behind a ridiculous F-250 truck. Beckett found Eve, whose lips were still stained red with blood. Beckett found it hard to focus as he wondered if he was part vampire—he wanted to taste that blood so badly.

The bathrooms at The Launch Pad were actually locker rooms, complete with showers. They were endlessly large, but deceptively limited in the number of people they could accommodate. There were two toilets in the ladies' room, side by side with no wall between them. Kyle always felt it was a little taste of prison when she went within arm's reach of a fellow female pisser. When she arrived this time, the line for the women's room was atrocious.

It would take extra time Kyle didn't have to wait in that line. The men's room taunted her with its empty doorway. She headed straight for it and turned her mind to the next challenge. *These leather pants are like a CapriSun—impossible to open.* Just as she was about to enter, two guys stopped her.

"Hey, sexy lady, where'd ya go?"

Both reached out to touch her. She'd given up all rights to her body on the dancefloor. These men were older than she was used to, and they were rougher as well. She couldn't actually place them from the dancing, but they breathed down her neck and layered compliments on her.

"Sweetheart, I love you," the taller one wheedled. "Come on, don't give me blue balls."

"Say that again." Kyle's voice was slurred and barely above a whisper.

The tall one steadied her. His copious chest hair mesmerized her—wild and curly like an old crotch. He smelled like sweat socks and beer.

He tried to focus on her face and spit with his words. "Don't give me blue balls."

Kyle laughed with her eyes almost closed. "No, fool, the other part."

He was stumped. "Uhhh…" Then he obviously remembered the best way to get in a drunken girl's pants. "I love you," he said proudly.

"You keep saying that, and you can do whatever you want to me." Kyle's eyes filled with tears, but her drunken suitors looked only at the smile she forced for them.

"Anything?" The tall one took a risk. "How 'bout the both of us?"

"Yeah. That sounds about right." Kyle let them lead her into the men's locker room.

The layout was a little different from the ladies', which turned Kyle's internal compass around. The men actually had walls around their toilets, of course.

"Let me pee first, for fuck's sake."

She locked herself in the stall, wrestled with her pants, and did what she needed to. She readjusted her outfit and stumbled out, narrowly avoiding falling onto the floor. Many drunken men in the past had not put forth the effort to aim. The tiles were dingy and sticky, with yellow urine puddled all around. The outer door was metal with a window like a ship's porthole. The solid-looking bolt was unlocked but made Kyle wonder what exactly usually happened in this bathroom. She wandered back into the center of the two men's ardor.

Kyle held still as the tall one mumbled, "I love you I love you I love you," until it became merely "ofyouofyouofyou."

He doesn't even know my name.

His short friend came around to test his luck on her breasts. Her top slid easily down. He added his "I love yous" to the mix like the phrase was the "Abracadabra" of sex. He watched her hands and remained ready to flee as he grabbed handfuls of her. Kyle felt the tears slip from her eyes and looked at her shoes.

She'd never been with two men before. She'd never been naked in a men's room before. She'd never had a man tell her he loved her before.

She could see herself in one smudged mirror, and the ones on either side were cracked into patterns like spider webs. Her reflection showed her the truth. She wasn't some beautiful siren being seduced by two men at once. She was a stupid girl getting pawed at by two balding idiots who didn't even know her name. She almost said nothing. *I've agreed to this, haven't I? I am this, aren't I?*

But then something glittering on the taller one caught her attention. Buried in his thick, graying chest hair was a gold cross. *Cross. I do not want this. Cole. I do not want this!*

Her head said it a few more times before her mouth had the courage to utter the words out loud. The shorter one had latched onto her right breast with his mouth like a leech. The taller one had untied her other heel and started working on her impossible pants.

Her voice was quiet at first. "I don't want this."

Their lack of response poured urgency in her words.

"I'm sorry. Stop. *I don't want this!*" Kyle began to shake when they still showed no sign of hearing her.

Then the taller one went from his "ofyou" mantra directly into a snarl. "Listen, sweetheart. This was your idea. This roller coaster has left the station, so just hang on for the ride."

He then stepped on one high heel's laces while the shorter one stepped on the other's, which bound her feet to the floor. She knew then that they'd planned this, at least a little. With her legs now immobile, each one grabbed an arm. Kyle had her voice left to fight with, but her shame gagged her quiet. The taller one finally figured out the two hook-and-eye closures on her pants, and she felt them loosen.

"I do not want this," she repeated. She sobbed now, and couldn't speak nearly as loudly as she wanted to.

Then all three looked up at the sound of the lock on the thick bathroom door clicking into place. Kyle looked in the mirror for a glimpse of her next attacker. *There are three of them now.*

But it was Cole's face she saw. For a moment she thought her heart was projecting his image into the mirror in sheer hope. But he was there, dressed like a dad in khaki pants and a plaid shirt.

Cole had no swagger. Cole had no menacing words. Cole didn't even wind up when he punched so viciously that the last unbroken mirror shattered with the impact of the taller man's head.

Beckett shook his head to clear it of his obsession with Eve's blood-stained lips. All business, she reported to him what she'd learned so far.

"The tags on that truck belong to a Chris Simmer. He's the one who Tweeted looking for Livia and Blake."

Beckett contemplated how to proceed. *Nothing rash.* Chris Simmer would die, of course, but Beckett's plans were too third-world interrogation room to implement in a parking lot with a crapload of eyeballs watching.

Beckett watched the lineup of cars sitting in the traffic jam. Though they were surely frustrated, the drivers refused to leave the safety of the painted lines that marked the pretend road in the lot. *Neat, orderly mother-erfuckers.* After a simple hand gesture from Beckett, two of his douchebags used their cars to block the front and back of the line of vehicles like beads on a necklace.

Beckett and Eve stood in companionable silence for a bit.

"What to do? What do you think, you sweet, sexy bitch?" Beckett stared into the headlights of the F-250.

"Now's not your moment, but you should scare him enough to stay away from Blake," Eve said.

Beckett nodded and headed for the truck. He jumped easily onto the running board and smiled like he was delivering Chris Simmer a big check and a bunch of balloons. Chris rolled down the window.

Beckett leaned in to look around the cab while he spoke. "Hey, dude! Are you here for some fun times and partying?"

Chris raised an eyebrow, emphasizing how unimpressed he was. "Yeah, dude," he accented the *dude.* "Why are we all boxed in?"

Beckett leaned back to take in the lineup of potential-Blake-beating watchers. He took a deep breath, his lungs filling with anger and menace. When Beckett met Chris's eyes again, Chris's whole demeanor had changed. He seemed to grow smaller in his seat.

"Chrissy, Chrissy, Chrissy. Give me your goddamn phone." All the while Beckett smiled.

"I'm not that comfortable with that—and how the fuck do you know my name?" Chris reached for the button to raise the window, as if a thin layer of glass could ever protect him from Beckett.

Beckett almost laughed. Almost. But he hadn't liked the use of the word *fuck* in Chris's response. Beckett waited for the glass to reach about halfway up before he grabbed it and leaned back until it snapped off in his hands. Chris kept his finger on the window button long after it was obvious nothing was left to respond anymore.

Beckett hated to repeat a request, so he just stared at Chris.

"What? My phone? Fine. Here." Chris rotated his phone off his hip clip.

Beckett scrolled through his messages.

Chris tried a threat. "My fiancée's dad is a cop, so I'd be careful what you say to me."

Beckett handed the phone back. "Oh, Chrissy, I'm going to be so careful with you. Have no worries."

Just then the club door flew open and Merkin came sprinting in Beckett's direction. Beckett felt his stomach curl in a ball. *What the hell?*

He stepped down from Chris's truck to receive Merkin's frantic whisper: "Cole's locked in the men's room with Kyle. Someone's screaming."

Beckett tossed a look at Eve that told her to finish threatening Chris. She sauntered over to the truck as Beckett took off running, through the doors of the club and straight to the men's room. He pushed through the crowd of his douchebags who'd formed a ring around the door so the regular crowd couldn't get a peek at the ruckus.

He grabbed the nearest minion. "Make that music as loud as you can and clear this club."

Beckett reluctantly turned his eyes to the porthole to the men's room. The tile walls were already sprinkled with blood, and inhumane screams emanated from inside. Beckett put his hands on the metal door. There were only a few feet of visible space before the locker room turned a corner, giving Cole privacy to do his worst. *Shit. Shit. Shit.*

"Cole, it's me! Let me in. For God's sake, Cole!" Beckett kept his hands flat on the door, wishing he could melt the metal with them.

The screaming stopped. Beckett tried again, yelling over the music to be heard. His phone buzzed and he checked the text from Eve:

Police r on their way 2 lock down 4 underage drinking. ETA 6 minutes.

Beckett gave a silent thanks that his crew monitored the police scanner as he texted Eve back:

Cl4ear the patrking lot of the purn#ks

"Cole, you have to let me in. I have to be *in* there to help." Beckett banged the door in the quick pattern they'd used in foster care. The code promised it was safe to open the door.

"Merk, where the hell's Blake? Where's Livia?" Beckett yelled.

"I'm on it, boss." Merkin headed for the dancefloor.

Beckett saw movement in the porthole. Cole approached in a red-stained plaid shirt and bloody priest pants. He didn't look at the window as he clicked the dead bolt open. Beckett opened the door and closed it behind him with a snap of the lock.

The scene around the corner was so bloody it was almost funny. Almost. And a scared Fairy Princess with her top around her waist sobered him immediately. Her fucking huge eyes stared at Cole. He would have to work quickly.

Cole's turned to face her as he whispered, "Kyle, I know you must be really afraid of me right now. I promise I won't move. Beckett will take you home, okay?"

Kyle stared blankly at them. Slowly she straightened herself, stood, and walked across the bloody floor to stand in front of Cole. Only then did she speak. "I'm so sorry. Look what I did. Now these men are...are they dead? All because I wanted to punish myself? You must be so ashamed of me."

"Can I remove my shirt?" Cole asked.

Kyle nodded. He unbuttoned his shirt and held it out to Kyle, who didn't move. Beckett sighed, took the shirt, and put it around Fairy Princess, covering her fantastic rack. He tried to button it up, but Cole's shirt had the smallest fucking toddler-sized buttons. He wound up getting them all matched with the wrong holes. But at least her tits were hidden now.

Kyle stepped into Cole's chest, and he wrapped his arms around her. They fit together like two quotation marks. Beckett didn't want to rush this sweet nonsense, but the cops would be here any freaking minute. He cleared his throat anxiously.

"Please leave with Beckett. Are you okay? Did I get here in time?" Cole spoke into the top of Kyle's head.

"I'm fine. I'm stupid, but I'm fine. I think I'm going to be sick." Kyle remained cuddled in Cole's arms.

Beckett heard the secret knock again and felt a surge of joy that Blake was safely on the other side. He grabbed Kyle's arm and led her away from Cole. He had a feeling if Kyle had had even one fewer drink, pulling her away would've been a whole lot harder.

"Wait — come with me, Cole." She looked confused and guilty.

Cole returned and took her hand. "Kyle, will you promise me something? It's all I'll ever ask of you, please?"

"Yes. I'll promise you anything." Kyle looked into his eyes.

"Don't let that girl inside you win. Ever again. Be the real Kyle. Promise me you'll be *you.*" Cole looked desperate.

Kyle shook her head, eyes pleading, but she responded in the affirmative. "I promise. Cole, what's next?"

Cole looked around the room sadly. One man was clearly dead and the other moaned softly.

"My sweet, beautiful Kyle, I have to atone for what I've done here. I want you far, far away when they put the cuffs on me."

Kyle's eyes widened, and she struggled valiantly against Beckett's instant grip on her.

He popped the lock and passed the bundle of squirming Kyle to Blake. "Bro, take Mouse and get her home. She'll be puking soon."

Livia looked furious and immediately pounded Kyle with high-pitched questions about the blood on Cole's shirt. Kyle stopped cursing and struggling long enough to tell Livia she was okay. Beckett slammed the men's room door and locked it again. He had just moments to make this right.

"Cole, you need to leave. Right now." Beckett started punching the wall to bruise his hands.

"I'm taking this, Beckett. *I* did this. I could have just disabled them. But when I heard her say no I just…" Cole seemed resigned to his fate.

"They were trying to rape her?" Beckett hit the wall with enough force to hear something crack—either a tile or a knuckle.

"She said, 'I do not want this,' and they were all over her." Cole glared at the men on the floor.

Beckett grabbed his brother by his shoulders. "Listen to me. The police are on their way. I know you want to take this and nail it to that giant fucking cross you're carrying around, but I can't have you in prison. Who the hell will take care of Blake?"

Cole looked unmoved.

"You and I both know I've already outlived my shelf life. Do you think I'll make it for another twenty years while you're locked up? Who'll make sure Blake gets what he needs if we're both gone? It has to be you. Let's face it, I deserve to be arrested—so many times over. So many times. Look at me."

Cole stared at the still-breathing man.

"How many lives will you save if I'm in prison?" Beckett continued. "Hundreds? Thousands? Do it for the people I haven't killed yet."

Cole turned to look at Beckett. *Success.* The combination of Blake and the yet-to-be-harmed had done it. Cole let himself be dragged to the door. Merkin was waiting.

"Take my brother and get our group out." Merkin looked puzzled, but he would never question Beckett.

Beckett left the door unlocked for the police. *No use making it hard.* Beckett Taylor gift-wrapped at a murder scene should make them cum in their pants.

Beckett hung his head and clasped his hands in front of his body. As he waited for the biggest punch of his life, the door creaked open.

"Do you have to kill people every time you take a piss?" Eve locked the men's room door behind her.

God, he loved looking at her. Even with her hair tucked in a baseball hat she was breathtaking.

"No, they killed themselves after I unleashed my colossal penis. It happens everywhere I go." Beckett smiled as she assessed the damage.

"What happened?" Eve felt for a pulse on the dead man.

Beckett told her without thinking twice. He trusted her implicitly. "Cole caught these two bastards trying to rape Fairy Princess."

Emotion flashed in her eyes. *Hate.*

"The cops are already here. Right about now…" She paused as they heard a ruckus outside and the music faded to silent. "All the douchebags are starting fights the police will have to break up. Do you trust me, Beckett?"

Beckett had never heard Eve use his first name before. It made him long for a home, a blanket, and her pussy all at once.

"Abso-fucking-lutely."

Eve moved to the dispenser that emitted rough, brown paper towels. She used one to withdraw a knife from her ankle holster. Beckett made no move to stop her as she walked toward him. She ran a hand through his hair, took the knife, and cut his scalp. She smiled as blood dripped onto his face.

"Fucking ouch." Beckett waited to see what she'd do next. Would this be the time she killed him?

She counted his ribs with her fingertips and found her favorite spot. She slid the knife in sideways and pulled it out. Beckett could only wheeze in response, feeling like all the air was instantly gone from his lungs. She yanked the gold chain off his neck and took the ring off his finger, ripping a good chunk of skin with it. Beckett put it together when she planted the jewelry on the dead man and carefully slid the knife out of its paper towel and into the grip of the corpse.

Fingerprints. Tricky bitch. She just made that dead fool my attacker.

He didn't complain when Eve hit him with a few precisely placed punches. She slid him down the wall and set him on the floor.

She arranged his legs and arms to her liking and whispered in his ear. "This was self-defense. You're unarmed. He wanted your gold. I'll call your lawyer." She put her hat on his head.

"What about the witness?" Beckett wheezed.

"There is no witness." Eve leaned down and placed a gentle kiss on Beckett's lips.

Our first fucking kiss.

Eve easily lifted the soon-to-be-ex witness. Apparently, he was not as bad off as he'd seemed because he was able to stand. Eve pulled another knife from around her ankle and inserted it into the fucker's lower back, essentially making the knife a handle to the man's kidney. She could steer him like a horse with a bridle. Eve commanded her hostage to open the door and look calm. She didn't turn around again, but Beckett knew what she'd done. She'd crossed some line she'd drawn for herself. She'd said his name, kissed him, and saved him.

She'd done what he couldn't do for himself.

19

Aftermath

Livia dug her keys out of her purse as Blake and Mouse hustled Kyle to the fire door. As they burst through, Livia braced herself for an alarm, but it remained silent. Four of Beckett's crew parted to allow them to exit, nodding at Mouse and Blake. They skirted the outside of the parking lot to find Livia's car, then stuffed Kyle in the backseat with Blake and Mouse on either side while Livia drove them home. As they pulled away, the night was on fire with red and blue lights. Halfway there, Kyle started throwing up. Blake handed her a plastic grocery bag he found on the floorboards to save Livia's upholstery. Livia pulled into the driveway but wondered aloud whether they should take Kyle straight to the hospital.

"I've been worse than this before," Kyle assured them between heaves.

Mouse helped Blake get Kyle upstairs, but returned immediately to the front porch. "I'll keep an eye on things," he explained. "I'm supposed to stay. One of the guys will bring a car for me. Can I have Cole's shirt back though? I'll need to burn it."

Livia nodded as the weird night got weirder.

Now that Kyle had returned to familiar territory, she lost some of her fight. She allowed Livia to put her in soft clothes, and Blake disappeared with Cole's shirt. Kyle collapsed in bed as Livia tucked her in.

Livia stepped into the hallway as Blake came back up the stairs. "I guess I'll stay in here to make sure she's doing all right," Livia said. "Kyle might decide she wants to talk, or worst case, she might choke on her own vomit."

Blake nodded and loosened his tie. "I'll keep you company if you'd like."

"I would like." Livia was thrilled he would stay, even without the promise of being alone in her bedroom.

Livia scooted past him to change into sweats. She selfishly didn't offer Blake any new clothes because he looked so magnificent in the loose tie and black pants. She came back to find him sitting on Kyle's floor with his back against the wall. She slid down to sit next to him, their legs touching.

"Blake, what do you think happened in there tonight?"

"I think Cole walked in on someone trying to hurt Kyle, and he handled it." Blake shrugged.

"Handled it?" Livia couldn't imagine how a would-be priest wound up covered in so much blood.

"Cole has a background that required him to fight like an animal," Blake said, seeming to choose his words carefully. "His dedication to the Church comes partly from what he endured as a child."

They sat holding hands in silence for a long time after that. Periodically Blake would peek over at her and smile.

Livia felt bold in the darkness of Kyle's room. "Blake, do you remember the first day your skin was like glass in the sun?"

Blake was quiet for what seemed like an endless expanse of time.

"I remember." He sighed.

Livia waited. He would tell her if he could. She would listen.

"You already know my mother was an alcoholic. She would get so frustrated with herself for failing me, but then she would take it out on me. Physically. When I was older, no matter which new housing program we were enrolled in—we always had to change and move—I was fortunate enough to be within walking distance of the Poughkeepsie library. I sort of used it as self-imposed daycare. I'd stop in after school and stay as late as it was open. In the summers, I spent my whole day there. The volunteers and the librarian did much more than organize the stacks." Blake stroked Livia's hand in his. "It was the center of the community, and those volunteers saw my need to learn and be mothered. They took it upon themselves to teach me, help me with homework, and give me lessons on the piano in the basement. I was like a stray cat with a dozen houses to call my own."

A smile crossed Blake's face at the memory. "Those ladies shaped me and ingrained my manners deeply," he continued. "Miss Joan would always say, 'Manners are everything, Blake. They're worth more than money.' But at home, my mother was getting worse. I was getting bigger, and I think that frightened her. She began increasing her episodes with me until there were times I couldn't go to the library because I didn't want them to see how I looked with bruises and think less of me."

Livia touched Blake's face, placing a soft kiss on his lips before he continued.

"When I was twelve, I made the worst mistake of my life. I didn't use my manners. I didn't respect my mother. The day my skin became glass, she used something other than her hands on me for the first time. She picked up my belt. She scared me. I was afraid to be hit with the belt. The metal buckle was headed straight for me." Blake rubbed his eyes against the memory.

"I punched her right in the face, Livia. My own mother. She was furious and hurt. I let her use the belt after I realized my mistake. She backed me into our coffee table and I tripped. I fell into the glass liquor cabinet that was her pride and joy. The glass shattered around me, and all the liquor bottles broke. Bits and shards embedded in my skin." He touched his forearm as if the glass was still there.

"My mother called the cops and demanded they remove me from the house. I was never sure if she had me removed because she was scared of me or mad that all her alcohol was in puddles mixed with glass and my blood. When the police and paramedics brought me into the sunlight, I saw. I saw the glass in my skin. The sun reveals what I really am, Livia. I hit a *woman*. My own mother. The glass and liquor seeped in, and I can't get it out."

Livia stayed silent and tried to quiet the screaming in her head. *Fuck your mother, Blake! She was a drunk and a coward. You were a child, not a man, and you were only trying to end your own pain.* She held tight to Dr. Lavender's advice. *Listen.* This was Blake's plane crash. Livia's silence invited him to continue.

"Social Services picked me up from the police station," he finally said. "The gentleman gave me a cardboard box with a few of my things in it, and he told me my mother had relinquished all her rights. My foster home was nowhere near the library, so my family there was lost as well. I couldn't have gone back in there anyway. They'd have known my mother gave me up and I hadn't been a gentleman.

"*My* manners were not impeccable," Blake added, his voice bitter now. "*My* manners were not worth more than money. I was medicated for my violent tendencies and spent a great deal of time either in a haze or totally numb, but I tried to uphold my library family's high expectations. A few years later the two little girls in the minivan paid the ultimate price for my cowardice." He took his hand out of hers and put it in his lap. "Now you know, Livia. All that I'm not."

So many people had tried for Blake, but so many had failed. *All it takes is one to be the glue. It's going to be me.* Livia moved quietly to straddle him. She put her hands on his scruffy cheeks. "I know all that you are. You almost don't belong here, your soul's so pure." Livia put a hand on his chest. "You're perfect to me. You're chivalrous to me. I adore your manners. You *can't* disappoint me. It's not possible." Livia leaned in and kissed him sweetly. *See? See how much I can fix?*

Blake became absorbed by her hair, grabbing handfuls of it. He pulled her to his chest, combing it out with his fingers as he hummed a soothing song in her ear. The liquid velvet of his voice lifted her into dreams.

The flames reflected in Eve's pupils matched her anger. She threw the rest of the gasoline on her private bonfire. The body of the witness produced almost-white flames and blinding heat. *I overdid it.*

But Eve wanted something tangible. Something to blister her skin a bit, to match her soul.

She was allowing herself to think of her past, which was a rare indulgence. She needed to relive it because she'd strayed from her purpose. She'd disregarded her calling. Eve chipped away at her decayed insides to find the little tiny piece of pink that was her heart now. She closed her eyes and let the waves of heat send her back to the accident.

The summer sun had been searing that day. Eve twisted the air conditioner on immediately as David started his old beater.

"Sweetness, a car needs to warm up to cool down." David chuckled as Eve blasted them both with fire-breathing dragon hot air instead of the instant relief she sought.

"That doesn't even make sense. Besides, being too hot can't be good for the baby." Eve's eyes twinkled. She tried to put the word baby in every sentence she could nowadays.

"She's probably already hot-tempered if she's anything like her mom." David put the car in gear.

Eve put both hands on her stomach. The description for week ten in her pregnancy book was her favorite so far. The baby had lost its tail, and its face had formed. There were even little fingers and toes. Eve couldn't wait to get her first pair of maternity pants. She was the only nineteen-year-old she knew who wanted to *gain* weight. David teased her when she flipped through the book, each chapter revealing new mysteries about her baby. *My baby.*

When she'd missed her period, Eve had gotten a pregnancy test—the most expensive brand because she wanted the best for her maybe-baby. She'd used it right when she got home, not even waiting to get David. She could hardly tell, but the test window looked like it might have two lines. *Two lines!*

After her call, David had made an excuse to leave his job as a mechanic for an hour so he could come to Eve's place in her dad's apartment building and peer at the stick in the sunlight. They waited together while she took the other two tests in the box in quick succession.

By the third test, she had been certain she was pregnant. Eve called her gynecologist immediately, as if being pregnant for five minutes was an emergency. David and Eve were too young and they weren't even married, but a baby was all she'd ever wanted.

Eve had planned to be a mom for as long as she could remember. In almost every childhood picture, she carried a baby doll. Before she was even of legal age, Eve was babysitting. She had an easy, natural way with children and found herself in great demand. Eve gravitated to babies, with their sweet cheeks and gummy smiles. They fit so perfectly on her hip, but she always had to give them back to their mothers.

Not this baby. This one is mine. With David as dad.

She'd made the best decision of her life when she convinced the easygoing David that, yes, he really did want to take her on a date. One year later they were inseparable.

He would make a patient, persistent father. He clearly adored Eve, but he also refused to put up with any of her drama. They solved their problems in quiet, respectful voices. Even Eve's father had seemed convinced that Eve and David would be together until they were old and forgetful.

"David, how can you be so sure the baby's a girl? It's way too soon to know," Eve had teased.

David reached over to cover both her hands, and much of her stomach, with one of his large, dark ones.

Eve let time freeze on his smile — his big, comforting smile. She wished the memory ended here and in that next instant, she'd just ceased to exist.

They'd been heading through a bad part of Poughkeepsie, on their way to get Chinese food because Eve had said the baby wanted it.

"Anything for my two girls." David had loved saying "two girls."

The accident that twisted the car into a searing, crushed pile of agony happened so quickly that Eve's mind couldn't process it. The noise alone was enough to make her think she was going insane. When the spinning stopped, Eve grabbed for David.

He was gone.

His eyes were open, but there was nothing left. Eve didn't realize she was the one screaming until her throat started to hurt. Time went by in great leaps forward, alternated with endless frozen pauses.

Sirens, eventually. Pain, eventually.

Eve finally looked down and saw a piece of maroon dashboard stabbing through her hand and into her stomach. *Oh, that's just plastic,* she thought. But the paramedics wouldn't let her pull it out.

She overheard one of them shout, "This is Dr. Hartt's daughter!"

Eve had no idea why those words came back to her at night. Over and over her brain repeated, *"This is Dr. Hartt's daughter!"*

Not *"Eve, we aren't showing a heartbeat on the baby."*

Not *"David Statford was pronounced dead at the scene."*

Not *"We can't stop the bleeding. She's hemorrhaging."*

Not *"If the infection continues, we're not going to have any choice. Eve, we're recommending a hysterectomy."*

Maybe it was because she'd still had hope when she heard those words. Maybe because she'd thought she'd be protected since her father was a surgeon at the hospital where the ambulance took her.

Eve grabbed the shovel and started to dig. After the witness was done smoldering, she'd bury him here in the woods. She'd dig so deep no one would ever find him. A murderer got caught when she got sloppy or got scared. Eve was neither of those things.

When she'd finally been released from the hospital, Eve found herself without a purpose. She had sat at home on her bed watching horrible daytime TV.

Her new mission — the one she'd so pathetically wavered from now — had been given to her by mistake. She never answered the phone in those days, but when she heard Officer McHugh from Poughkeepsie Police Department on the answering machine, she hit the TV's mute button.

"Ms. Hartt? This is Officer McHugh. I have some personal belongings from the car accident. The reconstruction team is finished. I'm so sorry for your loss. I'll keep the belongings at my desk, if you're interested in them."

Eve stared at the flickering, quiet TV for a while before she got up. Almost as if she were on autopilot, she drove her dilapidated Civic to the station. As the receptionist pointed out Officer McHugh's desk, Eve sensed that the people in the room were talking about her.

Two cops and a well-dressed woman discussed a car accident.

"That man's a bane to this community," the woman said, clearly in the midst of a tirade. "That couple in the wreck a few weeks back — did you know she lost the baby? The collateral damage that follows him around is amazing."

"Drugs and trouble," one cop said, shaking his head. "That's all he has to offer. What a sack of shit."

"Bad enough that they do those cowardly drive-by shootings, but they could at least wait until the victim's out of the car," said the second cop. "So they don't take anyone else out."

The woman shifted from one foot to the other. "Never any proof to nail that bastard. Beckett Taylor's one slippery asshole."

Eve hadn't noticed that the officer who'd called her stood behind his chair.

"Guys, take that somewhere else," he said. He gave a pointed glance in Eve's direction, and the group went silent. He ran a hand down his face and sat down. "I'm sorry. They don't think sometimes."

Eve used her voice for the first time in weeks. "The car that hit us…" The word *us* punched her in the heart. "The driver was the victim of a drive-by shooting?"

She appreciated that Officer McHugh told it to her straight. "Yeah, the driver had a fatal gunshot wound to the head," he said. "The car he was driving came at yours head-on."

"Who's Beckett Taylor?" Eve tried to form a picture in her mind. The name didn't sound menacing.

"You overheard quite a bit. I'm sorry for that. Mr. Taylor's a waste of skin, but we have no evidence tying him to this shooting." The officer tapped his fingers on his desk, like he was itching to do something.

"So David and my baby were 'collateral damage'?" Eve took small, sharp breaths.

"I wouldn't put it that way, but you *are* a victim of a crime, not just a tragedy. Would you like your belongings?" Officer McHugh looked under his desk.

"No, I'm good." Eve stood up and left. With every step she felt herself harden. She was a walking statue by the time she hit the police station's exit.

She had a purpose again. *Hate.*

Eve cuddled hate to her heart like a baby — like the only baby she'd ever have. Eve despised reliving the accident, but she had to do it to get harder. She needed to be angrier.

She'd spent the years after learning Beckett's name turning herself into a killing machine. Every time she felt a twinge of pain, she numbed it with a new skill. At first her father thought she might be interested in the police academy or the military. But Eve had no such plans. Her only goal was to kill Beckett Taylor. And she was nothing if not tenacious. All the fabulous capabilities she'd been proud to possess before the accident she now twisted into perfect means of causing pain.

Before she'd lost her purpose, Eve never let her CPR or first aid certification lapse. She prided herself on her work at the daycare, and someday she'd hoped to be a full-fledged teacher. She kept an eye on any child she could see, even in a store or at the mall, and she'd returned many a lost kid to his parent.

But now she used that watchfulness and vigilance to learn any deadly skill she could. Because once she was face to face with Beckett Taylor, she was going to kill the fuck out of him. She had no plans for after his death. She didn't give a rat's ass if she made it out alive. She wanted to be with David and her baby, but first she would end the man that had ruined it all.

Eve now knew how to kill without a sound. She knew every place on the human body that could be penetrated with a knife to induce death. She was better at killing than the man she hunted. Eve would never feel the soft, downy hair of her own baby against her cheek, but she knew she could kill at least three heavily armed men with a golf club.

All that was left of the witness was dispatched in just a few scoops with the shovel, so Eve now lifted the dirt back into the hole. Today she had to acknowledge that she was avoiding her mission. She could explain away all the other times she hadn't killed Beckett so far. *I'm just going to see what his inner circle's like…If I find out who he loves, I can kill them while he watches…If I make him fall for me, it will hurt worse when I kill him.* But there was no excuse for tonight. In that men's room she'd had another perfect opportunity. He'd gone willingly in front of her knife and fists.

But she'd spared him. She'd used all her deadly skills to save him instead. She'd spit on the memory of David and her baby to give Beckett a get-out-of-jail-free card.

She surveyed her work in the Hummer's headlights. *Perfect.* She'd done it so many times now it was second nature. *Now I'm just a murderer, not an avenger. I'm just like him.*

Eve drove his Hummer through the brush and back onto the path ATVs had made through the woods. It was almost morning.

She had to kill him. She had to kill Beckett the next time she saw him or all she'd done to become an exquisite monster would be for nothing.

20

D⊖n'† Run

Livia didn't immediately remember the details of the night before when she woke in her bed. Her blanket had been arranged around her. As she sat up, she noticed little paper-napkin roses tucked among her belongings. *Blake.*

He'd even given Teddy a spiffy bow tie. He must have taken a whole stack of napkins from The Launch Pad, and the sunlight trickling in her window explained his absence. His fancy clothes were folded neatly on the end of her bed. The prince was the one to run out of time in this Cinderella story. She smiled, then gasped as horror punched her in the stomach. *Kyle!*

Livia rushed out of her room to find Mouse happily knitting as he sat outside Kyle's open door. Seemed at some point in the night he'd decided to come in after all.

"She's doing fine," he whispered. "She'll feel awful today, but nothing a little time won't cure."

Hearing his squeaky voice in her house was bizarre. Livia ran her hands through her hair and studied Mouse for a moment. He was working on a different piece of knitting than last night.

"What do you have there?"

Mouse perked up at her interest. "I'm making ski masks to have on hand for bank robberies. Last night I finished the fingerless mermaid gloves for Eve. She likes her fingers free for gunplay."

Mouse's needles clicked together in a peaceful rhythm.

"That's, uh, nice. I loved the colors on the gloves." Livia wasn't sure how to complement Mouse's craft.

"Thanks. I'm proud of those. I like fall colors. They go nicely with her hair." Mouse smiled in the direction of his bag, which must have held his completed knitting. "My grandmother taught me to knit," he explained. "It's always good to keep the hands busy."

"Okay. I'm going to get some coffee started and stuff." Livia tried to leave.

"Wait!" Mouse popped a needle protector on the end of his tool. "Can you watch her for a moment? I have to take a leak."

Livia watched as his huge form eclipsed the hallway light, then peered through Kyle's doorway. She looked fine, just very asleep. Livia really wanted to talk to her, but it didn't look like that would be possible for hours. Next on Livia's to-do list was Blake. She needed to find him. They needed to face what he feared. Together. Livia slipped a freshly made ski mask out of Mouse's knitting bag. It was black and soft, with two holes for eyes and one for the mouth. *It's perfect.*

Livia walked silently down the stairs and closed the back door slowly, sliding her feet into the junk sneakers she always left on the back steps. Livia hoped she'd be two blocks away by the time Mouse realized she was gone and he was stuck watching over Kyle.

Livia leaped into the Escort and drove straight to Poughkeepsie Station, letting instinct and her internal Blake GPS be her guide. She tossed a mint from the glovebox into her mouth at a stoplight. The lot wasn't crowded on a Saturday, and she hopped out quickly, not bothering to lock the doors.

As she trotted down the stairs, she saw Blake stand up, tucking his piano in his pocket. The day's bright sun had him trapped in his spot in the shade. She stepped into his cover and kissed him.

"Thanks for the roses. And Teddy loves his bow." She brushed her hands through his hair.

"How's Kyle? I had Mouse watch her."

Such a normal question. "She'll feel like crap, but I think she'll be fine. I'm still waiting to hear what she's willing to tell me about the bathroom in the club." Livia kissed his chin. "Blake, I need you to do something for me. Will you do something for me?" Livia felt a little dirty about forcing him to agree before she told him how much she was asking.

"I'll do whatever you wish." Blake inclined his head in a solemn gesture.

Livia headed back to the car without explaining. She returned with a golf umbrella, a pair of leather work gloves, and Mouse's ski mask.

"Will you walk in the sunlight if these are covering you?" Livia held out her sunshields.

Blake looked at the items. Then he nodded and took the mask.

Livia knew this was a risk. Hell, she was half sure she was delirious with lack of sleep and desperation. But she had an insatiable need to heal. *I may lose him, but goddamn it, I have to try.*

Livia led the now overdressed Blake on a walk to his favorite clearing in the woods. Somehow she remembered the way, although at times he gave her gentle guidance with his hand. The golf umbrella's rainbow cloth kept them both shielded as they went. Blake wore his army jacket and the leather work gloves, but the real savior was the ski mask. At the moment it emphasized Blake's anxious eyes. Livia knew he followed her because she'd asked him to, and she was afraid he might run away.

When they arrived, Livia stopped and stood in the shade at the edge of the clearing.

Blake nodded toward the sunny center. "See those two saplings? In a little while, when the sun is just so in the sky, their shade will make a perfect heart."

"I can't wait to see the heart-shaped shade, Blake." She kissed his mouth. It was time to explain. "We're here because I think all that time ago you fell off the horse. I think you had the breath knocked out of you, but no one made you get back *on* the horse. No one was there to tell you to keep trying, that it's not okay to be afraid of the sun. But it's not okay. I'm here to tell you to try again."

Livia paused to assess the impact of her words, but the mask hid Blake's expression. "Running won't stop me," she continued. "I'll keep finding you. I'll keep dragging you back here — right to this spot — until you can stand in the sun. With me."

The knit mask framed Blake's lips. He bit one.

Livia let his hand drop. Now she'd set the boundaries so he could build his ladder to her. "Blake Hartt, if you touch me, your skin must be bare. Do you understand?" Livia looked into his green eyes. They seemed confused, but he nodded.

Livia wished she'd worn something more romantic, but no matter. This wasn't about clothes; it was about skin. Thank God it was unseasonably warm today. She kicked off her sneakers and stepped away from him.

Come get me, Livia said with her eyes.

She pulled off her sweatpants and felt the cool air snap at her skin. She walked further and stopped in the center of the clearing next to the miraculous saplings. She now stood right where they'd been before when they'd failed.

She took her jacket off and let it fall. She created a trail of clothes like little stepping stones to hope. Livia had always been shy about her body. She insisted on a one-piece bathing suit and a towel close to the ladder when she went swimming. But she could do this here, now. She was asking *so* much of him.

She pulled her sweatshirt off and stood in her bra and panties. She shook a little from the cold and the risk. She willed him to take the chance as well.

He hadn't moved, just stood squeezing the handle of the cheerful umbrella and watching Livia like she was walking a tightrope without a net. Livia reached behind her and unlatched her bra. She added it to her trail of clothes. Blake flexed and closed a gloved hand. Livia slipped off her white panties.

Now she was here—nude for him—if he could bring himself to walk across the meadow. She shivered and fought the need to cover her chilly skin. Blake kept his eyes on hers, not yet indulging in the sight before him.

"You're cold," he said softly.

Livia nodded. "I'm cold and alone out here." She longed to un-write that **Sorry** on his arm—if he could just take a chance.

The **y** in sorry erased as Blake braced himself and stepped into the full sun, leaving the umbrella in the shade. He moved as if walking through quicksand. But his eyes were on the prize.

Livia struggled to keep her tears to herself. She'd never witnessed such stunning bravery. She could only imagine the full nature of the walls, fears, and pain he climbed over to get to her.

She wanted to run and meet him in the middle, but she couldn't. He needed to come to her. *I* will *stay put. I will* not *cry. Come to me. Come to me.*

And he did. He made slow, steady progress until he stood in front of her.

Livia said nothing when Blake's masked face moved in for a kiss; she just turned her head. When he pulled back, she lifted a playful eyebrow.

He got it and did not try again. He took his piano out of his back pocket and set it reverently on the grass. He held out his leather-covered hands and ghosted her shape—almost touching, but not quite. He followed the lines of her face and arms. Livia bit the inside of her cheek as he outlined her breasts. He knelt in front of her and traced her legs in the air.

Livia held her breath. *Will he stay? Can he stay? Please stay.*

On his knees, Blake kept his eyes on hers as he slowly pulled off his glove, finger by finger, until the sun shone on his bare hand.

She saw the panic run through his eyes and lips. Livia broke her silence and grabbed his uncovered hand. "I don't believe your skin is glass, but I believe in you."

Blake took another breath and squeezed her hand. He smiled as he looked at their hands in sunlight together. He released her to take off his second glove and stood up. He grabbed both her hands, and they were joined.

The two **rr**'s dissolved from his tattoo in that moment.

Blake took off his jacket and blanketed her undergarments on the ground. He unbuttoned his shirt with the carelessness of a man standing in front of his dresser. His hands never hitched. Livia wanted to cheer as he revealed his chest to the sun. But Blake had other plans.

He put his chest against hers, and his sun-drenched hands ran from her shoulders to her lower back, pulling her to him with a hard jerk. He was a gentleman, but not necessarily a gentle lover. Their hearts beat as if they were trying to touch from the inside out.

Blake ghost-kissed Livia, not quite letting their lips touch. She felt his hot mint breath on her cheek. Blake reached for his pants, and Livia longed to release the button for him, but he needed to do this.

He removed his pants and boxer briefs in one swift motion. He kicked off his socks and shoes. All that remained was the mask. Blake and Livia stood apart for a moment before he gathered her again in his arms.

With no more material between their bodies, he touched every part of her. He spun her so her back pressed against his chest and he could warm her breasts with his hands.

"I always wanted to know if your lips were the same color as your nipples. But they're not. I think the sun has faded your lips just a bit." Blake's liquid silk voice tickled her neck.

Livia could feel the scratch of the ski mask. She remembered that the first time she'd heard his voice it was just like this, from behind her. She begged her hands not to remove his mask. They were having a hard time listening. She squirmed until she and Blake were chest to chest again. She kissed his shoulder instead of his mouth. Blake was glorious naked. *Powerful.*

"Livia, I can't get started if we can't finish. I can't trust myself to stop."

Livia smiled at his concern and grabbed her jacket, digging in the pocket. "Kyle had one, and I grabbed it." Livia held the condom up victoriously.

"Only one? I better make it count." Blake still had the mask on, so he left it to his fingers to adore her. "I'm going to paint my passion on your skin."

Livia used her mouth to warm any part of his body that felt cold. As she sucked his fingers, she heard a decision in his breathing. He would have her here, now. Blake gathered the clothes and helped Livia lay back on the makeshift bed. For a moment he took her in with a smile then he covered her body with his.

"Lying under me. You're lying under me," he breathed.

Livia felt him enter her and gasped uncontrollably in pure pleasure.

Alarmed, Blake stopped and looked inquisitively.

"Don't stop. Just don't." Livia clenched and unclenched her muscles, hugging him from the inside.

Blake's green eyes rolled into his head. There was no talking anymore. Just two together, struggling to give and take pleasure in the same movements.

Blake braced himself with one arm and traced her to where her pulse pounded the hardest against her skin. Livia offered a tangled mix of his name and assorted requests, each of which he indulged. When he lifted her leg to his shoulder, Livia wasn't sure she was that flexible. Then he moved inside her again, and Livia didn't care if she was that flexible. *Break my damn leg if you have to, just get deeper.*

Wave after wave of an orgasm broke over her, but soon it would be over for him. "Stop," Livia panted.

Blake paused as Livia swallowed to try to compose herself. She was here for a reason. "The mask. Take it off. I want you to kiss me." Livia watched his eyes. He was scared.

"Blake, you're inside of me. I'll keep you safe. You're *inside* of me." Livia squeezed him again, reminding him exactly where he was.

Blake smiled at the sensation. "Do it *for* me, Livia. Please."

And even though they were naked and locked in the most intimate embrace, this was the striptease.

Livia went slowly, rolling up the knit ski mask like a stocking. First his jaw came into the light. Livia slowed, tracing its strong line with her finger. Next, his lips lost their frame, then his eyes left their prison. He closed them. Finally, his wild, messy hair was free. Livia tossed the mask aside. And waited.

Open your eyes.

After a moment Blake looked around his sunny meadow. A breeze stirred the trees high up, and they released a shower of fall colors. In the silence of the day, the leaves hitting the ground sounded like applause. Quiet applause for a quiet victory.

The 0 in sorry vanished.

Blake looked at Livia beneath him. She smiled.

"Five hundred ninety-eight," he whispered.

Still counting. "Yes! Yes. I knew you could do this. I *knew* you could do this." Livia beamed with pride.

Blake blurred as her eyes became two pools of tears. He kissed her softly, but Livia wanted the rough thrusts back.

She pulled away and wiped her eyes. "Giddy up!" Livia spanked Blake playfully.

He gave a little chuckle before he put her out of her misery. If she thought he was going fast and hard before, she was wrong. Blake was almost done when he let Livia's leg slip from his shoulder. He kissed her with his clever tongue and moaned loudly into her mouth.

The S was now history. Blake collapsed next to Livia.

She grabbed his arm and traced the tattoo with her finger. "This Sorry is gone now. This is a new Sorry, and it's from me to you." Livia rolled onto her belly so she could see him lying in the sun. "*I'm* sorry I didn't say hello sooner. I'll never get those days I missed back. But I won't miss any more."

Livia kissed his sunny face. Blake held one fist in the air.

Even after they dressed, Livia and Blake stayed in the clearing. They left reluctantly when they grew too hungry. Livia wanted to stay forever. She knew this victory was one they'd have to fight for again in the real world.

21

Her Purpose

Eve put the finishing touches on her outfit. She wore big hair, her favorite spike-heeled boots, black leather pants, and a bra top. Her leather jacket topped off the look. *Battle armor.* She could *be* this girl if she dressed just like her. Eve tucked her knives and a gun into their hiding spots on her body.

A text arrived from Merkin:

Boss granted bail, wants u 2 pick him up

Eve typed back:

On it

She took her silver crotch-rocket to pick him up. When she arrived, Eve waited outside, leaning against her bike and holding her helmet.

Beckett pounded down the steps and smiled from ear to ear when he saw her. Eve tried to ignore the tremor she felt, the fracture in her shield.

"You're a sight for sore fucking eyes. Are you trying to kill me, hotness?" He walked with a fake pimp limp as he got closer.

"Yeah, I am." *If he only knew.*

Beckett stood within arm's reach. She could have her blade in his neck and be a mile away on her bike before he hit the ground. But her hands stayed still.

"You still an ass virgin?" she asked. "Did you have Mouse knit you a pair of iron panties to wear to jail?" Eve handed him her silver helmet.

"I'm still as pure as the driven fucking snow. Thanks for caring." Beckett looked around for another helmet.

"I didn't bring one. You wear it." Eve swung her leg over the seat and hit the kickstand with a clack of her metal heel.

Beckett stubbornly held onto the helmet, and they merged bareheaded into traffic, disregarding the law. Eve hated the way her body responded to his thick arm around her waist. She countered the feelings with a twist of the throttle, so the speed demanded all her concentration. The bike took the turns like a cheetah. Sooner than she wanted to, Eve pulled into the parking lot at Beckett's place of business. Beckett bumped fists with his hangers-on and the drug dealers in the parking lot.

Merkin appeared with an update on his brothers. "Cole's at the church and Blake's in the woods."

Beckett nodded as if these responses pleased him. Eve followed him into the building. No one would dare frisk her, and she entered Beckett's inner sanctum fully armed — not that she needed her weapons. They were just reminders about why she was here. Her purpose.

She closed the drapes and locked his office door. Beckett sat on his couch and kicked off his boots and socks with a shit-eating grin.

Bet he's thinking about our kiss. The weakness in that kiss was shameful. Eve let her horror at having wanted to comfort him last night fuel her. Her jacket slipped off her shoulders, and the seduction began.

A moment of uncertainty passed over Beckett's eyes.

"Stand up." Eve worked to keep her voice calm and in control. Beckett stood and waited with one eyebrow arched. Eve pulled out her favorite blade and smiled. She stepped close enough to feel the heat from his body. *There's just so much of him. Stop. Kill him. You're here to kill him.*

She tried not to let the sight of his banged-up hands generate any sympathy. Eve cut his shirt from his chest. With a quick slice up each arm she removed the sleeves, letting the blade scrape his skin gently. She put the knife in her teeth and used her hands to rip his shirt open. A bandage covered the wound she'd inflicted on him the night before. She used the knife on his jeans, the razor sharp edge sliding through the material quickly.

"I'm going commando today, Edward Scissorhands, so don't cut off anything precious. And leave a wide berth, if you know what I mean." He winked at her cold eyes.

Eve ignored his charm. It would do her no good to smile at him now.

"So that's how it is. Today's the big day." Beckett nodded with a wry smile.

He knows.

He was naked now. "How you want me, baby? Execution style? Or you want to look me in the eyes?"

Beckett put his arms behind his head like a prisoner of war. Eve threw her knife against the wall, where it stuck in the plaster. Here was where she was supposed to deliver her speech. The speech she'd recited so often in her head. She'd run through it over and over while running punishing miles. She'd delivered it after hours on the shooting range. She'd gasped it at the rear view mirror of her car after tae kwon do.

"Beckett Taylor, you killed my hopes and dreams. Now I'll kill you and everyone you care about. You'll leave this earth as empty as I am now."

Instead she stood looking at him. He looked around the room impatiently.

"Come on, sweetheart. I'm *letting* you do this. Do it." When she didn't respond, he added, "Listen, I know it's easier when they're not fucking looking at you."

Beckett turned and faced the wall. Eve tried to recreate the accident again, but she could only see him letting her have what she wanted. His own head on a platter.

"I don't know who hired you, but can I ask you for something?" He talked at the wall.

Here comes the fast-talking, the mojo, the shout to his employees.

"Could you make sure Cole doesn't take credit for his handiwork last night? And can you follow up on that Chris guy?" Beckett turned his head a bit, listening for her answer.

He still trusts me. He still trusts me with his brothers. I can't do it.

She then delivered a very different speech to his back. One she'd never practiced.

"I was pregnant, and then I wasn't," she said softly. "I was in love, and then I wasn't. *You* did that. *You* took those things from me. My family was collateral damage in a drive-by ordered by you."

She watched a tremor twitch through his muscles, but she didn't tense in defense like she'd planned, like she'd always prepared to. "I've hated you longer than I've done much of anything else. No one hired me. I'm here because it's the only way I'm still a mother to her. I can still be an angry mother even though she's not here. But I'm not even doing *that* right."

Eve hung her head in defeat. She felt the numbness crawl over her again. *Claim me. I have nothing left.*

Beckett dropped his arms and turned to face her. "Eve."

The odd sound of her name on his lips brought her eyes to his face. He was devastated.

"What's her name?" Beckett asked in an unsteady voice.

Eve bit her lip. She'd never told anyone.

"Anna." Eve's long-dry eyes filled with tears.

Beckett made no move to cover himself or call for help. "That's a beautiful name. Anna's very lucky to have such a dedicated mother. Once you're a mom, that title's yours for-fucking-ever—like a president."

He reached over and chose the quietest pistol from the wall. He held it out to her.

"No one will hear this one, so you should be able to get out of here. I'm so sorry. I caused you the most unimaginable pain. It would be my honor to die at your hand, if it gives you even a moment's peace."

Eve stared at the gun for a long while. "That's the worst part," she whispered, her voice soaked with defeat. "I'm not strong enough. I've killed so many. I can kill *anyone*. But I can't kill you."

Eve turned her back on the gun and the man. She heard the gun land with a soft thump on his couch.

He stepped close to her; she could feel his breath on her neck. "Eve, you make me not want to die."

She turned to see his face. "I didn't want to be this, and now it's all I am."

He put his hands on her cheeks. The look on his face did her in. He was kind, caring, and mourning her losses. Tears wet his cheeks. Eve felt a very deep sob choke her. If he was mourning, so could she.

He pulled her into his arms. "Cry. It's okay. Cry."

Eve felt her knees give. He caught her and carried her to his couch. He petted her hair and let her empty her pain and guilt onto his chest. He kissed the top of her head. For the first time, his actions toward her seemed to have no sexual intent whatsoever.

Eve let go of a rope she'd clung to for too long. And she fell. She fell right into him. Wrong or right, she gave up judging. Her lips found his, and he kissed her gently, not demanding any more than she was willing to offer.

Eve added her tongue, exploring his taste. She grabbed the back of his neck with one hand and traced his gunshot wounds with her other. He let her lead.

My call. Kill him or love him. He'll allow either.

Beckett smiled into her kiss when she started to shudder and fidget. She'd chosen passion.

"Are you sure?" He made her look at him.

She could only nod. Together they took off her leather armor. Then just before she could straddle him, Beckett stopped her.

"Shit! Hold on. Let me get rid of this. My luck I'll blow my balls off right fucking now." Beckett put the gun on the floor and kicked it away.

Eve put her knees on either side of his hips. She held herself just out of his reach and broke her last mental barriers. Then she slammed down on top of him with such force, she was sure Beckett was glad she had such impeccable aim.

Once she was committed and clearly enjoying the moment, Beckett allowed himself some breathing room. This woman seemed so hard but felt so soft. Eve was now lost to herself, letting her need rule her muscles. Beckett watched as her well-defined legs pumped at a maddening pace. She pulled him completely out of her, then slammed back down, taking him in roughly, over and over again.

Finally, she fell backward, and he reminded his hands to let go of the couch cushions and catch her by her hips. By the time he climaxed, Eve was arched and her hair touched the floor. Her face was as far away from his as it could get while still having him inside her.

They panted like this for a moment, until he realized she was too ashamed to sit back up and look at him. He'd just been at the center of her loss. He'd poisoned the only place she'd ever held her baby. Beckett looked at her long, white form. He ran his hand over a fine white scar he found just under her belly button—the scar somehow *he* had put on her body.

When she felt his hand she grabbed it. Beckett made a fist and watched her fingers on his forearm as they covered his **Sorry** tattoo. She maintained her grip and let him pull her up. But Eve looked to the right of his face, focusing on a mounted gun.

She let go of his arm and ran her hand through her long, tangled hair. Beckett could see the turmoil on her beautiful face. She didn't seem to know what to do with herself now. She bit her wrist and finally turned her blue eyes to him.

His eyes flared with shock when she backhanded him. Now she would empty out her anger.

"Fuck you. Fuck you, Beckett Taylor." She flexed her fist.

Beckett's jaw tightened. "Looks like you got that covered, gorgeous."

Eve full-on slapped his face in the opposite direction.

Beckett raised an eyebrow as he felt himself harden inside her.

"You like that?" she demanded.

Beckett just licked his lips. No woman had ever slapped him. But she did. Eve made her fingers into a claw and played a deep, painful game of connect-the-gunshot-scars on his skin.

He moved his hips against her. She growled, which just about undid him immediately. He grabbed her throat and cut off just enough oxygen to tinge her red lips blue while pushing harder against her. She could breathe, but just barely. He knew it would make the next moment insane for her.

Beckett stuck his thumb in her parted mouth. She bit him and sucked, as he'd expected. When he finally removed his thumb, it was moist and a little bloody. He smiled as he used it to touch her right above where his whole universe was embedded. She bucked at his touch, and Beckett assaulted her senses with pleasure. He knew just how to move himself and his thumb to make her die a little bit.

By the time he let go of her neck so she could take a gasp, she had the eyes of a predator. He stood and carried her to his perfect-height-for-doggy-style coffee table. He dumped her on the hard surface, arranging her on all fours. She seemed hesitant, but he knew she would submit. She needed him now. There would be no stopping.

Beckett let her know who he was. He let her know how many women he'd made scream his name as he slid into her from behind. He twirled her hair in his fist, yanking enough to make her curse. He added his favorite pimp ass-smack, alternating it with guiding her hips into him faster.

Beckett delighted in her screams and moans, and then Eve kicked up her game. She arranged her legs between his, crossing them at the ankles. She turned herself into a vice grip, and his dick was her happy prisoner.

By the time she was done squeezing him into a puddle of man, he was screaming so loud Merkin banged on the door.

"Merkin! Go...the...fuck...away!" Beckett yelled breathlessly as he staggered backward.

Eve collapsed on her back, looking up at him from the table.

Beckett wiped his mouth with his wrist. "If you're planning on fucking me to death, I'm so on board with that."

She gave him a sad smile. His heart actually stumbled when he remembered her pain. He immediately knelt by her head.

"Eve, how can I fix this? Tell me what to do. I'll do anything." He moved her hair out of her face.

Eve let his words lay in the room with them for a while before she uttered her blasphemous ones. "When I'm with you, it doesn't hurt as bad."

He picked her up again, surprised—now that he could think—at how much she weighed. *This girl's pure muscle.*

He sat on the couch with her on his lap. Starting over. "I'm so sorry, Eve."

Eve touched the new marks on his chest, lines that linked all his past violence with a path of red, new pain. "I know you are, Beck. I know you are."

22

ᴍᴇᴀᴛ Cᴜʀᴛᴀɪɴs

As they pulled in at her house, Livia gave the crumpled convertible a closer look in the late-morning sun. Kyle had really done a job on it. *Dad's going to lose his mind.*

Blake offered a gloved hand to take her keys, and she smiled at his ski mask-covered face. She tried not to see his desperate need to cover up in the sun as a setback.

"I'm safe in the meadow with you," he'd told her as they dressed. "But you, Livia, are extraordinary. You've seen me differently since that first day on the train platform. What if they still judge me?" He'd looked so longingly at the mask on the ground when they were ready to leave.

"Blake, you were amazing today," she'd told him. "If covering up makes you more comfortable, that's what you should do. You've climbed a mountain, so it's okay to rest." Livia had picked up the mask and handed it to him.

He hadn't removed it since. Livia handed him keys as they walked up the driveway, and he opened the front door for her.

Livia leaned up to kiss his considerate mouth as she passed. The brush of wool against her bottom lip sent a pulse of pleasure through her. They walked into the kitchen together to find Mouse still knitting away. Instead of being surprised by Blake's getup, he immediately began critiquing his own work.

"I think the eye holes on that one are bit too big." Mouse motioned for Blake to give it to him, which he did.

Mouse absorbed himself in comparing the hat in his hand with the pile of soft yarn he was knitting into submission. All three looked to the ceiling when they heard Kyle stumble-stomp to the bathroom. The door slammed. The old house had thin walls, and Kyle's voice carried clearly into the kitchen.

"Livia! My pussy smells like a monkey. Why do I wear leather pants to dance in?"

Livia felt her skin redden as she looked at Mouse. "She doesn't know you're here?"

He smiled widely. "Um, no. When she started waking up I came downstairs. I didn't want to scare her."

Kyle opened the bathroom door so Livia could hear her wherever she might be in the house. "Correction—my pussy smells like a monkey that got fucked by a dirty gorilla. Did I shower last night?"

The bathroom door slammed again.

Livia tried to choke an explanation out around her embarrassment. "She and I try to make each other laugh in the morning when our dad isn't here."

The distinct sound of the bathroom door opening again lifted Livia's eyebrows in alarm. She waved her hands uselessly in the direction of her sister's voice.

"I'm pissing straight alcohol," Kyle informed them from above. "Still peeing…still peeing….oh God, I'm bladdertastic!"

Livia grabbed her hair and shouted up to her sister. "Kyle, shut up! We have company. Shush!"

Blake and Mouse had cracked up as quietly as possible, but Mouse lost it first and started in with his full-volume hyena-like squeak. Blake actually had to sit down and put his head on his arms to laugh out loud. Livia gave them a grimace and took the stairs two at a time.

Kyle's wide eyes peeked out from behind the bathroom door. "Who's here?"

Livia shook her head. "Blake and Mouse, for God's sake."

"Now that right there is making my ass sweat." Kyle banged her head on the doorjamb.

"They can still hear you, Shakespeare." Livia smiled at her sister's horrified face.

"What the hell did we do last night? It tastes like I was sucking on a troll's dick." Kyle stuck her tongue out as if she might remove it.

Livia gave up trying to censor her sister. "Hairy Buffalo ring a bell?"

Kyle slapped her forehead with her palm. "Aw, man. That stuff eats me alive. I vaguely remember dancing with you."

Kyle fell silent, and Livia watched as her mind retraced its steps, then tripped and landed in the screaming, bloody end of the night.

"Oh, Liv, what happened? What happened? Cole and the men? Did that happen? What happened?"

Kyle looked even more pale than she had when she was vomiting. Livia opened the door the rest of the way and grabbed her hand. She dragged Kyle into her purple room and shut the door.

"All I know is you were in danger and Cole found you. You didn't want to leave him. What do you remember?" Livia wouldn't let go of Kyle's hand.

"There was dancing, and then the ladies' room line was too long. And then the men said they loved me. Oh, God. I told them I would do them both at once." Kyle squeezed Livia's hand tighter and looked down at the bed. "And then I didn't want to do it anymore. I told them no, but they didn't want to stop. I'd already said yes."

Livia's lips formed a straight, hard line. She had to be a sister now. She had to be a mother. Her rage would not help Kyle, so Livia swallowed it.

"Did they make you?" she whispered. *If they raped her and I was just outside. Oh please, no.*

"They didn't get that far before Cole showed up." Kyle took quick breaths.

"He helped you?"

"Of course he helped me. He stopped them. He stopped them so hard they couldn't even get up." Kyle covered her mouth. Her words became wobbly with emotion. "Those men—I think one of them was dead. His eyes just stayed open. That doesn't happen if you're alive, right? Cole tore them apart. He was so quick."

Kyle stood and rubbed her hands on her thighs. "I did that. What happened to them is on me. *I* made Cole do what he did."

Livia watched her sister tuck this new guilt into her essence. She stood and grabbed Kyle's endlessly rubbing hands. "Stop that right now. You said no. No one has a right to take what you don't want to give. Cole beat me to that bathroom by moments. I can promise you this, Kyle. Those men were dying last night, whether it was by my hand or his. And I should have been with you!"

"I hurt everyone but myself last night. I wanted to punish me. *Me.*" Kyle looked at the ceiling now.

"Well, then I'm going to have to kick your ass. No one gets to punish you. Enough of this shit, Kyle. You're more than this. You know better than this. Yes, Mom left. But Dad stayed. I stayed. You're more than enough for us. *This* is our family. You don't get to throw away your life. I'm sorry, but you don't. This is self-serving bullshit."

The girls looked at each other in startled silence. Livia was as surprised by her words as Kyle.

Slowly Kyle nodded. "You're so fucking right. God, I'm a sucking asshole."

"You're a huge sucking asshole," Livia agreed. "You have everything at your fingertips. You're healthy, smart, fun, and highly fashionable. But instead you're buying problems you don't even want. Let the death of at least one and maybe two scumbags have a little meaning. Be the real you. Follow your beautiful heart."

"You're not the first person to tell me that," Kyle said.

"Cole?"

Kyle smiled for a moment, then blanched. "Holy crap! Did he get arrested?" She searched Livia's face for an answer, but Livia didn't know.

Kyle rushed past her and down the stairs. Livia came scrambling behind.

Apparently, the walls were very, very thin because Mouse was ready with an answer.

"Good morning," he said as she came flying into the kitchen. "Cole was *not* arrested. Beckett was, but he was just released on bail an hour ago." Mouse stretched his fingers. "A douchebag checked in this morning and said he found Cole's car in the lot at his church."

"I gotta go." Kyle headed for the back door in her pajamas.

"Hey, monkey pussy, you might want to give those meat curtains a spit shine before you leave the house." Mouse pointed to Kyle's crotch with a knitting needle. Mouse looked around in the stunned silence. "What? I knit, but I'm still hardcore. Seriously."

Kyle swore-muttered something about "talking about my dick mitten in the middle of my own damn kitchen," and she stomped up the stairs again.

The squeaking scream of the hot water coming on in the shower filled the house for a moment, and Livia sat down at the table with the guys.

"What a stupid, crazy night," Livia said. "Good that Beckett's not still in jail. I have no clue what we're going to do about the convertible, but I'm pretty sure Kyle's either going to steal my car or make me drive her to church in a few minutes."

Blake held his hand out, palm up, and Livia slid hers into it. Her heart snuggled into its happiness. The sight of his fingers made her forget what she was about to say.

Mouse handed Blake back his mask. "You can have this. I need to rework the holes anyway." He bound off his knitting with a mysterious twirl of his wrist. "Well, I know a guy who works at a body shop. He could put the car back together. He owes Beckett a favor."

Livia saw an almost imperceptible shake of Blake's head. She didn't need to read his mind to understand.

"We would want to pay our own way," Livia said. She spoke to Mouse but kept Blake in her peripheral vision. He gave her a tiny nod.

Mouse pulled out his phone and pushed a button. "Bill, I got a convertible that needs attention...The two ladies are going to pay their own way." Mouse listened for a moment before he countered. "Beckett's fond of these two."

Mouse closed his phone. "He's ready for us now. Blake, can you drive my car? One of the douches brought it over last night."

Blake smiled easily at Mouse. "Sure, I'd be glad to."

Livia was grateful the cars wouldn't be here when her dad got home. Not only did she not want to explain, but the continued lack of police involvement had Livia wondering why Chris had kept his mouth shut about the accident.

Blake stood and joined Mouse by the front door. "Please drive safely," he told her.

Livia pulled her cell phone out and handed it to Blake. "I want to be able to reach you."

Mouse opened the door as Blake pulled Livia close. "I'll miss the hell out of you," he whispered.

Livia leaned into his ticklish breath. "I'll never look at fall leaves the same way."

Blake kissed her forehead and caught the keys Mouse tossed him.

"Just to the church and back, okay?" Mouse said, looking at her pointedly. "I have to check with the boss before you're free to roam."

Livia had just shut the door behind them when Kyle came leaping down the stairs with the grace of an elk running for its life. She wore a white sundress and flip-flops. Her hair was wet from the shower, and she hadn't put on makeup.

"Kyle, you *do* know you'll freeze your tits off in that outfit?" Livia shook her head.

"Sure, *now* you have a dirty mouth. I take it the boys are gone?" Kyle gave her the finger.

"They took the car to the body shop. We can say you decided to leave the car at a friend's because you'd been drinking when Dad asks."

Livia went to the front closet to find a coat for her sister. After some shuffling, Livia found the white trench coat Kyle had nicknamed "The Romantical."

Kyle took it without thanks. "I have to get to that church. He needs me today. I just know it."

Livia looked around the living room, then grabbed her keys from the key hook by the door. Blake had put them just where they were supposed to be. As they headed out the door, Livia wanted to call him just to hear his sweet hello.

I wonder how he answers the phone? I wonder how he likes his eggs in the morning? I wonder if he likes black or white lingerie better? Livia started the Escort and pointed the car in the right direction.

Kyle sat silently in the passenger seat, her hands folded and pulsating like a heart.

As she drove, Livia stole glances at Kyle's cell phone, which she'd carelessly thrown in the cup holder in the console. Livia took a breath to settle her itchy hands. She'd call Blake as soon as Kyle was safely delivered to Our Lady of the River.

In the meantime, Kyle wouldn't talk and kept a white-knuckle grasp on the door handle.

As the church appeared up ahead, Livia made an announcement. "Kyle, I'm going to stay in the parking lot in case you need me."

Kyle gave her a stern look. "Would you want me to wait for you if you were seeing Blake?"

Livia said nothing. She had a point.

"Cole needs me," Kyle said. "I don't know how long that'll take. He must be so confused and blaming himself. I might never leave his side again. You don't need to protect me." Kyle's lips became a straight line as Livia pulled into the parking lot.

She was out of the car before Livia came to a complete stop.

23

MURPHY OIL

Dressed in his cleaning jeans and a white T-shirt, Cole grabbed the Murphy Oil Soap, a sponge, and a bucket. Every time he looked down he thought he saw a spot of blood. He was way too early, but he needed to clean.

Cole filled the bucket with water and dumped in a glugging splash of the fragrant golden liquid. He took a deep breath and let the scent fill him like the Holy Spirit. It spoke more of the church to him than the incense at high mass.

It was the smell of his Saturday cleaning sessions with a selection of the dedicated parishioners from next door. The ladies on the "Pew Crew" spent at least two hours once a week to shine their cherished house of worship.

These Saturdays had shown Cole how competitive the older women were. Each lady took her swatch of the holy structure seriously and scrubbed and scrubbed until the honey tones in the wood glowed. In between the sounds of sloshing water and rubbing, he got a healing dose of their chatter. They had a wicked sense of humor, which had surprised him at first, then challenged him to join in their witty repartee. Bea was the ringleader, often regaling the group with tales from World War II or the Depression.

Cole took his full bucket to the pew where he'd once held Kyle. Seemed an ideal place to start. He began scrubbing, determined to clean until the screams in his head quieted. Last night in that bizarre club, in that dirty bathroom, he'd unleashed a part of himself he'd worked so hard to tame.

The feel of human skin parting like rotten fruit under his fists had brought it all back. For the first time in a long time, Cole remembered the crisis room at Evergreen Residential Home for Children. The Murphy Oil smell was overwhelmed by the memory of the odor of his own sweat and the gym mat he'd spent hours sitting on there.

When he was twelve years old, Cole had been at the residential home for two years. He'd spent much of that time glaring at his favorite adult in the whole word.

"Fuck you. Fuck you and your husband and your kids," he'd told her. "I hope your two dogs get run over by a car." He filled the rant with as much venom as possible.

Mrs. D had been unmoved. Very little Cole could think up was original to her. He knew that because she'd told him. His predecessors in this room— this small, windowless room—had already thrown feces. Had already threatened her family. Had already spit in her face. Still, she sat in the doorway with her coffee in a silver travel mug.

She had calmly taken a sip. "It's nice you're thinking of my family this morning."

Cole responded to her calm by growling and slapping the mat. Mrs. D just waited. Her eyes were an enigma. They'd spent hours like this, and Cole always tried to figure them out. *Are they green? Are they hazel?* The only thing he knew for certain was that he was safe when they were on him. She was what he imagined a grandmother could be like.

When he was quiet again, she spoke. "Are you ready to go back to class, or do I have to bounce you off that mat a few more times?"

Cole had known her threat meant a restraint. She was all of five feet tall, but when he lashed out, she could put him down before he knew what was happening. And he lashed out a lot. He did it more when she was around. This year she'd requested that he be in her classroom, which had puzzled him. No one *requested* Cole Bridge.

His connection with her was undeniable, but he couldn't understand it. She brought out the worst in him. He *wanted* to be restrained by her. Mrs. D would hold him tightly until he gave up. It could take hours. She always knew, though, when it was time, when he was ready. She'd ask him if she could let go of one of his hands, then wait until he nodded his assent. The process gave him back control over each of his limbs one at a time.

Afterward, Mrs. D would stay close, easily within his striking distance. She would listen. He would talk—about what had set him off in the first place or his fears for the future. He was a young boy with the concerns of a much older person.

"Shut the fuck up. What the hell are you anyway? A pissant teacher's aide? Get a real job." Cole rubbed his hands together.

"You've acquired a new curse word for your vocabulary. Should I add that to this week's spelling list?" Mrs. D smiled and took another sip.

It had infuriated him. *Enough! Enough with the smiling.* Cole stood. At twelve he was a good head taller than she, but he was so small inside.

She set her cup down and stood with him. Ready.

"You better leave, Mrs. D. I'm going to start hitting. I'm going. I'm going this time. I'm going out to the road and let the cars run me over." Cole spat to emphasize his words.

He was serious. He didn't want her to hold him close. He didn't want to pretend she was his mother. He didn't want to imagine going home in her car to pet her black labs. He didn't want to dream about sitting down to a home-cooked spaghetti dinner at her kitchen table with her family. Those things would never be his. He watched her eyes switch from hazel to green.

"Cole, I'm not going to let you do that." She had reached for her walkie-talkie. She wanted back-up. Somehow she knew he wasn't bluffing.

"Mrs. D, stop. I mean it. Stop." Cole felt his heart throw away its dreams. He walked toward her with a new, brazen self-indulgence.

"I need a crisis worker to—"

Mrs. D never got to finish her sentence because Cole punched her in the stomach. He had almost apologized as she crumpled from the blow. He knew she saw it coming. He saw the pain in her eyes, but it wasn't from his fist. She was disappointed.

Disappointed in me.

Cole started running. He hit the side door and let it bang loudly against the building. He ran full tilt toward the busy road. *This is it. I'm going down. Finally.*

The Evergreen employee who tackled Cole from behind wasn't intending to be a comforting presence. "You little piece of crap. How dare you hit Mrs. D? You have some nerve. She's the only one in this whole building who gives a rat's ass about you." He escorted Cole back to the crisis room.

Cole had curled into a ball on the mat. *Mrs. D will never spend time with me again.* He felt his brain crumble with sorrow. He'd been there a while before he heard her.

"Are you okay, Cole?" She'd walked in slowly.

Cole's head snapped up so quickly, he didn't have time to hide the love in his eyes. He looked at the floor immediately. He shook as she sat down next to him, easing against the wall.

Mrs. D had let the silence surround them. But time broke him. Cole could take it no longer.

"I hit you. Won't that make you go away? What else can I do?" he snarled. He'd fallen back on his old standby, anger.

"I'm not going away, Cole, so maybe we can cut out the assaults in the future. You don't want me to go away. I know that. You *love* me, Cole. That's the feeling that makes you so angry." She'd sighed and looked at the ceiling. "You don't know what to do with it, because the people you've loved in the past caused you pain. That's what you think love is. Pain."

She'd looked at his face until he met her eyes. They were still green.

"But, Cole, I love you. Have I hurt you? Ever?"

Cole had to shake his head. She hadn't. Not once.

"I'm showing you what to do with love, Cole." She stood and held out her arms.

A hug. A simple hug he didn't have to earn by throwing a chair. Human contact that wasn't required because he was trying to hurt someone. She still trusted him. She still saw something in him.

He'd stood like a baby deer. He lurched toward her with no grace at all. She enclosed him in a hug that was so much better than a restraint. She'd patted his head just like a mother. Like a mother who cared.

Cole's body had heaved with tears. She kept hugging him. She handed his heart back the dreams it had thrown away.

"That's it, sweetheart. Let it out." She rubbed his back.

Her shirt was soaked by the time he stopped crying. They sat down together again.

"I've read your file," Mrs. D said. "What your parents did to you was terrible. It was a horrible, horrible mistake. You should've been cherished. You should've been treated like the beautiful little boy you are. They were *wrong*, Cole." She held his hand. "I'm sorry for what they did to you."

Cole's mind had flashed with images from his time before Evergreen. *The cage. The belt. The drugs.* They still made him feel scared.

"You're going to make it. You'll be a great, thoughtful, proud man. I can see it. I know it as sure as I know my name." She wouldn't let go of his hand.

"I'm always awful. How can you know that?" Cole's voice remained thick with tears.

"I've been doing this job for twenty-five years. I know a good one when I see him." Mrs. D had stood and pulled on his hand. She walked him back to the living unit where he had his own room in a long hallway full of other boys' rooms.

Cole had never hit her again, though he did test her from time to time. He just wanted to be near her. By the time he was discharged from Evergreen, Cole had made huge strides. He'd been one of a very few to enter the foster care system instead of another residential program. Mrs. D got all dressed up for his Awards Day. She'd made sure to take a lot of pictures with Cole, and she gave him a gift: a picture of her two black Labradors in a frame.

Scrubbing the pew with renewed vigor, Cole wondered how disappointed Mrs. D would be if she knew he'd killed a man last night. He spilled the bucket in his haste to plunge the sponge back in and soaked his shirt. Cole pulled the T-shirt off and cast it aside. He'd have to turn himself in. How could he be a man if he didn't own up to his sins?

The Pew Crew would be here any minute, and he couldn't be half-naked in the church. He went to the supply closet and threw on the flowing black cassock Father Callahan never used anymore. He buttoned it up and worked to contain the soapy water from the overturned bucket. The church door creaked, and Cole stood to greet the ladies.

The air left the church in a *whoosh* as Kyle entered.

Kyle.

She waited in the doorway, her white sundress and trench coat fluttering like flags in the breeze. She ran a hand through her hair, all soft and wild. She looked like a heavenly messenger.

Cole headed down the side aisle, silhouetted against the stained glass windows. Kyle mirrored his movement, walking up the opposite side. They orbited one another, step for step, as they cast shadows that interrupted the splashes of color the sun painted through each window. They made a complete circuit, three-hundred-sixty degrees of anticipation.

When Kyle stood in the doorway again she shed her white trench coat in a puddle at her feet. The sunlight streamed in behind her, and the sundress became just a hint over her body.

Cole unbuttoned the cassock and let it fall as well.

Kyle took the first step, approaching him up the center aisle.

Cole took a breath and a step toward her, away from the altar behind him. They moved one step at a time, slowly—like soldiers from opposite armies.

But then Cole ran for her, sliding on his knees to close the final distance between his hands and her skin. Kyle wrapped his head in her arms, cradling him.

"My sweet Cole. That's better. That's better." Kyle braced her hands on his shoulders and slowly lowered herself to her knees. She put her hands on his cheeks and waited until he looked at her. "You forgot something last night."

Cole looked puzzled.

"You made me promise you something. Now you owe me a promise."

Cole nodded somberly.

"Be the real Cole. Promise me *you* will be you." Kyle's voice was strong and sure.

Cole felt his heart soar with her embrace, settling the feelings inside him. "Kyle, I've done so much wrong. I think I'm done being the real Cole. How much hurt can I cause?" He could hardly speak through his fear.

She smiled again. "I've done my own share of wrong, but look. Look around. We're in the perfect place."

The church looked like paradise. A frame of broken rainbows arched above the lovers on their knees.

Cole held her face to his, whispering, "Help me."

Kyle gave him the absolution he needed with her lips.

24

Fumigation

Once she'd parked in the church lot, Livia grabbed Kyle's phone and scrolled through the contacts, looking for her number so she could call Blake. She wasn't listed in the Ls—or under S for sister. Livia gave up and punched in her own number. Kyle's phone proudly reported that she'd dialed "Whore-a-saurus" as the line began to ring.

Livia rolled her eyes. She had her sister labeled neatly as "Kyle" in her phone and even had her in a red font to designate an emergency contact. Livia watched the church doors with the phone to her ear. She held her breath as it stopped ringing and connected.

"Hello, beautiful Livia," Blake answered.

"How did you know it was me?" Livia saw her wide smile in the rear view mirror.

"The phone looked sexier when it rang."

She could hear a matching smile in his voice and sighed. Livia hugged herself with her free arm. Just the sound of him made her skin beg to be touched.

"Is there a cloud going in front of the sun where you are, Livia?"

She leaned forward and peeked out the windshield. A fluffy white cloud defied the sun and tiptoed into its perfect circle.

"I see it, Blake." Livia put her hand against the glass.

"Does it have a shape for you?" he asked.

Livia ran her hand up to her neck, feeling his buttery voice everywhere. "Um…It looks like a—oh! It looks like a bunny. Aww, that's so stinking cute."

The sun melted the cloud a bit, like cotton candy in the heat. Eventually, the cloud finished its dance with the sun and escaped as a circular blob.

Livia bit her lip. "Well, that went from a romantic moment to horrifying bunny torture."

Blake laughed, and she wanted to put her head on his chest and feel it rumble through him like a happy earthquake.

"Where are you now?"

"Well, we're at the car place, but I'm in Mouse's car. I guess it's considered a car — it's actually a hearse with flames painted on it. I have a feeling it might even be bulletproof."

"Wow. You'd think I would've seen that bad boy rolling around town."

"I get the impression it's a new purchase," Blake said. "It's pretty crazy. He's got all this yarn lined up, like this is his storage closet. He has about three works in progress. The colors are amazing. This yarn in the passenger seat has perfect browns. It reminds me of your hair."

Livia touched her tresses, wishing they were tangled in his hands. "So is the mask up or down?" Livia wanted to know how to picture him in her head.

"Well, fortunately for me, Mouse's windows are tinted far beyond the legal limit. It's like sitting inside a giant pair of sunglasses. I'm wearing the mask as a hat instead."

"You're being courageous," she said. "I think you're noble." She felt her heart fill with the picture of his victory in the sun.

"I feel *very* noble talking on a pink phone." He gave a self-deprecating chuckle.

Sensing movement, Livia glanced in the rear view mirror. A slow-moving posse of women headed to the church. Livia gritted her teeth and saw that the church doors still stood open.

"Oh, no! The ladies from next door are headed to the church where Cole and Kyle are. What should I do?"

"Assuming they're being…amorous right now, I would highly suggest a diversion." Blake sounded amused.

"Hang on." Livia set the phone down carefully on the passenger seat. She hopped out and approached the ladies. She noticed Bea in her wheelchair.

"Bea! Ladies, it's so wonderful to run into you today." Livia smiled anxiously from one woman to the next, using friendliness to block their way.

A ripple of greetings ran through the crowd, but Bea was the spokeswoman.

"Livia, what a wonderful surprise. Look at her — isn't she just gorgeous? I swear her figure is fantastic."

Livia felt her color change to pink. "Thank you. Cole actually asked me to make sure no one went in the church for a little while." Livia clasped her hands behind her back to stop their wringing.

"Oh, well, we come every Saturday. We're the Pew Crew," Bea explained. "We have to keep the church fresh and clean." Bea and her friends nodded in tandem.

Oh crap. "He told me about that. But, ah, he's fumigating. For bugs. He needs to fumigate."

Do they even fumigate churches? Is there some sort of special mass that's said before they do something like that?

"Is it those pesky ants again? I do declare, if you leave one crumb of food on the floor the ants flock to it," said Bea. "We can't have the ants again."

Relief washed over Livia. "That's it. Ants. You got it. Hit the nail on the head. Can I help you ladies get back home?" Livia stepped behind Bea to turn her in the opposite direction.

The other ladies began animated swapping of bug-infestation stories. Bea kept insisting her wheelchair's brake was on. Then after Livia determined it was not, Bea complained she was going too fast.

Livia slowed to a snail's pace, and the Pew Crew was far ahead when Bea began her sly comments. "Fumigating can really hold things up. I can clearly remember fumigating with Aaron." Bea turned her head and smiled. "Some days I still miss fumigating. I did get three beautiful children from the process. Fumigation can be wonderful." She settled back into her wheelchair.

Livia jumped around to kneel in front of her. "Oh, please don't say anything to anyone. It's my sister in there with him. I bet he feels so guilty about it."

Bea gave a delighted cackle. "I'm sure guilty isn't *exactly* the right description of Mr. Cole right now." Her eyes softened. "Sweet Livia, young people can only learn with time, but maybe you can get a leg up. There's no shame in true love. And if Mr. Cole thinks he has some big secret, he's wrong. At my age, you can spot a man in love from a mile away. My friends and I probably knew before he did."

Bea's eyes got a little misty, and Livia reached for her hand. "Speaking of love, how's your beau?" Bea asked, brightening.

Livia's heart filled with joy. "He's great. He's doing great."

"That's wonderful news. You're a nice girl. Hold your head high. Now, Livia, I'm getting a bit of a chill." Bea rubbed her arms.

Livia popped up and wheeled her to the door of the retirement center.

As Livia parked her in the lobby, Bea offered a suggestion with her gentle hug. "You might want to go back and close those church doors. Fumigating is best done in private."

Livia nodded as she waved to the rest of the ladies and sprinted back to the church doors. At first, there was no hint of her sister. After her eyes adjusted to the dim lighting, Livia noticed Kyle's romantical white trench coat discarded like a crumpled dove. She said a silent prayer for Cole and Kyle as she secured the big doors, dividing the church from the world.

By the time she got back to her open phone, she knew Blake had probably hung up. Distracting the ladies had taken so long. But when she picked it up the screen showed she was still connected to Whore-a-saurus.

"Blake?" Livia closed one eye while she waited.

"Livia." He was still there.

"You waited," Livia whispered.

"Of course. I'll always wait."

Livia smiled wider than she thought possible.

"Maybe I could come to you?" Blake suggested. "Mouse looks like he's finishing up with the body shop gentleman."

Livia heard what sounded like a gunshot in the background.

"Oh, Blake!"

"I'm fine. That was a car backfiring. I'm fine. Here's Mouse now." Blake spoke to the man getting into the passenger seat. "Did that go well?"

Mouse's squeaky voice sounded even more comical over the phone. "Yeah, Pete's pushing the car up to the front of the line. I told them to work through the night. He'll give me a call when it's ready. Might be a few days."

"Well, Kyle will probably stomp around about that," Livia told Blake. "Please tell Mouse thank you from the McHughs."

After some manly discussion about the car, the damage, and ridiculous Ford F-250s, Blake politely requested a trip to Livia's car at the church. Mouse insisted Blake continue to drive the flaming hearse. Livia was almost positive Mouse was just trying to prevent Blake from having to step into the sun when they changed drivers.

Blake set the phone down, but left the line open for his entire ride. Livia listened to the car noises and eventually heard the clicking of Mouse's knitting needles.

When the hearse pulled into the church parking lot, Livia felt an inappropriate giggle bubble up as she looked from the flame-adorned car to the church to the retirement community.

Livia finally closed Kyle's phone when she saw Blake step out of the car. With the pink phone to his now wool-covered ear, he looked a little absurd. Mouse nodded in Livia's direction and folded himself into the driver's seat. He left the parking lot as quickly as possible.

Thank you, Mouse.

Blake climbed in her passenger seat and pushed his mask up to reveal his face—even with the sun out! Livia kissed him and kissed him and kissed him. When she started her car, she was sure her cheeks would crack from smiling so much.

"Do you think Cole will give Kyle a ride?" Livia asked as she pulled back onto the road. She contemplated making Blake drive. She couldn't keep her eyes on the asphalt.

"Absolutely." Blake reached for her hand and softly kissed it.

"I think I need to get home and talk to my dad. He'll be worried if he doesn't see us. Would you like to meet him?"

"I'd be honored," Blake said with a nod.

25

My Penis Rules the World

Chris parked The Beast in the Poughkeepsie Police Department parking lot. He'd spent a good chunk of the morning deciding what, exactly, to do about Livia and his current situation.

He brooded out the blurry plastic wrap that now served as his driver's side window. Thinking of the punk who broke it failed to give Chris the surge of adrenaline and testosterone he wanted. That fucker was scary. Beckett Taylor was his name; he'd learned that from the blonde.

Thinking about her made his jeans tighter. Again. She was one sexy floorboard wench. She was the kind of beautiful that people couldn't even touch. When he got Livia bent over in the bed of his truck again, he'd picture that blonde's face on her head.

When King Steroidiculous had taken his phone, Chris was sure he was about to have his ass whipped. Whatever had sent Beckett back into The Launch Pad had probably saved him a world of pain. Then the über-gorgeous chick headed right in his direction. She was even better up close. He relived the moment again.

Chris had realized he was breathing through his mouth when she gave him a snobby look. His tongue had swelled at the same rate as his dick.

Her voice was full of promising pussy. "Are you done staring yet?"

Chris shook his head no, but managed to pull his lips closed.

She looked around at the skeevy batch of thugs texting and pointing at each other. The blonde didn't fidget or bat her eyelashes like Hannah.

She settled her blue eyes on Chris. "Yet?"

He had to hear what she wanted to say. Maybe even get her digits. *Get control.*

"You're here for all the wrong reasons, Chris."

She knows my name. Fuck yeah. My penis rules the world. "My girlfriend is in there with a homeless dude. I need to protect her." Chris's voice was a lot higher-pitched than he wanted it to be at that fucking moment. He cleared his throat around his stupid tongue. Chris liked to tell ladies about his girlfriend. He always got a better response when they found out he was "taken."

He'd willed his voice go deeper. "My fiancée, I mean. We're engaged."

The blonde had looked puzzled.

Shit. I went too deep. Drag queen deep. Shit.

"Is something wrong with you?" She lifted her intense gaze to check her phone. She looked up, found a face in the crowd, and gave him some authoritative hand gestures.

Chris had been sure her hand would give a wicked beat-off to his power stick. He rolled his hips and tried to lick his bottom lip. He drooled by accident. He was busy wiping it off his chin with his wrist when she turned to face him again.

"Are you leaking? My God." She'd rolled her eyes like Chris was not worth her time. Like Chris was just dog shit on the bottom of her shoe.

"Ya know what, slut? How 'bout you get out of my way? I need to save my woman."

Chris had turned his truck off. He would leave it right fucking here. He had a line of people behind him waiting to see Epic Chris. A girl wasn't about to stop him.

She'd snatched the keys out of his hand and grabbed his face.

She'd brought his lips so close to hers, he'd thought for sure she was about to get a little Chris in her mouth.

"Beckett Taylor wants you gone. Leave. Leave now. Do you think I'm pretty? Do you?" She still held his face, but her fingers were becoming uncomfortably tight.

He'd nodded. "Mmhuh."

"I can rip your heart out of your chest and take a bite while it's still beating. I can kill your body before your brain dies. Am I pretty now, motherfucker?"

Chris could do nothing. Her words were terrifying. Her words should be in every horror movie ever written, but they were nothing, *nothing* compared to her cold alligator eyes. He instantly knew she could do everything she said.

She'd let go of his face and started his ignition. She threw the truck in reverse and spit words at him. "Go. And hope I have a lot more people to murder before I have time on my hands again."

She'd hopped backward off his truck and sprinted to the side door of the club. She was so fucking fast. The dirty drug dealer crew began the alarming process of tossing flash-bang grenades in the parking lot like snowballs.

The night had exploded around them. Chris watched his friends' cars take off. Several backed into each other in the mêlée. The dirty drug dealers moved the cars that had blocked Chris's crew in. *They want us to get away?*

Not one to miss an opportunity, Chris had kept The Beast in reverse and backed up. He'd had to do an embarrassingly slow five-point turn to get the massive vehicle free of the confining cars.

Chris paused at the exit. *Damn it. Livia! Livia's in there.*

Someone had sent him a picture. She was in there with him. They were all kinds of dressed up. He couldn't just leave…

Just then someone had noticed Chris's delay and tossed a flash-bang in the back of his truck. Luckily, he'd kept the bed door open and the grenade rolled out when he hit the gas hard, leaving the club and Livia behind.

The wind rattled his crappy plastic-wrap window, and his phone beeped at him, snapping him into the present. It was Dave.

"Speak."

"Hey, asshole. How're you doing after your fail last night? What the hell happened with that fuck-hot blonde?" Dave's voice was bubbly.

Chris glanced at the bath towel that covered his seat. It was soaking up the piss he'd only recently realized he'd released when that bitch had threatened him.

"She wanted to jump my bones, of course. That shit happens all the time." Now Chris could put on his tough guy voice.

"You're the king, man. The king. What're you up to? Want to know where Livia is?"

Chris felt his heart beat faster. "Yeah, you fucking prick. You still following her?"

Chris was really starting to wonder about Dave. He was too good at the whole stalking thing. And a little too interested.

"Let's just say not all my homemade porn is fake." Dave's laugh was hollow.

"You've followed Livia before?" No more tough guy. Chris was actually concerned.

"Oh, yeah. Man, she's just delicious, and so is her sister. I have a video of Kyle giving a football player a blowjob. I watch that every time I do exceptionally well on my video game. It's my reward."

Chris closed his eyes a moment to clear the cobwebs of weirdness Dave had just spun in his mind. "Where's Livia, freakyballs?"

"She's sitting in the parking lot at Our Lady of the River. I took a pic just a little bit ago. Wanna see?" Dave sounded more eager than Chris cared to hear.

"No. Back off, limp dick. Just watch for once." Chris pressed END as Dave started blathering about his fantasy world. *Holy fucksticks. I'm so going to cut ties with that nerd emergency as soon as Livia's back with me.*

Chris knew his time to hit was now. He felt like a tattletale, but with a little luck, Livia's new love life could be twisted to his benefit. He wanted to protect her; it was kind of hard to give up worring about Livia after all the time he'd spent in her life. Chris had been in the station before, and he knew John's schedule was like clockwork. Every third week he had an overnight, and Livia used to drag Chris along to bring him breakfast. John should be just finishing up his paperwork.

He breezed into the building and nodded at the receptionist. "Hey, Kathy. How are you this morning?"

"Chris. I'm doing good."

He could tell she was a little surprised to see him. Word must have gotten around about his breakup with Livia. He took another look at Kathy. She had that sexy teacher thing working for her. Sure, she was a little older, but she probably still had some snap in her snatch. He gave her a bigger smile. She looked him up and down in a way he really liked, so he puffed out his chest.

"I heard John's daughter broke up with you." She took out a sharp-looking file and started working on her middle finger's nail.

"We're still working on that." Chris tried his best injured-boy face. He was suddenly very interested in what color panties Kathy had on, if any at all.

"I bet you are. Livia's a real sweet girl." She looked at him pointedly and started filing the nail on her other middle finger, skipping the other fingers entirely.

She actually might not be liking me that much. "Officer McHugh in?"

Kathy nodded and pointed with her file. She kept her finger up though, either waiting for more filing or telling him to go to hell.

When Chris arrived at John's desk, he changed his demeanor again. For this to work he had to be the thoughtful ex-boyfriend. He arranged his face accordingly.

"Officer McHugh, may I have a word with you?" Chris remained standing.

John let out a tired-sounding sigh. Chris peeked at the paperwork in front of Livia's dad. Beckett Taylor's name was upside down and written in bold all over it. *Very, very good.*

"Sure. That would make this wonderful morning even more wonderful." Sarcasm filled every word to the breaking point.

"In private?" Chris looked in the direction of the conference room.

John shuffled his paperwork into a thick folder and motioned toward the room.

Chris let John have the chair at the head of the table. *You're the boss man.* He reminded himself not to smirk. He was about to play John like a fiddle. The long, black table reflected their faces and oily fingerprints from previous hands. Chris kept his hands in his lap

"How's your Grandma holding up?" John asked when Chris said nothing.

"She's super. She's a fighter, you know." Bringing Mrs. Grandma into the conversation was perfect. *Thanks, John.*

"What's up, Chris?" John looked at him expectantly.

With the door closed, Chris unloaded his pretend burdens. "Listen, Mr. McHugh. I know Livia and I aren't together any more. I'm having a hard time with it. I miss her. A lot." He paused.

John nodded and worked one hand over his tired face, smooshing it like Play-Doh.

"Well, I'm not proud to say it, but I've been trying to keep track of her," Chris confessed. "She seems to be hanging with a tough crowd. It's just not her style. I have to let her go, I know. And I'm going to — starting right now — but I had to tell someone. I had to tell you. If she were my daughter, I'd want to know she was hanging out with Beckett Taylor's kind." Chris stood up to leave. "Thanks for your time, Mr. McHugh. I'll leave you and your family alone. I wish you guys only good things and happy holidays."

Chris reached for the door handle.

Three... Two...

"Hold on a minute there, son. Have a seat."

...One. Bingo. John's such a fucking sucker. "Listen, I shouldn't even be here. Livia's choices are *her* choices. No matter how much I love her." Chris was surprised to hear his voice crack on the word *love*, but he worked it into his act. "I just don't want to see her hurt."

"Tell me everything you know. Now." John looked like he knew he shouldn't be pressing Chris, but he couldn't help himself.

"Okay. But I don't want her to know I came to you. If I have another shot...if she comes back to me..." Chris tried to will his eyes to tear up. They wouldn't.

"It's between us, son. Start from the beginning."

Chris tucked his smile out of sight and into his sad façade. He treated John to the alarming, agonizing tale of his fiancée dumping him for a homeless man and Livia's newfound friends. Thanks to Dave's big, banging geekiness, he could give John names, dates, and places. He put the cherry on top by describing last night's vandalism on his truck—first from Kyle and then finished by Livia's new best friend, Beckett.

John walked Chris out to the parking lot and took a look at the damage. "Well, Chris, I can't thank you enough for coming to me. Sounds like my girls need my attention. I'll pay for any damage to your truck. Please send me the bill." John reached out to shake Chris's hand.

"Blake Hartt, the homeless guy? I'd do a search on his background. I'm so relieved to know you'll take care of Livia and Kyle. I'll still keep my eye out for them. It's a hard habit to break. You all are family to me."

Chris climbed in his truck and pulled out of the lot. He waited to smile until he was back on the main road going a little too fast. *Perfection.* John would lock Livia in a closet and pay for The Beast. *I'm totally getting new rims and charging them to him. I deserve it.*

He texted Dave with one hand:

Stay on the hobo bastard.
Don't lose him no matter fucking what.

26

BRAILLE SUNDRESS

Cole held Kyle as gently as he could manage. He wanted to pull her inside of him. Kneeling with her in the church had saved him. He realized now that she was his angel. There would be no denying her again.

"Kyle, will you come with me?" He whispered the words against her forehead between kisses. His hands traveled over her back as if the Bible were written in Braille on her sundress.

"I'm your shadow now, Cole. I'll be where you are." Kyle smiled, her eyes steady on his.

He stood and held out his hand. She took it.

Kyle gasped as he swooped her into his arms. One of her hands touched his cheek as the other settled onto his bare chest.

The trip to his quarters was not smooth. He had to stop to kick open the door by the altar. At his bedroom, he awkwardly used his foot to un-latch the lever door handle. But he wouldn't put her down. Cole nudged the door shut with his rump.

He turned with Kyle so she could be his hands. "Lock it," he murmured.

She pushed the little button until it clicked. He set her on her feet, and she leaned against the closed door.

"I need to tell you some things," Cole began, gearing up for confession.

Kyle smoothed his hair. "No. No, you don't."

He continued as if she'd said nothing. "Kyle, I'm sorry for my past sins — especially because they may offend you. Help me to do penance, to do better, and to avoid anything that might lead me to sin." Cole paused to take a breath, then added, "Amen." He needed the ritual of prayer to make sense of the changes he was about to implement.

"Don't pray to me. Don't *pray* to me!" Kyle said, her eyes widening in alarm. "We're in this together. I've done things wrong too. We're human, Cole. We'll still make mistakes, but now we'll always have each other to hold when it hurts." Kyle's eyes filled with tears.

"It hurts now. I killed those men. How could I…" Cole's words failed him.

"*I* killed those men, Cole, before you even got there. How could I tempt them…" Kyle trailed into silence as well.

Cole hugged her to him again. He listened to her breathe and felt calmer.

"We have to go somewhere far from here." Her lips moved on his chest, tickling the skin there. "Where do we go, Cole?"

"You know in your heart that those men were wrong in the way they treated you. You *know* that." Cole's hands became two tight clenches of anger. "And they had no idea what lives inside me, what I can do."

"I know what you do to me," Kyle said, finding his eyes. "It's everything right, honest, and good." She stood on her tiptoes and kissed his lips.

"Kyle, I'm intense and devoted, and I need a lot of direction just to get through my day."

"Cole, I'm impulsive and devoted and hopeless. I have a filthy mouth, and I don't see it cleaning up anytime soon."

"I would like to make love to you. Here. Right now," Cole said, continuing his confession. "But I'm afraid I'll lose you, that you'll leave your body and go somewhere else. Will you stay with me?"

"I'm your shadow now, Cole. I'll be where you are." Kyle set her jaw, determined.

"Okay," he said. "This is how it'll go. I'm going to give you pleasure. And you're going to take it. No reciprocating." He instantly saw doubt in her face. "Please, this time—which will be the first of so many—let me make you happy. Let my touch cleanse you. When I'm done, I want your body to belong just to us." He could feel himself smiling, just thinking about it.

Kyle nodded and bit her lip. She looked nervous as a virgin. "This feels like jumping off a cliff," she finally said.

"I'll only do this if you want me to. Do you want me to?" Cole took a step back.

Kyle reached around and unzipped her sundress. She held her arms out like a sacrificial lamb.

"Say it, so I know for sure." Cole's eyes glowed with lust and reverence. "I want you to." Kyle watched him.

Cole gently took one of her outstretched hands and kissed it. Every place he christened on her skin became theirs. His lips took off layer after layer of mistake.

When he got to her dress strap, he watched her eyes as he slid it off her shoulder. She smiled her unquestionably Kyle smile. *Still present.* When the other strap left its perch, her sundress became a gentle puff of air around her ankles.

Now they were chest to chest. Skin to skin. Cole could see Kyle forcing herself to stay still rather than reach for him. She clasped her hands together behind her back.

In Cole's hands and mouth, Kyle's breasts were so much more than erotic tools. They were beautiful, able to sustain life. She moaned at his attention to them. He checked her eyes.

"I'm still here," she said in a playful voice. But she was. She was still there.

"Kyle, will you come to my bed?" Cole would take this so slowly.

"I will." Kyle followed as he led her to his simple twin bed, covered in a plain tan comforter.

The sun spilled onto the bed through his window, making sharp angles that wouldn't hurt at all. Cole kissed the standing Kyle until she was sitting. He nuzzled her neck until she lay on her back. Cole checked her eyes. She winked. Still there. When Cole's kisses lingered on her belly button, she crossed her legs.

"Are you okay?" He appeared instantly at her eye level, worried.

"I'm fine. I just, I never let a guy…um, well, they never wanted to. It's not what I do." Kyle's eyes looked everywhere but his.

"Is it because you don't think you'd like it, or you don't think you deserve it?"

Cole waited with patience that would have made him an excellent priest.

She bit her lip and looked away again. He saw her answer.

"You *do* deserve it," he said fiercely. "Can I give it to you?"

She accepted with a nod, and he slipped her panties down the smooth muscles of her legs. His kissing started at her ankles and moved up ever so slowly. By the time he could finally taste her, she'd gathered the sunshine and the bedspread in her hands.

Her thighs cradled his face, and when he added his fingers to explore with his mouth, her legs dropped open.

Cole felt her begin to shake as he increased the pressure of his persuasion. She arched her back when the inside-out magic he'd granted hit her. Then she relaxed, panting as her skin glistened.

Cole tucked his very proud self around her now-relaxed form. "Did you deserve it?" His voice was husky.

She sighed and tried to talk, but nothing came out. She just nodded.

Cole tilted her chin so he could look deeply into her eyes. "Kyle, you are my heaven. Will you come with me?"

"I will." Kyle snuggled deeper into his chest, gently tracing his Sorry tattoo.

Cole's heart beat like the pounding of an angel's wings.

27

FEED HIM

Livia put the car in gear and drove back to her home. She peeked at Blake and the ski mask on his head as he fiddled around in the passenger seat, touching her radio and the brush she kept in the cup holder.

"What's up?" she finally asked with a smile.

He looked up from his exploring. "You're so real. You have a bedroom and a brush. All the times I waited for you, I could never picture where you came from—what had made you so extraordinarily different. But *you* made you different." Blake ran his hand along his neck, smiling shyly in her direction.

"There are a million girls just like me." Livia almost hated to point that out.

"No. There's only you." Blake looked away from her and squinted into the sun.

Look at him looking into the sunlight! Livia reached in front of him and popped the glove box. She handed him a pair of her sunglasses. He looked so grateful as he slid on her oversized shades that Livia had to stomp down on a flicker of disappointment.

Livia refocused her attention on traffic lights and tricky turns. All she really wanted to do was study his face. Finally, parked in her driveway, Livia realized they'd beaten her father home from work. *Odd. He usually books it home after an overnight.*

The shade of the giant oak on the front lawn formed an umbrella for Blake, and he made it around the car in time to hold her door open and close it behind her. He kept his hand on her lower back as they headed for the house.

Halfway up the walk, she could take the tingling no longer. She whirled and hugged him. He squeezed her back and whispered something into her hair. She listened to his breathing and relaxed in the circle of his arms.

"Should we get inside before your Dad pulls up and finds me ravishing you on this cement path?" he said, more clearly now. She could hear the snicker in his voice.

Blake took the keys from her hands.

"The silver one," Livia said.

Blake held her arm with one hand and unlocked the door with the other. "I remember."

His attentions made Livia feel cherished. Blake removed his mask hat and took Livia's huge sunglasses from his face.

He takes his hat off indoors. Dad's going to love that.

Livia pointed to the catchall table in the foyer, and Blake set his hat and the sunglasses down. As before, he hung her keys on one of the three hooks by the door.

She stepped into him again, needing the contact to keep her heart rhythm steady. Blake rubbed the center of her back. It was a long, comforting moment before she was able to think of anything other than his strong fingers.

"Can I make you something to eat?" She watched his lips for an answer.

"I wouldn't want to trouble you." Blake smiled.

He knows I won't give up. "You're my favorite kind of trouble. Please?" Livia batted her eyelashes and pouted elaborately.

"Yes, tempting Livia, you may feed me. Thank you." He touched her lips with a single finger. "Can I help?"

"No." She led him to sit at the kitchen table. "I want you to relax."

The fridge was disappointing. Grocery shopping had not been on the front burner of her mind. She could see eggs and cheese. *Frittata!*

Livia set a pot of water to boil for pasta and combined the simple egg mixture. After a few minutes she drained the noodles. As she added and stirred and poured into a skillet, Blake wandered over.

"Smells good," he said.

Livia flipped the frittata over to cook on the opposing side, exposing the golden pasta.

"Wow. I think I just went into a frenzy."

Livia grinned. He peeled his attention from the sizzling meal and put his hands on the counter behind her, trapping her.

Livia held her spatula as Blake whispered in her ear. "I see us just like this a hundred years from now, old and deaf. I'll be the luckiest man."

Emotion caught her—this was all she wanted. Simple, beautiful frittata moments with this man.

"Someday, Livia, I'll be man enough to buy the food," he continued. "I'll give you an oven. I'll try so hard."

Livia leaned up and stopped his proclamations with her lips. After tender kisses, she gave her mouth enough room to promise back. "Blake, I'll never care if I have an oven. Just you."

The smell of the food roused them both, and she plated the meal as he sat again. He pulled his piano out of his back pocket and smoothed it. His fingers began flying.

Livia was certain it was a happy song. Uplifting. She slid a wedge of fritatta in front of him with a fork. She poured them ice-cold glasses of water and carried her plate to the table.

He stood and held out her chair, but he never put his fork down. He was so ready to eat. As they started, Livia felt her soul curl up around the edges. He ate so fast. He ate every crumb. *He was hungry.* She hopped up and plopped seconds on his plate as he shook his head no.

"Livia, I've imposed enough. I don't need to take any more of your food."

Livia shook her head as well. "Yes. Yes, you do. You really do. I need to see you eat until you're full. That will be a gift to me. A pleasure for *me*. Be full—that's all I ask in return for making you this meal."

He stood and held out her chair again.

Blake ate the entire rest of the frittata without objection.

"I'm full. It was so very delicious," he said when his plate was empty again. "She's beautiful and can cook. Every man's dream." He set his fork on his plate and cleared the dishes to the sink. "Can I put these in the dishwasher for you?"

Livia nodded. Seeing him puttering around in her kitchen, turning on the familiar faucet, solidified her feeling of destiny. She knew, staring at his back, that he would not go hungry again. She would have him, warm and safe, with her every day. It was perfectly clear. She would need to talk with her father. It was time for her to be on her own.

Livia looked down to wipe a happy tear. Her gaze fell on his cardboard piano. *The piano!*

"I'll be right back." Livia sprinted upstairs. For her fourteenth birthday, she'd wanted a key-lighted keyboard. She was convinced it would help her learn to play. Her father pulled through like the champ of a dad he was, and she had it in her hot little hands on her birthday. After numerous hours of listening to the preset songs and watching the pretty light show that corresponded to the notes, Livia knew her talents would be best applied to turning on the radio. She dug under her bed until she found it.

She dusted it off and prayed it would still work. She slid the button to on. Nothing. She popped out the corroded batteries and replaced each with a fresh D from her dad's endless battery stash in the hall closet. She hit the button again, and the keyboard flickered to life.

Livia almost fell down the stairs in her rush to bring it to him. She clattered into the kitchen and held it out, breathless.

He checked her face first to see if she was all right, then dropped his eyes to the keyboard. It was like someone had plugged *him* in. His eyes widened, his mouth dropped open, and he stretched his fingers.

"Will you play it, Blake? Will you?" Livia almost jumped with excitement.

Blake covered his smile. He nodded. Livia plopped the keyboard on the kitchen table, which was still moist from where he'd wiped it with the kitchen sponge.

Blake kissed her and then spoke solemnly. "I'll play it for you."

He studied the keyboard for a moment and then sat behind it. Livia leaned against the counter.

"What would you like to hear?" He seemed sheepish and nervous.

He has no idea I've heard him before.

"The happy one you were just playing on your piano, if you want."

He brightened. "Okay."

After trying a few buttons he turned off the key-light guide. He rolled his eyes and shook his head at her playfully. Then he began.

Listening to him play was like discovering an eagle in the wild. It was tumblingly bewitching. She could feel and hear genius — she knew it.

"Blake." She didn't have to say more.

He locked his emerald eyes on hers, and she could not look away. Not for anything. He let his happy song trickle into a more intimate one. Blake's fingers moved as he held her gaze. "I wrote this one while we danced the other night," he said softly.

The music washed over her. It changed her. Refreshed her. Made her more than she was. Blake stood and twisted the keyboard around, still playing with one hand. He motioned for her with the other. She nearly ran. He scooped her up with one arm and set her on the table next to the keyboard.

"This is what nibbling your ear sounds like." Blake created a soundtrack for his teeth.

"This is what looking into your eyes sounds like." The notes were deep and beckoning.

"This is what my mind hears when my tongue is in your mouth." The kiss sounded steamy and delicate. The rhythm was her heartbeat as he sampled her mouth.

"But when you smile. When you smile it's…" Blake scooted the keyboard around behind her. He needed both hands.

She put her hands on his face and smiled in amazement as the music exploded. She couldn't imagine how her simple facial gesture could inspire such a majestic sound.

He smiled back. "One thousand nine hundred and ten."

"So many? Really?"

"Yes, really. And it's not nearly enough. I want to lose count, Livia. Make me lose count." His hands left the beautiful music and grabbed handfuls of her hair.

His kisses were so mind-numbing that when Blake said, "Car door," it took Livia a few seconds to remember she spoke English.

"Dad. Oh. My dad's home."

Blake backed up and helped Livia off the table. He grabbed his cardboard piano and rolled it. He seemed to need it for confidence.

"Don't worry. My dad's a really great guy. He seems gruff, but he has a great heart." Livia rubbed Blake's back.

"You must take after him then." Blake eyed the door. "I just hate being inside before I've met him."

"It's okay. I'm allowed to have friends visit." Livia went to meet her father at the door.

She looked out the window beside the door and saw that he'd brought a squad car home, which was a rare occurrence. She looked back to Blake. He'd set his cardboard piano on the coffee table in the living room. He wiped his hands on his pants and practiced his handshake with an imaginary, friendly Livia's father. Her actual dad was headed down the path when Livia opened the door.

"Hey, Dad." She smiled as widely as she could.

Her father wasn't to the house yet when he started in. "Livia Marie McHugh, you and I need to have a serious sit down. A homeless guy? What the hell?"

28

ĪnvestmenT

Craig needed to meet with his contact again. After two years of frustration at having his construction teams cockblocked, it was time for definitive action. He knew that. He just needed a little encouragement.

At the root of it, this was not what he wanted. He didn't even think it was a good plan B — he just couldn't think of anything else. His phone beeped. The contact wanted to meet at a nearby fast food joint. Craig smoothed his hair and dusted off his suit. *Either shit or get off the pot.*

When asked, Craig described his profession as "investment dealer." It was a broad, sweeping term of his own creation that just barely defined what he did. He'd started as a realtor, but after buying a rundown building, he became a landlord, and his license to sell lay dormant. Landlording to mostly low-end clients tapped into Craig's darker talents. He could be a hell of a bully. His tactics for acquiring payments, when necessary, bordered on illegal. Luckily his renters had neither the knowledge nor the money to fight him. They just moved out, and he had more bait move in.

When the housing market heated up, he dusted off his real estate license and began flipping homes in his spare time. He became an expert in mirages. He could paint over the flaws in a house and hire his shady inspector to whitewash over shoddy repairs. At his disposal was a group of contractors who did exactly what he said and collected their money. End of story. He'd worked hard to cultivate a crew that had no concern about whether their creations would stand the test of time.

While his money flowed freely and his ego was limitless, Craig also invested in the part of town no one else wanted. He was certain he could revitalize the crappy, drug-riddled rubble—at least on the surface. It was within walking distance of the train station, for God's sake. Someday it would be "Soho in Pough"—a hipster-friendly selection of bistros, bookstores, and antique shops that currently existed only in his mind. Tourists would seek it out to dump their money into Craig's pocket.

Near as he could tell there was one, and only one, wrench in his plan. Beckett Fucking Taylor. His broken-down strip mall sat dead center, like a lead weight in "Soho in Pough's" potential. Any time Craig sent in his contractors to tear down a building in the area, they'd not only fail to complete the job, they'd refuse to ever return—no matter what tirade of disappointment Craig unleashed on them.

Then when the housing market bottomed out, the rest of Craig's luck went with it. Two lawsuits in particular had proved tough to shake. The duped owners of his flimsy rehabbed houses just had so much proof. Then the city condemned his building full of renters, and complete financial ruin loomed before him.

Before the downfall of his empire, Craig had had the luxury of waiting. He'd been willing to bide his time until the inevitable death of Beckett Taylor, whose lifestyle was bound to catch up with him. But Taylor wasn't cooperating. He had more lives than a bucketful of cats, along with a distinctly devoted staff of assholes. And Craig was out of time. He needed Soho in Pough to start happening *now*—before he no longer had the last of his money to finance it.

And so, despite his better judgment, here he was. The deal was simple: eliminate Beckett Taylor, however dirty the job became. Craig had hired a crew of trained mercenaries. They didn't come cheap, but they did come professional. And he'd never have found them without his contact.

Craig had never planned anyone's death before, and sometimes his hands shook when he thought of the enormity of his actions. But he was only speeding up the inevitable. Taylor would have been dead soon enough anyway, he often reminded himself.

He pulled his Jag into a spot at the burger joint. If he didn't pull this off, they'd finally repo this car. *I might have to get a job here to make fucking money. This has to work.*

The back booth contained a nondescript man eating an equally blasé burger. He didn't look up as Craig sat down.

After slowly polishing off his fries and looking everywhere but at Craig, the contact spoke up. "Now's the moment, if you're ready."

Craig swallowed the burning in his throat and felt cold sweat trickle into his suit pants. *I have no other options.* "Go over our deal one more time," he said, finding his voice. "Explain it like I'm a little kid." Craig clasped his sweating hands under the table.

"My boss will only respond to great force. You have to hit him hard and close. He has only two weaknesses that I've observed: his brothers. You get the brothers, you get the man."

The contact made a giant, crumpled ball out of his wrappers and ketchup packets. "The men skilled in the talents we discussed are on standby right now. All I need is the go from you."

Instead Craig finished the plan. "Then you'll run his organization because you're his right-hand man. You'll sell me the strip mall and clear out the riff-raff. We'll be partners in my new renovated section of town. Easy. Simple."

The contact looked bored. "It won't be easy or simple. Don't underestimate Beckett. I can handle my part, but you need to follow my directions to the letter."

"Go," Craig said. "You have my permission." He wiped sweat from his upper lip.

The contact nodded, got up, and disappeared. Craig looked at the ball of trash in front of him. It would all be over soon.

Beckett Taylor was a horrendous person. This opportunity had fallen in Craig's lap, and he'd simply jumped on it. *You have to be able to jump quickly with investments.*

Craig left the ball on the table, earning him a dirty look from an employee patrolling with a broom and an overworked rag. He sat for a moment once he was back in his Jag. One of the two brothers would be paying for their unfortunate connection to Taylor right about...now.

Merkin smiled as he slid into a drug runner's car. He texted the eight men he'd looked long and hard to find. His smile slipped for a moment as he stuffed down the gnawing pain that Beckett's brothers had to be involved. He still hoped he'd need only one to force Beckett out into the open. He texted the orders to his point man. The team had kept track of the easiest brother to find: Cole, always at his stupid church.

Merkin took a deep breath. He couldn't second-guess himself now. For at least a year he'd been looking for a way out—with a windfall. When he'd first joined Beckett's organization, he'd hoped to be chosen second in command. He was by far the most talented with technology. Christ, that was how he'd found Craig in the first place. Keeping watch on the local newspaper and following through with some backup hacking had paid off. He knew more about Craig's plans and finances than Craig did.

He hadn't wanted to do this. Mouse was close to Beckett, but the knitter had no head for business, so his path was clear—or so he thought. He kept waiting for something to happen, for Beckett to bring him into the fold. But he never did. Then Eve had come along and condemned Merkin to eternal second class. There wasn't jack shit she couldn't do. And judging from the screams in the office not long ago, her pussy was made of solid gold.

He was lucky if he was third in command at this point. Who really knew.

The point man texted back:

Subject in church. One female on premises. Terminate?

Merkin rolled his head on his neck; these were the kind of quick, hard decisions he'd have to get used to. He texted his answer and closed the phone. Merkin knew he had to get back to Eve *now*. Everything was about to happen real fast, and he needed her far away from Beckett.

He pulled in the parking lot of Beckett's strip mall office to find the usual stragglers milling around. Beckett's Hummer was gone, along with the vehicles that usually accompanied it, but a quick check of everyone's cell phone GPS chips let Merkin know where they were. At least he was still in charge of whereabouts. Mouse was in the fucking Jo-Ann Fabrics. Beckett was at a bank downtown, and Eve was inside Beckett's strip mall by herself.

He grabbed the douchebag guarding the front door. "Aunt Betty's coming to visit. Eve and I have the interior. Clear the exterior."

Soon the people in the lot scrambled. The code for "police on the way" worked like magic. Merkin knew this only bought him an hour or so, but he hoped that was all he'd need. He knocked on Beckett's office door.

"Enter." Her voice was husky and sexy.

She sat behind his desk, twirling a knife in her hand—flipping it from finger to finger like a secretary with a pencil.

"Better head out, Eve."

"You cleared the lot for the cops?" She gathered her hair in one hand and twirled it into a bun. She slid the knife in to hold it in place.

"I cleared it. Told the douchebags it was the cops, but it's not." Merkin tried not to let his voice trip. "The boss told me to tell you to leave. He's on his way with a few new hookers. He said to tell you, and I quote, 'I got what I fucking wanted. I'm a hit-it-and-quit-it kind of bastard. She's fired.'"

Eve didn't move. No emotion at all. Merkin had been very careful with his choice of words, and he really thought he'd gotten Beckett's curses down pat. *Come on...Believe me. Get mad. Leave.*

She stood. "When does he arrive?"

"He didn't want me to tell you. He said, 'She needs to be a man and leave. You play, you fucking pay.'" Merkin let the rejection marinate in her brain. "I'm sorry, Eve. I really thought you two were good for each other. He can't be tamed, I guess." Merkin looked at his shoes with faux embarrassment for her situation.

Eve went to a trunk in Beckett's office. She pulled out a huge duffle bag and began plucking guns off the wall. She grabbed fistfuls of ammunition boxes from the shelves and piled them in as well.

"You better get out of here, Merkin. Leave now." Eve slung two Uzis over her shoulders.

When she turned he got a glimpse of her eyes. She was furious. *Fantastic.*

She stomped out to the front lobby and cracked open the door to what Beckett had dubbed the "Oh Shit Closet." Merkin had to look twice to be sure, but she *had* pulled a rocket-propelled grenade launcher out of its depths. *Holy fuck.*

The actual rockets came next. Eve held the warheads with an unsettling expertise. She propped up the launcher and positioned the rocket with a sliding, metal-on-metal click. Watching her tuck the two other large rockets into her belt was almost comical — if they hadn't been fully equipped to blow everything to hell and back.

She kicked open the glass doors and headed for the center of the parking lot. Merkin jumped in his car. He realized that when Eve had said *leave now* earlier, she'd meant, "Leave at this moment. I'm not warning you again." Merkin floored the car and didn't even let himself look back. *Eve just might do this job for me!*

Cole finished making two peanut butter and jelly sandwiches on white bread. He added two cold cans of orange soda and put it all on the tray Father Callahan sometimes used as a table to watch TV while he ate in his room.

After laughing and kissing and promising, he and Kyle were starving. He'd left her in his room, waiting, with the door closed. Saturdays were Father Callahan's time to visit the housebound members of his congregation, offering them communion and prayer. Cole knew he had the church to himself for at least another three hours. He'd put two and two together and figured Livia had diverted the Pew Crew. He had to remember to thank her later. After investigating the parking lot, he knew her car was now gone.

He tried not to topple the tray as he hurried down the hallway to his small room. Kyle was all his for a few more hours. He let the happiness come from his feet to the top of his head.

But then the hallway felt wrong. There was too much air, lack of a barrier somewhere. His bedroom door was open.

Kyle probably had to use the bathroom.

That made sense, so Cole wasn't sure why his internal alarms were still going off. He could have done so many things differently in that instant—whether or not it would've changed the outcome, he'd never know—but he proceeded calmly. This was his safe, comforting church. His soul had finally found the arms of his beloved. *Kyle.*

The splintered doorframe changed his mind from human to reptilian. He threw the tray through the doorway and entered with a scream.

Two men held Kyle, who'd been silenced with thick duct tape over her mouth. Focused on her, Cole never noticed the man just inside the doorway. The taser hit him in the neck. He fell, numb, but started flailing as soon as his body hit the ground. Animal. Primal.

Another stun blasted him.

"Fuck—is he on crack or something?" one of the men asked. But Cole looked only for her.

His limbs tingled and refused to cooperate. The men in the room wore surgical masks. He screamed again. His own name coming from the stun gun operator stopped his flailing.

"Cole, calm down or we'll do more than kill her."

Rage nearly melted his brain. He saw the set of plastic ties just before his wrists were bound together.

Oh. God. No. My hands. I can't. Kyle.

She seemed to be nodding, calm for his benefit. Duct tape with a gag attached was wound around his head. They pulled him to his knees and bound his ankles. He almost looked like he was praying.

Cole willed himself to have superhuman strength and strained against the ties.

The man who'd tied his bindings whispered in Cole's ear. "Fun being the brother of a mobster, huh?"

Cole could not look away from Kyle's eyes. The whispering man pulled Cole's cell phone from his pocket. He scrolled through the options before pointing the phone at Cole. The phone's camera was still factory-programmed with a happy "Say Cheese" before the sound of a camera shutter.

"Now that's just lovely," the man sneered. He turned the phone to show Cole the image of himself, bound and gagged. "I'm gonna send that to a special recipient when the time is just right."

Beckett, of course.

It was a message, a warning, and a threat with the press of a single button. Cole was bait.

The picture-taker hefted Cole over his shoulder. Cole lost sight of Kyle's eyes.

"Did you get anything back from him? What'd he say? Kill her?" asked one of the attackers.

I love you. Dear Jesus. I love her. No. No.

Cole knew what the chemical smell on the cloth over his nose meant. He took one breath, and his last conscious thought was simple: *Kyle.*

29

Don't Give Up on Me. Please.

Livia cringed at her father's words and looked over at Blake. He'd stopped his practice handshake mid-swing. Livia watched hope die in his eyes. Blake had wanted to meet John man to man. But now...

Blake tried to smile at Livia, but only one side of his lip went up. Livia interrupted her father before he could say anything else.

"Dad, I have my friend, Blake Hartt, here to meet you." Livia tried to convey warning and begging with her eyes.

John stepped in and took off his hat. Livia felt every emotion her heart could hold when Blake stepped forward to greet her father, despite the words he'd just heard. John assessed Blake while rubbing a thumb over his mouth. Livia reached out to touch Blake's lower back. She outlined a heart with her finger. *I'm proud of you, no matter what happens here.*

Livia knew where to start — she'd learned from Blake's wonderful manners.

"John McHugh, this is Blake Hartt. Blake, this is my father." Livia left her hand on Blake's back, hoping to convey her attachment and acceptance.

Blake nodded and held out his hand, which John grasped firmly. "Sir, it's a pleasure to see you again. I owe you such gratitude for your many acts of kindness."

John stepped back from their handshake. "It's no problem," he grumbled.

Livia looked from one man to the other. Her father looked embarrassed, and Blake's shoulders showed a certain slump Livia recognized from before they'd first spoken — when they had just her smiles between them.

"Wait—hold the phone. You two know each other?" Livia felt a little lightheaded.

John shuffled his feet and observed the movement as if it was endlessly fascinating.

Blake turned to Livia. "We were never formally introduced. When your father sees me at the train station from his patrol car, he often stops by later in the day with a bagged meal that he refuses to let me turn down. You, Livia, inherit your generous nature from him."

Blake did his best to seem cool and collected, but irony coated the room, thick and palpable. Blake ever buying an oven seemed a reckless dream. His homelessness came into sharp relief.

Livia held tight to her heart. *This doesn't change anything. Blake's the right person for me.*

John twisted his hat in his hands and stayed silent.

"Dad, thank you. I had no idea. I wish I'd been smart enough to do that very thing for Blake sooner." She grabbed Blake's hand with both of her own and put a kiss on the back of it, forcing a jaunty wink and smile.

He looked at her, but he was only a shadow now. Livia gave him a warning look. He shook his head sadly and in total defeat. Standing in the house of a man who'd brought him food, with his daughter holding his hand, seemed to break some sort of honor code for Blake.

Livia felt her heart beating in her ears. "Don't give up on me. Please," she said softly.

He nodded and took a deep breath.

Livia looked at her father's uniform as if for the first time. His badge had just a number, nothing that said John McHugh and no way for Blake to know he'd been about to meet a benefactor who'd seen him at his worst and taken pity on him.

Livia watched Blake crumble like ash from a burnt cigarette. One stiff wind and he would disintegrate.

John seemed to note Livia's distress. "Hey, did you guys eat? Should I order a pizza?"

More food offered to Blake. Livia knew what he was thinking—that he hadn't earned it. *Crap.*

"No. Thank you, sir. Livia was kind enough to make me a meal. I appreciate the offer. I would imagine you might wish to spend some private moments with your daughter right now." Blake made a motion for the door.

Livia squeezed his hand. *I'm not letting you go.*

Blake turned to John. "I know you already know this, Mr. McHugh, but your daughter is the most exceptional person I've ever had the honor of meeting. She's a testament to your dedication as a parent." He squeezed Livia's hand back.

"Livia and her sister always do me proud. I only want the best for them." John said the words with kindness, but Livia heard them through Blake's ears. Disappointment and suspicion were sandwiched around fatherly pride.

"Again, sir. It was a pleasure meeting you." Blake leaned in and shook John's hand once more.

Livia looked at her dad. "I'll be right back. I'll whip you up something for dinner. Don't order in."

She watched as Blake slid the mask out from beneath her sunglasses and pocketed it discreetly. He held the door open for her and followed close behind. She smiled a little when she felt him sniff her hair. Under the little awning over the front door, Blake remained in the shade.

He seemed to be drinking in her face, looking *at* her instead of into her.

"Stop. Stop that. This isn't goodbye."

Blake pulled her left hand to his mouth and kissed her ring finger. "I'm still glad it's empty. He never deserved you. Of that, I'm very sure."

Livia saw moisture in his eyes. "You're saying goodbye. *No.* Here's what *I'm* sure of. I'll walk away from this house right now, wearing only what I have on my back and be happy. With you I can taste forever—it's right here." Livia pointed at her lips and then kissed his.

Blake allowed the kiss, but mumbled a question as well, "How many shotguns does he have?"

"Not enough to get me away from you." Livia traced his jaw.

Blake took her hand and kissed her palm, then her forehead, "Livia, go in there and let him talk to you. He's a father. I'd want to talk to my daughter at a moment like this. Let's give him that respect."

"I will not go in there. Where will you go?" Livia felt a gentle tug on her heart. She was torn. She wanted to comfort her dad and get him to understand who Blake was, but in as little time as possible so she could get back to Blake.

"My *inamorata*, you know where I'll be: where I'll always be. Waiting. For you." Blake began putting the mask on.

Livia looked around wildly, feeling close to irrational. "I don't want you to go." These words were inadequate to express her need.

Blake smoothed her hair away from her face. "I've often wished I had a father. Let me help him be that. He needs you to himself for a just a little while."

Livia's love for her dad gave her the strength to step back and nod. She stood on the porch and watched Blake's retreating form. Every once in a while he turned to wave, and just before he reached the end of her street, he stopped to look at her. Neither of them waved this time.

She watched with a crashing surge of pride as he reached up and pulled the mask off—he was in full sunlight. The orangey red light of the setting sun outlined him. Poughkeepsie's dusk set the mood. No matter how much Blake healed, Livia had a feeling nighttime would always be their favorite. He disappeared from view, but she knew he was strong. So much stronger so much sooner than she could ever have hoped.

Livia walked back in and leaned against the front door as she closed it behind her. She didn't throw the bolt because her dad was home. No one was stupid enough to rob the McHughs with a patrol car parked out front. She sighed as she felt his love settle even further into her soul.

Her father stood in the kitchen doorway with his eyebrows raised. Livia smiled. Out of the corner of her eye she saw the cardboard piano on the living room coffee table. Blake must have set it down to shake John's hand.

He left it! Livia hoped this was a good sign, not something that would cause a setback when he discovered it missing. *I'll get this discussion over with, then drive the piano over to him and pick him up.*

"Livia, I don't even know where to start with this nightmare."

Livia turned back to find her father winding up. His face flushed and the veins in his neck were more visible than they should have been.

"Blake's not a nightmare. I love him, Dad. I love him. Let's keep that straight." Livia felt her hackles rise.

"I'm not talking about Blake, though I have concerns about him. I want to know what happened to your sister and her car. I want to know why Beckett Taylor's hanging around *my* two daughters. Where the hell is your sister, anyway?" John had started pacing, as he tended to do when he was angry.

Livia felt some selfish relief. She loved the way her dad had said "Blake," just as he'd name any of her friends. "Kyle rammed Chris's truck when she found him spying on Blake and me. She's fine. The car's at a body shop. Beckett is Blake's foster brother. They're friendly. So yes, I know Beckett. I would almost call him a friend, but he does bad, bad things for a living." Livia had never been a good liar, and she wasn't going to try it now.

John ran his hand through his hair. Then he turned and walked upstairs. Livia followed him. He entered her room and sat down on the bed.

"I have to tell you, Chris came to see me. That's why I know so much right now." His voice seemed too loud in the small room. "Chris told me this. Not my own daughter. You're in love? So soon? Didn't Chris just ask me for your hand? Didn't you say yes?" He ran his hand through his hair again.

"He had no right to tell you before I had a chance. Was I not here? With Blake? Five minutes ago? I had every intention of telling you, Dad. It was not Chris's place, and I resent him for that." Livia found a paper rose and fiddled with it.

She and her dad rarely argued. Kyle went toe-to-toe with him on a regular basis, but Livia was always his girl, the one that understood him best. Being out of sync made Livia feel like her shirt was on backward. She came to sit next to him.

"No matter how I got the information, I got it," he countered. "Not saying Chris's intentions were pure. But going from what you just told me and what I learned today, I can't help but feel a little bit hysterical." He clenched his fists. "I spoke with Blake's old social worker. She does clerical work at the station, and she remembered his name, thank God." John put his severe voice on. "Now, I'm not proud of how I got this, but you need to know he's had a violent past."

Livia steadied herself internally. "I know about his past—what happened with his mom."

Having her father know Blake's deepest, darkest secret so soon felt improper. Livia wanted to cover him, hide the truth for now.

"Okay, so it's fine with you that he punched his own mother? Let's just say that's water under the bridge. As nice as he seems, he had an excuse, or he was young. Let's just pick a reason and run with it. But how about this? Blake, Beckett, and his other foster brother were unofficially considered suspects in the case of a missing, and presumed dead, male. He was the last foster father all three of them had together. The man left one Saturday and never returned. Murder, Livia." John stood and began pacing again.

"Were any of them found guilty?" Livia could barely take this all in. Blake would play no part in a murder. He'd even been reluctant to have the cooler stealers punished.

"No. No, they weren't, but that question scares the hell out of me, Livia. There wasn't enough evidence to even question them. But I don't need a guilty verdict to worry about my daughter. Will you make murder fit into your lifestyle now? Is that where this is heading?"

Livia knew she needed to be sensible. How could she possibly make him understand? She needed to buy some breathing room. She halted her father's words with her hand. "Dad, Blake and I have only known each other a few weeks. It's a brand new thing. It might not even last."

He seemed to take a deep breath. Livia thought he looked a little less red in the face.

"What about his foster brother, Beckett Taylor?" he asked. "Do you know what we call him down at the station, Livia? The Bloody Bastard. I don't even want to get into how much that's not okay. Even if in some dream world Beckett is decent, his enemies won't be. And Blake? Your brand-new boyfriend?" John clenched and unclenched his hands. "He has a violent past I know about, and maybe plenty more I don't know about. Has he ever hurt you?" John stopped pacing like a lion and waited for her answer.

No! Never. Livia felt the words start to form, but then her first time in the clearing with Blake surfaced in her memory. She thought of being thrown to the ground. She thought of Blake running at her. She didn't want to lie—surely her father could understand Blake was a work in progress. *Aren't we all?*

"Did he?" her father questioned again, his eyes growing bigger and bigger.

Livia took a breath and spoke calmly. "He scared me once, but he's dealing with some stuff, Dad. He didn't do it on purpose. I don't ever think he'd do it again. At least he wouldn't want to. I just need to learn when to give him some space." Livia knew her words were not telling the story the way her father needed to hear it.

"Liv, do you know how many times I've heard those exact words from the mouth of a woman with her face beaten in? The men are always gonna change. The woman needs to learn. Christ Almighty, I never thought I'd hear those words from my daughter. Are you on drugs?" John held his palms out to her as if she could lay the answers he needed in them.

"No. Jeez, Dad." Livia sighed. *Can I even begin to make him see things my way?*

"He's homeless, Livia," her father continued, moving on to a new concern. "Do you want to know why people are homeless? I'll tell you, because I've seen a ton of them. They're homeless because they're crazy. Normal people don't sit in one spot all day. I've seen that kid sitting in one spot *all damn day*, playing with a piece of cardboard. Now you're dating him? You want to know what I think?" He didn't wait for her assent. "It's the university. I think it's great for you to go—first McHugh to go to grad school and all that. But all those psychology classes are putting ideas in your head. I think you want to try to fix a crazy man, and one was conveniently located at the train station. Is he like a class paper for you?"

Livia rubbed her hand over her face. She pictured Blake's distant form removing his mask. "I'm a person who can help him, Dad. I even met with a professor about his problem, and I got great advice. It's working. He's doing great. Right now, he's doing great." Livia looked in her lap and realized she'd untwisted the rose. It was just a wrinkled napkin. She busied her hands trying to put it back together, nice and tight.

"Livia, I can't tell you what to do anymore. You're a grown woman. But I can give you my opinion, and I think Blake's a mistake. You're a beautiful, smart young lady with a head on your shoulders—up until this point anyway. Getting romantically involved five minutes after breaking up with your fiancé and hopping into the arms of the train station hobo while making friends with murderers is not who I raised you to be. I expect more from you, Livia. I have to say, I'm disappointed. And I'm worried sick."

John sat again and pulled her into an uncharacteristic hug. "I just love you too damn much. You're my perfect girl. I want perfect things for you. That's all I want. Happy and safe. I want you happy and safe."

Livia could hear a sob in his voice. She could only imagine what he must have read and heard at the station. Beckett probably had his own roomful of paperwork documenting his evils. Considering that, her dad was holding up pretty well.

"I love you, Dad." His police uniform was scratchy against her cheek.

Livia caught movement outside on the front lawn in her peripheral vision but didn't want to break from her dad's rare hug to look. She turned her attention to her father's face.

"I have to tell you, Blake's not a murderer or a woman beater. When he hurt me, it was an absolute accident. He actually saved Kyle and me when Chris seemed to be getting out of hand. I can't apologize for Beckett, but he's not the man I love."

Here it goes, the hell with breathing room. Dad needs to know how it is.

"It happened so quick. I just knew. In my heart, Blake and I are already bound. Remember the story about when you met Mom? How you knew she was special right away?" Livia waited to see if he was following.

He nodded.

"You took a risk marrying her. You took a risk having kids with her. You knew she was flighty, to say the least, but you did it anyway. Do you regret it, Dad?" Livia took his hand.

"Never," he said immediately. "I got my girls. You two are why I get up in the morning."

His eyes were angry, but Livia could see the glow of pride as well. She'd known that would be his answer, and it made her smile.

"That's because it was the right thing to do. You followed your heart, even though it might get broken. You let it lead you to the path. I've found my path, Dad. Blake's someone I'll never regret. I can't promise how it'll turn out, but my heart can't make any other choice."

Livia squeezed his hand; he had to understand. "You're the first man I ever loved. He's the second. I couldn't have one without the other. Please, Dad, stand with me on this."

He squeezed her hand back and made a sour face. "I hate when you use logic against me. It takes my knees out. I'll give him a shot, but if he ever hurts you…"

Livia put the paper rose down on her dresser. She couldn't get it back together correctly and wished she hadn't messed with it in the first place. It looked deflated and sad.

John sighed when Livia turned to his arms again. She decided right then to hug him more often. Every day he needed to know how much she appreciated him. The ringing of the house phone broke their embrace.

They then played the McHugh family's most hated game. They had three cordless phones and after talking, Kyle would toss the handsets aside and return to whatever she was doing at the moment. They could be buried in the couch, on top of the fridge, or nestled in the pantry when she was done.

Livia and John ran from room to room, looking. Livia swore she heard one in the living room. She froze when she saw the coffee table empty. She dropped to the floor and checked all around. Blake's cardboard piano was gone. She ran for the door and tried the knob. It was locked. No one in her family ever locked the knob, just the bolt.

But Blake would, just to be courteous and keep Livia safe. Blake would have picked up the piano, locked the door, and closed it behind him. Blake had been in the house to get his piano. Livia knew it for sure. She ran through her conversation with her father.

"*Dad, Blake and I have only known each other two weeks. It's a brand new thing. It might not even last.*"

"*Has he ever hurt you?*"

"*He scared me once…*"

Livia grabbed her car keys. She had to get to him.

She ran out, only to remember father's cruiser blocking her in. She turned just as John found one of the phones. The answering machine clicked on and became a loudspeaker, booming voices throughout the house.

"Sorry. The machine got it first. Hi." He was gruff on the phone, as usual.

"This is Nurse Susan Weiss at Poughkeepsie General Hospital. May I speak with Officer McHugh?" She sounded stiff and professional.

"This is John McHugh." He spoke slowly.

Livia tried to get back out the door before hearing this woman possibly ask her father on a date, but the next words stopped her cold.

"Your daughter, Kyle, was just brought into the ER. I'll need you to come as soon as possible."

"What happened?" John asked, his voice robotic.

"Sir, I just need you to drive safely and quickly to the hospital. Do you need directions?"

"Tell me what the hell has happened to my daughter! Is she okay?" John appeared in front of Livia, squeezing the phone tightly.

"Officer McHugh, is Kyle allergic to any medications?"

John looked at the phone like it had sprouted wings.

Livia took the phone from his hand. She led him by the arm and grabbed the cruiser's keys off the hook. They rushed outside together.

"This is Livia. I'm Kyle's sister. She's not allergic to any medications. You need to tell me right now what we'll be facing when we get there." Livia landed in the passenger seat as John threw the cruiser into reverse.

The phone could almost reach the end of the block before it went out of range. Livia had walked out of the house thinking she was on her cell phone instead of the house phone on more than one occasion.

"Livia, Kyle is unconscious. One of the police officers at the scene recognized her. I can't tell you why, just yet...B..fr..." Susan's voice faded.

John looked at Livia's pale face and flipped on his lights and sirens. He hit the accelerator and turned the cruiser toward the hospital.

30

RESTLESS COCK SYNDROME

B eckett parked the Hummer in front of the bank's outdoor ATM. It had its own drive-thru spot, which looked like a teller window, and that pissed him the fuck off. Windows should have people in 'em, not machines.

He hopped out of the Hummer and grabbed his wallet. He ran his fingers through his hair and felt the scab from Eve's knife on his scalp.

Eve. That torpedo mind-fuck sex was outrageous and fantastically titil-lating. *Titi*-fuck-*illating*. But there was something else as well. *Emotional,* a small voice in Beckett's head suggested. *Connected.* Well, shit. That seemed just about right. Definitely something new.

Beckett smiled to himself as he pulled open the bank's thick glass door and held it for a middle-aged mom-type glued to her iPhone.

"Thanks," she mumbled as he followed her into the building. A line of people snaked into the maze of red velvet ropes. *Son of a bitch.* A long line did lots of bad things to Beckett and his spotty attention span. He called this condition Restless Cock Syndrome. But he liked to do his wheeling and dealing at the window—when he actually used the bank—so Beckett stepped into the dreaded line. He flipped a toothpick out of his pocket and put it in his mouth. A good fifteen people were ahead of him, so he had to dig deep to stay sane.

He peeked over middle-aged iPhone lady's shoulder. Her screen had nice, large print. He figured she needed eyeglasses to read, but was too vain to wear them. He almost turned his attention back to his toothpick when the word *pussy* caught his attention. Girl was reading some porn. Beckett put the toothpick away. *Hot damn.*

He decided to fuck with her head and read the male's part of the conversation. "Let me slide my fingers into your pussy while we slap your ass with this whip," he whispered nonchalantly into her ear.

The lady dropped her phone and stood stock still. Beckett stooped and picked up the phone, handing it back with both his dimples on full display.

"Hey, sweetheart. Don't be ashamed. It's hot." He waggled his eyebrows.

A key chain decorated with pictures of kids' faces dangled from her jeans pocket. She smiled at him and accepted her phone with a blush.

"Do you know why I like moms so much?" Beckett couldn't stop himself now. His restless cock needed entertainment.

"Why?" she whispered, her eyes riveted to him.

"Because a lady with a little vintage can usually take all of me. And I like *all* of me taken care of." He reveled in the heat that rushed to her cheeks and neck.

Beckett gave her one last wink and turned his attention to his own phone. He enjoyed the back and forth, but as cute as she was, middle-aged iPhone chick could never shake Eve out of his mind.

He stared at his phone and thought of having her surround him. Her smell when she wanted him. Even the soft curve of her lower back helped make Beckett sure what he was about to do was right.

Beckett clipped and unclipped the closest red velvet rope from its post and tried to avoid thinking about how close the guy in line behind him was. He pulled his phone out again and checked for missed calls. None. He played a little Tetris, then trashed the whole game with his lack of concentration. He returned the phone to his pocket.

Finally, the stealth porn reader sashayed up to the next teller. Beckett breathed more freely with the space in front of him clear. A contractor with ridiculously droopy pants finished up what must have been a fucking elaborate transaction that apparently involved an assortment of questions from the Spanish Inquisition. Beckett rolled his head on his neck and shook out his hands. As soon as the contractor and his pants were out of the way, Beckett appeared in front of the vacated teller. He hated to wait to be called like a dog when he was obviously goddamn next.

The teller finished writing the previous customer's receipt with big, loopy handwriting. Her fancy script took so motherfucking long that Beckett knocked on her clear, bulletproof window. She jumped and dropped her pen. "Shannon Waltus," according to her gold-etched nametag, gave Beckett the most polite dirty look he'd ever received.

He felt a little bad about scaring her. "I'm sorry, dollface. I know we're not supposed to tap the glass. But are we allowed to tap fine, fine bank teller ass?" He let his two winning dimples come out to play again.

Shannon snickered and tried to look disapproving. His eyes twinkled, and he knew she forgave him.

"How can I help you, sir?" she asked.

Beckett pulled out his wallet and sifted through a few different licenses with his mug on them until he found the one that worked at this bank. He slid the New York ID under the little pass-way to the other side. Shannon entered the information with her quiet keyboard.

"I need to close a few accounts, Shannon." Beckett put his mouth a little closer to the circle of air holes punched in the barrier between the money and the customers and settled his elbows on the counter in a friendly gesture. Without the glass, they'd be very close to each other.

Shannon glanced from the license to the computer monitor to his ridiculous biceps. "I'm sorry to hear that, Mr. Taylor."

Beckett could tell the moment the total of his first account appeared on her screen. She kept her mouth closed in a testament to her professionalism, but her eyes widened slightly. After a few more clicks, she handed his license back to him.

"Sir, let me call the manager. I'm sure she'd like to handle this herself." Shannon looked like she would gnaw off her own leg to get an on-the-spot promotion.

Beckett sighed. Merkin or Mouse usually did his banking for him. He kept his elbows on the cold marble. *Fuck. This is going to take forever.*

In just a few moments Bank Manager Diana Grint motioned him to her office and closed the door behind her. Beckett endured her endless verbal gymnastics after he told her the purpose of his visit. He let his eyes go numb and daydreamed about his plans.

Beckett wanted his money out where he could hold it. Eve deserved everything he could give her. Watching her lay herself open in front of him had cracked his iron resolve to exist solely for his brothers' protection. Beckett knew Kyle and Livia were sure things for Blake and Cole. It was a feeling in his gut, so that decision was made. He'd give bonuses to his employees and cut out of town with his whole fucking family and everyone who mattered to them.

Diana slid a piece of paper with his total liquid assets circled across the desk, and even Beckett was impressed. Plenty enough money to support some crazy commune of his favorite people. He knew his plan was a little spur of the moment, but for crap's sake—it was all he really needed.

He tuned back in to Diana in time to hear her say, "Your associate, Jim Hern, has done a wonderful job with your investments over the years. Does he do that professionally?"

Mouse. I haven't thought of his real freaking name in a million years.
"Did he now?" Beckett said.

Diana tapped a few more keys and turned the thin monitor to face him. "See here? And here? This was the starting sum. And this is where you've ended up."

Hot damn. "He'll get a big-ass raise, I promise." Beckett felt a rush of love for the squeaky-voiced henchman. Mouse wasn't a brother, but damn, he was close. He was definitely a friend.

"So when do I get my paper bags filled with money? I've still got a lot to do this afternoon." *I gotta do Eve in the shower. Eve in a bed, swirled in sheets like cotton candy. Eve in my arms so I can whisper in her ear.*

Diana seemed done begging and pleading for him to reconsider his withdrawals, but she now gave him some solid advice. "Mr. Taylor, I highly suggest transferring these funds. If you want some cash to work with, I'll be more than happy to bring you whatever amount you desire. But I suggest we set you up with an overseas account. Traveling around with this kind of money..." Diana shook her head. "I just can't recommend it. I'm sure Mr. Hern can assist you on a more personal level with the overseas funds."

Beckett knew how to listen to expertise, and he thanked her for offering it. He still got quite a large wad of cash in an envelope, but he also took along all the new account papers he needed to look over with Mouse and Eve.

Beckett was surprised by the twilight when he came out the front door of the bank. His transactions had taken some time. He shook his head, realizing no one had dared say anything to him about the bank needing to close. He looked at his watch—it was nearly six—and smiled to himself as he trotted around the building toward the Hummer.

Then he heard an explosion. The dread climbed up his legs, slapped at his balls, and clung to his neck. Another explosion sounded. Now he could see the smoke. It created a thick, black freight train across the sky, right above his mall.

Eve's in the mall. He ran for his Hummer as a third blast rocked Poughkeepsie.

Beckett wanted to call her, but he needed both hands to drive the Hummer as the crow would fly to his den of evil, especially in the gathering darkness. Beckett tore through front lawns, crushed pretty fences, and maneuvered around dogs. His headlights bounced wildly, and he could barely see the ground around the image in his mind of her sitting behind his desk watching him leave. *Don't be in the mall. Fuck!*

Beckett careened into his parking lot. The entire structure of the strip mall was a seething, angry monster of flames. Its heat would melt the sun.

"EVE!" Beckett screamed as he leaped out of the Hummer. *Where the fuck is everybody?* "EVE!" Beckett ran for the building, only to be thrown back by an onslaught of fire.

When he picked himself up off his ass, he couldn't hear the roar of the flames anymore. Actually he couldn't hear anything but a muffled silence. His ears had quit working. He looked at the building, trying to find a way in, but there wasn't even a hint of the doorway, no trace of a window.

"EEEVE!!" He had to trust his mouth to do its job, even without proof it was working—or that anyone was around to hear him.

Beckett dropped to his knees in the parking lot. He knew he was too close to the fire. His clothes were so hot. His skin prickled with pain as he rose and geared up to join her. He had to find her, even if she was gone.

31

The Sunset has a Flavor

The sunset was glorious: orange and purple and red. But Blake's mind reeled. Standing in the sunlight, battling his glass skin, he tried to find the positive. The rays felt so beautiful on his face; Blake thought he could taste the colors. The red was his fear, the orange was hope, and the purple — the purple tasted of tomorrow. He just wasn't sure he knew what tomorrow would bring anymore.

Stupid piano. He wished he'd never gone back inside Livia's house. But maybe it was better he knew how she really felt. He slid the mask back on even though there was little sunshine left now. His mind refused to stop blaring the worst parts of what he'd heard over and over again. *"Dad, Blake and I have only known each other for a few weeks. It's a brand new thing. It might not even last."*

Blake wondered why Livia hadn't told him she studied psychology at her school in the city. But deep down, he knew. A glass-skinned, cardboard piano-lover had to be an amazing case study. A sure-fire way to make a name for yourself — or at the very least a professional challenge too tempting to resist. Had she been taking notes all along? *While I was counting smiles, was she proving her thesis?*

Blake knew he needed to calm down. He needed to think. Over his shoulder he noticed a small car following him too slowly. He hopped a fence and let his inner tramp take over. He picked through backyards and driveways with about as much concern for human boundaries as a squirrel would have.

Blake bit his tongue. *Of course she's not perfect. Of course she has ulterior motives. God, she was good at pretending.* The soulful gray eyes. The tender heart drawn on his back. He had to admit he would never have guessed. Stupid, trusting, loyal Blake.

Hasn't life taught me well enough? Love is not mine to find. I'm a fool. Damn it to hell.

As his thoughts raced, Blake picked up his pace. Without realizing where he'd been going, Blake soon stood at the top of the stairs to the train platform. He shook his head at his stubborn, still-believing feet. While his brain was numb with pain, they'd brought him back to where it all began, as if that could somehow make things better.

Psychology. How could she not tell me?

The only reason he could fathom was deception. It was such a small piece of information, until it remained unspoken. Then it became everything.

"It probably won't even last...He scared me once..."

Blake trotted down the steps and pulled off his mask. He'd have to return it to Mouse. He'd done fine without it before her. He just needed to go back to being what he was.

He stood in his shady spot, which was ironically the brightest place on the platform once the lights came on at night. Against his better judgment, he considered his possibilities. *I could be her guinea pig—let her try her best on me. She could strap me to a board in the sunlight in the center of town. At least maybe I could still kiss her. Maybe I could still touch the soft skin inside her elbow.*

Blake knew Livia had given him more than pain, more than a mask. She'd given him worth—such soaring worth, he'd been wealthy with it. Even now he still had a little to draw from. He had enough not to make himself an experiment for her.

He dug in his jacket pocket and pulled out his heart-shaped stone. When he'd found it after she kissed him that first time, he'd taken it as a sign. Even his woods knew he was in love and had given him a present. He'd used a knife at Beckett's place to scratch the B+L on its face.

Beckett had eyed him with suspicion as he worked. "A chick got you by the balls? Or is it a dude? You know I'm not a hater, baby."

Blake had told Beckett all about her and the kiss.

"Good for fucking you," Beckett said, pounding him on the back. "If I told you once, I told you a million times: you're a handsome motherfucker. I'm almost gay for you." Beckett pulled out a wad of cash. "Now, you go spoil that pussy."

Blake waved his hands, rejecting the money. "No, Beckett, I'm telling you, I really think she might like *me*. Just me—the way I am."

Blake rubbed his finger over the stone. Now it was testament to a broken dream. It was just a rock in the right shape, not a message from the universe. She *did* want him just the way he was: a diseased brain she could try to fix.

He set the rock down in his spot. He needed to give her something to tell her he knew. He knew it was over. Livia would find the rock when she came to the train station. She would know he'd been there, and that he was gone.

Maybe she'll be proud I could walk away. Maybe she'll know that's a good thing.

He turned from the spot as the train pulled loudly into the station. Distracted by his thoughts and the roar of the train, Blake barely noticed the dazzling brightness that appeared for a moment in the sky. A second and third flash and accompanying rumble got Blake moving. *Rain must be on the way.* He trotted up the steps. There was one more thing he had to do. It would cleanse him. He had a new purpose now.

A short jog later, he peeled back the fence to the woods past Firefly Park. A little ways down his familiar trail, he stopped at the tree with the hole in its trunk and dug out a coffee can that kept a few things safe for him. By the time he got to the clearing, the moon was high enough so he could see. *This is good. I can say goodbye.*

Livia had ruined this clearing for him. He could never again be here without picturing her hair fanned out around her. He'd never find peace here now. He'd always picture the love he'd seen in her eyes when she'd taken off his mask.

Thought, he corrected himself. Thought *I'd seen in her eyes.* Blake felt the lump of wool in his pocket. *This very mask.*

He would start with that. Blake pulled it out and clicked open the lighter he kept in the coffee can. The yarn took a while to catch and was mostly disappointing in its smoky smoldering.

He pulled out his piano. *No. It's all I have,* his mind screamed. *But she's in here. All the songs I wrote, all the hope I had. It's all in here,* he argued back.

He tried to make his heart hard as he smoothed it out on his knee. He held the very top corner and clicked the lighter on the bottom. The cardboard went much faster than the wool. An angry red line preceded the flame, as if warning his beloved cardboard of its eminent death. Blake pictured Livia's smile as the cardboard blackened and curled.

He tried to remember the feel of her hand when she'd shaken his. "*I'm Livia McHugh. It's nice to meet you.*"

Smoke poured from the cardboard as he remembered his response. "*Blake Hartt. It's a pleasure to make your acquaintance.*" He'd said his name, but what he'd been thinking was: *She touched me. I am someone. I count.*

Blake held the piano until the flames licked his fingers. Then he dropped the tiny, glowing piece, and it landed on top of the smoky pile of mask.

He felt no relief. He felt no closure. He knew then he would have to leave Poughkeepsie. He'd go very far away so he wouldn't be tempted to come back. He looked down at the ash that had been his piano and missed it. He missed it already.

His sadness slowly solidified into anger as he scraped piles of leaves together with his feet and lit them with the lighter. He kept going until the center of his clearing had a floor of flames.

He watched the yellow and gold with tears forming in his eyes. The flames had a taste. They tasted like Livia never really loving him at all.

32

TRUST NO ONE

Eve let the motorcycle have its head. She felt her tears drying into itchy, salty tracks on her cheeks. This was everything she'd dreaded. She blew through a red light without even looking for oncoming cars, desperate to outrun her pain.

She felt a wave of disgust. She'd reacted the way she'd trained herself to do — Find something and destroy it. Feel something else, so pain won't be the only thing inside — but blowing up the strip mall had not been gratifying. It hadn't even been worth the trouble. And now she should want to find him and kill him, which she could easily do. But she couldn't. Even if he'd used her and thrown her away. She sped by an empty parking lot. She couldn't end someone she loved, even if she hated him.

Through her anger, something in Eve's mind twitched. *An empty parking lot.* Where was she even headed? *An empty parking lot!*

Eve whipped the motorcycle around in an intersection. She only registered the swerving cars to avoid them. *Fucking Merkin.*

It all clicked together like a stack of Legos. Beckett would never have told Merkin to clear the lot before he fired her. Beckett didn't believe in crying wolf, especially about the cops. And he'd never send Merkin to fire her. He knew she'd be likely to kill the messenger. *I'm so stupid. Damn it.*

She'd let her worst fears cloud her vision. She hadn't seen Merkin's deception. Eve raced back to the strip mall, something guiding her to the fury she'd just left. She pulled in just in time to see Beckett blown backward by an explosion inside the blazing building.

Son of a bitch. The motorcycle clattered to the ground on its side, and Eve sprinted to him as he pulled himself up and screamed her name. He looked at the wall of fire tensed like a runner on the starting blocks.

He thinks I'm in there.

The heat stung Eve's skin and sirens wailed behind her as she reached Beckett and wrapped her hand around his throat, the most immediate means she could think of to stop him. He stiffened, then relaxed as she molded herself to his back and began pulling him away from the flames.

Irregular pops and explosions punctuated the ongoing blaze as the weapons inside the building discharged in the heat. But Beckett never flinched. She felt his throat vibrate as he sighed her name with relief. He tilted his head back until it rested on hers.

"Don't ever die in my head again. Please, never again," he told her, his voice raspy.

Eve continued to guide Beckett until they stepped backward over the firefighters' hose and the air began to cool. When she released him, Beckett spun to face her. He didn't smile until he met her eyes.

She pulled on his hand. "Come on, baby. We've got to get out of here."

Beckett dropped her hand and grabbed her face, his big thumbs tracing her cheekbones.

"IS EVERYONE OUT? DO YOU KNOW WHO DID THIS?" he shouted at a volume too loud even for the fire-ravaged parking lot.

Eve realized then he couldn't hear. She mouthed silently, "Everyone is out." Then she pointed to the discarded rocket-propelled grenade launcher in the parking lot, back at her own chest, and finally at the mall.

"YOU BLEW THIS SHIT UP?" Beckett looked puzzled, then smiled.

She nodded.

"EVE, I LOVE YOU. I LOVE THE HELL OUT OF YOU. YOU'RE ONE CRAZY BITCH!" Beckett would not be pulled from the spot.

With the mall fire blazing high in the sky behind him and the emergency vehicles' lights dancing across his face, he swept Eve into an I-just-got-off-the-boat-after-the-war-style dip kiss. Finally he set her on her feet and smacked her ass. He strolled over to the firemen and police officers.

"GENTLEMEN! THE BUILDING IS EMPTY. PLEASE STAY CLEAR AND LET IT BURN TO THE GROUND. THERE ARE DANGEROUS WEAPONS INSIDE." He nodded when they gave him thumbs up.

Beckett waved away a paramedic who gestured toward a waiting ambulance, and Eve picked up her scratched motorcycle. Beckett threw himself into the seat of his Hummer, and they tore out of the parking lot.

They were a few miles away when Eve pulled ahead, then signaled him to pull over. Beckett parked alongside her on the shoulder. He stomped over to the motorcycle and stood in front of her with a huge, winning smile. She started speaking immediately. "Merkin's a traitor. We have to find him—get everyone together. I don't know what he's up to. Can you hear me?"

"When your lips move, it makes me want to take my pants off right here." Beckett went in for a kiss. He spoke loudly, but he wasn't screaming anymore, which Eve took as a good sign.

Eve accepted the kiss and pulled his phone out of his pocket. She used the texting feature to type and then handed it to him:

Merkin told me u fired me. He cleared the lot. I blew up the mall because I believed him. He's up 2 something.

After a moment, Eve pulled his phone out of his hands as he began to shake and growl. She made him look at her.

"I'm sorry I believed him. I shouldn't have believed him. I don't believe him now." Eve spoke slowly and watched as Beckett waved away her apology. He rubbed his hands over his face, turning away.

He didn't hear his phone beep to announce an incoming text, so Eve clicked *open* and stared at the picture sent from Cole's phone for several seconds before *what* she was seeing hit her completely. The message wasn't from Cole.

When Beckett turned to her again, Eve's horror was illuminated in the twilight by the phone's screen. He pulled it out of her hands and looked for himself.

Silence.

Then the night echoed with Beckett's anguished wail. "NOT MY BROTHERS!"

Eve grabbed his angry face, using all her strength to force him close to her. Beckett's eyes had rolled back in his head. He was losing his mind.

"Look at me! *Can you hear me?*" Now Eve was the one yelling too loudly.

Beckett breathed quickly and through his teeth.

"We're here together. We'll get him back. I promise you," Eve said. "Merkin has no idea I'm with you. I've practiced killing for years, and tonight I'm going to use everything I've learned to save Cole. Do you believe me?"

Beckett still sounded like an angry bull, but he nodded.

"I will not let you lose your family. I won't let it happen to *you*." Eve's hands circled his big, tense neck.

He shook his head and let out a defeated breath. "I'm so sorry, Eve. I can't even…Well, now I guess I can imagine what I did to you—just a little."

Her words had hurt him, knocked him down. That's not what she'd intended. She would have to lay it out.

"Beckett, I'll save you from that fate because I love you. I love you." She let her hands slip to his chest.

His heart. His beautiful heart, surrounded by thorns, guns, and pain. Beckett kissed her again, and together they began to plot like two evil bastards. Beckett had Eve send Mouse a text to catch him up and get his eyes on Blake; she signed it so he'd know why the spelling was so perfect coming from Beckett's phone.

33

Hobosexual Healing

Chris could have strangled Dave — if he didn't need him. Dave texted every thirty freaking seconds with an update.

Hobo on road!

Hobo still on road!

Lost Hobo!

Found Hobo!! ☺

The smiley face made Chris want to punch Dave in the fucking taint.

Holy Crap! Explosions!

I'm ok! U ok?!

My balls r tingling!

Hobo still alive! Hobo headed to Firefly Park!

Chris put his truck in gear and started rolling. After this whole show went down tonight, he planned to build a life-size exclamation point and beat Dave to death with it.

Got my work buds!

Great. Dave's work buds were the fools that got off on throwing pennies at bums. He'd known them since high school. Losers. All of them. Chris honestly wondered if they could tell real life from gaming.

Hobo headed in woods!

Waiting for you, Robin Hood!

Dave seemed to be living out every nerdtastic dream he'd ever had. Would he be wearing a goddamn beanie and his mother's pantyhose like Little John?

Chris pulled into the parking lot and cut his lights. Immediately Dave bounced over with Wilson, Jamie, and...Dorkalooza. Chris couldn't remember that last asshole's name. He unlocked his truck box, pulled on his hunting jacket, and slid some tools into the pockets and holes. *Flashlight, check. Rope, check. Cell phone, check. Pliers, check.*

Dave nearly blew off Dorkalooza's head as he flashed his dad's Sig Mosquito .22.

Sweet Baby Jesus in a waffle cone! Leave it to Dave to come armed.

It was a nice little pistol with a ten-round magazine—simple enough for even Dave to fire. Chris took it out of his hands and double-checked the safety.

"Hey, fuck nugget!" Chris thumped Dave on the forehead with his middle finger. "We're not in a video game. This doesn't take batteries. You can't masturbate with a real fucking firearm."

Dave rubbed his forehead and looked at Chris with wounded eyes. "You're a shit. Who followed this bastard all over Poughkeepsie for you tonight?"

Chris knew he needed to keep the peace. "You're a solid-gold ass avenger, Dave. Which way did he go?"

Dave trotted ahead like Quasimodo getting ready to hump a giant bell. Chris tucked the gun in the back of his waistband.

"Right here!" Dave pulled the fence out of the way.

Chris said nothing. They didn't have a wild ass-pimple's chance in hell of finding this bastard in the woods. Chris had hunted long enough to know his way around a forest, but the hobo was a hobo. He'd have to send up a goddamn flare for them to locate him.

Trudging along the dirt path, Chris almost didn't believe his good luck when he saw the glow of fire hovering over the next hill. After a brief foray off the path, he realized it was an all-out bonfire. *Son of a bitch.* It couldn't be him.

Chris rolled his eyes as he listened to his highly prepared-for-nothing crew behind him. They kept trying new plays on the word *hobo* like a gang of fucking second graders.

"We're about to commit hobocide." Wilson's observation was met with girly cackles.

"It's hobo-smashing time," added Dorkalooza.

Dave snorted through his laughter and proclaimed, "I want some hobosexual healing," in a sing-song voice.

Everyone stopped to stare at him. Chris aimed his flashlight right at Dave's face.

"Dude. Too much," Wilson said and took a step away.

Dave blinked in the harsh spotlight. "What? Whatever. I'm excited. I even put a condom on!"

Dorkalooza shook his head in disbelief. "You put a love glove on your limp dick?"

Dave shrugged. "Who said it was limp?"

Chris rolled his eyes. "Your mom, asshole." He was headed into war with a gang of crotch-lobsters. "You bastards couldn't sneak up on a dead whore," he hissed. "Shut your traps and try to staple on some balls."

The butt-munchers quieted down and followed Chris like a group of baby ducks. When Chris finally stepped into the flaming meadow, the hobo stood right in front of the fire like he was roasting marshmallows on his dick.

Chris nodded as he wordlessly sent three of the assholes across to get him. They grabbed the hobo's arms. He didn't even flinch. It was like he knew they were coming. Chris felt so powerful. This was better than killing deer.

When Wilson, Dave, and Jamie turned the hobo around, Chris smiled at his forlorn face. *I only shoot the ones that don't run*, he reminded himself. This was totally justified. It was open season — the hobo had just given him permission.

Merkin stayed in the back of the mercenaries' cargo van and tried to look tough. The men surrounding him — with the exception of Craig sitting uncomfortably in the passenger seat — were as manly as they come. He opened his laptop and checked the locations of Beckett's crew via cell phone GPS. Eve was off grid. Probably ran over her phone with her motorcycle. She was too smart to let Beckett track her after she blew up the mall. Beckett was in the woods, and Mouse was, predictably, still at Jo-Ann Fabrics.

Merkin nodded and got to his knees when the hired gun came to tie him up and gag him. They needed to set the stage for the next part of the plan. Merkin put his hands behind his back and lay next to Cole's motionless form.

He closed his eyes as the man took his picture. Merkin wrote the text to Beckett himself after the mercenary released him:

Got 2 of ur men. Meet at Symbols Warehouse. Come alone.

The abandoned warehouse was a great spot for his assassins to entrench themselves. So much to kill one man. Maybe too much. But bringing big ol' Beckett to his knees would gain Merkin respect in so many places.

"You got the other guys in place?" Merkin made his voice a little deeper.

The driver just nodded. Merkin suspected a trace of annoyance. *Fuckers think they're the only professionals.*

"Tell them it's go time," Merkin said. "The mark they're following will be driving a flaming hearse. Find him and you find Blake Hartt."

Of course Beckett would send Mouse to protect his other brother. Merkin knew that as sure as the sky was blue. Beckett trusted Mouse implicitly. Merkin nodded smugly as the driver relayed this information to the others via his wireless headset.

Really, Blake wasn't needed. Merkin *could* get the job done with just Cole, but tonight would be legendary. Craig would witness it, and all these hired men would see that Merkin was deadly.

Cole moaned, and Merkin looked over. His face was pressed into the dirty, metal floor of the van. One of the hired guns prepared another hanky full of the chemical that had taken Cole's consciousness the first time around.

"No, I want him awake," Merkin said.

The hired gun recapped the canister of liquid.

"He's gonna puke." The man sat back as if Merkin's decision was a poor one.

"Take the gag off and let 'im puke then."

After Cole was done, he glared at Merkin. "Where is she? Where is she!" Cole threw up again. Speaking was asking too much of his ravaged body.

"Shut up, Cole. Don't make me drug your ass again." Merkin tried to ignore his burning stare.

"WHERE'S KYLE??" Cole screamed at a deafening level.

The mercenaries rolled their eyes and looked annoyed.

"Damn it. Just gag him again. Shut the fuck up, Cole. Do you want to die?"

Cole struggled to keep his mouth free. "Merkin, tell me!"

Merkin took a deep breath. "Cole, if you sit pretty for the man, I'll tell you all about Kyle."

Cole stopped struggling instantly and let the mercenary replace his gag. But the burning stare never wavered.

"Kyle was not even raped, Cole. Do you see how much respect I have? Do you see how nice I am? She's with more of my men. You do what I say, and I'll be true to my word. I won't kill her."

Merkin watched hate climb into Cole's eyes like a tiger. For the first time he doubted his decision to grab the priest instead of the homeless brother.

34

PATTERNS BEGIN

Patterns.

Patterns had set the tone of Mouse's day since early in his life.

Poughkeepsie's Jo-Ann Fabrics store was one of his most vivid memories of childhood. He could picture his grandmother picking her way through the towers of fabric. Mouse had loved to reach up and touch the ones with the patterns. The happy ones with colorful animals were always rough on his fingers. The white borders on the ends had been perplexing. *Why did the fun have to end?*

Inevitably, his grandmother would catch his small hands roving over some cloth. When she smiled her eyes would crinkle, and she'd quickly cover her teeth, which were far from perfect, with one hand as emotion filled her face.

"You want the puppies, Jimmy? I make you a great shirt with the puppies." His grandmother could carry the bolts effortlessly.

He loved when the women would smooth fabric over the impossibly wide table and decide just how much they needed to cover Jimmy now. He knew he was small for his age, but they always made a fuss over how big he was getting.

Mouse would stare at the silver ruler embedded in the white laminate as the correct amount of fabric was cordoned off and cut. His grandmother would then head for the yarn. The yarn aisle was Mouse's favorite. Each bundle seemed like a puzzle waiting to be solved.

"Meemaw, this green is really great, don't you think?" Mouse grabbed it by the white paper that kept the yarn from spilling out.

"It's perfect, Jimmy. Just like you." She put it in the cart on top of the puppy fabric.

Meemaw plucked vibrant colors from the wall of choices like ripe apples from a tree. Her grand total was always a little more than she expected, and she usually said exactly that with a chuckle as she dug for her wallet.

Then Jimmy and Meemaw would walk home, dragging her metal basket behind them. They didn't have a car, but Meemaw swore she didn't need one. She could walk everywhere she needed to go. When they got home, Meemaw always immediately organized her sewing pile and sorted her new yarn into her current collection.

"Too much yarn, Jimmy. Why you never stop me?"

Mouse knew this was a rhetorical question. He would never stop her from doing anything. Mouse loved his grandmother with all his heart. She was the only family he'd ever known. They had each other in this special little world they'd created, and that was fine by him. But Meemaw often brought his mother into the conversation. Her picture could be found in little frames all over the house.

"Your mother loves you very much," Meemaw would remind him. "She wishes she was here." She spoke with conviction, but her eyes were always sad.

Mouse knew his mother was in prison, and he eventually figured out it was for drug possession. She'd burned through her three state-mandated chances to be his mom before he was even old enough to remember her. She didn't have a possibility of parole until Mouse would be thirty-two years old.

"That last charge was a doozy, Jimmy. Your mother tried so hard, but the call of that stuff—it never stopped for her." Meemaw always called drugs "that stuff," but she was honest about everything else.

Letters from Mouse's mother were filled with talk of finding Jesus and the love of the Holy Ghost. For a while, Mouse thought jail was a big game of hide and seek where the winner got a bag of treats, like at Halloween. But eventually he figured that out too. His mother said Jesus was in her heart, and Jimmy figured they had to let you take your heart to jail, so Jesus could keep her company until he was thirty-two—unless the stuff called to her even then. Either way, Meemaw was his.

Patterns.

Meemaw loved patterns as much as Mouse. She liked to do her grocery shopping with coupons on Monday, her laundry on Tuesday, housecleaning on Wednesday, and shop at Jo-Ann Fabrics on Thursday.

Full-grown Mouse stood in the yarn aisle of the very same store, although today was Saturday. He picked a few colors out of the wall. He grabbed the green from his memories and decided to make a scarf. The store had been remodeled since his days with Meemaw, but he still saw her here, out of the corner of his eye. She was average in every way—her body soft and smooshable for hugs. Mouse missed her terribly. Some days the pain wound around his neck like a snake.

Meemaw and Mouse had had a quiet relationship. She'd look up from her knitting on a nice day and ask in a playful voice, "Jimmy, you want to go to swings? Yes?" Her thick Polish accent made her sound angry when she was far from it.

At the playground, Mouse sometimes wished one of the stylish moms with the big sunglasses would claim him as her own. But Meemaw sat in the shade, knitting away, always waiting. She'd call him over for a sip of water every once in a while, commenting on how hard he was playing. Mouse would unscrew the top and take a drink from the jam jar Meemaw saved for just this purpose.

Eventually, he dreaded the park. Once the other kids picked up on his high, squeaky voice that refused to sound any different no matter how hard he prayed to his mother's Jesus, nothing was fun anymore.

On the way back from the park, if it happened to be a Friday, Meemaw would take Mouse into the accountant's office to discuss her finances. Friday was for accounting. She insisted he be included in the decisions. "Is his money too. We do everything together."

So he watched and learned how his grandmother turned her measly Social Security check into enough money for a woman and child to live on.

The most soothing thing Mouse learned from Meemaw was knitting. She was a miracle-worker with yarn and needles. Colors that would never imagine being neighbors in the store found harmonious comfort together in Meemaw's knitted blankets. No ruffle was too complicated for her. Mouse had watched Meemaw slyly examine a pattern on someone else's hat in the grocery store, and the next day create it from scratch.

"Meemaw, can you teach me to knit?" The question that bubbled out of Mouse one rainy, drippy Thursday lifted his grandmother's eyebrows and made her blue eyes sparkle.

"Yes? Very well, Jimmy. Sit next to me." Meemaw patted the worn couch cushion.

That day Mouse learned the magic handshake of the creative. The slipknot and the gentle ladder of lovely that built on his grandmother's needle instantly made sense.

"You're a natural, Jimmy." She sounded prouder than a bird watching its fledgling take flight.

They formed the defining bond of their relationship that day. After that Meemaw would bring his current creations to Jo-Ann Fabrics and brag to all the employees. Mouse stood looking at the floor, blushing at their compliments and encouragement.

Patterns.

Meemaw was as reliable as clockwork. She dressed him each day in dime-store clothes, which they'd carefully counted out the money to buy. She walked Mouse to school every morning, and gave him a sack lunch, which was equally predictable. The sandwich was always some horribly smelly meat that his classmates complained about, like tuna or liverwurst, wrapped in wax paper. And the glass jar had followed him from the playground to the lunch table. His special treat was juice instead of water.

All the things that reminded Mouse of Meemaw made him different. And he learned that different wasn't good as quickly as he'd picked up knitting. Meemaw made it to every event at school, even ones that no other parent showed up for, but her metal basket filled with knitting squeaked into the school lobby like a loud, dying cat. Mouse hated not being proud of her.

Patterns.

Mouse soon learned the patterns of the bullies at his school. When the meaner children figured out that taunting him about his grandmother got a response, they grabbed onto his self-worth with their jaws and never let go. His teachers stepped in if they could, but they weren't always around.

When Billy made fun of his grandmother's teeth and her squeaky basket in the cafeteria, Mouse felt something snap.

He jumped up. "Meemaw is a wonderful person! She's all I have!"

Billy's immediate and perfect mimic of Mouse's outburst brought a roar of laughter from the lunch crowd. Mouse sat and hid behind his lunch bag, filled with shame. He couldn't eat a thing. When he brought home his uneaten meal—he wouldn't dare throw it out and waste it—his grandmother questioned him.

Mouse gave in to her concerned eyes and told her the whole story. Meemaw's eyebrows rose higher and higher as he spoke, and when he'd finished she released a torrent of angry Polish. She called the teacher, principal, and the custodian that evening.

"My grandson was tormented today! If happens again I will handle that *psia krew* myself." She was so angry she had to sit down. Mouse brought her water. She looked so pale and worn. He was worried.

"Jimmy, you are small now. I know that. But your heart, so big. Don't let them hurt your heart. You are big to me."

Mouse patted her back until she looked better. He never told her about the bullies again. Perhaps her calls put the adults at school on higher alert, but Billy and his crew were skilled at finding their moments. The worst, by far, was lunch. The cafeteria monitor had a habit of sneaking outside to have a smoke, and Billy had an incredible talent: he knew exactly how long it took to smoke a cigarette. He would devise tortures that lasted precisely that amount of time.

Most of the time Mouse said nothing as Billy spat in his milk or threw his sandwich in the garbage. Because when he did get a reaction, Billy got more creative. Then one day when Mouse spoke up, his life changed.

Billy stood in front of him as soon as the lunch monitor clicked the exit door guiltily behind her.

"Hey, squeaky ass, what stinky lunch do you have today?" Billy tore into Mouse's bag. Mouse felt revulsion crawling up his spine when he saw a thick slice of cake in Billy's grubby hand.

He hated his voice, but used it. "Put it down, Billy. That's not cool, man."

The cake was from Meemaw's birthday celebration the night before. Mouse had knitted her a shawl using her favorite colors and made the dessert.

Billy imitated him, his go-to tease.

Mouse made a fist, then unclenched it. Finally he smacked Billy in the chest.

"You smacking me? You smacking me?" Billy asked, incredulous. "That's it. Get him, guys. He's asking for it now." Billy's friends grabbed Mouse's arms, which were thin and lacking anything resembling muscle.

"Let's make him moon the cafeteria!" Billy smiled as Mouse made a grab for his pants.

Together, like a pack of dogs, they brought him down. All the hands began working at once. Mouse felt tears of shame roll down his cheeks.

"NO! NO!"

Billy laughed harder at his screams.

When the air hit his rump, Mouse's inside hurt so much. Everyone in the cafeteria would see him like this. The bullies stood up, mission accomplished, and pointed. Mouse yanked on his dime-store pants, but the buckle that hadn't helped to keep his pants on during the attack now sprang into action to prevent him from covering himself.

Mouse heard Billy's voice again as he worked at his belt. "Get back to your seats," Billy shouted. "The monitor should be back by now."

Mouse heard footsteps and squeezed his eyes shut, fearing another assault. When he felt a cover over his exposed rear, the sense of relief was so amazing, he opened his eyes. It was a denim jacket. With this cover in place, Mouse hastily got his pants back in order. Instead of a teacher, as he'd expected, the new kid, Beckett Taylor, had bestowed dignity upon him.

Mouse had heard Beckett was bad news, but he'd never been so grateful to anyone in his life.

"Dude, what's your name?" Beckett held out a hand so Mouse could stand up.

"Jimmy."

"I was in the can or I would have stopped this crazy shit sooner. Which fool started it?" Beckett followed Mouse's pointing finger.

Beckett walked up behind Billy just as the cafeteria monitor snuck back into the room.

Billy gave Beckett a smug smile over his shoulder. "You better sit down, new kid. You'll get in trouble for standing up during lunch."

Beckett smiled back. "Hey, fucker, some trouble's worth it."

Mouse's mouth dropped open. Never in his eleven years on this planet had he heard a kid use that word.

Beckett grabbed Billy by the jaw. "If you ever touch Jimmy again, I'll kill you. It's that simple."

Billy tried to pull away from Beckett.

The lunch monitor shouted "Hey, *hey!*" in the loudest voice anyone had ever heard her use.

Beckett began punching Billy in the face. The violence was quick and decisive. Billy couldn't get up from his chair, and blood spurted from his nose, but that didn't stop Beckett.

When Billy's head slipped backward, Beckett changed his grip, grabbing a fistful of Billy's hair, and continued on. Flecks of Billy's blood splattered all over Beckett's face. The cafeteria monitor called for assistance on her walkie-talkie and grabbed Beckett's arm to stop the pummeling. Beckett let himself be pulled from the now-unconscious bully.

He smiled at Billy's friends. "I got more where that came from. Never do that shit again." He found Mouse's eyes. "Jimmy, you hold your head high."

That moment changed Mouse.

Beckett never came back to school, and Mouse wondered if his mother's Jesus had sent him like a guardian angel. By listening to the hushed conversation of teachers, Mouse learned that Beckett had gone to juvie, but Billy and his cronies gave Mouse a wide berth for years afterward. Their memories were better than an elephant's when it came to that pain, and Beckett's protection covered Mouse long after he wasn't physically present to provide it.

Once he made it to high school, Mouse's tall genes kicked in, and he grew to look down on most kids his age. Even though his voice kept its squeakiness, he never forgot to hold his head high. Beckett had paid dearly to defend him, so he made it count.

He occasionally heard Beckett's name tossed around, and he knew his savior's reputation hadn't changed a whit. Stories of his drug running and vicious ways became legend in the school hallways.

When he was seventeen, Mouse's sweet Meemaw succumbed to congestive heart failure. For weeks after her passing, he sat in her house, drenched in heartbreak. He'd known she was old, but she seemed timeless. Soon creditors called looking for money. Mouse grabbed his grandmother's knitting bag and slung it over his shoulder. He walked the streets and asked about Beckett. Every person he passed got grilled. His persistence paid off and Mouse was finally pointed in the direction of a convenience store.

Beckett held court in a booth at the back, and his disciples were decidedly shady characters. His loud voice and filthy mouth echoed off the walls, but Mouse smiled when he saw his defender all grown up. He looked just the same, except bigger and full of muscles.

Mouse held his head high and cleared his throat. "Sir, I would like to work for you."

One of the dirt bags laughed and mimicked Mouse's high voice. "Beckett, you're stupider than I thought if you hire this bastard."

Mouse backhanded the dirt bag in a move eerily reminiscent of the one that had freed him from his shame so many years ago. He grabbed the asshole by the throat. "Don't make that mistake again, fuckbag."

Beckett lifted an eyebrow at the man in Mouse's grasp. "Last time you'll make fun of his voice, huh?"

Mouse shook his head and locked eyes with Beckett. "He can make fun of my voice all he wants, but if he ever calls you stupid again, I'll eat his brains for breakfast."

Beckett nodded. Mouse nodded back. The moment held a pact only those two men would recognize. Without a word, Mouse became Beckett's bodyguard.

Mouse got his high school diploma and began helping Beckett with his finances. He tried not to think about his Grandma's opinion of whores and drugs. He could only believe in the pattern he'd learned from Beckett—a pattern of respect and kindness.

Mouse learned quickly about the three brothers, and he remembered clearly the state his boss had been in when they buried the body of his last foster father. Mouse would be lying if he said he hadn't hoped Beckett would consider him a brother too. So many times he'd looked on as Beckett wrapped his wrist around Cole's or Blake's arm and wished he had a tattoo as well. But he resigned himself to being a help to Beckett, keeping him alive and out of jail.

To celebrate five years of protecting his defender, Mouse had made a discreet visit to Chaos. As he laid his head on the dirty bunk in Chaos's shed, he'd made a silent wish that someday he could show Beckett his tattoo.

An employee disrupted Mouse's reverie. "Can I help you?"

Jo-Ann Fabrics appeared again around him.

"Thanks, no. I'm all good." Mouse slung his grandmother's treasured knitting sack over his shoulder.

The vibrating phone alerted him to a text from the boss.

Merkin's a traitor, kidnapped Cole. Find Blake, keep him safe.
Trust no 1. -Eve

Mouse dropped his merchandise and swiftly left the store. He hopped in his new hearse and had his laptop open before he'd closed the driver's door. He pulled up the GPS tracker he and Merkin had installed on everyone's phones.

Eve — or at least her phone — was off-grid. Merkin was speeding along Route 9, and Beckett was headed south on Franklin Road. He raged at Merkin's deception. Mouse had never been totally thrilled about Merkin. There was something off, something about his demeanor that reminded Mouse of Billy from the good ol' days of getting the crap tortured out of him every day. Merkin would die a painful death if Mouse got to him first.

35

Aпd ᛗᴇ

Livia held the door handle with one hand and braced the other on the dashboard. Her father was usually a sensible driver, but now Livia discovered his well-honed high-speed skills. In her near-panic over Kyle's unknown condition she kept forgetting to breathe.

When the police radio crackled to life, John listened for a moment, then translated the cop speak for Livia. "They're at a fire and saying there's ammo in a building—that mall where Beckett Taylor conducts his...*business.*"

John gave Livia a withering look as he bottomed out the cruiser in the drainage ditch at the entrance to the hospital. When he pulled up to the ER, Livia was out before the car came to a stop. She headed straight for the closest check-in window.

John, on the other hand, busted right on through the swinging doors. "Kyle! Kyle McHugh!" he yelled.

Livia hesitated only a moment before she followed her father. He was armed, after all. He went from one curtain to another, sliding them aside with a noisy swoosh. He would look at the patient and move on, not bothering to put the curtains and their flimsy privacy back in place.

A pretty, brown-haired nurse stepped in front of the rampaging John. "Officer McHugh, Kyle's in a room, not behind a curtain. Please come with me." She kept talking as they moved down the hall. "I'm Nurse Susan Weiss. I spoke to you on the phone. Kyle's doing fine. She arrived unconscious, and we're monitoring her. We ran a tox screen to see why she's unconscious, and she just got back from an MRI to double check for any head injuries. Her vitals are great."

John stared at the nurse like he could burn all his worries into her face.

"She's still unconscious, but the doctor thinks she'll be coming out of it soon," she finished as they arrived.

She opened the heavy hospital-room door and pulled back the curtain. Kyle seemed so small in the bed. An IV stand and a heart monitor that beeped with assuring regularity stood at her bedside, along with a doctor.

"Dr. Hartt, this is Officer McHugh and Livia, his daughter." She touched John's arm. "Dr. Hartt's the best we have. Kyle's in amazing hands." Susan then busied herself with Kyle's IV.

John stared at his daughter and choked back a sob. Livia felt tears hit her eyes at the sound of her father's emotion. They both moved to Kyle's bedside. John held her elbow, carefully avoiding the IV needle taped to her hand.

Livia smoothed back her sister's hair and murmured, "Hey, I'm here."

Kyle had a red rash around her nose and mouth that had been dressed with salve.

"Yes, I'm Dr. Ted Hartt. Kyle's under the influence of some form of an inhaled anesthetic," the doctor began. "Under different circumstances I might think she'd overdosed, but the paramedics on the scene felt she'd been attacked. There were signs of a serious struggle at the church."

John looked confused, but Livia could feel her anger brewing. *Cole did this to her?*

"The people who live in the building next door witnessed a group of men leaving the church. A woman named…" Dr. Hartt consulted a sheet of paper fastened to his clipboard. "Bea Florentine had an aide wheel her to the church and found your daughter. She said their multiple calls to police were not taken seriously."

Bea. Sweet Bea was so brave to enter the church.

Another nurse popped in and handed Dr. Hartt an MRI film and a folder. He placed the MRI results on a light-up display.

"The MRI is clean," he said after a moment. He opened the folder. "Looks like she was exposed to a chloroform-based chemical."

"Cole. Cole. COLE!" Kyle's eyes snapped open. They searched the room and seemed to register none of it. Finally, she found Livia next to her and delivered her desperate message. "Cole! They kidnapped Cole. Cole!"

"Okay, it's okay," Livia said, her own panic rising. "I'll find him."

John began grilling the doctor about the paramedics involved. Now that his daughters were safe, he seemed to shift into policeman mode. He wanted to know who did this to Kyle and exactly what had happened.

Livia stood back as her sister began to vomit. The nurse closest to John grabbed a bedpan with the reflexes of a pro basketball player. She had it under Kyle's mouth before she could do any damage to the blankets.

Livia backed up as Kyle tried again to yell something about Cole. She clawed frantically and tried to pull out her IV. Dr. Hartt gave terse instructions for a sedative, which Nurse Susan delivered. Kyle fell asleep again, her mouth open in the middle of saying Cole's name.

Livia put her hand on Susan's arm while she still stood close. "Ms. Weiss, was Kyle okay *everywhere* else?"

Susan nodded quickly. "She showed no sexual trauma." The nurse patted Livia's arm. "And please call me Susan."

Livia bit her lip and continued murmuring to Susan, ignoring the bustling men in the room. "Tell me what effect this chloroform is having on my sister, please."

Susan looked at Livia with kind eyes. "Kyle's going to be fine. The vomiting is to be expected. She'll have a headache, but assuming she has no allergic reactions or underlying problems, I'd imagine she'll go home within a day or so." Susan looked back at the patient.

Livia felt relief wash over her. Kyle would be fine, if she'd just stay put. But Cole, wherever he was, was in serious trouble. Livia had to tell Beckett. *Blake. Oh God.* Her pocket began ringing.

"Please take that outside," Susan said.

Livia walked obediently down the hall, but when she pulled out her phone there was no call—just a text from a number she didn't recognize:

> *Livia, this is Mouse. Where r you? Is Blake with u?*
> *U stole a mask from me (Just so u know it's really me)*

Livia texted back quickly:

> *I was going to meet him @ train station. But I'm @ hospital with Dad and Kyle. She said Cole was kidnapped. She is ok.*

Mouse's response was alarming:

> *Cole was taken. Beckett knows. We have traitors in the group.*
> *Stay put. Tell ur father 2 keep u next 2 him. I'll find Blake.*

Livia put a hand over her mouth and leaned against the wall. All hell was breaking loose, and Blake was out in the open, hurt. It was all her fault. From Kyle's room she heard her father trying again to get a detailed description of what his daughter had been through. Livia took comfort in the fact that the doctor's last name was Hartt. *Is that common?*

She'd just have to wait for Mouse to find Blake. Would he even be at the train station? Livia felt a sudden chill. *I wouldn't be there if the situation was reversed.*

Livia considered explaining what was going on to her father, but she knew he would handcuff her to Kyle's bed and stand with his gun pointed at the door, frisking anyone that walked through it. She couldn't add any more stress to his night — not if she could quickly solve this problem on her own.

When the idea hit her, she felt a certain kinship with Beckett. *Sometimes you gotta do what you gotta do.*

Livia returned to Kyle's room long enough to lift her father's keys from the nightstand. After surveying the bustling activity, she knew she could slip out unnoticed. She needed to get to Blake. Quickly. Safely. She blew a kiss in her sleeping sister's direction.

Livia ran down the hall and out of the ER. The police cruiser was still just where they'd left it, lights blazing. At least her dad had turned off the motor and locked the doors. Livia hopped in and left the lights on as she accelerated out of the parking lot.

She drove to the train station. This would be hard to explain later, but right now it was perfect. She tore into the parking lot and stopped right in front of the stairs. Livia was taking them three at a time before she realized she was out of the car.

Blake wasn't there. She tried not to feel hopeless as she stared at his empty spot. She knew for sure he'd heard what she said to her father. She felt a crack in the place where she kept him in her heart. She walked over to his favorite spot, as if somehow he might materialize, and noticed a familiar stone. She stubbed her fingers as she grabbed it from the cement. It was the rock from Blake's pocket. *B+L*

She put it to her lips and tried to imagine what finding it here meant. Had he left it in anger? Had he been kidnapped like Cole and left it as some sort of sign she was supposed to understand?

She turned to trudge back up the steps. She might as well wait for Mouse and tell him what she'd found. Her cell phone made an ominous beep. Low battery. *Damn it!*

Livia looked to the sky in anguish and saw a glow in the distance, just past Firefly Park. She began to run. When she reached the car she turned off the cruiser's emergency lights. There was definitely a hazy orange hovering in the trees. *In the woods.* It hit her like a punch in the teeth. *Our spot in the woods. His clearing is on fire.*

Livia jumped back in the police car. She punched the buttons of her phone, only to hear the jingle of it shutting down. She picked up the police radio instead.

"Hello? This is Livia McHugh. I need police assistance at Firefly Park!" She listened as the dispatchers' voices overlapped each other. They seemed to completely disregard her in their buzz over the recent explosions.

Livia looked around, surveying her options, and felt like throwing up when she saw Chris's Beast parked in the lot with stupid Dave's crappy little black car next to it.

Livia drove the cruiser right up on the grass and tried one last time to make contact with the rest of the world. "Send cops to Firefly Park," she ordered. "There's been another explosion." *Maybe...but I definitely need help out here!*

The idea of walking into the dark woods was not appealing. She looked in the car to see if her dad had anything worth bringing along. Peeking out from under the driver's seat was Kyle's favorite weapon. A Mag light! She dragged it out and hefted its comforting weight in her hands. *A Chris-basher.*

She felt a trickle of courage like an IV straight from Kyle. Livia ran for the woods, ducked under the fence, and turned the flashlight on the underbrush. She moved quickly, trying not to speculate about what she might find at the clearing.

Deeper into the woods, the inky black threatened to engulf her tiny beam of light. But everything was so clear in its path. Within that beam, she and Blake had danced in the club, twirling in the corner. She had felt his white shirt under her fingers. She had kissed the hollow of his neck. He had touched her so gently, and when his eyes sparked with a naughty idea, he'd tightened his hold on her. *Blake.*

She heard the crackling of the fire, and its ominous glow appeared over the next slope to compete with her beam. She set herself on a direct course. What the hell could Chris be up to? *All I have is this flashlight. And me.*

She heard the shouts before she saw the men. She heard the punches before she saw the fists. Livia entered the clearing to find Chris and Dave taking turns punching Blake while two others held his arms. Blake spotted her and returned her gaze with indifferent eyes. Another punch from Chris broke their stare.

At that moment, Livia discovered a volcano inside of her. Her mind exploded, and she flung her body between Blake and his attackers.

"You will stop. *Now.*" If she could have killed with words, four bodies would be lying in the clearing.

She felt Blake behind her, just where he'd been the first day they'd spoken. She wanted to tear out her heart and hand it to him, so he'd know she hadn't meant to hurt him. But first she had to get them out of danger.

36

PRAYER OF A DEVIL

The roadside plotting continued, but Beckett and Eve had taken seats inside the Hummer for both comfort and cover. Beckett's phone beeped and Eve read the message from Mouse, holding the phone so Beckett could see it too:

Livia and Kyle r @ hospital. Both r fine. Heading 2 train station 2 look 4 Blake.

Beckett nodded. "Tell him to watch his ass."

Eve closed the phone almost the same instant he was done talking.

"Damn, girl, you type so shitastically fast. You should be a fucking secretary or something." Beckett still talked too loud, like he was at a rock concert only he could hear.

The phone beeped again as Eve rolled her eyes. "Mouse is pretty fast too," she commented, flipping open the phone again. But instead of a text from Mouse, she found another horrific picture of Cole. Still bound, he now lay in a heap with Merkin, who was lumped next to him. Beckett pounded the steering wheel, and the night filled with sporadic honks. Eve read the message accompanying the picture.

"They want you to come to the warehouse," she told Beckett, but turned to find he was gone.

Beckett was out of the Hummer and cursing at the top of his lungs. "Motherfucking, ass-crunching, donkey-slutting cocksucker!" He prowled around and seethed.

Eve crawled onto the hood of the Hummer and timed a jump onto his back. Beckett kept going like he didn't notice.

"Ball-sniffing, pussy snot-fuckers. Mother of fuck!" He ran his hands through his hair, almost poking Eve in the eye.

As if the horror hit him from above and pressed down, he collapsed on his knees and beat the ground. Eve slid off his back and crouched in front of him.

Beckett registered her presence by venting. "Safe! All I wanted to do was keep them safe. How do you protect your brothers at eight-fucking-*teen?* How do you make enough money, get enough respect to do that? I wasn't smart, Eve. I'm a big, dumb fucking bastard. I couldn't even get a job as a bagger at the A&P. I wanted to make their lives worth living. That's what they'd done for me—made my life worth living. They're my family. I can't…I just can't." Beckett pounded his chest.

Eve didn't touch him. She didn't reassure him. Now was not the moment.

"They would've been better off without me," he continued. "Blake would still be homeless, but Cole made his own damn way. But I wanted in. I wanted to belong. I was too fucking selfish to walk away. I should have walked away. But I didn't and now—" Beckett choked on a deep, angry sob. "Now, they're paying for it. All my stupid decisions. They'll die tonight. They'll both die, and I can't stop it. I can't plug it with money. I can't bring them back from the dead, even if I act tough or kill more people."

Beckett looked at Eve, his eyes brimming with hopelessness and panic. She grabbed a handful of his balls through his cammo pants. She squeezed until his eyebrows lifted.

"Are you done twisting your nipples and crying like a pigtail-wearing girl?" she asked in her loudest voice. "I can't work with this shit. You're no good to me right now. You need to stand up, tuck your junk back into your pants, and be a hardcore killer right now. The sobbing, self-hating bullshit will not get those boys out alive. We're wasting time, and frankly we don't have it to waste. Are you on board? 'Cause otherwise I'm leaving now to go get your brothers." Eve's eyes flared, and her gaze was constant.

Beckett ran a hand over his face and managed a smile. "All right. Fuck-ing *all right*. Let's make a plan. You can keep your hands on my nugget sack, though. I find it comforting."

Eve leaned forward and gave his lips a quick kiss. She stopped being his nut warmer and returned to the phone. Together they looked at the poorly lit picture. There was at least one leg in the frame that didn't belong to Cole or fucking Merkin. Add that to the dude taking the picture, and you had at least three assholes against them.

Beckett reached for the phone. "You know that tampon-chomper is tracking this."

Before he could crush the device, Eve shook her head. "No, the minute you smash this, Merkin will know we're on to him. I killed mine because he just thinks I'm hiding from you. I'll get there and scope it out before you come on to their radar."

They discussed the layout of the warehouse and snooped through the weapons they had with them—not enough to take out an army, but enough to singe the ball hairs off a nice group of people. They hashed out a plan that was a little unlikely, very determined, and mostly crazy and headed for the warehouse.

"Save Cole," Beckett told her as he straddled the motorcycle. "I don't intend to put my life at a premium, so no matter what happens, just get him out."

Eve got in the Hummer and raised a quick hand as they separated to take different paths to the same destination. She tried to ignore the dread in the pit of her stomach. She set her mind on the positive. She wanted Cole *and* Beckett breathing when this confrontation was over. She gently tweaked the plan she and Beckett had developed as she drove. She knew in her heart he'd roll with the punches when she changed shit up.

She parked the Hummer a good distance from the destination. She grabbed her guns, checked her knives, and tucked an envelope of cash into her jacket. Eve had no idea what type of weapons she might need tonight, but she wasn't opposed to monetary ones. Eve walked half a mile or so, then climbed a tree for a view of the meeting spot. The trap did not actually seem to be in the warehouse. The activity currently centered on a long expanse of asphalt between the warehouse and various outbuildings. Whoever they were, the men were well-placed and well-prepared. The closest assassin to Eve's tree was outfitted with a Kevlar vest and bulletproof helmet.

These guys were the real deal. And Beckett's plan was to walk unarmed into the middle of it all and talk. Then Eve was to provide cover for him while he made a play for Cole. Beckett wanted only to get his brother on the motorcycle and out of Dodge. He'd refused to discuss his own options, and Eve didn't see a whole lot of opportunity for Beckett to get out alive—no matter how well she picked off the enemy. Beckett was ready to martyr himself for brotherhood and past mistakes.

Eve waited until the sentry walked under her branch. She pulled a knife from her hair and dropped from the tree. She let her knees bend to quiet the impact, but he still turned toward the sound. Eve stayed in her squat for another split second, then lunged up and stabbed the man through the bottom of his jaw, nailing his tongue to the roof of his mouth. No scream.

She cracked his thick forearm on her thigh, using his own strength against him. His gun fell from his hand.

She pulled her knife out of his jaw and inserted it in his temple, just inside his protective helmet. He went down instantly. Death was quick. Eve stepped back swiftly to avoid his limp body. She retrieved her knife, and a quick inspection of his body yielded a two-way transmission earpiece tuned to the enemy's channel. Her frisk also turned up two handguns, which she tucked into the back of her pants.

Her earpiece clicked to life. *"All men in position. Target approaching. Alpha One ready up top?"*

She scanned the roof to find Alpha One lying on his belly behind a bi-pod, which steadied his weapon.

Shit. Eve set a ridiculously brisk pace and slunk her way to the building in question. She kicked off her boots so they wouldn't make noise and made the leap onto the roof-access ladder. She felt it creak under her weight. *That's not good.*

Eve climbed a few more rungs, and her earpiece chirped again. *"Target arriving on motorcycle. Any moment now—look alive."*

Eve looked up to gauge how far she had to go—about fifteen steps. She felt her knife slip out of her hair as she tilted her head, and a quick second later she heard the metallic clatter as it struck the ground. *Damn it.* Eve knew she had next to no time. She ripped her top roughly off her body. With her breasts exposed, she pulled herself up the remainder of the ladder in a hurry.

The dude had to get up off his stomach to come see what's up. I just need to get my hands free.

Alpha One came to the top of the ladder just as Eve made the last step. He wore a Kevlar vest, but no helmet. Eve knew then how he would die. She smiled her biggest come-hither grin as she climbed over the edge of the rooftop, and Alpha One's mouth fell open. Her glorious rack had struck him numb from the penis up. She rolled her shoulders to make her boobs bounce, mesmerizing him like a cobra.

He missed the motion of her hand as it found the knife latched to her belt. She whipped it at him and ducked to avoid a counterstrike. It hit him in the voice box. Eve ran behind him and grabbed his jaw and the top of his head. He seemed to know the maneuver and tried to swat at her, but he could only use one hand. His other was useless, hovering over the small knife protruding from his throat. Eve gave his neck just enough torque to snap it from his spine. He fell in a lump at her feet.

Her earpiece was alive in her ear. *"Alpha One, signal if you're ready. Alpha One?"*

Eve took a diving belly flop in the direction of the fallen bi-pod and gun. She felt little bits of gravel from the flat rooftop embed themselves in her chest. She took a wild guess and held up one fist, ducking her blond head under the lip of the building.

"Alpha One is in ready position."

Eve propped up the firearm and used the gun's scope to get the lay of the land. Cole and Merkin stood side by side between the warehouse and another building, their hands bound with rope and still gagged. Merkin seemed to be sending frantic messages with his eyes to the men around him, who included a dude in a business suit and two more attackers. Eve swung the scope to find Beckett tearing in on her bike.

Be safe, Beckett. And forgive me.

Beckett roared the motorcycle up to the meeting point. He'd be damned if his choices were going to make Cole road kill. Beckett cut the motor and stepped off the bike with a huge smile on his face. These bastards would never know he was a wreck inside.

He looked at the hostage and the fake fucking hostage, and it took a big-ass load of restraint to resist popping Merkin's eyes right out of their sockets.

"You guys all right?" Beckett refused to acknowledge the armed men or the shitbag in the monkey suit.

Merkin nodded. Cole just stared at Beckett, but there was no hate in his eyes. With that tiny kindness, Beckett cursed his own evil being.

"So which of you cum cowboys called this little meeting? Whose dick is so infinitesimally small that he had to gather a huge posse to put one bullet in my brain?" Beckett rocked back and forth on the balls of his feet.

He'd thrown down the gauntlet, and due to his wording no one really wanted to pick it up.

Finally, Craig cleared his throat and spoke. "I brought you here, Mr. Taylor. We have business dealings."

Beckett landed his jovial smile on the speaker. "And you are?"

"Craig Ledert. I own the property around your building. You've been thwarting my efforts to develop my real estate." Craig straightened his back like there was a rod in his ass.

"Back the truck the fuck up," Beckett said, shaking his head. "You're, like, a real estate agent? You wimpy-ass ball nibbler. Seriously? You kidnap people? Did you ever think of taking out an ad? This is the crappiest way to build a business I've ever seen. Then again, if you're ignorant enough to pay money for a roach-infested nightmare in my part of town, you might also think you stand a chance in hell of living through this night." Beckett had inched closer to Cole during his tirade.

He'd left Eve's motorcycle angled toward the road. As soon as Cole was free, he could fire it up and get the hell out of here. His brother *had* to leave.

The men tensed and seemed to wait for a signal. Craig looked at Beckett and swallowed.

"You can say I'm idiotic, but me and your man here will improve the community for the better." Craig motioned to Merkin, who miraculously freed himself from his loose bindings.

Beckett was about to tear into Craig again when a dull pop sounded and a red dot appeared in the center of the man's forehead. Another pop and Merkin's forehead had a matching dot. They hit the ground like collapsing dominoes in perfect synchronicity.

Beckett wasted no time in dragging his brother to him and pulling a knife from his waistband. He slashed at Cole's ropes. "Take the bike and go!" he yelled.

Eve was jacking shit up, changing the plans. The remaining men seemed to be listening to their earpieces with their guns trained on the two brothers.

"Go!" Beckett didn't care why the men were slow to kill. He wanted his brother gone.

Cole ripped the tape off his mouth and spit out a wad of gauze. "I'm not leaving you here. I'm not." His voice was raspy and angry.

"Kyle's okay," Beckett countered.

He fully expected a bullet to find his head at any moment, and he wanted his brother to know his lady was safe. At least he could give him that. The men lowered their weapons a fraction and gave Beckett a thumbs up. *What the fuck?*

"Is what she's saying true?" asked the taller of the two.

"Absolutely. You have my word," Beckett said seriously. *About what, I have not a twat's clue.*

Eve walked out from around the warehouse with Beckett's envelope from the bank. She had her leather jacket buttoned up and a high-powered sniper rifle slung over her shoulder. She gave each man a wad of cash.

"Like I already arranged with your pal—" Eve tapped her earpiece as proof of the dead man's compliance "—if you don't kill us now, we'll use you in the future. Beckett keeps his employees well-paid."

They nodded and started packing up their gear.

Fucking genius. Pay the paid men. Of course.

The other rooftop sniper stood and collapsed his gun support.

Beckett sidled up to Eve. "Hey, gorgeous. This wasn't the plan."

Eve ignored him and spoke to the wirelessly listening mercenaries. "Yup, come on down and you'll get your share."

Eve turned to the brothers and gathered them in an uncharacteristic hug. Then she slid a handgun to Beckett and passed another to Cole. She covered the speaker on the wire and murmured in their ears. "This is all going to hit the fan when they find out I killed the other two in their group. Be ready."

The three turned around and made a triangle, shoulders touching, as they faced the mercenaries and waited. When the remaining men failed to make contact with Alphas One and Four, they suddenly scrambled for their guns.

Eve put her hand on her earpiece and spoke over her shoulder. "I'll get the roof. NOW!"

The remaining mercenaries turned their guns on the three, but the triangle of family was faster and ready. Cole's bullet hit the taller mercenary in the head. Eve's ludicrous rifle blew out the rooftop man's vulnerable neck as he tried to rearm himself. He fell off the building in spectacular fashion like a stunt man in an action movie. Only there was no cushion to prevent the crunching noise his body made on the pavement. Beckett riddled the shorter one with a pistol full of bullets. Start to finish, this crazy mercenary ambush had lasted less than thirty minutes.

"There were eight," Cole said in the silence of the stilled guns. "They sent three to follow Mouse so they could grab Blake. How many dead, Eve?"

"Five here." Eve knelt by the nearest dead man to ransack his pockets.

Beckett turned to his brother. "Cole, take the bike and go to Kyle in the hospital. You need to be with her. Keep an eye on Livia too."

Cole held his arm out. "I want to help you make sure Blake's okay."

Beckett wrapped his arm around the one Cole offered him. "Bro, go to Kyle. Stay out of this next fight. I won't be able to deal with you behind me and Blake in front of me. You can't ask me to decide which one of you to defend first. Please, Cole. Give me peace of mind."

Now sitting on the ground, Eve scrolled through a complicated-looking communication device.

Cole leaned in for a back-pounding and murmured in Beckett's ear. "Blake and I need you alive too. Don't forget that."

Beckett inclined his head toward the motorcycle. Cole lifted it and revved the motor to life. He stuck the handgun Eve had passed him into his waistband.

"I'll pray for you." Cole said. Then he set the motorcycle in the direction of the hospital.

Beckett watched him leave. At least one was safe now. Cole had been his biggest concern—kidnapped, for Christ's sake. But now Blake and Mouse moved to the forefront. He wanted three miracles tonight. It was the prayer of a devil. How dare he even ask? But Beckett had no shame. The thought of Blake walking around with a trail of trained killers behind him stopped his heart. He had to give Mouse some backup. Eve was mumbling. He turned to listen.

"According to their last communication, they found Mouse and they're tracking the hearse." Eve looked at Beckett's phone. "Mouse's last text said he's almost to the train station."

"Text Mouse and tell him how many guys to look out for." Beckett stomped over to try to make sense of the gadget in Eve's hands.

"I did. I'm waiting for a reply. Let's roll out." Beckett and Eve quick-marched the distance out to the Hummer, and the engine rumbled to life in the stillness of the night.

As he drove, Beckett's eyes found the beautiful, fierce soul next to him. She bit her lip and watched his face like it was a TV.

Beckett curled his lip into a sneer. *Thank the fuck outta you,* he told her silently.

Eve's eyebrow rose in return. *You're welcome.*

"Baby, I want to take you far from here. I'm going to take you where the water's as blue as your fucking eyes." Beckett leaned in for a tender kiss, with one eye on the road. "I'm going to take you there as soon as this is over."

Eve grabbed the roll bar as Beckett accelerated like a mad man. A lot had to go wrong for this evening to turn out right.

37

PATTERNS END

Mouse had been through a bunch of shit with Beckett, but tonight felt all wrong. This was different. Their control had finally slipped.

As he drove like a maniac toward the train station, Mouse tried to plan a strategy. As soon as he had Blake, he'd take him to the outskirts of town. Mouse desperately wanted to be at Beckett's side during this uncertainty, but he'd never stray from a command. At least Beckett had Eve. Mouse adored Eve. If he could admit it to himself, he had a bit of a crush on her. But he never would—that would feel traitorous. He would *never* be that. *Fucking Merkin.*

He approached the train station parking lot just as a police car came blazing in with its lights on. Mouse changed his path and pulled alongside the woods near the platform. The cops grabbing Blake right now might be the best thing. Maybe Livia's dad had sent a cruiser.

Mouse tiptoed to a place where he could see the platform. The police lights pierced the night and made it hard to focus on the form running up the stairs. *Is that Livia?* There was clearly no Blake here, and the person who now definitely seemed to be Livia reached the cruiser and killed the lights for a moment. Mouse stepped out from the cover of the trees and jogged toward her. *What the hell is she doing here? Did she steal her dad's car?*

He was almost to the steps when he started shouting. "Livia! Wait, Livia!" She ignored him and climbed back into the car. She hit the gas and the cruiser jumped off the curb by the staircase.

Crap. Mouse double-timed it back to his car and slid into the driver's seat. He'd assumed she was headed for the main road and overshot the parking lot. But then he saw her car again, the white of the police cruiser almost glowed in the dark. *Why the hell is she parked there?*

Mouse dialed Livia's number, but immediately got her voicemail. *What the fuck?* He stashed the hearse near the abandoned police cruiser at Firefly Park. He pulled his Glock from the glove box, and when he cut the lights, he noticed a glow coming from the center of the woods. He slammed his car door shut. Thoroughly confused, Mouse reached for his phone in his grandmother's bag. As he retrieved it from the tangle of yarn and knitting needles, he heard a rush of air and footsteps that were a whole lot closer than they should be before he'd even seen the men.

On pure adrenaline Mouse sprinted in a zig-zag pattern for the treeline. He found a thick tree and used it as cover. The pine needles that carpeted the ground softened the sounds of the feet headed his way. He tried to concentrate on how many. *One, now two. Two to deal with.* Was this part of the group moving against Beckett?

He took a quick peek, but the woods were too dark. The men were professionals. They moved sporadically, not making their path obvious. Everyone seemed headed for the fire. Mouse moved as quietly as he could and slid his cell phone back into Meemaw's bag. They might be tracking his phone. It vibrated, like an angry bee, just before he let go of it. Mouse looked at the screen:

We killed 5. 3 on ur tail. Pros. Kevlar vests n helmets.
Cole and Beckett safe -Eve

There could be one more than he'd thought. Mouse slid the phone between two skeins of yarn. His hand grazed one of his wickedly sharp, double-pointed metal knitting needles. Using an old Tom-and-Jerry-style trick, he threw the needle as far away as he could. It made an impressive clatter in the quiet night. He saw one of the men step out of the darkness next to his cover tree and motion to those behind him to head in the direction of the sound.

He was extra thankful for Eve's text. In the dim light Mouse would have gone for a head shot, but now he settled his aim on the side of the mercenary's neck. The Glock seemed loud, even with the silencer, and the man dropped before the noise had finished repeating in the dark.

Mouse's tree immediately lit up with automatic gunfire. A bullet pierced his upper arm, and his own shout of pain was louder than the gunfire. These bastards had silencers too. Mouse made sure his Glock was in ready position. He had to take a chance to get the two remaining men. He waited for a break in the gunfire and did a forward-roll out from behind the tree. His maneuver gave him a perfect shot at mercenary number two.

Mouse aimed for the belt and hit the man just below his navel. Another quick pop and the man was hit in the thigh as well. Mouse hoped he'd ruptured the femoral artery. The man would bleed out from the gut shot and leg wound within seconds.

The third mercenary was well-hidden and had fabulous aim. First, he hit Mouse's hand, blowing the gun from his grip. Next Mouse felt his center invaded by metal. His lungs felt like raisins as he tried to remain standing. Gravity pulled him down. The landing jarred his back, and his legs felt bent in the wrong direction.

The third mercenary came to stand above him. "Tell me where the homeless one is, and I'll just kill you. Don't tell me, and I'll figure out how to skin you with my pocketknife."

The voice had a hint of an accent Mouse had difficulty placing. Mouse's breathing was shallow and his brain seemed not to fit in his skull. Pain brought sound from his body even as he willed himself to be quiet. He knew now that he was going to die. But he had one last mission from Beckett. *I have to finish this.* Mouse took quick stock of what parts of him still worked. He could move one of his hands, and one eye seemed good. The other was open, he was pretty sure, but it saw nothing.

I'm scared, Meemaw. Her spirit filled him to the brim, gently plugging the open hole in his center. He wasn't surprised to find his working hand in her knitting bag. He wiggled his fingers and begged them to grasp. Soon they had a tenuous hold on another double-pointed needle. It took more effort to curl his hand tightly around it than anything Mouse could remember.

Mouse spoke and was surprised that now, this close to the end, his voice finally sounded a little deeper. "I'll tell you, man. I'll tell you."

Mouse didn't have to try to make his pretend confession quiet; the words were almost ghosts of themselves anyway. The man leaned in close, and Mouse jabbed his arm out and up, thrilled to see the speed his hand provided for his final act as Beckett's bodyguard.

The needle lodged deeply in the mercenary's eye. Mouse pushed it deeper until it robbed the man of all his functions. He fell backward in a spectacular show and kicked up a pile of leaves, one of which landed over Mouse's gasping mouth.

All three were dead. *I did it, Beckett. I saved your brother.*

But Mouse had two more tasks to perform before he drifted away in the pool of blood forming below him. He dragged his hand to his shirt and ripped it aside to reveal the tattoo above his heart.

This fucking leaf. I want one clean, last breath. His hand wouldn't move from his chest. *Come on. Please.* The leaf tasted like dirt. Mouse wanted this last pattern, his breathing, to be pure. But he had a greater goal. *Meemaw. Please help me.*

Her spirit surged through him again. His hand inched up. Close to his neck. Close to the goddamn leaf. Mouse's hand kept moving right past the leaf and his dearest wish for a last fresh breath. He heard the rhythmic clattering of his grandmother's needles and knew he was almost done. *Almost.*

His miraculous hand went higher still, past his head. He stretched it as far as it would go and pointed it in the direction of the glow he'd seen from the parking lot. Mouse pointed to where he believed Blake might be. *Just in case you need it, boss.*

In the night, on the soft carpet of pine needles, his body was still. The leaf that had hampered his last breath fluttered to the ground beside his head.

The glistening beauty of the rising moon illuminated Mouse's bare chest and revealed a familiar tattoo with a music clef, a cross, and a knife. But in this case, Chaos' mark featured an addition. The knitting needles fit perfectly into the montage of brotherhood.

Patterns.

But this pattern had to come to an end.

38

You're My Friend

Kyle.

Hearing the words from Beckett had provided little comfort. Cole needed to see her. He needed to touch her sweet face without the duct tape. The chemical the mercenaries had used against him wafted up nauseatingly, burning his throat. The white button-down shirt he'd thrown on to make a snack for Kyle at the church had been through much more than he'd intended. He had to be rid of the smell. It was awful.

Kyle. He twisted the handle of Eve's ridiculously fast motorcycle. It responded willingly. Cole took one hand off the controls and ripped his shirt open. He let the wind take it off his body. He looked quickly to see it flutter behind him like a flag of surrender before it deflated on the asphalt.

Kyle. Now clad only in his jeans and socks, he leaned into turns and took the sidewalk when the traffic impeded his forward motion. The blue signs with the H guided him toward the hospital and called to him like sea nymphs. As he rolled over a bridge, he tossed the gun Eve had given him. When he finally saw the building that held Kyle towering formidably in front of him, he took a deep breath. Channeling Beckett, Cole aimed the motorcycle straight at the ER's automatic doors.

He filled the waiting room to the brim with the engine's growl, but after a quick glance at the shocked people in carefully lined chairs, Cole moved the motorcycle forward.

When he got to the curtained maze that kept the sick from having to look at one another, he cut the engine and laid the bike on its side. The hospital personnel looked mildly surprised and curious to see a shirtless, shoeless man and a motorcycle. Anything could happen in an ER and often did. Calmly and without moving too quickly, one of the nurses paged security over the intercom.

"Kyle?" Cole looked around wildly. He was beyond functioning as a rational human being.

"Kyle!" His need for her strangled him.

"KYLE!" Cole beat his chest with his fist, bending at the waist with the force of his cry. His head snapped up. He'd heard her soft, sleepy voice.

"Cole? Cole? Please, Cole?"

All the people who should spring into action in the presence of a screaming, half-naked man in a hospital now started in his direction. The door to his left was open. He darted in and pulled back the privacy curtain.

Kyle. There she was, propped up in a hospital bed. Only one of her eyes was completely open, but she smiled and held her arms out to him. Cole crawled onto her bed, right over the footboard and up to her arms.

"Kyle, I was so afraid." Cole lifted his head from the comfort of her bosom to see her face again.

She smoothed back his wild, knotted hair. "It's you. It's you. It's you."

A crowd in the doorway interrupted their loving revelation. Nurse Susan stormed into the room.

Cole ignored them all and kissed Kyle's sleepy lips. "I love you, Kyle. Thank you for being alive. They didn't hurt you, did they?"

Kyle sighed. "They hurt me so much when they took you, Cole. That's the worst pain on earth. The worst." Kyle kissed his forehead and ran her hands over his back. "I'm your shadow. I love you too."

"I take it you're the Cole she wanted so badly we needed to sedate her?" Susan ran a quick visual check on him while he took inventory of her official patient. "You have a nasty head contusion, young man."

Cole nodded, touching Kyle's cheek.

"What the hell is this?" John bellowed, pushing his way in roughly. "What's going on?"

Susan stepped in front of him. "This gentleman is your daughter's best sedative," she said. "I suggest a gentle approach."

John met Susan's eyes. "Fine."

Susan bustled off, mumbling about ice, and chased away the security personnel and other employees who came to help after the commotion.

Cole noticed Kyle could open both eyes now.

"Daddy, this is Cole Bridge," she said. "He'll never be far from my side."

Cole shook off the magic of her touch and stood to greet her father. "Sir, I'm sorry to meet you under these circumstances. This is all my fault. I didn't protect your daughter."

Kyle tried to get up immediately.

"Stay in bed." John pointed to the crumpled blankets she nested in.

She reclined, but remained as focused as it seemed she could in her groggy state.

John sighed as he looked Cole up and down. "Cole, is it? Do you have a good goddamn reason for screaming and climbing into my daughter's bed with no shirt? What the hell do *you* do for a living?"

Cole fidgeted and tried to look more clothed. "Sir, I've been working at the church. But..." He turned and smiled at Kyle. "That situation may be changing."

John rubbed his eyes. "This has been the weirdest goddamn night."

Kathy, the receptionist from the precinct, tentatively knocked on the door. "Excuse me, John? I just wanted to drop by and make sure you guys didn't need anything. I heard from the boys what was going on." When one of their own was in trouble, the wall of blue tightened up around him.

"Kathy. Hey, thanks. Yeah, I made a lot of calls trying to figure things out. Could you grab Livia for me? I'm sure she'll want to see her sister now that she's awake."

John turned to face Kyle and her half-naked, half-holy boyfriend. Then he froze. He held up a finger as if to stop someone from talking, but the room was silent.

"Where's Livia?" he asked.

John turned back to Kathy. He had the panicked look of a parent whose toddler has wandered off.

Kathy held up her hands. "I didn't pass her on the way in."

"Can you stay with these two? I'll tell security to keep close."

With a nod, Kathy stepped into the room and set her purse on the chair.

John soared through the door, but returned just a few minutes later—before anyone left in Kyle's room had thought of what to say to one another. They'd watched silently as Nurse Susan brought Cole a scrub shirt and an ice pack.

"The cruiser is gone," John announced. "And not just because Livia thoughtfully parked it somewhere. I gotta reach the station."

He opened his cell phone and dialed. "Burt? We need an APB out on my daughter, Livia. I think she took my cruiser. No, she's not dangerous! But she's *in* danger—I just know it."

Returning his attention to the room, John asked, "Cole, what do you know about Livia?"

Cole stood again, though he kept hold of Kyle's hand. "Beckett told me Livia was here at the hospital with Kyle. He was going off to find Blake and protect him from the mercenaries that are left. We believe there are three still looking to harm him."

John had visibly tensed at Beckett's name and clenched his teeth at the word *mercenaries*. After a couple of false starts, he finally asked, "Is there a way Livia could've known Blake needed protecting?"

Cole didn't bother to explain. "It's possible."

John grabbed his jacket and looked at Kathy, who nodded. He looked out the doorway just as an orderly attempted to lift Cole's abandoned motorcycle. He struggled with its weight in the lacquered hallway.

"I'll take that, son," John said as he exited the room.

Cole and Kyle looked at each other with wide eyes as the bike roared to life just outside the door. It seemed Kyle's father had decided to leave the way Cole came in.

It didn't take Beckett a long fucking time to figure out that whatever was going down with Blake was not at the train station. Eve pointed toward Firefly Park, where there were way too many vehicles for this time of night. At quick glance they ID-ed Mouse's hearse and AssFuck's ridiculous truck in the parking lot, and most surprisingly, a police cruiser parked on a nearby hill.

They changed course immediately, and when they drew close, Eve hopped out of the Hummer while it was still moving. She used her elbow to crack the top left corner of Mouse's driver's side window. Beckett threw the Hummer in park and trotted up next to her, scanning the parking lot for any movement. Eve retrieved Mouse's laptop, and after some quick typing into the GPS program, she looked up at the stars and back at the forest.

"Mouse should be in the forest just a little way ahead." She went back to the Hummer and pulled out a gun. She tossed Beckett a flashlight.

"Eve?" Beckett had a million questions and suspicions. Something was wrong.

She shook her head quickly, and they walked carefully into the woods on full alert. Eve lifted the screen on the laptop and reoriented herself every few feet. They walked steadily forward until, despite his light, Beckett kicked something. He trained the flashlight on the obstacle. A leg.

He turned the beam on the body — a mercenary, or former mercenary, actually. Eve noted his discovery with wary eyes. Beckett swung the flashlight even with the ground and picked up a second massacred mercenary. *Good ol' Mouse.*

Eve now used the light of the laptop like a glowing torch. Beckett registered two more bodies in the blue haze offered by the screen. *Two more. Two?*

Eve snapped the laptop shut and walked back toward him.

"Eve?" he questioned, forgetting to be quiet.

"Beck, let's get back to the Hummer." She stepped in front of him and tried to turn his massive body around.

"Tell me, Eve. Tell me." Beckett had done the math. Only three were supposed to be dead. Only three.

Eve took a deep breath. "Mouse didn't make it." She stood next to Beckett, looking up at the canopy of dark leaves.

"I don't believe you. Fuck that shit! He's bulletproof. He's fucking bulletproof. Let me see him." Beckett hadn't moved.

Eve shook her head. "Don't. It's too much…" Her tears were silver on her cheeks in the moonlight.

Beckett stepped around her toward the bodies. He swung the flashlight and found the third mercenary with a knitting needle sticking out of his eye socket.

Then Beckett knew. He knew deep inside that his friend was dead. *No. Fucking no.*

He tried to put the flashlight on Mouse gently, reverently, but it was still too harsh. Mouse's eyes were open, like haphazard shades on a vacant house.

Beckett fell to his knees. "Ahh…I never thought they'd get you. Never. Fuck."

He dropped the light and balled his fists, jamming them into his eyes. Pain seared from his head to his heart. He took another look, putting one fist in his mouth. His breath came in loud, shaky gasps. It was the sound of someone coming apart at the seams.

"Fuck it, Mouse. No fucking way. Not tonight. I even fucking prayed tonight!"

Beckett gathered his courage and closed his friend's eyes. He put one giant hand across Mouse's chest, just to make sure there was no heartbeat. Mouse's skin was cold and clammy. The discarded flashlight illuminated the darkened, bloody pine needles around Mouse.

"Ah, son of a bitch. Mouse, you fucking deserved more than this. More than dying in the goddamn dirt. You're more than this to me. You're my friend." Beckett's emotions got him again, and he sobbed deeply into the dark.

He felt Eve's hand on his shoulder. "We have to make sure Blake is okay. I have no idea why Chris Simmer's truck is here." Her voice was hushed and sad.

"I can't leave him here. Not with them. Not in the fucking dirt." Beckett grabbed his flashlight with every intention of handing it to Eve so he could carry his friend—no matter how fucking big he was—to someplace better, when the light landed on Mouse's bare chest.

"What the hell?" Beckett touched Mouse's chest again, and Eve took the light and centered it on the tattoo in question.

Beckett traced it for a moment, his finger lingering on the knitting needles that set it apart from his own, and bowed his head. "Now that's too fucking much," he said softly. "That hurts too fucking much. Eve, not Mouse. He can't be gone."

"Wait." Eve stopped Beckett from scooping Mouse into his arms. She positioned herself at Mouse's head.

She gently touched Mouse's arm. "Beck, I think he's pointing." She stood up and tracked the path Mouse's finger had given them. "We need to head that way."

Beckett saw what she saw. Mouse had died working. Working for him. And not for the fucking money—Mouse's tat proved that. Beckett longed to get Mouse off the fucking dirt, but he needed to find Blake.

"Listen, Mouse wants us to find Blake," Eve pleaded. "That's why he's pointing. That's why he took out three assholes on his own like a gladiator. I want to sit and cry. I want to get him in the back of his own hearse and treat him like a goddamn king. But right now, we're going to finish what he started."

Beckett stood and nodded. As wrong as it felt, he needed to leave his friend—*no, my brother*—lying dead here. At least for now.

John used the handbrake to stop the wickedly fast motorcycle at the light. He was pleased that his old motocross skills seemed to have resurfaced. He was less pleased because he knew he was a sight to see: still in his uniform and disobeying the law by going helmetless. But Livia was out in town somewhere involved in who the hell knew what. He braced the bike with his legs and did something he told the girls never to do while they were on the road: he took out his phone.

He dialed Kathy's number and waited. "Hey, Kath. How's Kyle?"

He could hear the smirk in Kathy's voice when she replied. "Kyle's definitely fine. I was about to call you. I spoke with the station — someone spotted your cruiser at Firefly Park. It was abandoned on a hill with the door open."

The light in front of John changed to green. The honks of frustrated drivers behind him just added to the urgency of his thoughts. *Livia, baby, what have you gotten into?*

"Kathy, I want you to send an ambulance, an advanced life team, SWAT, and anything else you can think of to Firefly Park." John stared at the green circle beckoning him to go.

He whipped his badge out of his pocket and held it up for the irate drivers behind him to see. The honking ceased.

"John, are you sure?" Kathy asked.

"She's my daughter. I need everything. Everything. Please?" John watched as the light flicked to yellow.

"Consider it done. Go get her, cowboy." Kathy hung up, and John could picture her fingers already placing the next call.

He hung up and slipped the phone into his pocket. The light turned red, but John used the heartbeat before the opposing light turned green to rocket the bike through the intersection. *Oh God oh God oh God. Livia, be okay. I'll give anything. Just please, Livia, be okay.*

39

GLASS

So many things in the clearing should have had Livia's attention—Chris, stupid Dave, the fire, the weird noises all these crazy men were making—but all Livia could do was feel. She could feel Blake's crackling presence behind her. Her skin prickled in each place she knew they'd make contact if she just leaned back into him. She turned her head to try to see his face. But Chris advanced, so she held her ground; she couldn't succumb to Blake's pull on her body.

"Livia, so nice of you to show. You're late. I'm glad you got my text telling you to meet me here." He grabbed her shoulders.

Livia tried to make sense of his words and slapped at his arms. He yanked her away from her place as Blake's shield.

"No. What are you talking about? No! Chris, let me go." Livia dug in her heels.

He wrenched her harder and wrapped an arm possessively around her shoulders. "I told you I'd get this bastard for you, baby. Nobody touches my girl and gets away with it."

Livia slipped out from under his arm. All these boys from high school gave her a feeling of déjà vu. Their voices and mannerisms were so familiar. She had a hard time taking any of them seriously. She turned to see Blake silhouetted by the glow of burning leaves as Chris seized her bicep.

How could they do this? I know them all. "Chris, just stop this. Let go of me right now." Livia pulled until he released her and almost fell with the sudden lack of counterbalance.

"Don't be mad, sweet tits. I won't hurt him too bad. I know you have a soft heart. It goes with your soft head." Chris wiggled an eyebrow at Wilson. "I swear, she's such a wuss. But you're *my* little wuss, aren't you baby?" Chris held out a hand to Livia.

Her mouth fell open. She dismissed him with a shake of her head and looked at Blake. He wasn't even straining against Wilson and Francis as they held his arms.

His indifference told her she had a mountain to climb. She needed Blake out of here and somewhere safe—safe from the nimrods of her teen years and safe from whoever had kidnapped Cole. But mostly she needed him safe from the anguish her words had caused him. The fire slowly reduced to a smolder.

"Blake, I'm so sorry. We need to discuss what happened earlier. Let's go, okay?" Livia focused solely on assessing Blake's facial expression in the darkness. *Apathy. Blake, damn it. At least look like you hate me. Apathy is the* opposite *of love.*

Dave snatched her as she took a step toward Blake.

"Enough!" she shrieked. "Guys, this is over. We have to leave. Dave, let go. Why do you all think it's okay to put your hands on me?" Dave pulled her arms uncomfortably behind her back, locking her into place.

The fire was dwindling so quickly. Soon the only light would come from the full moon that now levitated above the tree line. In the slices of illumination, she saw gashes on Blake's face.

"You bastards. How dare you?" Livia turned her hands to claws and tried to scratch Dave. He evaded her nails.

"She's really head over heels for you, Chris." Wilson laughed.

"Seriously, that pussy is just begging for you." Francis yanked Blake's arm to make him stagger.

Chris stepped in front of Livia, his voice was low and menacing, "Don't embarrass me in front of these guys. It's bad enough you've been throwing yourself all over this homeless asshole. Tonight I'm setting things right. And you're helping me."

He cracked his knuckles and his neck. She hated that, and he knew it.

"No, I'm leaving," Livia countered. "And I'm taking Blake with me. This is crazy. I don't know what the hell you thought you were doing, but it stops right now." Livia waited for Dave to let go of her arms.

Dave, who'd borrowed her glue stick so often in fifth grade that she had to buy a new one, was just a child. What was he thinking? He pulled her into him and ground his hips against her lower back. Finally Livia realized how high the level of testosterone was flowing through the clearing. Pack mentality was in full effect, preventing any of them from behaving rationally.

Shame. I'll just shame them out of this. "Dave, quit poking me with that tube of Chapstick." Livia made sure her voice carried.

"I don't have Chapstick," Dave said indignantly.

"Damn, she's calling your dick Chapstick," Wilson said through a snort. "That burns." He laughed like a seventh grader in the boys' locker room.

Dave leaned close to her ear. "Chris ain't gonna want you any more 'cause you're a hobo whore," he whispered. Then he tried the words more loudly to compete with Wilson's ribbing. "Hobo Whore! Hobo Whore! Livia's banging a ho-bo!"

Livia's breath came through her teeth. *Will Chris defend me?* He had to pick a side, but as she met his eyes, Livia knew before he opened his mouth what his decision would be. She wore a scarlet letter now.

"What Dave says is kind of true, Livia," he said thoughtfully. "You know you're fucking this bum. You're slutting it out like a crack-hungry street whore. And that's disrespectful to me." Chris's face had changed in the bluish light.

Livia now faced a very different Chris. Like a long, spindly hair caught in a floorboard, she'd thought Chris was harmless—annoying, but harmless. Now that she'd pulled on the hair, she could see it was the leg of a big, black spider, full of venom just for her. *How the hell am I getting us out of this, Blake?*

Dave snickered in her ear. "Chris's not happy. *He* called you a whore. Maybe he'll let me have you." He followed his desperate wish with a high, nasal cackle.

Livia turned her mouth in his direction. "Dave, you throbbing nimrod, I've flushed things more useful than you down the toilet."

She stomped on the toe of his sneaker and was rewarded with a shriek of pain. Dave let go, and she started toward Blake.

Chris stepped in and took hold of her arms. "You can't do this," he hissed. "You can't pick him over me. You *can't* pick him. I'll look like a fool." Rising panic topped his voice like an overflowing soda.

"God, just get out of the way. I need Blake." Livia tried again to free herself.

Chris squeezed her arms hard. She hated the smell of his cologne, the highlights in his hair. All of it was so ludicrous.

Wilson repeated her words in a high-pitched voice. "'Just get out of the way, I need Blake.' Hey, Chris, maybe the hobo wears crack-coated condoms. Your girlfriend's probably getting it up the ass. Crack in her crack. Get it?"

Dave stopped squealing like a guinea pig and grabbed Livia from Chris with renewed vigor. Chris turned to gesture to Wilson, affording Livia a glimpse of Blake. When he saw her looking he refocused on a spot above her head.

Damn it to hell. I need to tell him why tonight is so dangerous. I need this parade of assholes to go away.

Then Francis decided to jump in. "Chris, you got to be pretty lame to lose your girl to the homeless. You could've just given the shitbag a dollar, not your regular bearded clam."

Livia let the fighting dissolve out of focus around her. She'd have to connect with Blake here, among the idiots—with Dave grinding his pencil dick into her back and Chris making angry hand gestures at Wilson. With smoke blowing in the wind to make her eyes tear up.

"Look at me. Please." It was more than a whisper but less than a shout. She got quieter. "Blake, please."

His green eyes found hers. She spoke as if they were alone.

"I made a mistake," Livia began. "I know you overheard me talking to my dad. I needed him to understand who you are, but I had to talk on his level. As a father he needed to know I was being decisive. I don't think you heard the last part when I told him you were the path I wanted to take."

A flicker. Was it hope? Livia smiled.

Blake's lips moved, and she knew he'd counted her smile. Wilson, Francis, and Chris continued their heated exchange. Every other word was *cocksucker.* Dave sniffed the back of her neck, and revulsion rolled along her spine. Hope made her weak and strong, all at once.

"I'll make mistakes. I know I will," she continued. "I want to be perfect for you. But I'm human. I can only be me. That probably isn't enough for a soul as beautiful as yours. But if I hurt you by accident, can't we stay and hold hands until we fix it? Can't we fix it?" Livia now spoke louder than she wanted to, but she had to be heard over the cacophony.

"Chris's a loser!" Dave shouted.

Livia refocused to block him out and keep her bond with Blake.

Blake bit his lip. "You're perfect."

"No, sweetheart. I can't even pretend to be perfect. Look where we are right now. That's my fault, Blake."

Dave's "Chris's a loser!" mantra grew louder. Chris whipped around and pointed at him. "Don't call me that! I'm not a loser. I'm *not* a fucking loser." His eyes blazed with manic intensity.

Dave tried his luck again. "Whoever smelt it dealt it."

All the bastards fell quiet. Dave had turned the tables on Chris, the wounded alpha. The clearing now offered only an occasional pop from the smoke-drowned leaves.

Here. I need to tell him now. "Blake, I love you," Livia confessed quietly.

The tears in her eyes had nothing to do with smoke this time, and Chris began to shake with fury. Livia leaned toward Blake and tried again, louder still.

"Blake, I love you."

Chris closed the distance until he was inches from her traitorous face.

Livia shouted in the silence because now her soul was free. "I love you, Blake!"

She smiled as he mouthed the words back to her.

Chris slapped her viciously — once, twice, three times without pause. Livia's neck and face pounded with pain. The inside of her cheek was stuck on her top molar.

"Fuck you, Livia. I'm not a loser," Chris shouted in her face.

She spat out a mouthful of blood and looked at his angry, red features.

"I'm so ashamed." Livia felt blood filling her mouth again.

She kept her eyes on Chris, but saw Blake finally taking action against his captors in her peripheral vision. He slammed an elbow into Wilson's face and gave a twisting crack to Francis's throat. Both men fell to the ground, writhing.

I'm almost glad Chris slapped me.

Chris pointed a shaky finger at her. "You *should* be ashamed. It's about time."

"I'm ashamed of *you*, Chris," Livia said fiercely. "I'm ashamed I ever let you touch me. I should have saved myself for Blake." She topped off her statement by heaving bloody spit into Chris's face.

As Chris reached to grab her, Blake sprinted and took a flying leap that hit him in the side. Chris almost folded in half with the force. The two men hit the ground, and Blake executed a graceful forward roll. Chris lay prone, the wind knocked out of him.

Blake was up and punching before Chris could move. Three solid punches to the jaw were the swift justice Blake deemed appropriate. Chris curled into the fetal position and moaned. Blake pushed himself to standing and got to Livia. He put his hands gently on her face.

Dave seemed frozen. Blake took his gaze from Livia long enough to growl at him, and Dave took off running. The moaning twosome that had been Blake's restraints now got to their feet. Wilson made his plans known immediately: "Fuck this shit. Let's get out of here. I'm not being all revenge for the nerd. Chris Simmer's an ass clown." The two helped each other stagger away like rats from a sinking ship.

Blake rubbed Livia's cheekbones gently with his thumbs. "I can't believe you came for me. My brave Livia." He kissed her lips and looked concerned. "You're bleeding."

"I'm fine, Blake, but we have to get out of here. Some of Beckett's enemies are after you." Livia stroked his bruised face.

"Then why are you out here?" he asked, eyes instantly angry.

Livia gave the perfect answer. "This is the only place I knew I'd get to see you."

Blake kissed her lingeringly on the forehead, then grabbed her hand and pulled her toward the trees. He took care to go a different direction than their attackers-turned-victims had fled. Livia smiled, in spite of the situation. In the woods Blake could keep them safe for days.

Then the distinct sound of a gun being cocked stopped Blake like he'd just stepped on a landmine.

"Now hold the fuck up, you two shitty lovebirds," Chris's voice echoed through the air. "That's not how this plays out."

Livia could hear Chris stepping through the leaves. Closer, closer.

"Livia, when I count to three, I want to you to run into the trees," Blake whispered. "And keep running. Promise me." He sounded calm and determined.

"Absolutely not." Livia turned from their escape route. "I'm never leaving you."

"Livia, please." Blake squeezed her hand and tried to force her in the right direction.

She squeezed right back.

Chris seemed to think the gun meant he could call the shots. "Come the fuck back over here. We got some shit to discuss."

Blake kept his body between Livia and the gun. Chris motioned the couple to the center of the clearing.

"See, they were calling me a loser, and I just can't have that. Livia, you're making everything so tough for me. You playing Juliet to this bastard's Romeo affects *my* reputation. Do you know what people will say? I had witnesses here tonight. It'll be all over Twitter what a punk I am. A fucking loser punk. Livia, those are the kind of people I beat up. I can't be one of them."

He paused for a moment to reposition the gun in his hand. "So you need to understand, I have to do this. I need to do this. Really, it's what you want. It's what you asked for. Maybe a murder-suicide will let those guys know who's in fucking charge around here, eh?" A sick plan solidified in Chris's eyes.

Livia tried to see him around Blake. "You're delusional," she said. "This has gone way too far."

Blake crouched slightly, as if trying to calculate Chris's next move.

"Murder-suicide? Now you're going to kill yourself? What the hell?" Livia wished she could slap Chris back into reality.

Blake squeezed her hand and spoke over his shoulder, "Don't say any more."

"No, Livia. God, you're a stupid fuck," Chris said. "Now stand next to each other so I can see you."

Blake hesitated.

"Fucking do it." Chris's voice had a desperate edge.

Livia stepped up next to Blake. She had to talk Chris down.

"I'll make this work," Chris said. "Homeless bastard goes apeshit on the chick too stupid to stay away from him. It'll be a good lesson for other ladies."

The gleam in Chris's eyes sent a silent scream of terror through Livia. "Chris, it won't work like that," she quickly countered. "You're just angry. You make awful choices when you're angry, remember?" Livia held an open palm to him, trying to soothe his unhinged mind.

But in an instant Blake stepped in front of her, turning his back to Chris and the gun. The shot was so much louder than anything else in the woods. And it seemed to echo forever. Livia watched Blake's face in horror as he fell toward her, leaning for a moment like the Tower of Pisa. She staggered back, trying to hold him as they both collapsed to the forest floor. Livia knew he was tremendously injured when his body hit hers so hard. If he could have, she knew Blake would've softened the blow.

His breath was a sucking gasp that sounded more like a draining tub than a man filling his lungs with air. Then she heard him form the words "Play dead."

So Livia did. She closed her eyes as much as she dared. She could still see outlines through her lashes. She squeezed her hands against Blake's chest. *Hold on, Blake. Stay with me.*

A sharp pain in her side reminded her of the Mag light in the inside pocket of her jacket. She snaked her arm out and found the opening. She could hear Chris cursing.

"Motherfucker. I shot them both. Fuck my life."

Who he was talking to, Livia wasn't sure—maybe the devil in his head. She wrapped her hand around the flashlight and waited. Her heart pounded so hard it felt like one giant explosion, not individual beats. Blake's body pressed on her ribcage. *Is he playing dead or being dead?*

Chris stomped over to the pile of lovers and yanked Blake off of Livia. As soon as she had Chris's head in her sight, she sat up and swung the flashlight as hard as she could. It bounced off his skull with a thud.

For years John had trained his girls in self-defense. "Just common sense stuff," he liked to say. "Hit your attacker three times and run." This mantra kept Livia swinging. She pushed herself to her knees and onto her feet. She hit Chris again, her blow landing on his neck.

He crouched from the pain and moaned. "Ow, ow, ow."

His hand still held the gun. Livia hit that hand with the flashlight, and the weapon thumped to the ground. She gave Chris a quick sidekick that was not nearly as powerful as she'd hoped. He grabbed her foot and dragged her down with him.

As she fell, Livia found her knee right above his testicles. She put all her weight on that leg, pressing on his soft parts. Chris flung her off and grabbed his privates. She lifted her body off the soil with a mouthful of leaves.

"Fuck. Rrrr." Chris seemed to be trying to get away from his own balls as he writhed on the ground.

Livia traced the ground with her hands and found the warm gun. As soon as she had it pointed at Chris, she hazarded a look at Blake, but she already knew things weren't good. He'd never let her fight Chris on her own if he had a choice. She gritted her teeth at the sight of his motionless body and turned back to Chris, who she found propping himself up.

"Don't move. Just don't move." Livia's voice was laced with agony.

"Liv, we can do this. We can say the bastard attacked you, and I saved you. I'll do that." He used one hand to massage his nuts.

Maybe it was the word *bastard*. Maybe it was Chris using the word *we*. But Livia leveled the pistol with his head.

"Livia, you're not a murderer." Chris spoke quickly now. "You won't kill me. I had our whole life planned out — and you couldn't do that to my mom," he suddenly added. Chris's face was as serious as he ever got.

This was Chris *trying* to be the Chris from years ago, when they'd first met. She approached him, keeping the gun pointed between his eyes. She stood with her feet apart and her shoulders squared. *I want him to die.* Her hands shook as she looked at him. He lacked the sense, it seemed, to run away. *I can't be like him. I won't.*

Livia changed her aim and Chris breathed a sigh of relief. "Thank God, Liv. I thought you — "

Bang.

Livia fired the gun into Chris's right knee. As he reeled, she took aim at his left.

Bang.

Chris's screaming made the sounds of the cold night into a horror movie soundtrack. Livia put the safety on the gun and slid the hot metal into her pocket.

She turned her back on him. He couldn't chase her now. She sprinted to Blake's side and found him blinking, so she knew he was alive. She actually sobbed with relief.

"Blake, where were you hit?" Livia dropped to her knees to feel his chest. The moon gave him an ethereal bath. His breathing was shallow and wet.

"Livia." He coughed and winced.

"I'm right here." She searched her pockets for her cell phone, then remembered it was in the cruiser with a dead battery. *Of course.* "Do you have a phone?" Livia lay her hand on his forehead. He was cold.

Blake gave the slightest headshake. *No.*

Livia set her jaw. She knew Chris always had his phone in his left jacket pocket. His screams had turned to whimpers. She pulled out the gun and lifted the safety. Cautiously, she inched closer to Chris and reached in his jacket pocket. He grabbed her wrist as soon as she made contact with the phone.

"You shot me. What the hell?" His voice and his grip were weak.

He was just a talking monster in her head. She ignored him. Livia slipped out of his grasp and dialed the phone while sprinting back to Blake. She propped it on her shoulder and put the gun's safety back on before shoving it back in her pocket. She heard nothing, so she took a closer look at the phone. There was no goddamn signal.

She kneeled at Blake's side again.

"Hey, handsome. I don't have a signal. We're going to have walk a bit. Let's help you up." Livia slipped her arm under his and tried to help him sit. He shouted, and Livia laid him down quickly.

"I'm so sorry. Is it that bad?" Frustration curled her fingers.

"Livia, it's not good." Blake hardly moved his lips.

His voice was just a hint. Just a whisper. Panic poured into Livia's system.

"It's okay. It's going to be okay. I'll just drag you out." Livia put down the flashlight.

"Wait. Why don't *you* go get help?" Blake panted with the effort of his words.

"I can't leave you here. Beckett's enemies and Chris's asshole friends are still out there. I can't leave you." She situated herself behind his head.

She heard him suck in a wet gasp as she lifted his shoulders and attempted to pull him out of the clearing. She tried so hard, fighting and straining to tow him. But he was too heavy. She hadn't moved him at all. Livia gently laid his head on the ground.

"Oh good. You stopped. That hurt."

Livia grabbed handfuls of her hair. "I'm sorry. That was stupid. You're not supposed to move someone who's injured." Livia took off her jacket and made a little pillow for his head. "I don't know what to do, Blake. You're hurt. I can't move you. The cell phone's got nothing. I've no idea if they heard me over the police radio earlier." She put her hands on his cheeks.

He kept his eyes closed for longer and longer periods of time, and he offered no answer to her problem. He seemed to be working on staying alive. *Are his lips that blue? Or is it the moon?* Livia knew she'd have to go for help.

"Hey, look, I'm going to run toward the road. I'll call 911 as soon as I get a signal, and then I'm coming back. Does that sound right? Is that right?" Livia begged and told at the same time.

Blake opened his beautiful green eyes. He tried to smile, but it was just a grimace. "Livia. I love you too. Smile again."

She hated his words. They were a goodbye. "I can't smile, I have to run. I have to get help." She tried to stand and felt the gentle pressure of his hand on her thigh.

"Smile again." He worked to keep his eyes open.

Livia picked up the hand that had stopped her. She lifted it to her lips and kissed every knuckle. By the time Livia tried to smile, only one of his green eyes was focused on her face. Her forced smile used all the wrong muscles.

"Good enough," he joked.

"I'm going to be right back. Hang on. All this love is stealing time." She pulled herself from his side. "Stay right here, Blake. Hang on. Okay? Hang on."

Livia found the flashlight she'd pummeled Chris with, and it still worked. Chris had stopped making noises altogether—not that Livia cared. She forced herself out of the clearing and to the edge of the woods and begged herself not to turn around. If she saw Blake lying helpless, she wouldn't be able to leave. A few more steps and the trees enveloped her in their darkness, adding fear of the unseen to everything else she was shouldering. She steeled herself and began to sprint. Twenty steps in, she felt her soul grind to a halt. *Go back.*

She couldn't even argue. She doubled back and stared at Blake's form. Something was different. He wasn't there. *No.* She ran to him. Setting her ear to his chest and hushing her own panting, she waited. And waited. She put two fingers on his neck to feel for a beat. She watched for a breath. *No beat. No breath. Nothing.*

In theory, she knew just what to do. Her dad always made sure his girls got in on the CPR recertification down at the precinct. It hadn't even been three months since she'd resuscitated a cold, white CPR dummy. Thirty to two. *Simple.*

But this was far from simple. She second- and third-guessed herself. *What if he's breathing and I can't see it?* She sat back and looked at her still, beautiful love. *Do it now.*

Livia positioned Blake's head and plugged his nose. She clasped her mouth around his. One breath, two breaths.

The metallic taste of his blood met her lips, joining the blood from her mouth's wound. She positioned her hands, almost an inverted prayer, and committed herself to the act. Livia pushed her hands straight down from her shoulders, as she'd practiced time after time. The tearing and popping sounds were unexpected, and she powered through a wave of nausea.

"One and two and three and four and five and six…"

Oh, God don't let me hurt him.

"…and seven and eight and nine and ten and eleven…"

Am I really doing this? Here? Is this real?

"…and twelve and thirteen and fourteen and fifteen…"

We're in the middle of nowhere. No one is going to find us. Even the fire has gone out.

"…and sixteen and seventeen and eighteen and nineteen…"

He's dead. I'm just beating on his body.

"…and twenty and twenty-one and twenty-two and twenty-three and twenty-four…"

My arms hurt. How can my arms hurt now? Blake. I can't. I can't be here without you.

"…and twenty-five and twenty-six and twenty-seven and twenty-eight and twenty-nine and thirty."

The next step was simple: cover his mouth and fill his lungs with air. Breathe into him with life's breath. Livia did so, licked her lips, and started compressions again.

"And one and two and three and four and five and six and seven…"

I've got to be positive. I have to know he'll make it.

"…and eight and nine and ten and eleven and twelve and thirteen and fourteen…"

We're going to grow old together, Blake. We're going to hold hands and kiss.

"…and fifteen and sixteen and seventeen and eighteen and nineteen…"

I'm giving you all my energy. All this love and hope. It's going from my heart to yours, through my hands.

"…and twenty and twenty-one and twenty-two and twenty-three…"

Feel it, Blake. Feel it.

"…and twenty-four and twenty-five and twenty-six and twenty-seven…"

I love you so much. I'm going to love you forever. Can you feel that, Blake?

"…and twenty-eight and twenty-nine and thirty."

Livia leaned down, repositioned Blake's head, and filled his lungs twice more. As she put her hands on his chest to keep her rhythm, she looked down at his face, at his skin.

"And one and two and three and four and five and six…"

Am I imagining that? Your skin?

"…and seven and eight and nine and ten and eleven…"

Blake! Blake, your skin! It's just like glass, Blake. You're really sparkling. I can see it. I can really see it. Your skin is amazing!

Livia's tears landed on her hard-pumping hands. Nothing would stop her from beating Blake's heart for him now. Nothing. Not even the sound of people crashing through the woods.

"…and twelve and thirteen and fourteen and fifteen and sixteen and seventeen…"

You're glistening, Blake. I'll never stop. I'll never stop.

40

İF İ WAΠTED YOU TO CRY

E ve had a horrible feeling. She and Beckett had been doing their best to
walk quietly in the direction Mouse pointed when they heard the first
gunshot. They let go of each other's hands and broke into a run, weaving
through the thick trees. A few minutes later, they heard two more quick pops.

Eve kept herself at a dead run mostly so she could get to the situation,
whatever it was, before Beckett did. She couldn't look at him again and see
guilt and horror. Losing Mouse had already been too much. If Blake had
been taken from him too...But despite her best effort, the underbrush and
haphazard trees were doing an excellent job of slowing her the hell down,
and Beckett lumbered close behind.

They should still have been trying to be quiet, but Beckett would go
in guns blazing, so she needed to have his back *and* his front. Eve briefly
entertained shooting him in the foot or knocking him out, just to keep
him safe. He was a charging bull, but after having planned Beckett's death
for years, she would not allow it to happen now.

When they stumbled together into a clearing, even in their panic the
blue moonlight made it ethereal, like a fairy ring. But in the center knelt
Livia, counting out compressions.

Beckett stopped in his tracks. "No no no no no no."

Livia looked exhausted. Eve knew the marathon toll CPR took on your
arms. As she moved to join her, Eve took fierce pride in the brave beauty
of a woman alone in the woods, working her hardest with no help on the
horizon. Livia never stopped; she just kept on counting as Eve knelt on
the other side of Blake.

"...and fourteen and fifteen and sixteen and seventeen..."

Eve spoke over the precious numbers. "Livia, I'm going to take over compressions and breaths on the next cycle. I know what I'm doing, okay?"

Livia nodded and pushed. "...twenty-nine and thirty."

Livia placed a hopeful open-mouthed kiss on Blake's pale lips. Eve set up her arms and continued where Livia had left off.

Her arms suddenly free, Livia stroked Blake's face and whispered. "I see it, sweetheart. I was right—you're beautiful when you're glass."

Eve kept the steady metronome of artificial heartbeats in her head. They needed to move rapidly. *Blake has a fucking chance. I have to believe that.*

Eve shouted to Beckett just before her two breaths. "Beckett, do you hear that? You need to run as fast as you can and flag down those sirens. They sound close. Go, baby. You have to run!"

Beckett seemed energized by having a job and took off faster than she'd ever seen him move. Eve resumed her chest compressions. *Nice and constant. Pump the blood. Keep it moving.* She looked around the clearing. It seemed empty, but there was a pile of something off to one side near the trees.

Livia rubbed Blake's unresponsive hands and talking of their future. "Blake, we'll walk in the woods together. We have forever. Just wake up, okay? That's the deal we're making right here. You wake up and we get to have forever."

Eve tried to ignore the words to give Livia privacy. Two more breaths. *Crap, this is hard. How long has Livia been doing this?* "Livia, do you know how many cycles you gave him?" Eve asked when Livia paused.

Livia put Blake's hand on her cheek. "I'm not sure. I was counting to thirty." Her eyes never moved from Blake's still face.

"You did great. Do you know what happened to him? Are there any dangerous people around us?" Eve finished a cycle of compressions and leaned down for Blake's mouth.

"Blake stepped in front of a bullet for me. It went into his back. I have no idea if we're safe." Livia smoothed Blake's hair.

"Listen, I need you to put pressure on his wound to stop the bleeding," Eve said. She felt an ache climb up her arms.

Livia took her shirt off and faced in the cold night in her bra. Eve helped lift Blake up a bit so Livia could find the source of the blood. As Eve resumed the cycle, the noise of what had to be Beckett's Hummer came crashing into the clearing. Headlights bounced around like two tandem falling stars. Beckett's demanding voice filled the night.

"Right there—that's my brother. Right fucking there." The paramedics descended, breaking out bags and tubes and needles.

Eve gave them all the information she could. As they prepared the paddles to shock Blake, Eve pulled Livia away, not sure if she'd realize *Clear!* meant she had to let go of Blake's hand.

A police officer came and took Livia from Eve's arms, hugging her hard and kissing the top of her head. "Livia, dear God."

Livia turned into the man. "Dad, I did CPR. He's going to make it, right?"

His eyes held little hope. He slipped his jacket off to cover his freezing daughter as a flurry of alarming words clouded the night.

"Epinephrine."

"Atropine."

"GSW."

"Possible lung collapse."

The officer kept his arms around Livia, keeping her from getting involved. The paramedics argued with one another, trying to figure out how to get the ambulance closer. They were still a few hundred yards from the scene, having followed Beckett's tree-crushing trail. They put a stretcher on the ground to accept the seemingly lifeless Blake.

"I've got a rhythm," one of them shouted. "Go, go, go!" They whisked Blake away without a backward glance.

John caught Livia as her knees gave out and lowered her to the grass.

"Rhythm means good, right? That's his heart? Beating?" Livia looked almost childlike as she questioned her father.

He knelt and patted her back. "Blake's going to fight real hard to be with you. He knows how much you love him."

"Is the ambulance gone?" Livia seemed to emerge from her shock for a moment.

"Sounds like they're off," he assured her.

Eve noticed Livia's eyes flickering to the pile across the clearing.

"Daddy, Chris's over there. He may be dead—I don't know. He tried to shoot me, and Blake—" Livia's eyes filled up, and she began to shudder.

Eve watched as Livia visibly stabilized herself to deliver the news. "Blake stepped in front of me—the bullet meant for me. He told me to play dead, and I did. When Chris came to shoot me too, I hit him with the flashlight. I kept hitting until he dropped the gun, and then I…" Livia held her hands out from under her father's too long jacket. "I shot him in the knees. Both of them. But he should be still alive."

All eyes turned in the direction of the villain. Beckett's flashed with anger.

"I'll find out," he said.

As Beckett walked over, Chris began crying like a kitten. Beckett pointed at Chris's whimpering form. "Shut up. If I wanted you to cry I would've kicked ya."

Eve made it to Beckett in a few long-legged strides.

Beckett kicked Chris in the head. "Now you can cry, motherfucker."

Eve pulled Beckett forcibly away and stilled the hand she knew was headed for his firearm. "Please don't commit murder in front of the cop," she whispered.

Beckett was coiled like a tight spring. She knew he wanted to snap, wanted a release for all his frustration, anger, and worry. Instead she had to help him focus. "Blake needs someone to take care of Livia until he gets back," Eve suggested, looking at him intently. "Take her to the hospital and wait with her. Blake needs you there."

Beckett wound up to kick Chris again, but stopped himself. He turned his back and closed his eyes for a moment. "I'll keep Livia safe until Blake's better. Okay."

Beckett trained his eyes on Livia as if she were an extension of his brother. He walked to the huddled lump of father and daughter.

"I'll take Livia to the hospital." Beckett held out his hand for hers.

"No, you fucking won't!" John glared angrily.

Beckett dropped his hand. "Ahh, okay. I see how it is. I can't say I blame ya." He clenched his fists, his purpose shriveling like a wilting flower.

Eve sighed. Beckett needed to feel useful, and she needed to help him. She had no choice.

She recognized John as the officer she'd spoken with the day she decided to kill Beckett. It was like having a tiny piece of Anna and David with her here; Officer McHugh's grumbly voice brought it all back. The smell of shattered glass and broken dreams filled her mind.

"Officer McHugh, may I have a word?"

He looked reluctant, but carefully pulled his daughter to her feet along with him. He glanced across at Chris for a moment, but then looked back at Eve.

Livia pushed him in Eve's direction, and he took a few hesitant steps. Eve closed the distance and spoke quietly, making sure only he heard her confession. Beckett gave her a shield of privacy by talking boisterously to Livia. He offered the shocked girl endless platitudes about Blake's condition.

"Officer McHugh, I remember you. Do you remember me?" She waited. His eyes narrowed as he tried to place her. "Eve Hartt? My fiancé, David, was the victim of a drive-by?"

Eve watched as he made the connection. He raised one eyebrow and gave a slight nod.

"I've got you. You were expecting," he said.

Eve accepted the crack in her shell and kept the prize in sight. "Livia will be my responsibility. We have only a few seconds before your buddies are standing here with us and Livia has to explain why Chris has been shot. You know what that will be like for her."

Eve paused to let her words sink into the soil of his fatherly impulses. "Blake's not doing good—you know that. It's more than possible he won't make it. Being with the one you love at the end is almost as important as the beginning. It's a mark in time, before and after. That tiny bit of time in the middle? You never stop thinking about that. She needs to be with Blake."

Eve found herself unable to continue. Those were all the cards she had to show. She'd been Eve again for a moment—an Eve she hadn't seen since she turned up the air conditioner in David's car all those years ago. She swallowed and replaced her armor.

"And *you* need to stay here and make sure none of that comes back to bite her in the ass," Eve finished, jerking her finger toward Chris.

Officer McHugh nodded. "All right. Get her to the hospital and have her call me when you get there."

Eve could see disembodied searchlights as she sprinted for Beckett and Livia and hustled them out of the clearing. She drew her gun as soon as they were in the trees and miraculously found a detour around the storming troopers. Beckett located Eve's motorcycle in the parking lot, heaved it from its side, and started it up.

Eve made a big show of hugging Livia as she whispered, "Who else was with Chris tonight?"

Livia hesitated. She seemed to know giving Eve names would have serious repercussions. She looked at her shoes.

"Dave was here, wasn't he?" Eve prompted, and a sudden widening of Livia's eyes told her everything she needed. "Don't worry. I'll sort out the rest," Eve promised.

Livia's eyes remained wide, but she nodded slightly as Eve helped her climb onto the bike. Livia hugged Beckett's waist and laid her exhausted, worried head on his back.

Eve put a possessive hand on Beckett's throat. "I'll be along in a little bit. I'm going to get Mouse and clean up the mess we made tonight. I'll come as soon as I can. Be strong for her. I know you can do it." She tapped her forehead against his, like two tigers home from the hunt. Beckett revved the engine and took off.

Now doing her best to be silent in the forest, Eve picked her way back to Mouse's body. She'd dropped his laptop in this battlefield when she'd left to follow the gunshots. She knew Mouse was too big to carry alone, so she picked the laptop up, tapped out a few quick emails, and headed back to wait by the hearse.

She tried to ignore the distinct Mouseness of the vehicle: a death mobile that exploded with colored skeins of yarn inside. She brushed the window glass off the front seat as another ambulance came and went with Assfuck's worthless waste of skin taking up space in the back.

Fifteen minutes later, two mid-level douchebags — the best of what she had left available to her at the moment — arrived in an astoundingly old pickup truck. Eve noticed a tarp, quick-dry cement, and a shovel in the back. They seemed to have a little brainpower working for them. The first hopped out quickly and looked ready for direction. The second got out more slowly and added a stylized limp to his gait.

Eve nodded at the first and turned to the second. "When you walk like that, it pisses me off."

He sneered, but walked smoothly after the reprimand.

"Mouse's body is in there." She pointed — just as Mouse had done, she realized with a wince — and sent the minions on their way.

Eve returned to the hearse to make room for her friend. She opened the back door and shifted the yarn and partially finished projects around. Then she too headed in the direction of the corpse.

It took all three to carry Mouse out, and it was much less dignified than Eve had hoped. She had to climb in backward while holding Mouse's armpits just to get him into his flaming vehicle. She arranged his body and covered him with a lovely afghan he was almost done knitting. Purple and white. She smoothed the patterns over his broad form.

The two henchmen had moist eyes as they watched the unusual preparations, and they had the brains to maintain a respectful silence. Eve swallowed her pain. She would face this moment again and again — she just couldn't face it now.

She turned and gave them the additional task of cleaning up the horror she and Beckett had left in their wake. She outlined how tricky it would be, because the cops were close, even if they were occupied in the clearing for the moment. The douchebags would hear from her after the bodies were buried.

She left them to it. Before moving into the driver's seat, Eve felt around Mouse's body for a weapon that would fit her evening's purposes. She needed to move quickly and get back to Beckett. She wanted to hold his big hand and make sure he didn't kill anyone when Blake died.

If. If Blake dies, she admonished herself. Blake had a rhythm—that was the best news. She refused to think about brain damage or infection.

Still, she needed to be prepared to give Beckett some peace. If the worst happened, he would only want revenge. Her hand closed around a familiar shape, and her eyes teared up a little.

She decided to talk to this man she admired, even though he was covered with intricate yarn knots and would not respond. "Mouse, you sexy bitch. You have a crossbow?" Eve pulled it out and examined it in the streetlight's gleam. "You hot piece of man." It was cocked and ready to fire.

She turned away from the car and took aim. With barely a whoosh the arrow, complete with custom-made point, embedded itself deeply in the trunk of an unsuspecting tree. She grabbed the quiver of arrows as well.

"One last mission together, big guy. Let's go get 'em."

Eve hot-wired the hearse because she didn't have the heart to go through Mouse's pockets for the keys. Once the engine hummed to life, Eve typed quickly into the laptop. She found Dave Tweeting, like the nimrod he truly was, about the evening's exploits with two others who also seemed to have been involved. A few more clicks through a search engine and Eve had their names and addresses, along with a helpful selection of photos. *Just put it all out there, why don't you, boys?* She shook her head. One of the guys Dave was Tweeting with lived close by. Seemed at least worth a visit.

When Eve arrived at Wilson's house it looked empty, but it also had a big backyard. She left Mouse and the hearse down the street and trotted through backyards until she heard voices, just as she'd suspected.

After a moment, the two idiots she sought blazed up a joint and gave her the moment of light she needed for a positive ID.

"Man, that hobo coulda beat the shit outta us." Francis took an exaggerated inhale, then immediately began to cough.

"Wonder if Chris had the balls to bust out Dave's gun," Wilson said. "If he did we're gonna have to help him clean that shit—even if he is sort of a loser. Guess he can't help it his lady prefers hobo dick. He's gonna need an alibi."

Eve had heard enough. There was a mess brewing here. She braced her legs and readied her crossbow. She'd be kinder to them than Beckett would be if she let this play out. Mouse had done his homework; everything about the bow was modified to be silent. Only because she knew she'd released the arrow could she detect its death-filled slice through the air. Wilson crumpled without a sound. Francis looked perplexed at his now-prone friend. But before the horror of realization could reach his eyes, he was also on the ground.

Eve trotted away stealthily. *Two down, two to go.*

POUGHKEEPSIE

She slid back into the driver's seat. Mouse's presence was as tangible as his afghan-covered body.

"Hey, big guy. We got two. Now I'm going to get Photoshop Dave." She glanced in the rearview mirror, as if she might see Mouse sitting up instead of lying flat. "I can't imagine Blake living through the night," she confessed. "If you can see him from where you are right now, tell him Livia did a good job."

A few more quick taps on the laptop and Eve had a map to Dave's parents' house. The outcome for this one was already clear. Dave's misguided geek skills had earned him this reward.

The hearse rolled quietly into the driveway of a completely dark house, and Eve rearmed herself with the bow. After a few careful circles around the perimeter, she determined that Dave's room was in the garage. The blinds covering the only window were partially open. Eve waited, still as a statue as she inspected the room from the outside.

Black velvet posters had been hung on the cement walls with packing tape. The huge flat-screen TV was the only thing of any value in the setting. Dave sat sniffing a thick black marker and hitting the remote. Eve felt the disgust crawl up her throat.

He had the fake topless photo of Livia and the penny-whipped Blake pictures up on the screen. Grotesquely large, the photos apparently turned the idiot on. He began what looked like an extremely well-practiced maneuver of jerking himself off.

Eve decided then to kill him with her bare hands.

The garage door was unlocked, and she yanked it open with a thunderous roar. She stepped in and surveyed the room as Dave cowered on the couch, his face a mixture of fear and lust. Eve spotted a woman dressed very much like herself—and holding a crossbow—on the cover of a videogame on the coffee table. She dropped the bow and let a Mona Lisa smile form on her lips.

Eve closed the door behind her and went to work. She filled the room with the horrendous thumps of a body being tossed like a rag doll and the cracks of a fist smashing into Dave's bones. A quick spray of blood splashed the blinds like unruly paint, and Eve left the same way she came. She thoughtfully turned out the light as she closed the door. Back in Mouse's hearse, Eve knew she'd given Beckett a little less to do, especially if Blake gasped his last breath.

Beckett had many types of people and businesses on retainer, loyal to his money and at his beck and call. The liquor store, the florist, and the mayor all received regular calls for their services. But one he rarely, if ever, utilized was now finally in demand.

Eve banged on the owner of Coot's Funeral Parlor's door. His house was conveniently located next to his business. When he stumbled down the stairs to answer, she didn't make small talk.

"You owe Beckett. The man in that hearse needs to be…" Her voice faltered; she had to speak around her emotion. "Attended to. No police or hospital involvement."

Mr. Coot looked around nervously. "Is he already, um, expired?"

Eve couldn't bring herself to voice it, so she just nodded.

She watched while the funeral director and his teenage son removed Mouse from his hearse. They were efficient and reverent. Eve put her wrist in her mouth. She had to get out of here. Seeing Mouse like this was grinding her down.

"I'll be in touch."

Eve collapsed back into the hearse. The vehicle was so empty without him. His presence had gone with his body. Eve drove with blurry eyes, trying not to let the sorrow reach her center. She had one more kill to make.

41

I'll Love You Forever

Livia pressed her cheek against Beckett's back. She held on tight, though she wasn't afraid of falling. Instead it was her soul that wanted to fly away. All the ties that bound it inside her body seemed numb. She kept her eyes closed and hugged him tighter. Beckett was the string that kept her tethered to earth, like a trapped balloon.

She knew he was going fast; his back twitched as he shifted gears. His black shirt absorbed her tears, and she should have felt ashamed at the wet mark she was leaving, but she didn't care. When the motorcycle finally stopped, Livia just hung on. Beckett quieted the engine. The unlikely pair sat together for a moment, and Beckett wrapped his arms around hers.

"Hang in there, Whitebread. We just gotta get inside." He unpeeled her arms carefully and got off the bike.

Livia sat as if made of stone. Beckett waited next to the bike for a moment, then cocked his eyebrow and held out his hand. Livia kept her hands on the warm seat.

"What if I go in there and my whole life changes? I can't even feel my insides anymore. Beckett, I'm not strong enough." Livia didn't wipe her tears and instead let the hospital blur.

"Livia, I've never seen anything stronger than you tonight with my brother. You're the whole reason he's here." Beckett jabbed a finger at the building. "I'm not asking you to be strong by yourself. I'll be with you. Honestly? I'm not man enough to go in there alone either."

Beckett extended his invitation again, palm up. This time Livia's shaky hand, still covered in Blake's blood, fell into Beckett's like a leaf from a tree. Livia had felt glued to the seat, but once she was up and walking, her senses brought everything into sharp focus: the sound of their feet on the asphalt, the smell of the crisp night air, the sight of the broken automatic doors whooshing open and holding their place with a click.

He's here. Somewhere in the bowels of this building that was drenched in florescent lights and antiseptic cleaner, was Blake. All at once she wanted to run. She needed to run. But Beckett's firm grip on her waist kept her harnessed. He approached the check-in desk.

"My brother was brought here with a gunshot wound to the back."

It wasn't a question. It wasn't an order. Beckett presented the fact and waited to see which way common sense would twist it.

The receptionist did not seem flustered by the word *gunshot*—or Beckett, for that matter. "I'll page someone to come get you," she said.

Beckett returned his attention to Livia. He rubbed her shoulders and set to the task of rolling up the sleeves of her father's too-big jacket to reveal her hands. The simple act almost took Livia's breath away. The basic kindness in this criminal was all she'd prayed for from Chris in the forest. But instead he shot Blake.

Beckett held her shoulders again and stared into her eyes. "Whitebread, you sure you're not hurt? You look a little fucking pale." Beckett pulled her into a thick hug, burying her face in his chest.

Livia inhaled his scent—masculine, but fresh from the very chilly motorcycle ride.

"Who's looking for the gunshot wound?" The nurse who spoke was at least ten years past reasonable retirement age. Her whole demeanor screamed, *I'm only here because the economy sucks; otherwise I'd be in Boca playing shuffleboard and doing water aerobics.*

Beckett faced her and kept an arm around Livia. "I'm here for my brother, Blake."

The nurse glared at Livia. "Family only."

Livia bit her lip.

"This is my wife," Beckett explained smoothly.

The unmovable nurse raised a skeptical eyebrow at their naked hands.

Beckett smiled. "We don't wear our rings because we like to fuck other people too." The geriatric nurse blushed deeply as Beckett gave her a leering onceover. "Don't be shy, baby. I'm not afraid of a little senior lovin'."

"Follow me." Whether flattered or mortified, she was at least compelled to action.

Beckett's voice was kind in Livia's ear. "Sorry. Hope that didn't make you feel slutty."

Livia just shook her head.

The nurse's voice was nasal and grinding as she spotted someone from the ER. "Kim! I've got gawkers for the GSW."

The nurse she spoke to was small with brown curls she kept tucking behind her ears. She stepped around the elderly woman without acknowledging her at all.

"I'm so glad his family has arrived," she said, smiling at Beckett and Livia. "I'm Nurse Kim Powell. Please tell me what you can about this gentleman." She gestured over her shoulder at a large curtain.

He's right there.

"Blake Hartt is my brother," Beckett began. "He was shot in the back. Livia and Eve gave him mouth to mouth…"

Beckett's words stopped registering in Livia's consciousness. The curtain had a life of its own, blowing and rippling with activity. Scuffed-looking sneakers behind it bustled around.

Kim's voice cut through. "Does Blake have any allergies?"

The sun, Livia stopped herself from saying out loud. *But we're fixing that. We're fixing that.*

Beckett grew more and more agitated as the nurse spoke. "So what you're saying is his heart stopped again? He died again?"

Kim laid a comforting hand on Beckett's forearm, and her touch seemed to settle him enough to make eye contact. "No, Blake has not died. He's fighting, but I'm not going to lie to you—there are a lot of obstacles in his way right now. He's lost a lot of blood."

Beckett moved quickly. In one motion he snagged the pen out of Kim's scrub pocket, stepped back, and stabbed his forearm. The ballpoint produced an instant stream of blood.

"Here, take mine," he begged. "I've got plenty of blood."

Even in the depths of her shock and despair, Beckett's desperate act got Livia's attention. *Of course, he's as overwhelmed I am.* She stepped next to him and rubbed warm circles on his back.

Kim observed his offering unfazed while she snagged gauze from a nearby cart. "Baby, we've already got plenty of blood in bags, but if we need any I'll let you know—and I'll bring an IV."

Her words seemed to soothe him. He just needed something to do, a purpose here in the hospital. Livia suddenly realized how deeply affected he'd been by the evening's events. Beckett had parked legally in a parking spot, waited for someone to come help them, and inanely stabbed himself with a pen—all completely out of character. *She* needed to be here for *him* as well.

Kim held pressure on Beckett's wound. "All right, you two hang tight. I have to go scrub in. Blake's almost prepared for surgery. I'll keep you posted." She motioned another nurse over with her head. "We're going to need this bandaged. Thanks, Sue."

Livia recognized Sue as Susan Weiss, Kyle's nurse, and continued to observe closely as the two nurses said a hell of a lot more to each other with their eyes than their words. Nurse Susan deftly steered Livia and Beckett to a pair of hard plastic chairs outside the restroom.

"May I tell your sister you're here? She's been sick with worry." Susan finished wrapping Beckett's forearm with medical tape.

"That's fine. Please tell her—I need to tell my dad I'm here." Livia looked around for a phone, but lacked the motivation to leave her seat. "How's she doing?" Livia kept her eyes on Blake's curtain and her arm around Beckett's shoulders.

Susan gave Beckett a motherly pat before she stood. "Kyle? Medically, she's doing great. We're going to release her in the morning. You guys can go visit her in her new room. It might be more comfortable," she suggested carefully.

"I need to touch him." Livia waited for the curtain to open.

She realized she'd started rocking and rubbing Beckett's back in a measured rhythm. With a slight nod, Susan went off down the hall.

"Livia, he's got to make it, right? Right? He's at the hospital. We did everything right." Beckett's voice grew louder.

Livia's worry stretched to include Beckett as well. It was so big now, she couldn't imagine it ever fitting back where it belonged. She knew what Beckett was asking, and she realized her battle had just begun. The energy she'd felt in the woods—the energy that made Blake glisten—she needed to find it here too.

She turned inward for a moment, then placed steady eyes on Beckett. "He's going to make it, Beckett. I know it."

He nodded.

The curtain skittered open, sounding like loose change hitting the floor. Blake was bare to the waist. Tubes, gels, and angry red marks criss-crossed his chest. Livia focused on his 𝖲𝗈𝗋𝗋𝗒 tattoo, one of the only things she recognized with any certainty. She got to her feet and headed for the gurney as the teal-clad army rolled down the hall to fight for Blake's life. She had to trot to keep up.

Center it, Livia. Healing energy. Golden energy. She laid a hand on his arm, covering the Sorry. The touch was everything she needed it to be. She didn't think about goodbyes, only beginnings. *I love you...*

She let him slip from her fingers so those who'd trained for years could take his life in their hands. As the gurney made the turn, Livia knew she saw it. It was no figment in the moonlight. It was no exhausted CPR hallucination. His skin glistened — it shone like glass.

Livia stood in that hallway, trying to ignore the hole that formed as soon as Blake was out of sight. *Stay positive. Positive.*

She turned to find Beckett, who also stared down the hall. She smiled. "He's going to be fine."

Beckett looked away from her and toward the sound of running footsteps. He was out of his chair and standing in front of Livia before even a hint of adrenaline hit her system.

Kyle came down the hall at a dead run, with Cole barely keeping up with her. Beckett stepped aside to allow the sisters to collide. In a well-practiced movement, Livia accepted Kyle's crushing leap.

"Holy fucking dogs! You scared the uterus out of me." Kyle squeezed Livia's face.

Beckett and Cole wrapped arms as Beckett shook his head. "Bro, he's in there. I...he...he was shot in the back." Cole bypassed the usual man-hug and embraced Beckett like a father would a son.

The clatter of another fast-moving gurney replenished the volume and urgency that had departed with Blake's team. Livia spotted a flash of familiar T-shirt and overly gelled hair as it raced by. *Chris.*

Livia saw her father coming down the corridor much more slowly. He heaved a sigh of relief as his eyes met hers. Livia set her sister's feet on the floor, and suddenly felt the world moving in slow motion. Cole's hug became a restraint as Beckett realized who'd just sped by on the second gurney.

"Let me go." Beckett's voice was deadly.

Cole tightened his hold. "Over my dead body."

John continued past them down the hall and disappeared. He was on the job now, part of the busy epicenter behind the curtain. Livia could hear him ask a series of official-sounding questions about the events of the evening, but he received no audible response from Chris. Livia hugged her sister a little tighter, then quickly pushed her aside.

Daring to approach the brothers' tension-filled embrace, Livia touched one of Beckett's coiled arms. "Beckett." She waited until his furious face turned toward her mouth. "I still need you. Here. I can't wait for him without you. You promised. I'm not man enough. Remember?"

Livia held her breath.

"You've got your sister," he said quietly.

"Let go of him, Cole. Please." Livia nodded at the puzzle of arms, each with its own agenda.

Cole looked reluctant as he stepped away, keeping his body between Beckett and Chris.

"It has to be all of us. Don't ask me how I know, but I do. We all have to sit here and hope for the best. Pray for the best. Even with that pile of shit right there." Livia didn't have to point; they could all feel pulsating of the evil that was lodged in Chris.

"We have to think about Blake—getting fixed, getting healed, getting back to us. Adding murder to tonight is wrong. It's all wrong. You have to make a different choice. I trust you, Beckett. You can do this."

Livia's earnest words seemed to make Beckett want to curse. His face boiled red for a moment. Only Beckett could hear Livia's gentle breath that pleaded, "Please."

Rather than leaping to action, he rubbed his forehead and took in great gasps of air. Finally, he grabbed her head in a giant hug. "For you, Whitebread. Only for fucking you."

Livia tried to hug him back, but he had her in such a way that she just had to let her arms hang.

On another pass down the hall, Susan approached the group, oblivious to their drama. "Hey, kids, can you take it back to Kyle's room now? This isn't exactly a hangout spot."

Beckett twirled Livia so he could wrap his arm around her shoulders. "We ain't moving. My brother's in there, and we have to know what the fuck is going on." His eyes, despite his promises, found the billowing curtain that hid Chris from view.

Susan's demeanor and tone remained professional. "How about I promise to tell you what the fuck is going on as soon as we know anything?"

Livia didn't like the idea of being any farther than she had to from Blake, but she also didn't like the longing in Beckett's eyes. *We have to stay positive.*

"All right, Nurse Susan. I think that sounds good. You'll tell us as soon as you know anything?" Livia tried pushing on Beckett's side.

"I'll go in there specially to find out what's happening," she promised. "I just need you all to clear out of my ER." The choice was clear: They could be on her good side or her bad side.

Kyle led the way, and Cole kept a hand on her lower back, holding her hospital gown together. Livia loved the sight of this man covering her sister. And thankfully someone had given Kyle a pair of scrub bottoms. They were at least three sizes too big, and with all Kyle's running and jumping they'd come unrolled at the bottom. She flopped the long legs around like penguin feet.

Kyle's room was now one floor up from the ER. Kathy looked up from her reading but said nothing as the herd shuffled in. Kyle climbed back in bed, and Cole curled his long body around hers. Beckett collapsed in a chair and pulled Livia into his lap. They began a séance of silence. Susan was true to her word and appeared with hourly updates.

Though they listened carefully, without internet access Livia couldn't look up the fancy terms Susan tossed around. Her complicated descriptions did little to assuage fear. On her first visit Susan detailed blood transfusions and chest tubes. John popped in and hugged his girls. He begged their forgiveness, but needed to get to the precinct to sort out the evening's mess.

"You might have to come in later to answer a few questions, Liv," her father said reluctantly. "Shouldn't be a problem, but you know how it is. I'll try and make it fast."

Livia kissed her father's cheek. "Thanks, Dad. I'm so lucky to have you."

John shuffled his feet and looked shy. Kathy stood and walked with him out of the room.

The second Susan visit included words like *bullet penetration* and *cavitation*. She seemed to think the fact that there was "no fragmentation" was a good thing. As the nurse bustled out, Eve appeared silently at the door wearing jeans and a T-shirt — completely normal apparel that on her seemed outrageously out of place. She nodded once at Livia, who found herself instantly alone in the chair as Beckett headed for the hallway.

Soon his too-loud voice drifted back into the room. "He shot *my brother* in the back. He's mine. That's a fucking order. *Mine.*"

Eve's gentle murmur was indecipherable.

"Do what you gotta, Eve, but I swear to fuck, you better not touch him." Beckett huffed back into the room.

He paced and punched his own palm for a bit, then finally sat and held his head.

The third, fourth, and fifth Susan visits were just updates that Blake was still alive, but her lips seemed tight. Kyle shifted between leaning into Cole's chest and putting little braids in Livia's hair. The TV flickered from its perch in the corner of the room, but no one could keep their eyes on it.

Beckett did a cafeteria run. He came back with a trash bag full of food and drinks and announced, "The cafeteria was closed." No one asked him how he got food from a closed establishment.

"Eat up, Whitebread," Beckett held out a granola bar to Livia.

She shook her head.

"You know what's going to fucking happen? You're going to pass the fuck out," he told her. "You'll hit your damn head and be a useless sack when Blake gets out of surgery. You want to be a sack on the floor with your ass pointed in the air, Livia? Will that help anyone?"

Livia almost smiled at his awful mothering. She took the bar and unwrapped it, then nearly choked as Beckett pounded her back in encouragement.

The sixth Susan visit was tortuous. She described the effect of severe blood loss and oxygen deprivation on the brain, and she kept saying "traumatic injury."

Like we don't already know.

"He should be out of surgery in the next hour. One of you can accompany him in the recovery room. Then you can take turns visiting when he gets to his room." Susan smoothed her scrubs and left them to think.

Beckett blew out a noisy breath. "Well, that doesn't sound very fucking good. He's gonna be a vegetable. Son of a bitch."

Livia stood and looked out the window. Her own eyes stared back at her. "We need to pray. Cole, say some prayers for us. Please. Healing prayers." Livia kept her eyes on her reflection.

Cole cleared his throat. "Um. Okay. Let's see."

Kyle stroked Cole's lips gently with her thumb. "Go ahead."

Cole pulled the room's Bible out of a top drawer and flipped through it for a moment. His voice took on a different tone as he prayed, as if he painted the air with the solemn aura of the church.

"The Lord is my Shepherd; I shall not want. He maketh me to lie down in green pastures: He leadeth me beside the still waters. He restoreth my soul: He leadeth me in the paths of righteousness for His name's sake…"

Livia watched as Beckett folded his hands into a thick sailor's knot of hope. He bowed his head. She couldn't have loved him more if he'd been her actual brother. She let Cole's words lift her.

She pictured Blake and closed her eyes. He lay under the bright surgery lights, tubes in place, beeping monitors, Sorry tattoo. It was as if she stood in the room with him. She poured her energy around him, surrounded him with sparkling, champagne-colored sunlight. *Heal him. Strengthen him. Heal him.*

"…Yea, though I walk through the valley of the shadow of death, I will fear no evil: For thou art with me; Thy rod and thy staff, they comfort me…"

Livia pictured herself holding Blake's hand on a walk in the forest, the sun prickling through the leaves to dance on his face. She pictured his smile. She imagined she felt the gentle touch of his finger on her cheek. She pressed her lips together. *He will kiss me again. I know it.*

Cole's lilting prayer continued, almost like music. "Surely goodness and mercy shall follow me all the days of my life, and I will dwell in the House of the Lord forever."

Cole lifted his head, and in the pause, the four spoke together: "Amen."

Susan appeared as if the word was her name. "Okay, who's going to visit Blake?"

Livia smiled as three fingers pointed at her.

She followed Susan into the surgical recovery area. The recovery room was a giant cube of yet more curtains. Walls, it seemed, were a precious luxury. Susan fitted Livia with a paper jumpsuit, explaining that Blake was susceptible to infection. Livia washed up to her elbows with antibacterial soap and snapped on a paper mask. Susan approved with a nod and walked to a spot two curtains away. She parted the fabric with reverence.

Livia took in the sight of her love. He fought a still, silent battle against death, but he looked pale and helpless. Livia hated that. She knelt next the bed and kissed the mark of his tattoo through her paper mask and around the tubes. An IV chugged liquid straight into his veins.

"Go ahead and talk to him, sweetheart. It helps," suggested Nurse Kim as she monitored Blake's machines. She checked off a few things on a clipboard, and Susan rolled in a computer chair for Livia to sit on as she held Blake's hand and stroked his tattoo.

"Hey, handsome, I'm right here. You're doing an amazing job. I'm so proud of you." Livia's voice cracked a bit, and she swallowed her tears. "The ladies here are working real hard. Beckett's here, and Cole is too. We're all just waiting for you. But you take the time you need. I'm not going anywhere. Well, I may have to pee once in a while, but I'll come right back."

Susan gently laughed and rubbed Livia's shoulders. "There you go. Keep it honest for him."

As the nurses busied themselves with other patients and statistics, Livia slid her hand over his. She needed to feel his skin. She tucked his hand under the thin blanket and held it without protection. The same tingling she'd felt when they first held hands flooded her skin. *He's still in there. They can tell me anything they want. Blake's right here.*

She scooted her chair closer to his head. The deep, monotonous breaths the ventilator forced him to take sounded scary, but Livia held tight to his hand.

"I love you, Blake Hartt," she whispered. "I'll love you forever."

42

EYE FOR AN EYE

D r. Hartt had put Blake in a medically induced coma, as even waking might be too much for his recovering system. He was moved to a private room, and Livia began a hospital vigil. No one mentioned payment or insurance, but Livia had a feeling Beckett would provide cash.

After three days, Blake was weaned off the drugs that kept him asleep. Told he could wake at any moment, everyone but Livia was concerned. They all found time to try to prepare Livia for the worst. Each time she would listen, thank them for their concerns, and turn back to Blake with a smile.

They couldn't feel the tingling. But she could. Nurses Susan and Kim had arranged for Livia to stay in Blake's room, and she left only when she felt Blake's gentleman's code would be compromised if she remained. During one of these brief moments, while Livia stood in the hall, her father decided to stop by.

"Hey, Liv. Kathy picked these out for you," he said, handing her a bag of fresh clothes.

"Thanks, Dad." Livia looked over her shoulder, but Susan was still fixing Blake's bedding. How she changed the sheets with Blake still in the bed seemed like a magic trick.

"Well, your sister moved out," her father began in a matter-of-fact tone. "She'll probably be over to tell you all about it." He shook his head in a constant "no" motion while delivering the news.

"Did you guys have a fight?" Livia had always been the filter for her sister's impulses.

"Oh, no. She was busy rushing around sighing about the new holy boyfriend, saying things like 'shadow' and 'my other self,' yadda yadda. You know how I feel about living together before marriage."

Livia sighed. If he only knew how wonderful it was for Kyle to be settling down.

"She's going to be fine, Dad. Cole's good for her." Livia crossed her arms and looked again in Blake's direction.

"There's something else," her father said, capturing her attention again. "Your friend Beckett? If he shows up, I need you to call me right away." Livia watched as discomfort and resolve took their places on her father's face.

"What happened?" Livia asked a little sharply. But she knew before her father told her.

"You got a lot going on here. We'll talk about it later," he said, backing away.

"Just tell me, Dad." She gave him a pointed stare.

"Chris was murdered right in his hospital room. Beckett Taylor is wanted for questioning."

Livia closed her eyes. *Beckett.*

"I can't say I'm sorry to hear that," Livia finally said. "I damn near did it myself. How are you so sure it wasn't me?" Livia watched as her father smirked then looked solemn.

"The way Chris went? You could never do that — ever." He shuddered.

Livia did feel sorry for Chris's family — for the beautiful Mrs. Grandma. But she couldn't muster any real regret for Chris's demise.

Susan rolled a cart full of used linens past father and daughter. "Hey, Princess Charming, Sleeping Handsome is all yours."

Livia was grateful. Her hand had started to ache, missing the tingle Blake's skin provided. Her dad held his arms out for a hug, a new custom he'd adopted the night Blake was shot. Livia hugged him and returned to Blake's side, the door closing softly behind her.

She arranged Blake's hair so it looked more like it was supposed to, then pulled the now-familiar recliner over and held his hand. She'd put on her fresh clothes later. She focused on her favorite machine in the room: the one that kept track of Blake's heartbeat. With slow breaths and concentration, Livia could make her heart beat in tandem with his.

Beckett sat in the hospital parking lot in a Lincoln he'd commandeered from one of his douchebags. Its windows were so black the car looked like a Matchbox toy. Behind them, Beckett's eyes fixed on what he knew was Blake's window. Whitebread was in there, waiting like the fucking pillar of strength she was. That little brunette had out-couraged pretty much every damn person he'd ever met—exactly what Blake needed.

Beckett's gaze fell on the discarded scalpel on the floor of the car. It was covered in blood. He sat here at the scene of the crime like a first-time pussy, with the goddamn weapon right next to him.

When Eve had appeared at the hospital to tell him she'd killed the other assholes involved, Beckett had been relieved. And she'd been ready to finish the job. Eve wanted to eliminate Chris and keep Beckett's hands clean. But Beckett wanted his hands dirty. He wanted to avenge his brother. Almost equal was his desire to protect sweet Whitebread. Eve was not pleased, but there was nothing she could do. She'd left to hide the corpses she'd created.

As he had strolled the hospital and broken into the cafeteria to get food for his people upstairs, Beckett had formed the weak outline of a plan. He knew he owned a few beat cops. Mouse always made sure to keep a selection on the payroll—at times it was truly the only way to stay out of jail.

Mouse. Beckett put his grief away.

He'd fed his people, and Livia had even convinced him to pray. But Beckett's prayer had nothing to do with Cole's mumbo jumbo and all the "ths" at the end of every other damn word. Beckett wanted one simple thing. A shot. A chance to kill the fuck out of Chris.

The next day they'd sent Kyle home, so Cole went back to his church and Livia followed Blake to his new room. Beckett said goodbye as if he were heading out, but instead did some stalking while flirting with the nurses. Over the next twenty-four hours, Beckett figured out their schedule, and he also scoped out Chris's room—just one cop sitting outside his door. *Guess they aren't afraid of a double-kneecapped bitch running away.*

When he spied O'Malley, one of the cops on his take, starting a shift in front of the bastard's door the next day, Beckett grabbed the first weapon he could lay his hands on. He found a packet of shiny tools for surgery and ripped it open. The scalpel's blade was sharp and very small. *Perfect.*

"Hey, O'Malley!" Beckett sauntered up to the uniformed officer.

They shook hands like friends, but the cop's eyes clearly said, *What the hell?*

Beckett's big smile never left his face as he issued orders. "Go get coffee for an hour. Then you can come back."

O'Malley's mouth opened, but nothing ever came out. He put his head down and walked quickly down the hall.

Beckett slipped into the room and let his eyes adjust to the dim light. Chris had cartoons on the TV like a dickless woman. He snored with his mouth open. Guaranteed, his IV was chock full of pain meds.

Beckett stood looming over Chris, letting the image of his brother's chest being shocked in the night fill his mind. At his core, Beckett was a killer; no one could find mercy in him now.

A cracking punch on the bruise on Chris's face was the patient's good morning kiss. Chris woke, shaking like he was having a seizure. Beckett plunged the scalpel into Chris's neck, slicing his vocal cords to keep him silent. After yanking the IV from Chris's arm, Beckett let him know why he was visiting.

"Hey, fuck-a-doodle-doo! You soggy-ass pussy. You shot my brother in the back. Know what that means? You're gonna die, bitch." Beckett didn't put on gloves; he wanted to feel the warm, sticky blood. "Let's get started. Eye for an eye, they always say." Beckett began carving as Chris's mouth formed the circle of a noiseless scream.

Beckett looked away from the instrument on the floor of the Lincoln. Chris had died a horrific death, even by Beckett's standards.

But his death didn't give Beckett the peace he craved. Until Blake woke up and talked like a normal motherfucker, Beckett was going to want to puke. All the doctors and nurses assigned to Blake had that sad look in their eyes, like they were treating a damn dead dog or something. And he knew those bastards had seen shit like this before.

He guessed that was why he'd committed Chris's murder like an amateur. Like a butt-munching serial jack-off. He'd left more DNA, proof, and motive in his wake than he could shake his dick at.

Eve was going to kill him.

And now he was back at the scene of the crime. His ass was getting stupider by the second. But he had to see Blake and bask in all the hope Whitebread tossed around like confetti.

"Fuck it, here I go." Beckett squared his shoulders, walked in the front door, and continued on to Blake's room without incident. He found Whitebread curled up in the chair like a cat, her hand touching Blake's. She was sleeping, and Beckett had almost turned tail to leave her in peace when Blake's eyes snapped open.

"The fuck!?" Beckett ran to Blake's side as his brother's face registered the room in panic.

Whitebread popped up and was almost nose-to-nose with Blake immediately. Beckett leaned around her and held his brother's flailing arms.

Livia spoke in a soft, urgent voice. "Blake? They have you on a ventilator; this thing in your mouth needs to be removed by the doctor. Just calm down. Look, I'm here. I'm here. See? It's okay. Just try to be calm."

Whitebread stroked Blake's cheek.

Beckett held his breath. *Is this flailing, panicked dude the new Blake?*

43

A Real Human Heart

Livia had been thinking about this moment since Blake came out of surgery. She'd talked herself through all the possibilities for when he woke up: he might be confused, and the ventilator sure as hell would freak him out. But now, sitting almost on top of him and holding his alert, scared face was enough to make her cry. His vibrant green eyes looked everywhere but at her.

"Beckett, go get a nurse or a doctor," she said as calmly as possible. She sensed Beckett's reluctance. "Let go of his arms. It's okay." Livia felt the bed react as Beckett removed his huge body.

Blake's hands covered hers. She could see the trapped feeling in his wild eyes.

"I'm so happy to see you. I love you so much. Thank you for waking up," Livia spoke quickly but calmly, trying to capture Blake's attention.

Finally, his eyes locked on hers, and she gave him a huge, teary-eyed smile. She couldn't tell if he counted because his lips were stretched around the appliance that had kept him breathing. *Be in there, Blake. Please. Please, God.*

Livia turned to see Beckett run back into the room literally carrying a nurse. Nurse Kim, to be exact. He set her down, pointed at Blake, and shouted, "See!?"

"Our boy's awake," Kim said simply, not even acknowledging her strange entry. "Hey, Blake. Good morning."

She kept a happy banter going as she efficiently checked the machines surrounding her patient. Susan arrived within seconds, and the nurses slipped into easy conversation. They seemed to be demonstrating for Blake how relaxed they were.

"Blake, glad to see you awake. Good timing—we were prepping to wean you off of the vent to see how your lungs are doing. Would you like to try that now?" Susan waited with a gentle smile.

Livia sat frozen. She hadn't asked Blake a direct question yet. This simple yes-or-no answer would tell everyone in the room a million things. *Can he understand words? Will he be okay? Is Blake still here?*

He looked perplexed and strained against the tube in his throat.

Livia centered her energy again. *You can do this.*

Blake nodded once, then twice, then three times. Yes, he wanted the tube out.

He understands!

Beckett scooped Livia off the bed and twirled her. The nurses filled the space she emptied.

"You did it, Whitebread! You saved him. You're amazing. My brother. My brother." His voice breaking, Beckett set her back on her feet and hugged her.

When she saw Blake staring at her over Beckett's shoulder, Livia stumbled a bit. His gaze was so intense. So Blake. Beckett kept her steady. She could feel his whole body smiling.

They both stayed through the meticulous process of removing the ventilator. Blake's first breaths on his own were gentle and sure, thanks to Kim and Susan's expertise. He coughed when he was supposed to, following yet another command, and Livia's heart soared. Finally, when they asked him to speak, he found her gray eyes.

His voice was husky and raspy, but his words were clear. "Livia. You love me."

Beckett let her go as she climbed back onto Blake's bed. Blake moved slowly, but he seemed determined and winced only a little as he reached for her shoulders and pulled Livia against his chest. She wanted to say something, but her sobs took those words from her.

His raspy voice moved her hair with his precious, perfect words. "You're here. With me."

Livia grabbed a fistful of his hospital gown. The strength that had sustained her dissolved into gratitude. To see his light, his face, everything that was Blake again brought relief like she'd never known. He rubbed her back as her body shook with sobs.

After surveying the scene for another moment, Susan and Kim stepped into the hall and hovered just outside the door. Beckett held up his fist, and

Blake paused his rubbing to salute by grabbing Beckett's arm. Her sobs quieting, Livia turned to watch as the brothers said nothing but nodded solemnly at one another, which said everything. Beckett then turned to exit through the open door.

As he stepped into the hallway, Susan looked Beckett up and down. "Livia's dad told me to watch for you and give him a call if you turned up."

Beckett froze. His hands gripped the doorframe where he stood.

"So, as soon as I'm sure Blake is on the mend, I'm going to make that call," Susan continued. "It should be within the next ten minutes." She finished her speech with a pointed look.

Beckett's smile filled his voice. "Thank you."

"Don't thank us, just go," Kim replied. "We don't approve of what you might have done."

Beckett kissed each woman's cheek and said, "Ladies, I was saying thank you for taking such beautiful care of my brother. You're angels. Selfless, beautiful fucking angels. I'll get out of your hair." After the briefest of looks back into Blake's hospital room, Beckett disappeared down the hall.

Livia closed her eyes to steady herself for a moment. Her sobs had subsided into small, rhythmic sniffles. When she opened her eyes, she was ready. She sat up and tucked her hair behind her ear. She filled a cup of water and added the straw. The cup was steady in her hand as he took a few sips.

Livia decided she loved watching things go into him. Food, water, love — all these things she could give him.

"You look tired. Would you like to nap?" he asked. Blake was definitely back. There was less rasp and more smoke in his silky voice.

"No, Blake. I never want to sleep again. Just this." Livia touched his face. "Only this."

The pride in his eyes almost changed their color. He turned his face to her palm, kissed it, and said, "Come, my love, put your head on my shoulder. Your burdens have been heavy."

In that moment, Livia realized her eyelids were drooping, and the crook of Blake's arm seemed perfect for her head. His lips stayed on her forehead as he hummed a serene song. Livia fell into a deep, dreamless slumber.

Blake's cough woke her sometime later. He shrugged and looked apologetic when she checked his face, touching him again for reassurance.

"You're doing great, Mr. Hartt," said the therapist who Livia now noticed in the room. "We'll work on those breathing exercises again later." Blake gave a quick wave as the man in scrubs left the room.

He returned his gaze to Livia. "I'm sorry I woke you. You were so out. You need the rest."

Livia touched his limbs, his blankets, and his hair, taking inventory. "Having you wake me is worth it every time."

"Did I pass inspection?" he teased, watching her roving hands.

"Yes. You're still here. That's what I need." Livia reached to refill his cup.

She had a flash of her effortless forever: Feeding Blake, tucking a blanket around his body when he fell asleep on a couch, saying thank you any time he passed her the salt at the table.

"The nurses told me what you did, Livia. You made my heart beat in the woods." He looked at her lips and continued, "You gave me breath. Were you scared, love? I'm sorry."

"You're apologizing because you stopped breathing?" Livia wrinkled her nose.

He nodded reverently. "I left you in the clearing again."

"You took the bullet that had my name on it and let it lodge in your back," Livia responded. "You never left me in those woods. You gave me strength when I needed it. You don't need to apologize, but it's perfectly acceptable for you to never, ever stop breathing again." She touched his *Sorry* tattoo.

At his slow smile, she gathered him into a gentle hug again. *Will I ever be able to stop touching him?*

"Brave Livia, you never cease to amaze me." He lifted her chin with his finger. "I've never been more thankful to be alive than right now."

After soft kisses, they pressed their hands together palm to palm. The tingling scattered all over Livia's body, warming her.

"Do you feel that?" she whispered with a smile.

His lips moved in his silent count. Blake wrapped his fingers around her hand. She copied the movement. Their hands together now resembled a heart—not a cartoon rendering of the shape, but a real human heart.

He touched her lips with his and murmured, "I've been feeling it since you first smiled at me."

44

COOL, CLEAN WATER

D r. Hartt usually kept his past from his friends, colleagues, and patients. There was just never a great time to bring up childhood. His
wasn't necessarily something he had to hide; he just chose to omit it from
his present-day life.

His parents had announced they were separating the night before his
sixth birthday. Then his father was remarried and Flora, Dad's new wife,
announced he would be getting a baby sister or brother soon. Her belly
grew, and Ted watched the house fill with more and more baby toys each
time he visited.

When he first met his half-sister Elizabeth, she was angry, red, and
crying. Flora made him sit in a big rocker and hold the terrifyingly loud
bundle while she took a picture. But by the time Flora had found the camera,
remembered to remove the lens cap, and added the flash, Elizabeth had
quieted in his arms. She put one of her flailing hands in her mouth and
settled her grass-green eyes on her big brother's face.

Ted was hooked. Every visit to his father's after that was filled with
Elizabeth. And it seemed she felt the same. Before she could even walk,
Elizabeth insisted on getting a handful of Ted's cheek by way of greeting.

One afternoon Ted overheard Flora on the phone. "I'll tell you what,
Pam, Ted has such a way with Elizabeth. She adores him. I swear she cries
for hours when he goes back to his mother's. That boy will make an amazing dad someday."

Over the next four years, Ted and Elizabeth created a world all their
own. He built her grand forts using blankets and chairs. Flora took hundreds
of pictures of the two of them, and she liked to call them Hansel and Gretel.

Then the night before Ted's twelfth birthday, his father sat him down. "I'm sorry to tell you this, son, but Flora and I are separating. She's not taking it real well. She needs some time is all, and she's taking Elizabeth down to her grandmother's."

Ted's father seemed resigned to the loss.

"Are you done with Flora like you were done with Mom?" Ted wanted him to say no.

His father answered as if Ted was a full-grown man. "I can't get it right," he sighed. "Another one keeps catching my eye. I have trouble with forever, you know?"

That night Ted went through the photo albums and took a fistful Hansel and Gretel pictures. He had no problem with forever, even at his tender age.

Ted refused to visit his father after that. His dad was soon married for the third time—to an even younger version of Flora. During their infrequent phone calls Ted always asked his father about Elizabeth. He never received solid answers or any information he could act on. The door to finding his sister closed permanently when an aggressive cancer suddenly ended his father's life.

In the years after he finished med school, Ted took advantage of all the technology at his fingertips. But his searches for Elizabeth or Flora Hartt yielded too many results. Desperate for something to do, Ted decided the obvious choice was returning to work at Poughkeepsie Hospital. His mother still lived close, and the house where he used to visit Elizabeth still stood in one of the old neighborhoods. In Ted's mind, this was a way to honor them both.

He'd plunged himself into his work and set his past aside, but his new trauma patient had piqued his interest. The green eyes and strong jaw were so familiar, and coupled with the matching last name, Ted was inspired. Maybe it was time to take things a step further. He'd hired a private investigator.

He'd received the report not an hour earlier, complete with arrest records, a death certificate, and a birth certificate. The young man who'd so recently beaten the odds and emerged alert and aware from his medically induced coma was most likely his nephew. After looking over the hospital records and intake papers, Ted had learned Blake was a vagrant. So he had a homeless, injured nephew whose childhood had been a casualty of his half-sister's descent into alcoholism and death.

He now struggled to find a way to explain this bizarre connection to the man behind the hospital-room door in front of him. He glanced down at the photo he'd brought: Elizabeth giggling happily with Ted in the center of their sheet-made castle. He traced the face of the little girl who still held his heart. How terrible to learn what she'd become.

His surgeon's hands shook as he opened the door. A curtain of light brown hair obscured Blake's face as he was thoroughly kissed by his girlfriend. Ted cleared his throat. Livia sat back and gave a sheepish smile with a matching blush. Blake reached up and touched her cheek. Ted felt like he'd walked into a confessional.

"Dr. Hartt, good afternoon," Blake said warmly, ending his discomfort.

"Mr. Hartt, good afternoon to you as well. Ms. McHugh." He nodded formally to her. But he didn't know where to start, his easy bedside manner was lost for once. He just forged ahead. "Blake, I had a sister named Elizabeth—she was my half-sister. I lost touch with her when I was twelve. I've been looking for her ever since, and I think she was your mother."

Ted held out the report with Elizabeth's digital mugshot printed in color on the bottom. Blake looked at the picture and turned to stare out the window. He made no move to accept the papers.

Livia took them from the doctor's hand and touched Blake's arm. "Is this her?" she asked. "Is this your mom?"

Blake's nod was barely perceptible.

"That's great. You have family." Livia rubbed Blake's arm.

"You're my family," Blake said coldly.

She looked confused and handed the report back. "I'm sorry, Dr. Hartt. Can we have a moment?"

She asked politely, but Ted could tell she would enforce whatever Blake decided regarding his newfound uncle. He had to try one last time before he left them to their own conclusions. He stepped up and set the picture from his childhood on Blake's bed, where the two could see it.

"*This* is your mother to me, this little girl," Ted explained. "I adored her. My father's poor choices took her out of my life. I'm not trying to do anything other than tell you I'm here, and I was looking for her. Whatever she became, she was a wonderful little sister. I miss her."

Ted left the picture and walked out. He felt not the least bit professional. Why hadn't he waited until Blake recovered? *That was selfish, just like my goddamn father always was.*

"You look pale. Are you hungry? We don't have to talk about this now." Livia watched as Blake lifted the snapshot from the fuzzy splash of blanket.

"That's your mom?" She looked at his face as he studied it.

He nodded. "I never imagined she could smile that big."

Livia felt the deluge of hate fill her to the top. Blake should've received limitless smiles as a child. Every time he entered the room his mother's face should've lit up. His counting of Livia's smiles made even-more-painful sense.

"Your future will be full of smiles. I promise."

He looked surprised by the vehemence in her voice. "My past was worth it," he said evenly. "All the trials brought me to this: you holding my hand." He trailed his fingers up her arm to her shoulder and finally around the nape of her neck. "Kiss me."

Livia leaned into his full lips, relishing the taste that was Blake. The little slice of Ted's past slipped from between them and landed on the floor. The kiss led to embarrassing moaning, and they pulled away, laughing at the need between them.

"Being with you might just kill me right now." Blake held her hands and took slow measured breaths.

"I'll wait until you can pant properly." Livia looked at him from under her lashes.

"Oh crap. That's not helping." Blake pretended to do CPR on his own chest.

"What are you going to do about Uncle Dr. Hartt? He's been really wonderful while we've been here." Livia got off of the bed and retrieved his picture from the floor.

"I don't want to be anyone's charity case. Not even my new uncle." Blake's raspy voice cracked a little.

"Well, you're all mine now, Blake. We can handle anything; we will or won't be charity cases together. I don't think he's offering to diaper you and buy you a wagon. Maybe just a cup of coffee?" She touched his hair.

He softened. "*Together* makes this easier to swallow. I guess there's no harm in talking to the man."

"Uncle or not, he did save your life," Livia pointed out.

Blake bit his bottom lip and shook his head. Livia felt a wintry shiver as he licked his lips.

"*You* saved my life, Livia. Only you."

Blake's hospital stay lasted two more weeks, and when he inquired about the bill, Kim informed him it had been covered by an anonymous donation. A cash donation.

"The billing department actually had to call the hospital president for instructions on how to deal with all the large bills," she explained in a secretive voice. "In the end, hospital security escorted the head of accounting to the bank in the middle of the day." Kim shook her head and laughed, but Blake's eyes hardened. When they were alone he vented to Livia.

"Beckett and his goddamn blood money. This feels all wrong to me." He sat in what Livia had come to think of as *her* recliner as she helped him lace up his boots. Their soles were still dulled with a coating of soil from their traumatic night.

Livia wasn't sure how to comfort Blake. She certainly didn't have a big pile of clean money to take the place of Beckett's. "Beckett is all sorts of bad because of what he does, but who he *is*—that's very beautiful. Sweetheart, he really stood by me while I waited for you to come out of surgery." She rose and held out her arm.

"I would've been a wreck waiting for you for hours like that," Blake said. He leaned on her arm as little as possible as he stood.

"And Beckett would've been right next to you the whole time." She shrugged. None of this changed the fact that Beckett was a murderer and the funds probably came from merchandise customers injected into themselves.

Checking out of the hospital was a process that had started in the morning and now continued into the afternoon. Kim and Susan popped in before their shifts were up to give Blake and Livia hugs and praise. The nurses waved away the thanks Blake and Livia showered on them. Directions from the respiratory therapist, prescriptions for rehabilitation and pain pills, and consent forms made a little pile on Blake's hospital bed. And still they sat. Waiting. The TV was off. The room felt claustrophobic. Blake and Livia had made all the hard decisions already. Now they just needed to *go*.

True to his word, Blake had spoken to Dr. Hartt every day since he revealed their connection. They'd even progressed to calling each other by their first names. And Ted's answer to Blake's housing predicament was almost perfect.

Ted owned the apartment building he lived in, and he told Blake that his property manager had moved out a few months ago, and he needed someone new to fill the job. In exchange for collecting rent and making minor repairs, Blake could live in the building's basement apartment. It was small, but it came furnished, Ted explained.

Livia had a sneaking suspicion he'd filled an empty apartment with belongings just for Blake, but he was trying very hard to be respectful and sensitive to Blake's pride. She was thrilled when Blake agreed to take the position.

Around four p.m., Cole and Kyle gave up waiting for Livia's "Come get us!" text and appeared in Blake's hospital room. Cole greeted Blake with the usual arm hug, and their eyes locked in silent conversation.

Where's Beckett? Blake's asked.

Cole quickly shook his head. "Blake, you're looking great," he said instead.

Blake nodded. "Livia wouldn't have it any other way."

He smiled at her, but Livia was busy watching her sister hop from one foot to the other.

"Do you have to use the ladies' room or something?" Livia asked.

"No. No, I don't. I just can't wait. I'm having all sorts of problems with the waiting."

Livia knew her sister's secret would bubble out of her soon.

Cole put a hand on Kyle's shoulder. "You wanted to wait, remember? Tell her if you can't stand it anymore."

At that, Kyle exploded. She waved her sparkling left hand in front of her. *"Oh my God! I'm engaged! I'm marrying Cole!"*

"What?!" Livia squeezed her sister hard. "Let me see. When did this happen? Did you tell Dad? When is it going to be? How did he propose?"

The men stopped their congratulatory handshake to stare at the speed-talking ladies.

"Last night, not yet, four weeks from today, naked!" Kyle blurted in response.

The girls became a moving, jumping circle of hug.

"Cole, you popped the question in your birthday suit?" Blake teased.

Cole put his face in his hands. "Did not think she would share that bit of information."

Blake slapped his brother on the back. "Pretty sure Kyle lacks any kind of editing mechanism."

"So, seeing as you know all the details already, can I count on you to be best man?" Cole watched fear creep over Blake's face. "The ceremony is at night," he added quickly.

Blake said nothing, just opened and closed his fist.

"If Mr. Old Timey is still all jacked up from being a bullet catcher, we'll put it off," Kyle added.

Blake smiled and held his arms open to the female ball of fire. "I'll be fine, Kyle. I wouldn't want you to spend one extra day not married to Cole because of me."

Kyle hugged him carefully. "Your being well is one of the only things that could ever make me wait."

After an extra squeeze Blake unclasped Kyle and she found her way to Cole's hand, as surely as a river finding the bay.

Blake answered Cole's question still hanging in the air. "I'd be honored to serve as your best man."

Neither mentioned Beckett, but both touched their tattoos. Then a nurse appeared in the door with some final paperwork and a wheelchair. Livia took the papers and pen over to Blake, whose gaze was riveted on the wheelchair.

"I'd prefer to stand when ladies are standing," he said quietly to Livia.

She longed to smooth a balm on all his wounds. "Blake, I'm exhausted. What I really need is a nice, strong lap to sit on to get me out to the car."

He reached up and stroked her hair. "I could be a lap for you, my tired angel."

Blake settled into the wheelchair and patted his lap for Livia.

"That's against policy. Patient only in the wheelchair." The geriatric nurse made a face as if the sight of gentle, new love was a pile of crap under her nose. "And I'm not pushing two people's weight."

Kyle stepped up to the tip of the nurse's formidable bosom. "Hey, Tit-tanic, you're absolutely going to allow it, or I'll show you my projectile-vomit-at-will skills. And he has a touch of food poisoning that might just kick in before he can get to the crapper," she added, pointing to Cole.

Cole hung his head and shook it.

"And I'll fucking push them myself." Kyle grabbed the wheelchair. "All aboard!" She started toward the elevator, and Cole quickly joined the parade of laughter.

All four exited the hospital standing, as they sent the chair of contention on an elevator ride back up to Nurse Grouchy's floor. Cole pulled the car up, and Livia insisted Blake sit in the passenger seat. She sat behind him and kept a hand on his shoulder.

"Livia told me Beckett's wanted for questioning about what happened to Chris Simmer." Blake grasped her hand.

Cole drove slowly and meticulously, pausing to look and look again at each stop and curve. "It was Beckett," he confirmed. "He couldn't take it. The knowing." Cole checked his rearview mirror.

"So what now?" Blake wondered aloud.

Cole blew out a frustrated breath. "Eve's keeping tabs on him. He's in hiding."

Blake turned to catch Livia's eye. "You okay?"

She nodded.

Cole looked repentant immediately. "I'm sorry, Livia. I didn't think before I spoke."

"I'll never be sorry Chris's dead," Livia said. "Not after what he turned out to be. I should have shot him in the chest and saved Beckett the trouble."

"Stop this," Kyle said suddenly. "We're not eating this pity pie right now. Liv, you were about as likely to shoot Chris in the fucking cold, black thing that passed as his heart as I am to give the Pope a big, sloppy, wet one." Kyle closed one eye. "Sorry, honey."

Cole bit his lip to keep from laughing.

"Beckett's the mayor of Murderville," Kyle added with a shrug. "We aren't going to sit around and pretend he's an innocent schoolgirl."

The sedan was quiet.

Kyle looked out the window. "But I do wish he could make it to the wedding. That would be nice."

Cole pulled up to the curb in front of Uncle Dr. Ted's building. Eve stood waiting with him on the sidewalk, dressed again in an uncharacteristic jeans and a sweater. Livia was out of the car and opening Blake's door before anyone even finished waving. He looked apprehensive, and Livia was grateful for the huge awning outside the building's entrance. Blake went easily from the shade of the car to the shade of the walkway.

It's new. Ted did this for Blake. Livia held his arm as Dr. Hartt made the introductions he didn't realize none of them needed.

"Blake, Kyle, Cole, and Livia, this is my daughter, Eve." Ted looked from Blake to Eve and back again. Eve gave them each a wry smile and a wink as she grasped their hands with a firm grip.

Ted motioned the group to the entrance. "Please, this way. Blake, your apartment's the first one on the bottom floor."

He passed him a set of keys. Livia watched as they shook a bit in Blake's hands. She tried to keep her eyes from filling with tears but failed.

They walked down the carpeted hallway to the door. His hands steady now, Blake turned the key in the lock and stepped inside. He looked around with a small smile. "This is wonderful, Ted. I appreciate your kindness."

Ted ran a hand through his hair. "Truly, you're doing me a huge favor. Eve's hardly ever here. It's nice to have a full-time person." He gave his daughter a pointed stare. She shrugged.

Cole stepped to his brother and held up his arm. They wrapped forearms and nodded. Then Cole held out a hand to Kyle. "Livia, we'll drive your car over here for you, unless you want a ride now?"

Livia was not ready to leave. She wanted to explore Blake's cabinets, make sure his bed had fresh sheets, and hold his hand. She opened her mouth to say so just as Ted spoke.

"I was actually hoping to have a few words with Blake." Ted met Livia's eyes. He looked like he was not beyond begging for some time with his nephew.

"I'll let you guys catch up," Livia said quickly. "I'm going to run home and shower, then I'll bring dinner by. Okay, Blake? Do you feel okay?"

Blake pulled Livia to him and whispered in her ear. "I'm fine. That's great—just come back." After a quick kiss on the lips, Livia left the apartment with Kyle riding her piggyback as Cole held the door.

The door clicked shut with an amazingly solid sound. A sound that indicated private space. Blake stood mesmerized for a moment, then remembered his manners and motioned to the basic, brown couch. The three sat.

Eve broke the awkward silence. "Blake, my dad wants to tell you we're cousins. Well, we're, like, half cousins or whatever. This is supposed to be a touchy-feely conversation where we tell you, 'Don't worry, you'll always have a family here with us.' And then we may or may not have sappy music piped in."

Ted rolled his eyes. "That was tactful, Eve. Wonderful."

Blake held up a hand. "I understand what you're trying to do here, Ted, and I have to tell you I'm working to make this all okay in my head. It's not easy for me to learn to trust now, this late in life, but I'll try. And when someone shows me kindness, I don't forget it."

Ted stood and waited as Blake rose as well. They shook hands.

"Okay. Well, I guess this is pretty good then," Ted said.

Blake walked Eve and Ted to the door. *My door.* The littlest things were amazing.

"I'll be upstairs if you need anything," Ted added. "My home number and my cell number are on your fridge. You can reach me as your physician or your uncle or just the guy you know upstairs."

Blake closed the door behind them and was alone. Walls surrounded him, giving him complete privacy. Moments later, a soft knock disrupted his relishing. Eve had reappeared in the doorway, and he let her back in, closing the door behind her.

"Blake, I failed you in the woods," she began, getting right to the point. "I should have been there sooner." She held up a finger to stop his argument. "You're Beckett's brother, and that means something to me. It matters. And now I know you're my cousin as well. That matters too. For what it's worth, I won't be late again if you need me." Eve turned and grabbed the doorknob, evidently having said what she came to say.

"Eve?" Blake waited as she turned back. "Thanks. It matters to me as well. It means something."

She almost looked him in the face as she nodded.

"Tell me about Beckett," Blake said. The simple request seemed to light a fire in her.

"Son of a bitch. I told him I'd get Chris. But no. 'That's an order,' he says. And why did I listen? Why did I think he was in his right mind? He's a basket case. Wait until he hears about Cole's wedding. He'll be knocking down the walls." Eve shook her head sadly.

"Beckett's probably the hardest man there is to love," Blake said. "He does life wrong for all the right reasons."

Eve finally met his eyes. He could see the pain in them.

"Are you going to make sure he's safe? Because if you can't, I have to." Blake stood tall.

"I'm here," she promised. "If I have to leave, I'll let you know."

Eve held up her fist, and it took Blake a beat to realize she wanted it bumped. He complied, and she let herself out of the apartment.

My apartment. He pictured Livia naked on every piece of furniture in the room. He ran his hand across the soft fabric of the old couch. There were cold, bitter nights when he would've given his soul for a place like this. *And* a throw blanket to tuck around his freezing feet. That bit of the dream was draped carefully over an armchair.

He turned on the faucet in the kitchen and watched the silver sink turn to glistening mercury from the water. *My water.*

He opened cabinet after cabinet, looking for a cup. His hands found a mug, and he filled it greedily, drinking once, twice, three times. *Clean, fresh water.*

He could hear a clock ticking somewhere in the apartment, and the pipes in the building clanked. Blake circled his new living room with a slow, measured pace. He wanted Livia back. Kyle probably wanted to talk her ear off all about the wedding, but he needed Livia here. He ached for her.

45

21

Eve threw her keys on the round hotel table. Beckett lay still with every pillow from the two queen beds crammed behind his shoulders. He held the remote, but the TV was off. Eve placed her hand on the set's black plastic. It was cold. He'd never turned it on—just sat in front of the murky black screen while she was gone. A still Beckett was not a well Beckett, and Eve was concerned.

"'Sup." She waited until he transferred his attention from the blank screen to her.

"Did he look okay? Was he all right? Did the door have a good lock?" Beckett kept the remote pointed at the TV like he was threatening it.

"Of course—he had a great lock. What the hell?" She rolled her eyes.

Beckett finally dropped the remote and dragged himself off the bed. "Sorry. I just wanted to be there. You know, to make sure. I've wanted to close a door with him behind it for seven fucking years. Cut me some slack."

Beckett began to pace. Restless Beckett worried Eve as well.

"He's doing great. Very courteous to my dad." Eve leaned against the sink.

"Of course he's fucking courteous. It's Blake. What the hell? He has to be fucking grateful for every damn thing? He's not a charity case, you know." Beckett seemed to be looking for a target for his anger.

Eve tried not to take it personally, but that was becoming more difficult. "The funeral home said Mouse's ashes are ready to be picked up." It was a low blow, but she wanted him to remember there were worse things than his current predicament.

"We need to give him a proper burial." Beckett stopped pacing.

"How're we going to do that? We can't have a regular funeral. I've looked into it. He had a grandmother, and she's buried here in town. We can do it at night—dig a hole and leave him there." Eve hated the idea. She wanted Mouse's name on a respectable stone.

"He gets buried in the full light of day. He had nothing to be ashamed of. I will not bury him like a coward." Beckett pointed at Eve angrily.

"You won't bury him at all. That's my job. When you went all Cuisinart on Chris Simmer? That's when you decided not to bury your friend." Eve felt hot rage grabbing her heart.

"I'll put Mouse in the ground, Cole'll pray, and Blake will be there to see the man who took his place in the grave. That's how it's going down. If I get arrested doing it, so be it." He stuck his chin out defiantly.

Eve walked closer to the boiling man. "You think that's what Mouse wants? You in jail? He's not the pile of ashes we're going to put in the ground. His soul is free in the woods." Eve wanted to comfort Beckett, but all her energy went to combating her frustration.

"I'll see him buried," Beckett said again, slightly less confidently. "I'll see my brothers. I have to. I can't not see them. I…" Beckett looked at his reflection in the mirror. "My life is worthless if it's not about them."

This time Eve hugged him. She rested her forehead on his lips. He did not return her hug.

"This is so hard for you. I know that. You want to do something. But you have to get it through your thick head that by doing nothing, staying here, you're doing exactly what those boys need."

Beckett looked at the ceiling. Eve waited, feeling his hot, angry-bull breath on her hair.

"I want to bury Mouse." This time Beckett put his words into the universe quietly.

Eve was ready for shouting and cursing, but the pleading, small voice broke her resolve. She looked into his eyes. "I'll make it happen. I don't know how, but I'll do it."

Beckett wove his arms around her, pulling her in. "Tell me what else."

Eve snorted. "What do you mean what else?"

"You're still all tense. There's something you don't want to tell me." He moved his hands to her shoulders. "Spit it the fuck out."

"Cole and Kyle got engaged." She rubbed a hand across her face.

"That's really good. Great for them. I knew they were a good match. Fairy Princess will keep his hands full." Beckett watched Eve's face. "And?"

"They're getting married in a month. There's no way I can get this murder mess fixed in time for you to go to the ceremony. They've got you. There's *so* much evidence. Damn it, Beckett. You knew better than that. And now I'm scared you're going to want to go to the wedding, and it'll be a big fucking mess." She put her hand on his heart, where she knew her next words would land. "You can't go to the wedding."

Beckett pushed her away. He made a fist and held it to his forehead. After turning it into a claw that raked through his hair, he used it to punch the nearest wall. The plaster cracked around the meteor-crash print his fist left.

Eve knew his anger was far from spent, but the hotel room corralled him. He sat on the edge of the bed, pounding a fist on his thigh. She knelt in front of him, brave inches from his angry knuckles.

"This is it, Beck. This is the hardest part of loving someone: not being with them when you want to be. It's so bad you can taste it." She put her hand on his knee, daring his fist to smash it.

He stilled his hand. "I'm going to need my brothers with me for Mouse. And call Chaos. Tell him to bring his ink. Then I'm outta here. I leave and don't darken their fucking doors again." He looked at her.

His pride was dying, and she couldn't save it. Her finger traced the marking on his forearm, and she raised one eyebrow in question.

Beckett nodded. "Yeah. I need Mouse to be permanent."

Eve went to work and finally arranged a way to have Mouse's funeral while the rest of the world planned celebrations of their beloved winter holidays. Cole agreed to bring a Bible and say a few words at the gravesite. Blake said he'd attend as well. Eve wanted to tell him she'd bring an umbrella, but it just seemed too awkward. He had to know a cemetery would be outdoors.

When the cold December Monday finally arrived, Eve set out her distractions for the police. She'd designed two very real-looking fake bombs and put one at the mall and the other under a busy intersection. Then she'd dug a small hole at Mouse's grandmother's grave. She wished there was some soil beneath her fingernails, some sort of testament to her preparations, but she'd been too careful; her nails were clean.

Beckett was at the hotel putting on the all-black suit and tie combination he'd requested. He was handling his confinement well, which surprised her. She knew he had a touch of claustrophobia, but his other option was leaving the country, and he'd refused to do that.

When she arrived to pick him up, Beckett was ready to say goodbye to his brothers. Before she put him on the back of her motorcycle, she made a phone call alerting the authorities of the two bombs. She had extra remote detonations set up in an abandoned house on Beckett's old stomping ground. She would listen to the police scanner, and if they figured out the bombs were decoys too quickly, she'd give them a little more—all so she could get Beckett in and out of the cemetery with as little risk as possible.

They both wore helmets as they rode through town, more for disguise than protection, and they arrived to find Blake and Cole had brought Livia and Kyle as well. As if a gift from Mouse himself, the sky was overcast with a thick gray batting of clouds. Beckett was off the bike before she could put the kickstand down, a full black messenger bag bouncing on his back.

He grabbed his brothers. All three pounded each others' backs and gave grumbling, cursing acknowledgments.

"I can finally fucking breathe, seeing you goddamn bastards."

Everyone smiled at Beckett's exuberance, despite the somber occasion.

"Where's the bride-to-be?" Beckett held his arms open for Kyle and gave her a gentle hug. "Good on you, Fairy Princess, making an honest man out of my boy here. Jesus was treating him like shit; he was never getting laid. I hope you two have a million damn kids and name them all Beckett, boys or girls."

Kyle returned the hug and smirked. "We might name our dog Beckett, if you're lucky."

Beckett laughed a bit too loudly. He seemed desperate to make up for lost time.

He locked eyes with Livia, and his face became serious. "Com'ere, Whitebread." He held out his hand and enveloped her as soon as she got close.

She started to cry softly in his chest.

"Don't cry. I'm so motherfucking proud of you. You hold your beautiful face up. Stand proud."

He rubbed her back and motioned Blake over with his head. Beckett twirled her into Blake's arms. She looked back to give him a sad smile from her warm place by Blake's heart.

Beckett slid the messenger bag around and without preamble began to speak. "Hey, this here's Mouse's ashes. He was an employee of mine. I know you all knew him. If you knew him, you liked him. He was smart. Fucking loyal. And big. He didn't deserve to end up in a jar. He didn't deserve to die in the dirt a-fucking-lone. He was following orders. Orders to protect Blake at any cost, at all costs. They were my orders. And this was his cost." Beckett held the urn up higher.

"And I know Blake had a bunch of fucking problems going on the night he was shot. But Mouse here made sure the hired guns were dead before they could hurt him. I don't know if I get to call him a hero, if that's allowed, because I'm a bad man, and he was my friend. But he was a hero to me." Beckett handed the urn to Blake.

Beckett pushed back the sleeve of his jacket, unbuttoned the cuff on his expensive shirt and revealed the brothers' mark. The addition of knitting needles and twirling yarn made Beckett's forearm ink the exact replica of the tattoo on Mouse's chest.

"He was my friend and my brother." Beckett looked at Cole, who stared at the mark on Beckett's arm.

Seeming to feel Beckett's eyes, Cole shook himself a bit and pulled out his Bible. Blake stepped forward and placed Mouse's urn gently in the hole Eve had prepared. Although he'd told Eve he'd just recite a simple rosary, Cole now opened the Bible instead.

"Beckett, you've reminded me of one of my favorite passages," he explained. "This is from First Corinthians thirteen."

He cleared his throat and spoke in a lyrical tone. "Love is patient and is kind; love doesn't envy. Love doesn't brag, is not proud, doesn't behave itself inappropriately, doesn't seek its own way, is not provoked, takes no account of wrongs done to it."

Cole looked up from the Bible and met each person's eyes before he continued. "Love doesn't rejoice in evil, but rejoices with the truth. It bears all things, believes all things, hopes all things, endures all things. Love *never* fails. And now these three remain: faith, hope and love, but the greatest of these is love."

After the murmured "amen" Beckett wiped his eyes. "Yeah, Cole. That was it. Right there."

Eve retrieved the shovel she'd stowed behind a tombstone.

"Wait." Beckett reached into his bag and pulled out a semi-automatic pistol. All present watched with wide eyes.

"They do the twenty-one-gun salute for the good guys, right? So I brought this." Beckett pointed the gun in the sky. "For Mouse."

The gun gave such a loud crack, it seemed to split the sky. Livia jumped, and Blake pulled her closer, his eyes wary on his brother.

One, two, three, four, five, six, seven, eight, nine, ten, eleven, twelve, thirteen, fourteen, fifteen, sixteen shots exploded from Beckett's gun. Then he lowered his arm, wreathed in smoke. He ejected the empty clip and pulled a full one from his bag. He palmed it into the gun, but suddenly Beckett's arm seemed too heavy for him to lift.

He hung his head. "Who am I fucking kidding? What the hell does a gun shot by *me* mean? Nothing special, that's for damn sure. Fuck it."

Livia left the comfort of Blake's embrace. She put her hands on Beckett's elbow carefully. She lifted his arm and angled it skyward.

She spoke, staring into Beckett's sad eyes. "For Mouse, who watched over my sister and saved Blake and me from more than we could've handled in the woods that night." Livia nodded at Beckett, and he squeezed the trigger. When the sound had cleared, she counted out loud. "Seventeen."

Kyle stepped forward and replaced Livia at Beckett's arm. "For Mouse. I didn't know you well, but I wish I had." The air snapped with the shot. "Eighteen."

Cole rubbed Kyle's shoulder as he approached. He took the gun from Beckett's hand. "For Mouse, who protected Beckett from himself for years." The gun popped again. "Nineteen."

Cole waited as his brother came forward. Blake thought for a moment with the gun pointed at the ground, then aimed it at the sky. "For Mouse, who saved Livia's life when I couldn't. Thank you is not enough." The gun took his gratitude to the heavens. "Twenty."

Beckett watched with pride, occasionally pounding his chest. Eve remained a few steps away, listening to the police scanner on her earpiece. She now looked at the gun in Blake's hand and brought a shaking fist to her lips. She walked over and pulled the technology out of her ear.

As she took the gun from Blake, the hand that had been shaking steadied. "Mouse, I wish you were still here. This place was better when you were part of it." The last shot was the most jarring, juxtaposed with the perfect silence of its wake.

As if the bullet was a key in a lock, the gray skies opened and a quiet, lovely snow shower filtered down. The flakes decorated the hair of the six mourners like glistening knit caps.

Eve turned her face to be bathed in the fresh flakes. "Twenty-one," she said softly, replacing her earpiece.

Beckett picked up the shovel and brought moist soil to cover the urn-filled hole. He smoothed the small mound with the back of the shovel and wiped his hands on his suit. Eve gathered the used ammo clip and tucked it and the gun back in Beckett's bag.

Eve met his eyes. "The cops have reports of gunfire here, so we've got to go."

Beckett groaned, and for a moment a look of sheer panic flashed in his eyes. His brothers stepped to him quickly, rushing to join their tattoos for possibly the last time.

"I think a call to Chaos is in order," Blake said, looking at Cole.

Cole nodded, and Beckett smiled. "Thanks," he said.

Eve had Beckett back on the motorcycle within moments and they sped away, leaving nothing but a flurry of snowflakes behind.

46

İ'ṁ Dꙩİnꙩ Ṁy Jꙩв

Christmas at the McHugh home was a sweet scene. The girls spent the morning with their father before gathering with their favorite brothers in the afternoon. Gratitude and love were the most cherished gifts exchanged. But then Livia watched as her sister took less than a week to turn their father's house into a Tasmanian devil's bridal boutique. For every wreath Livia put away, every ornament she wrapped in paper, Kyle came in with an armload of wedding options.

Kyle taped flowers, fabrics, and pictures to the walls in every room, and she ate, drank, and breathed wedding. She could work it into any conversation. But the one thing she refused to talk about was her dress. She wouldn't even let Livia mention it, and she also let her know she need not worry about her maid of honor gown.

"How come she has more crap here now than when she lived with me?" their father grumbled as he came down one morning.

Livia moved a few bridal magazines off the stove to make him some scrambled eggs. She knew he must be crumbling a bit on the inside. The whirlwind wedding was scary, especially for someone not ready to lose his baby girl.

Livia waited until her father had eaten and muttered his way out the door. She picked up the phone and dialed Blake's number. His silky *hello* made her smile.

"You're smiling, right?" His voice was so intimate.

"Of course," she murmured. "Does it still count if you don't see it?"

"It counts when I feel it," he replied.

Livia longed to smell his skin. "I want to come over." She knew she was losing the fight to live any life outside his apartment. She listened to his hum as he considered the possibilities. Livia moved a bundle of wedding favor bags out of the way.

"You have to go work on your papers," he finally said. "I'll meet you at the station."

She knew he was right. Dr. Lavender had worked hard on her behalf. After Livia explained about Blake's injury and the precariousness of his situation, Dr. Lavender had contacted Livia's professors and requested lenience for her absences and a generous opportunity to make up her work after the semester's end. Whether the other professors had kind hearts or Dr. Lavender had twisted their arms, she wasn't sure, but Livia still had a shot at making this semester count.

"I do have to go," she agreed. "Did you get the rent collected?"

"I've got one tenant left and then everyone will have settled up," Blake reported with pride. "Actually, I have something to ask, and then I know you have to get ready."

"Go ahead." Livia tried to picture what he might be wearing.

"Ted has a friend that owns a club. They're looking for a piano player on Thursday nights. I was thinking about it…" Blake trailed off.

"I think that sounds wonderful," Livia said immediately. "You'll be terrific, and I'll be front and center, every Thursday night." She smiled again, wondering if he could feel it.

"I'll see you at the station," he said before they ended the call with a click.

Neither said goodbye. They never could.

One week before the wedding, the place cards had been filled out, and the candles for the tables were decorated with little hand-painted daisies. Livia's dress had been revealed as crisp red with a white sash, and the matching shoes were surprisingly comfortable. Also, everyone except Cole was pretty much done with Kyle. She was snippy, frenzied, and angry.

Kyle stood in the doorway to Livia's room as she tried on the gown again. "That looks good. Your tits aren't too pointy," Kyle said, narrowing her eyes. "Hair up on the day of—I'll help you with all that shit. No bedraggled librarian hair. Do you hear me?" Kyle jabbed her finger in Livia's face. She'd taken to pointing a lot lately.

"I don't have a choice. You keep talking." Livia gave her sister the finger and stuck out her tongue.

"If you didn't have your dress on, I'd pummel you. I owe you a pummeling now…" A florist's catalog on Livia's bed distracted Kyle from her threatening. "I think I'll carry red flowers. You carry white and red. These ones, right here." Kyle jabbed her finger at the pictured bouquet. She rolled her eyes when Livia refused to look. "Damn it, Livia. If you're not helping, how in holy fuck's sake am I going to be ready? I have so much to do." She flopped backward on the bed, covering her eyes.

Livia took a risk and sat next to her sister. "Your wedding is going to be beautiful. In the end, it'll be you and Cole, and that'll be perfect."

At the mention of Cole's name, Kyle uncovered her eyes and a hint of a smile found her lips. She ran her hands through her hair.

Livia looked out the window. Her father's SUV crackled bits of gravel in the driveway as he arrived from work.

"Dad's home."

Livia said it out loud, but Kyle had already started to sit up. They listened in silence as their father went through the coming-home routine he'd followed for years. Putting away the hat and shoes, taking off his gun, and unloading it all made distinct noises.

He must have known Kyle was home because her now-restored convertible sat outside. The bill for fixing it had been ridiculously low. Kyle and Livia suspected that Mouse had paid the bulk of it.

The girls waited as their father climbed the stairs. When he arrived, he looked so big in Livia's doorway, just like he had when she was a child.

"Girls," he said in greeting. "Have either of you heard anything on Mr. Taylor?" He sent his best dad stare from one to the other.

Both looked away and shook their heads.

"Do you know that my two daughters are the best leads I have to find Chris Simmer's murderer?" He took a deep, steadying breath. "No one can find the other boys who were in the woods that night either." He looked solemnly at the girls again. "I don't want to be in this position. But I have to find that man."

Livia twisted her hands in a knot. She hated not helping her dad, but she could still picture Beckett standing by Mouse's grave.

Kyle's fragile temper exploded. "Oh, so we're defending Chris's dead ass? The animal that tried to kill your daughter? Livia? My sister? I've never been happier that someone was dead. He pointed a gun at her, Dad. And those twits in the woods were right with him, I'm sure. How can you ever blame Beckett for doing what you weren't man enough to do?"

Kyle covered her mouth. The words were so harsh, even she knew she'd gone too far.

Their father closed his eyes. He nodded.

"Kyle, I'm doing my goddamn job. The same job that's kept a roof over our heads and food in our stomachs. This is what I do. I'm slow, and I'm calculating. You don't think I could've killed Chris that night? You don't think my co-workers would've had my back? I had a gun in my hand. And I didn't kill him. Not because I couldn't, but because I would never, ever want either of you girls to be disappointed in me. You know what you get when it comes to your father. I'm sorry that's not enough for you, Kyle. I'm sorry a drug dealer commands more of your respect than I do." He turned in the doorway, suddenly seeming a little smaller.

Livia hopped up. She couldn't let them leave it this way. "Dad, stop. Please." She put her hand on his arm and he turned, as if powerless to resist her. "The only reason Kyle and I are worth anything at all is because you've set the most stellar example. I stood up to Chris because I knew that's what you'd expect—for me to do the right thing. We love you so much. You're everything we could want or need in a parent. Please know that."

He looked from Livia to his younger daughter and found her crying silently into her hands. He took Livia under one arm and spoke to Kyle. "Come here, little girl."

Kyle launched herself at them and into a three-way hug, just like when they were small.

"I'm sorry, Dad," she said.

Their father hugged them both hard and kissed the tops of their heads. After a time, he patted their backs to end the hug. "Well, I got to get out of this uniform. But Kyle, just a word, you've been snapping and harping at everyone trying to help you with this wedding, and you need to knock that off. Everyone knows when they're being a bitch." He looked pointedly at his daughter.

Kyle gave him a pretend glare.

Livia patted her sister's shoulder. "It's true. You're being a bitch."

Kyle threw the floral catalog at her as she headed downstairs.

47

KYLE'S JOY

The morning of the wedding was a cold January Wednesday, which made no sense to anyone except those in the wedding party. Midnight mass would be even more special this week. The residents of the retirement community were deep into the preparations and had turned out to be wonderful coordinators. Many of them had sons, daughters, and grandchildren who were willing to provide services or help out.

Kyle still had not shown a single soul her wedding dress, and Livia was a little worried. Would fashion-forward Kyle strike a pose in some crazed, super sexy version of a runway gown? Offering no clue at all, Kyle did her makeup and hair at home wearing a baggy sweatsuit. Livia was also coiffed—and dressed—long before the sunset. Kyle insisted on doing Livia's hair early, and it looked wonderful, but the curls were crispy to the touch. After dinner, the girls and their contrasting ensembles piled into Livia's Escort for the ride to the church. Kyle had at least said she was planning to change into her dress there.

When Livia parked in the church lot, the slow-moving caterpillar of angels from next door was already swinging and rocking the way forward to the church. Livia and Kyle blew kisses and curtseyed to the clapping that ensued when the seniors spotted them. Wednesday night seemed to be celebrating its unconventional use for a wedding. The stars blinked like Christmas lights and wintry air smelled of crisp snow—although thankfully the weather had stayed clear, eliminating the need for a whole lot of shoveling. The trees were stark and bare now, outlined against the night sky.

Loaded down with cardboard boxes of flowers and a garment bag holding Kyle's dress, the girls made their way inside. Once they'd deposited their goods, Kyle requested to dress in private, so Livia led her sister to the "crying room" at the back of the sanctuary. Livia closed the curtain over the wide glass window that separated the room from the rest of the congregation, then closed the door quietly behind her. Her sister would don her mysterious dress in a space that usually kept noisy babies from disrupting a worshiping crowd.

With Kyle tucked away, Livia began her inspection. The pews had little bouquets of lilies tied with gossamer slips of fabric that connected each one to the other—like a train, Livia instantly thought. The candles flickered, and the wood shone from the Pew Crew's tireless ministrations.

Blake pushed open the door by the altar. His rented tuxedo was crisp, the bow tie perfectly straight. Livia stopped and let the sight of him evaporate her common sense.

When his eyes found hers, he placed a hand over his heart, as if it might stop again. "You are so lovely," he said.

Livia wrinkled her nose and blew him a kiss. Cole poked his head through the door as well and ruffled his brother's hair.

When he spotted Livia, he hollered, "Is she here?"

Livia nodded but kept her eyes on Blake. Cole, usually calm, now seemed to be bouncing like a rabbit and dragged Blake back through the door. The guests had started to trickle in, and Livia knew it was time to help Kyle. She knocked on the door that sequestered her sister. She waited and knocked again. Nothing.

"Kyle, enough with the secrecy. I'm coming in." Livia opened the door, entered the room, and shut the door in one spinning motion so no one else would see in.

Livia turned to face her sister, who was admiring her reflection in a framed full-length mirror. Kyle smoothed a short blue dress.

"It's time to get dressed. Can I help? Is the dress very complicated?" Livia stepped forward so she too was reflected in the mirror.

Kyle bit her lip and looked at Livia in the mirror. "This is my wedding dress."

Livia raised her eyebrow and waited for some explanation. This was the dress Kyle had picked for *her* to wear on the night of the revenge partying. It seemed an odd choice.

"I was going to wear this dress when Mom came back," Kyle finally said. She ironed the material again with her hands.

"Kyle, Mom's not coming back. She's not going to show up here today. I'm sorry." Livia rested a tentative hand on her sister's shoulder.

"I know. I know she's not coming. But I'm going to wear this dress to start my life with Cole. I'm this person now." Kyle clenched her fists.

"Wait. What?" Livia turned her sister to face her. "The dress doesn't change who you are. Don't get me wrong, I've never seen a more beautiful bride, but you've always been this person. It's not that you didn't earn a mother, it's that Mom didn't earn you." Livia waited until Kyle looked her in the eyes. "Do you understand that?"

Kyle nodded. "Thanks, Liv. You look great too."

Livia smiled and busied herself with the bridal accessories. "Well, that dress gets a lot of things out of the way." She lifted Kyle's headdress of fresh flowers from its box. There was no veil.

Kyle gave her a questioning look as she clipped the blossoms in place.

"Something old: the dress. Something new: your attitude. Something borrowed: I'm pretty sure you got those earrings from my jewelry box."

Kyle rolled her eyes.

"Something blue: the dress again. The last thing we need is this." Livia slipped off her shoe and turned it upside down until a penny fell in her hand. "This bad larry comes pre-warmed."

Kyle kicked off her high heel, and Livia dropped the copper piece into the shoe. There was loud knock on the door.

"Ladies, I believe I have a job to do."

Their father's gruff voice made them smile. "Come in," they said in stereo, like they had when they were kids.

Livia watched her father's policeman's entrance, as if a room that held chirping girls was harder to face than an armed robber. He gave each of them a nervous smile and said nothing about Kyle's unconventional dress. Perhaps her delicate beauty or the emotion of his little girl getting married blinded him, but Livia had a feeling her dad just knew when to keep his mouth shut.

Livia patted his shoulder. "It's time."

The bells in the steeple began to reverberate through the very foundation of the church. They wouldn't normally ring them so late at night, not wanting to disturb the neighborhood, but tonight was special. Twelve full-bodied tones notified the town that something spectacular was about to happen.

Livia dared to peek out of the crying room and into the foyer of the church. It was empty. She nodded at her sister and waved her little family out of the room. Her father waited with an awkward arm crooked for Kyle's hand.

The first strains of organ music filled the church.

Blake. His playing brought Livia a wide, warm smile. The music was supposed to be reverent. It was supposed to slow the world down for prayer. But Blake infused hope in his music. Love was the only song he knew how to play.

Livia faced the crowd. She commenced her slow, practiced step-to-gether-step march. She felt like she was onstage without knowing her lines. All eyes were on her, and really, she just wanted to crane her neck to see Blake's hands on the organ.

She focused on smiling at the guests as she passed. Dear Bea gave her a wink, and Eve stood on Ted's right, looking effortlessly exquisite in a black A-line gown. She seemed to tip her sparkling hummingbird brooch toward Livia as she passed. And there was Nurse Susan, looking beautiful in a silvery dress, rather than her usual scrubs.

As Livia finally completed her journey, Blake switched to Mendelssohn's traditional wedding march. Cole came through the altar door and assumed his spot next to Father Callahan. He nodded at Livia and watched the door where Kyle was about to make her appearance.

The door swung open, and Kyle and her father stepped into the archway. Livia heard a gasp from the crowd. In the middle of a classic church wedding, Kyle's blue dress was shocking, simple, and entirely casual. But one look at the bride's face should have obliterated any other considerations. Her smile was unadulterated joy. She almost hopped between steps. Her father looked pained and proud as he walked her down the aisle.

When Kyle was finally firmly in front of the groom, John held out his hand. As Cole shook it, the men had the most important conversation in the world without saying a word.

John stooped to give Kyle a kiss on the cheek. Kyle held her hand out to Cole, and for a brief moment their hands didn't touch. The tiny sliver of air between their palms seemed to contain the energy of an entire universe. But when his hand eclipsed hers, instead of an explosion, there was only calm. Only peace.

Livia set down her flowers and scurried over to the spiral staircase and up to the organ. As Blake put the finishing touches on the march, Livia lifted her long skirt and ascended the stairs. Blake nodded at the newly appointed, and seemingly rather nervous, church organist and motioned to the bench for the changing of the guard.

With his shaky replacement in position and continuing to produce sound from the organ, Blake turned to descend the stairs and join the wedding. His eyes widened when he found Livia waiting, still holding her dress out of the way of her feet. She motioned for him to join her as she began walking backward down the stairs. Blake had been doing well for the past month, but he still became winded and a bit dizzy at times. Livia was taking no chances.

He looked amused as he placed his shiny dress shoes on each stair as she vacated it. The church organist slammed her way into a little improv, providing some filler so Blake could get to the altar. Livia looked at Blake and tried not to burst out laughing.

"What exactly, my love, do you think you're doing?" Blake looked down at her.

"These stairs make me nervous. I just wanted to make sure you got down them okay." Livia felt silly now. He was obviously fine. Their slow spiraling dance actually made her a little dizzy instead.

"And if I trip like the delicate flower that I am?" Blake asked, drawing near.

"I was hoping I would break your fall, if you fell…which you won't." Livia stepped backward again. The edge of her train caught under her heel, and her careful steps stuttered.

Blake reacted swiftly, grabbing her around the waist and righting her balance in one smooth swoop. He held her close and used the railing to keep them steady.

"Oh. Damn." Livia pressed against his chest as she caught her breath. Instead of keeping him safe she was about to break both their necks. The organist decided to drop some vocals on the captive crowd.

Blake stilled even though they should have been rushing at this point; everyone was waiting. "Livia, I'm going to be okay. You have to believe it."

The nape of his neck was just inches from her lips. The only things stopping her from tasting it were red lipstick and one hundred pairs of eyes.

"I've always believed it." Livia tilted her head so she could see him.

Blake held his lips close to hers. They were lost in each other until Kyle had enough.

"Get the hell down here!" the bride shouted. "You're stealing my thunder."

Livia could hear Bea's distinct laugh over the organist's shrill rendition of "Closer My God to Thee." Blake transported Livia back to her spot next to Kyle, and Kyle slapped Blake's shoulder in greeting. Cole and Blake executed a subtle tattoo touch.

The wedding proceeded, and the ceremony never veered from the time-honored, familiar words. The well-practiced clergyman rarely consulted his prayer book. His homily was filled wonderful advice about patience and listening to one another. When it was time for the promises in front of God,

Cole repeated his vows in a voice well-practiced at filling the whole room. Kyle's words were quiet, small, and for his ears alone. They exchanged shiny new wedding bands.

Communion took forever, and the guests chatted quietly as everyone was served the sacrament. Cole and Kyle looked anxious and wildly in love.

Blake held out a hand to Livia, who felt like she was cheating on an exam as she took it.

"I can't stop looking at you," he whispered. "The candlelight, the dress, the curls." He pressed a reverent kiss on her forehead.

Livia inhaled his cologne. Maybe he'd borrowed Cole's, and the warm scent made Blake a present begging to be opened.

By the time Father Callahan had concluded his work, he had to hold up a hand to quiet the crowd. "I do believe we have a bit more business to attend to."

After a gentle round of snickers, quiet blanketed the church.

The crowd knew what was next, and although there was no sound, the anticipation itself was shouting.

"I present Mr. and Mrs. Cole Bridge. You may kiss the bride." Father Callahan gave Cole a nod of approval.

Cole faced Kyle and wrapped her in his arms. He pulled her off her feet and closer to his face. Livia and Blake were the only ones close enough to hear Cole's private vows.

He kissed her once, gently and almost chastely. "For our past."

Cole kissed her again, just a breath of a kiss, lightly touching her lips. "For today."

The last kiss was deeper, but still maintained church decorum. It was the intimacy in his gaze that made the guests feel voyeuristic. "For the rest of our lives," he said softly as he set her back on her feet.

Kyle looked stunned and deliriously teary and happy as she turned to face the crowd, which clapped and whooped. The processional music burst forth, and the organist's exuberance propelled it through the sour notes. Cole picked Kyle up as soon as they were down the few steps from the altar. The ladies in the crowd sighed and smiled as he carried her down the aisle.

Blake and Livia were next to exit. He took the steps before she could and turned to offer her his hand, like a knight escorting his queen. Livia took Blake's hand and hugged his offered arm. Bea's photographer-nephew's flash blinded them as it captured their moment for all time.

Kyle and Cole's reception was to be hosted in the community room at the retirement center. The couple multitasked with the slow conga line of seniors heading back home by greeting them as they passed like a receiving line. Kyle got on her tiptoes to search the crowd every few minutes.

"What's up?" Cole asked. "Are you looking for someone?"

Kyle waved his questions away.

Livia leaned down to her sister. "Beckett?"

Kyle made big eyes and shook her head.

Eventually, Kyle seemed to find what she'd been looking for and became less agitated.

As they drew close to the building Livia was pleased to see Bea in her wheelchair, decked out in a lavender dress and bright rosy blush. A string of pearls completed her fancy look.

"I see your young man has accompanied you today." Bea accepted Livia's hug with a gentle pat.

"He has. I'm so glad he gets to meet you." Livia held Bea's soft, delicate hand.

"I've noticed he always has his body angled toward yours," Bea reported seriously. "It's a good sign, my dear. I do believe you've found yourself a winner." She smiled.

Livia leaned back to catch Blake's eye. As if he heard her heart calling his, he leaned back as well. Livia motioned for him to come over.

"Blake, this is Bea," she said as he came to her side. "She's that friend of mine who gives great advice." Blake touched Livia's lower back before he took to one knee.

With his eyes sparkling, he turned Bea's offered hand to kiss it. "Lovely Bea, it's a pleasure to make your acquaintance. Thank you so much for befriending Livia. She speaks very highly of you."

Bea giggled and swatted at him playfully with the very hand he'd kissed. "What a gentleman. Aren't you a looker?"

Blake stayed on his knee, giving Bea his full attention.

"I hope you know how rare a girl like Livia is."

Blake nodded, but said nothing.

"I've only met a few souls as crystal clear as hers," Bea continued. "One of them was my Aaron; we were married for sixty-two years. Souls like that, my boy, are a gift. Cherish her."

"I will." Blake stood and gave Bea a formal bow only he could get away with.

Kyle glared at Blake. He jumped and kissed Livia quickly so he could get back into his Kyle-approved position, next to Cole.

A small lady moved on after greeting Livia to address the wedding couple. "Cole Bridge. Look at you!"

Cole's mouth dropped open. "Mrs. D?" After a shocked pause, he scooped her into a hug. "You're here?"

"Of course I am, sweetheart. Your wonderful wife delivered the invitation by hand. She insisted it be a surprise." Mrs. D rubbed Cole's arm.

Cole turned to Kyle. "Thank you so much. I didn't know you were going to do this."

Kyle nodded. "I know how much she means to you," she said.

Livia smiled, making a mental note to ask Kyle about this later, as the bride turned and held her hand out to Mr. D. He looked like he'd been to a million weddings. Livia suspected Mrs. D was important in a lot of lives.

After greeting each of her guests, Kyle was in for her own surprise. The seniors had been preparing the community room for weeks, and Kyle and Livia both held a hand to their mouths when they saw the intricate decorations.

Nothing was hung very high, but what the residents could reach was touched by love, wisdom, and heart: knit-flower centerpieces, carefully cut paper shapes, and streamers arranged to look like expensive fabric.

The DJ had set up in the corner, and he looked old enough to have started his career by knocking rocks together to entertain dinosaurs, but he was excellent and provided the best oldies in existence. The buffet was served by some of the seniors themselves, their fancy clothes complemented by hairnets.

Cole led Kyle to the center of the room when the DJ announced their wedding dance and Etta James did the honors with "At Last." When Cole kissed Kyle deeply to show off at the end of their graceful dance, the bride bent one knee and pointed her toe like a smitten cartoon character. The spectators laughed out loud.

Though they spanned an unlikely range of ages, everyone in the crowd was ready for a good time. Kyle twirled endlessly around a mostly stationary Cole, and the older couples schooled their younger counterparts. The seniors seemed to slip from one delicate, complicated set of steps to another, reacting to cues in the music only they understood.

The entire wedding party was adopted by a blue-haired beauty who tried, with varying degrees of success, to teach them some classic moves from the musical past. Blake and Kyle were quick studies. Cole and Livia just shrugged and smiled. Livia watched as Blake sought out Bea for a dance, twirling her chair gently in circles.

Cole tried his best to dance with Mrs. D, but she was much shorter and by far the better dancer. Mostly they rocked back and forth, smiling at each other.

Mrs. D hugged Cole's middle, hard, and the music cut out just in time for her compliment to carry across the room. "I *knew* you would be a magnificent man."

When it was time for the father-daughter dance, John politely left Kathy, his date, sitting with Nurse Susan and Dr. Ted. Kyle waited for her father in the center of the floor as the opening notes of Nat King Cole's "Unforgettable" swept through the air. John was not a dancer, but he was determined. He put his arms around his daughter, and Kyle rested her head on his chest.

Halfway through, the DJ suggested others dance as well. Blake swept Livia onto the dancefloor, and she gazed at her sister and father as she basked in his arms.

"Kyle, I love you. I'm always here," she heard her father murmur as the song came to an end.

Kyle gave her father a kiss on the cheek. "I know. I love you too."

With the formalities out of the way, the wedding party gathered in the corner with the bride and groom, and Cole grabbed Eve to join them. Beckett's absence was a looming hole in the joy of the evening, and the friends offered a toast to their absent brother. Eve turned her whole body to gaze at each person in the circle for a moment.

Blake lifted a plastic champagne flute filled with bubbling apple cider. "To Beckett—we wouldn't be here without him."

"To Beckett," the others agreed.

The dull thump of the plastic was unsatisfying, but it would have to suffice.

It was early morning with the sun creeping into view when the room's harsh fluorescent lights came on. Instead of leaving to collapse in bed, the guests stayed to help clean up. With everyone working together, they had the community room back to its original state and ready for the day's activities within an hour.

Though Beckett remained confined to the same claustrophobic hotel room that had housed him for weeks now, he'd attended the wedding in every sense but literally.

He dressed for the occasion, and Eve helped him get his bow tie just right before she left, promising once again that her hummingbird pin would send him every detail it could.

Riveted to the live feed from Eve's transmitter on his hotel room TV, Beckett stood when the congregation stood, and he sat when they sat. And when he noticed that the camera had bounced even lower, Beckett knelt.

As Kyle came fluttering down the aisle in her simple blue dress, Beckett swore aloud in the empty room. "Shit, Fairy Princess, you're an angel."

He fought with himself through the entire ceremony—despondent to be separated from his family, but bursting with pride over every single one of them. With no one around to preserve church decorum, he began toasting his sorrows and lining up shots to drown his frustrations about the same time as Cole and Kyle began their vows. By the time they'd reached the reception, he was a rumpled mess on the bed.

But he did see them dance. He laughed out loud remembering when he'd danced with Kyle. She hardly seemed the same person. And Cole needed some *serious* help in the moves department.

"Fuck, brother, you're making us all look bad!" Beckett shouted at the screen.

Everyone had a glass in their hand at the reception, so Beckett helped himself to a little more. He was just finishing off the bottle when he saw them raise their glasses to him—to *him!*—via Eve's hummingbird camera. At that moment Beckett was glad he was alone. After joining the toast, his eyes blurry with tears, Beckett threw the bottle against the wall where it shattered spectacularly. This video was testament to exactly how normal his brothers' lives would be without him.

He lay back on the bed and balled his hands into fists.

Cole shut the bedroom door and gazed at Kyle. His eyes said he'd married his salvation, and Kyle knew what he meant. Two souls in need had finally found resolution with "I do."

"Wife. You're the most stunning vision I've ever seen. Will you always be mine?" Cole held out his hand as he unbuttoned his shirt.

"Husband, I already promised you that." She accepted his hand and cuddled into his chest. "I, Kyle McHugh, choose you, Cole Bridge, to be my husband, to respect you in your failures, to care for you in sickness, to nurture you, and to grow with you throughout the seasons of life."

"Why did you leave out the good parts?" Cole tilted her delicate face toward his.

"It'll be easy to stand next to you during good times. It's the bad times, the scary times that are tough. I'll never leave—no matter what life hands us." A tear shone on Kyle's cheek.

Cole wiped it dry with his thumb. "To the bad times then, my divine bride. I pledge my heart to bad times as well."

He leaned down, changing his hold so he could pull her body into his and deliver a passionate kiss. She buried herself in his chest when they needed to catch their breath.

"I have to ask you something—promise me you'll be open-minded?" She looked tentative.

He nodded.

"I've got some mad skills. Some mad *sex* skills. I want to do stuff to you, without you worrying about me." She looked at him with one eye closed.

"I can *never* promise to stop worrying about you," Cole said, smiling. "You're all I think about. But I'm sure my body is up to this task. Do as you must. I won't fight you off," he said with a resolute sigh.

Kyle stepped up and unbuttoned his pants. He put his thumb in her mouth. She smirked around it and swirled her tongue in a circle. Kyle kicked off her heels and switched to her dancer's toes, en pointe. As she unzipped his pants she kicked her leg up to rest a foot on his shoulder. Cole couldn't keep his hand from tracing the muscles of her smooth leg. Kyle used the moment to arch into a back bend, carefully dragging her legs over in a display of flexibility. She tucked her knees at the last moment to kneel in front of him.

"Don't worry." She watched suspicion cloud his eyes. "I'm going to give you pleasure. And you're going to take it."

She waited until his grin formed, then kissed him everywhere she could reach with her lips. She magicked his pants away from his ankles and slipped off his shoes and socks.

Now she would show him—show him that she loved him enough to stay with him, to be present as she wrapped her mouth around his length. She looked up so he could see her eyes and be sure of her. She kept her hands busy, increasing the friction and finding the places that made it hard for him to breathe. She could feel him tense with pleasure. Kyle cupped him and adjusted subtly until she found the spot.

"Damn it," he gasped as she pressed gently.

She continued stroking and sucking, planning to finish him still standing, just so she could see his knees shake. But Cole stepped back and away from her tender touches.

"Get on the bed, Kyle." His hands trembled.

"Cole, you promised. I want to do this for you." Kyle was suddenly worried. Didn't he trust her?

"That's not it. I just—your legs, your head moving, your hands. I need to taste you. Get on the bed." Cole offered a hand to her, helping her from her knees.

She smiled when she realized what he meant. Soon they were twisted into each other, unobstructed by clothing in a yin and yang of pleasure. She now had to fight through her own ecstasy to concentrate on his manhood. But this new angle gave her mouth more to work with, and soon together they became a shimmering convulsion of gratification. Cole untangled himself to stand over her, glistening.

"Mrs. Bridge? Would you care to shower?"

Kyle accepted his hand and swatted his bottom. "Yes. Mr. Bridge, I would love to." She giggled and tried to get away as he spanked her in return.

Cole did the honors of adjusting the water to the perfect temperature. He stood outside the shower as Kyle stepped into the stream. The curtain remained pushed aside as Cole watched Kyle soak her hair, her skin warming and glowing with the liquid heat. She peeked out at him every so often, thrilled every time to find his eyes on her body.

Droplets of water beaded on Cole's chest, and Kyle ran her hands over her body. "There's water everywhere, Cole. Get in. Come inside me this time."

Water covered the patchwork of scars on Cole's back as he pounded into Kyle. She opened her hands to steady herself against the tile as he pressed her high against the shower wall. She was blessed by the hot water, by his touch. He was baptized by the warm, inviting spot inside her.

The steam that poured out the open bathroom door created a blurry cloud. It seemed to pulsate in time with Cole's deep thrusts into his bride. Her hands moved from the tile to caress his neck. He sounded almost as if he was in pain as he thundered with the ecstasy of his release.

After lathering up and rinsing each other, Cole toweled Kyle's body dry. As he wrapped her in white terrycloth, Kyle eyed his lingering hardness. "Again?"

Cole turned his bride to hug her from behind, nuzzling her neck. "I'll have you in my bed next," he said. "I'm going to make love to you so thoroughly that, tomorrow? You'll walk like John Wayne."

Her laughter sounded so free.

Far from Kyle's joy, back in the lonely hotel room, Eve opened the door to find the drunken Beckett. She sat on the bed and leaned her back against the headboard. Beckett could barely manage the coordination it took to crawl to her and set his head on her chest.

"How wazzit?" he slurred.

He started to snore between her breasts before she could answer. She stroked his hair, letting his rhythmic noise free her tears. She watched the camera in her brooch project a picture of the TV to the TV, creating a sort of bizarre, M.C. Escher-style modern art—so fitting for the girl whose problems became her answers, which had then become her problems all over again.

Eve had wet cheeks when she finally answered a completely unaware Beckett. "It was amazing. It was everything I'll never have." She leaned down and pressed her lips to his hair. "Loving you is more of a curse than anything else."

48

Hummingbird

Eve's bike ate the pavement. She didn't bother with blinkers or inconvenient road signs. She just flew — weaving in and out of traffic. Most of the other drivers didn't even register her presence until she was long gone.

The routine she'd established in the last few months would be broken today. She'd have nothing more to report to Beckett. Blake and Eve had made an unlikely pair on his quest for freedom from his paralyzing fear, but this had been her last morning with her cousin.

Soon after Blake had moved into her father's building, Eve had been back to check on him — at Beckett's request. Beckett had been crawling the walls with his desperate need for his brothers' companionship, so Eve was to be his eyes.

She'd entered the apartment building and gone downstairs to find Livia standing just inside Blake's apartment door, her hand on the knob, ready to leave.

"Blake, I need to make the time. Dr. Lavender said a little at a time, every day, would be the way to go." Livia seemed angry with herself.

Eve's silent ways made eavesdropping part of her personality. She scarcely breathed. She noticed a crack in the hallway had been puttied over and painted, no doubt by Blake the handyman.

"You have too much going on," Blake insisted. "I can do this on my own, really. I'll try tomorrow. I will." Blake's voice sounded shaky.

Eve heard what had to be a gentle kiss.

"You said that about today," Livia added softly. "No, don't look at me like that; I'm so proud of you. This is a huge task, and I want to help."

The rustling of clothes had to be a hug.

"I never want to disappoint you, Livia." Blake sounded stronger now, determined, but still anxious.

"That's not possible. Ever. God, I have to go. The test is tomorrow, and I haven't even looked at the material."

Livia stepped backward into the hall. Eve slid into the cover of another doorway.

"You should definitely go," Blake said. "Will you please call me when you get home? So I know you're safe?" He closed the door behind them and walked with Livia down the hall and up the stairs, presumably to her car.

Eve watched silently, and unseen, as they passed, wondering if now was really a great time to be Beckett's nosy emissary. A few minutes later Blake walked past her hiding place in a furious, stomping rage. She was still debating with herself about visiting when she heard a crash. She arrived instantly at Blake's slightly open door.

"Goddammit! Man up and do this. Just do it. How can she be with me? I can't even...I won't try hard enough."

He was utterly defeated. Eve knew it without having to see the slope of his shoulders.

She pushed the door open, and it creaked on its hinges. Blake whirled and was instantaneously relived. Eve knew he'd been afraid he'd find Livia. She looked from Blake to the water glass he'd thrown against the wall. He must be seriously twisted up; he treated everything in the apartment like it belonged in a museum.

"Beckett says hi. Can I come in?" Eve waited until he nodded.

"Eve, I apologize for this broken glass. It's an extremely disrespectful way to treat these belongings." Blake fetched his broom and dustpan, kneeling to gather the destroyed kitchenware.

"Dude, I blew up Beckett's strip mall. I'm not judging." Eve strolled into his kitchen behind him, listening to the tinkle of broken glass as it found its resting place in the trash.

Blake lifted one eyebrow. He'd been in Beckett's world too long to be shocked by destruction. He put the broom away and faced Eve.

"Hey, I overheard part of your conversation with Livia." She tried to sound friendly.

Blake shook his head. "Yeah. I'm not doing so great at getting used to the sun." His hands were restless. "It's supposed to be little steps at a time, but I..."

Eve nodded. "I'm going to come tomorrow morning. We're going to get a cup of coffee at the place down the road. We'll walk, so be ready." Eve watched as he calculated the shadows, sun, and shade on the way to Cup O' Joe's.

"I wouldn't want to trouble you. Thank you for the offer, though." Blake held his own clenched fist.

Eve waited. They both looked around the kitchen. Blake cleared his throat.

"It's not an offer. I'm going to be here," she said. "We're going for a walk. Real simple." She watched as he changed his fingers' grip, once, twice, three times.

He needed convincing.

"Hey, I'm not your girlfriend. I'm no one you can disappoint. I'll just make sure we work through the fear that keeps you in the dark. Plus it'll be good exercise after the gunshot wound and all."

Blake looked at the ceiling and blew out a breath. "Why, Eve? Why would you do this for me?"

His suspicious eyes found her face again. That question caught her off guard. She pulled herself up to sit on the counter. Of course—Blake hadn't known her before David's accident. He had no idea she'd once honestly liked helping people.

"I used to be a human being," Eve said. "I used to care if people lived or died." She thought of Mouse and knew her emotions were not entirely buried. "You puttied the crack in the hall. You're letting my dad be a part of your life. I owe you, and this—helping you get coffee? I can do. You'll have to trust me." She hopped off the counter and held out her hand.

Blake stared, and instead of shaking it, he opened a drawer, retrieved a velvet ring box, and placed it in her extended hand. She opened it while Blake watched the box like it was a bomb. Inside was Eve's great-grandmother's engagement ring. She'd know it anywhere. Great Gran wore it every day of her fifty-eight years married to Eve and Blake's great-grandfather. She'd left it to Ted.

"Ted gave that to me," Blake said. "But I want you to have it. It was your great-grandmother's." He watched her carefully.

Eve took the ring out of the velvet slit that held it tightly. A shiver ran through her body. She jammed it back into its box and snapped it shut. The small, perfect diamond had taken a bite out of her soul. She tossed the box back to Blake. He caught it, looking puzzled.

"I can't wear that. I won't wear that." Eve turned her back on Blake. "I can't wear stuff like that in my line of work."

Blake said nothing, letting the silence ask his questions. Eve realized she was expecting a lot from him. She wanted him to trust her in the sun, so she'd have to do something that scared her as well. Time to show Blake what was left of her tiny, crumpled pink heart.

"I was going to wear that once. It was going to be mine. My boyfriend and I would have gotten married." She turned to see his reaction.

He was waiting patiently.

"David died in a car crash. It's a—he was my future, you know?"

It was the way he received her pain that made her tell him more. He looked at her intently, like what she told him would be part of him forever.

"I was pregnant with his baby. She died too." Eve shrugged, but her wet eyes betrayed her casualness.

Blake took the distance in two quick strides and enveloped her. Eve's stiff body was ill-prepared for the hug. But Blake held on until she softened against his chest.

"The sun's on the inside sometimes, huh?" He patted her back.

Eve patted his in return. "It burns in there."

Finally they parted, and Blake found Eve a tissue.

"Well, I can't very well give this to Livia," he said matter-of-factly, looking at the box on the counter.

"You're getting engaged?" Eve smiled at the thought of Blake and Livia.

"I want to, but I don't know if I have any right to ask her." Blake tucked the ring back into its drawer. "Your dad talked me into accepting this ring in a weak moment. He got me talking about my future and—"

Eve interrupted, imitating her father's voice and stance. "Don't put off happiness you can have today. Tomorrow is a hope, not a promise."

Blake laughed. "Yes! Exactly. Glad to see it was a real original speech, just for me."

"I hate to say this—ever—but my dad is right. I'll tell you what, I wish I'd married David." Eve's eyes got a faraway look. "I wanted to wait until after the baby and when we'd saved up enough to have a real, big wedding."

Blake was stoic as she picked the right words.

"But to have heard him say I do…" She trailed off and ran her hand through her hair.

Blake touched his heart, perhaps remembering his own brush with death.

"And that ring deserves another sixty years and more of love on it," she said, gesturing toward the drawer. "I'd never say this out loud to anyone, but I guess we're getting all touchy-feely: Livia? She's the bravest chick I've ever met. Let her have it, Blake. Let her have what I never did." Eve nodded and headed for his door.

She let him catch up to open it for her, knowing his chivalrous behavior gave him peace.

"I'll be here tomorrow." Eve patted his forearm.

Blake took a deep breath and nodded.

It took an entire week to actually get to Cup O' Joe's—even with the sun shields Livia had found for Blake. But Eve turned out to be just what he needed: a firm, uncompromising taskmaster. She always seemed to know how far to push him before she'd let him stop and try again the next day.

One day Beckett asked her what her trick was.

"His pupils," she answered immediately. "When a man gets so scared he's close to losing his mind, his pupils dilate." She shrugged. "When he gets there, we get to shade."

Over the next few weeks, Blake grew stronger and began to set aside his coverings. Now better able to see him, Eve studied him closely as they walked. His eyes never stopped watching the faces of those passing by. He seemed truly astounded that they had no reaction to the sight of him. They couldn't see his past etched into his skin.

The day Blake finally made it to the coffee shop uncovered, he and Eve touched paper cups of steaming brew in a toast. And they talked for a long time about his mother and what had made his skin glass. Eve tried her best to listen for him the way he'd absorbed her story about David. He seemed to be gaining some perspective on his situation, which Eve believed to be as crucial as the minutes that ticked by with sun on his skin, right out in public.

As they left, Eve watched him slide the coffee sleeve off the drink and put it in his pocket.

After they'd walked a few blocks, she questioned him. "Why'd you keep the sleeve?"

Blake pulled out the cardboard and looked down at it. "Just to remember I could do it."

Eve grabbed it from him quickly, ripped it in half, and threw it in a trashcan on the sidewalk. Blake held his hands up and gave her a *What the hell?* look.

"Don't tie your success to anything other than what's inside you." She stepped up to him and gently patted his heart. "*You* did this, Blake. You. Not the coffee, not me, not Livia. You did this."

Blake nodded. He motioned for her to continue walking, and she did.

Building up suited Eve much better than tearing down ever did. She recounted Blake's careful steps for Beckett each day when she returned to him at the current safe house in the evenings. There was little else she could do to ease the frustration of his imprisonment, other than tend to the sexual beast in him.

A couple weeks later Blake worked up to walking to the coffee shop by himself—and most other places too. Eve had watched from behind a tree the afternoon she found him sitting on the patio, just basking in the sun. That very night Blake had proposed to Livia with their great-grandmother's ring. And Livia had said yes.

Eve had been thrilled, with only a tinge of regret, as Blake recounted his betrothal and early wedding plans over their coffee that day. But now Eve grew uneasy. She had to tell Beckett there was another wedding to attend from a distance. Blake had refused to appoint anyone else as best man. He said it was Beckett's place, whether he filled it or not. Cole would officiate.

Beckett would have to make some decisions, and this news might put him over the edge.

Beckett rode the four-wheel ATV over a huge mound of dirt, and the vehicle went airborne. His helmet slipped, nearly covering his eyes. He hated it, but he didn't have a choice. Eve demanded the security and privacy it provided. *Like anyone could find me here.*

Eve had stashed him in Rhinebeck, New York, in a place off the road, off a driveway, then off a dirt path. The house had at least forty acres of woods surrounding it and very few neighbors. It belonged to some half-dead celebrity who never used it anymore. Eve paid the rent in cash, and the agreement was verbal. Beckett allowed himself the luxury of expecting this sort of perfection from her.

He pulled the ATV to a stop and unzipped the leather jacket he wore, revealing his shirtless, chiseled chest. *No need to get dressed up. Only deer and chipmunks buttfucking each other out here in the boondocks.*

He managed a smile, cracking himself up a little, as Eve pulled up on her motorcycle.

"How's he doing?" he hollered as soon as she cut the engine.

Her eyes paused on his naked, damp chest. He made his pecs dance to get a smile. She looked away.

"It may technically be spring, but it's cold out here, Beckett. What's wrong with you?" Beckett just smirked, so Eve continued. "Blake's doing great. He was in the sun for hours today. Beckett, he asked Livia to marry him. He says you're the best man. He says it's your place and he'd rather have it empty than have anyone else." She peeled off her riding gloves.

Beckett hung his head. The news hit him right in his heart's nuts. Hungry for physical connection, he pushed himself into her personal space, corralling her with his arms against the bike.

"I got to get to town before the store closes. I just came back for the minivan," she said quickly. "We don't have time for this." She didn't push him away, but he could feel the chill rolling off her.

"No need to bruise my dick. It's all good. Why don't you get a steak? I'll grill it."

Eve did finally smirk a bit. "After the sun goes down it's going to be twenty-eight degrees. You planning on grilling them with napalm?"

The change in her face made him try harder. "Fuck buying steaks. I'll torch us some raccoon. I saw some back there."

He pointed over his shoulder. Eve put a hand on his chest.

"Upstate raccoons will kick your ass," she said, digging in with her nails. "They'd have you crying like a bitch and wearing a dress in no time." Her hand traced the fine white scars she'd put on his skin during these two months of lying low.

He was insatiable these days. Beckett knew the time without social interaction was making him even more depraved and twisted. She'd been trying to convince him to leave the country with her—probably because she'd begun to fear he'd fuck her to death.

But as attractive as a tropical island alone with Eve might be, Beckett knew he could never go. He couldn't be that far from his brothers. What if one of them needed him? What if Eve's dad needed her? Family was family.

Beckett was so fucking proud of his lady and his brother. His heart threatened to swell out of his chest whenever he thought of her patiently, diligently working to get Blake into the sun. He just wished it could have been him. Maybe he'd send Eve to be Blake's fucking best man. Jesus. He grabbed his helmet and thought for a moment about chucking it as far as it could go, but instead he stuffed his jealousy deep inside and turned to walk with Eve back to the safe house.

Just one month later, as May began, the next wedding date arrived. Once Blake had conquered the sun, he let nothing hold him back from creating the life he'd always wanted. Livia and Blake had worked quickly to arrange their train-platform nuptials, and when Livia had suggested a wedding after dark, Blake shook his head. He'd insisted the ceremony be held in the full beauty of the sunset.

Eve dressed quietly after lunch that afternoon, choosing the same dress and hummingbird pin she'd worn to Cole and Kyle's wedding. As she checked her hair in the bedroom mirror, he appeared behind her. Beckett wore a crisp, white button-down shirt and jeans. They'd agreed he would stay home and watch the live feed again.

"Why did you pick a hummingbird for the camera?" He reached around and touched the gold wings. "'Cause they're so cute and pretty?"

He dared to tease her on this day, this twisty, pointy, dangerous day.

"They're vicious loners," she said quietly, speaking to her reflection. "Did you know that? They spend most of their time alone, protecting what's theirs."

Beckett's forehead wrinkled. "Is that how you see you?"

She shrugged. "It's what I am. What I am now."

She knew regret shone in her eyes before she closed them, and Beckett took a step back. She could sense the guilt rolling off of him and opened her mouth to speak when the high-pitched whine of one of her tripwires pierced the heavy atmosphere.

She kicked off her heels and had a gun in her hand before the alarm stopped. She nodded at Beckett, and he went to the closet to wait. They'd been through the drill before: a slow deer, a meter reader, a hunter.

He turned to watch her slide by him. He leaned against the doorframe. He didn't want to hide any more. His brother was finally out in the fucking sunlight, and here he was cowering from what might be a fat squirrel. He heard Eve trot down the stairs and exit the house through the back door. She was a machine, really. She knew all the right moves. She was a hummingbird. *No, not really. She's a freaking happy canary that I've squeezed into a rubber hummingbird costume.*

Beckett heard barking. He sidestepped his way to the window he should have been avoiding and stood behind the sheer. He watched as a dopey-looking beagle sniffed and skittered its way onto the front lawn. He heard another high-pitched whine. The alarm had sounded again.

He stepped to the center of the window and had to scan the lawn to find Eve. Her blond ponytail was the only thing he could see. She was behind a tree for cover. Beckett hit the window with one knuckle. Her eyes found the noise he made instantly. He pointed to his ear and held up two fingers.

She nodded once and gave him a glare that clearly said, "Get back in the fucking closet."

He ignored her and stepped behind the sheer again. Up the rocky path pedaled the most unlikely of assassins. A little girl about six years old pumped her chubby legs on a pink-and-white bike. The tassels on the handlebars swung in a steady rhythm, and she had a stuffed dolphin crammed in the basket in front of her.

The little girl was freaking adorable. Beckett watched through the murky sheer as Eve put the safety on her gun and knelt to hide it behind a root of the tree. She seemed to stay on her knee a moment, catching her breath. *That's a first.* Beckett was mesmerized by Eve's reaction. He carefully slid the window open a crack so he could hear their conversation.

The beagle bounded over to the now unarmed Eve, tongue lolling. Eve offered her hand for the dog to sniff, which it did and then took off in another direction.

"Peanut! No! Bad dog, come back. Lady! Lady, grab him!" The little girl had an even more adorable voice.

Why the hell is she out here in the middle of nowhere? She's so fucking little.

Eve looked at her new self-appointed boss. "Did he run away?"

Her voice was so warm. Achingly warm. Beckett almost didn't recognize it.

The little girl stopped her bike and took an elaborate, deep breath. "Peanut is not a good dog. He ran away when I tried to put my sister's dress on him. He likes to run away. Mommy said, 'Go get Peanut!' So I went to go get Peanut, and he saw a bunny and took off down the road, and my sister's crying, and she's just a baby. I'm a big sister. I know how to give her a bottle, and Mommy says I'm a big help. Peanut! Don't poop! Oh, I'm sorry, lady. He's just on a streak of bad."

Beckett stepped from behind the curtain so he could see Eve's face clearly. He knew she was beautiful, but the smile on her face for this little girl made him grab the windowsill.

Eve was magnificent. Her eyes were soft, her body language welcoming. Her guard was not only down, it was gone. In just a few sentences, this child had broken through to the Eve he'd only seen hints of.

Eve got down to the girl's level. "What's your name?"

The big-eyed girl had the audacity to bounce her pigtails while she recited her full name: "Emily Anna Whiteside."

Anna. Beckett watched as Eve's chest caved ever so slightly with the blow.

She recovered, as she always did, to deal with the task in front of her. "Hi, Emily. I'm Eve. There are no houses close by. How long have you been riding your bike?"

"It feels like hours. And I have to go potty, but I won't give up. Peanut's bad, but he's mine."

The unacceptable dog now licked his hindquarters with abandon a stone's throw from where the two were getting to know one another.

"Okay, Emily. I'm sure your mom's worried. I'll get Peanut, and we'll get you home." Eve put her hand out like she might like to touch the top of the girl's head, but she pulled it back at the last second.

Would soft hair hurt that much to touch? Beckett dropped to his knees, trying to see this tender Eve more closely.

Eve headed for the dog. "Here, Peanut. Here, boy."

The dog trotted eagerly toward her, then veered away just as Eve got close.

The little girl laughed and scolded the dog at the same time. "Go, Eve, go! Peanut, stop."

She dissolved into giggles. Like a husk of ice cracking and falling to the ground, the giggles changed Eve. She began exaggerating her movements to make the girl laugh, and she pretended to growl and bark at Peanut, who stopped and cocked his head to one side.

Little Emily had to hold her middle as Eve finally dove at the dog, tackling him efficiently. All dressed up for the wedding, Eve was now covered in clinging leaves and smudges of dirt. Emily clapped her hands at the sight of her beloved pooch captured and safe. As Eve knelt to get a better grip on the dog's collar, she faced the house.

Maybe he could have changed his mind. Maybe he could have continued thinking only about himself. But Beckett had seen her face. He'd been looking at her eyes when the grateful girl reached up to give Eve a hug.

Emily was so excited she forgot. She was so happy she made a mistake and said, "Thank you so much, Mommy!"

Beckett watched baby Anna die all over again on Eve's face. Her raw agony was worse than any bullet he'd ever taken. As the icy husk crystallized again around this beautiful woman, he made his decision, determined his future.

He watched as Eve took Emily in the front door, disappearing beneath him. Evil Peanut's paws made regular clacks on the wood floor as Eve showed Emily the bathroom. Eve's murmurs and the little girl's bright-voiced answers decorated the house with life. Too soon Eve had loaded the little girl, her pink bike, and the wayward dog into his minivan.

After they'd pulled away Beckett found a blazer to wear over his shirt. He went out on the porch and waited in the rocking chair until she returned and parked the minivan just where it had been before.

Eve sat for a split second in the driver's seat before she leaped out and slammed the door. He waited until she'd come to lean against the porch railing before he looked up at her face again.

"You can have that life," he told her. "It's right there for you to take."

"I love you," Eve quickly countered.

"Loving me hurts you, doesn't it?" Beckett asked, looking down. "No, you don't have to tell me. I know. I can smell it. I can smell the pain coming off of you," he said, looking at the floor. "You had love before and a future. What does loving me get you, Eve? What does it get you?" He stood, angry with himself.

"I don't need to *get* anything from you. It's the way it is. There's no changing that." She gripped the porch railing.

Beckett stepped close to Eve and tenderly tucked a lock of hair that had escaped her ponytail behind her ear.

"You're saying goodbye," she said, her eyes full of questions.

"Do you know there are other little girls out there like that one? I lived with a few of them. They would sell their souls for a mother like you."

At the word *mother* Eve's chin crumpled. She tried to hold back the tears, but they wouldn't obey.

"See that? It's what you need. You need that—a little kid calling you Mom." Beckett put his arms around her as she shattered.

The pain she kept hidden surfaced from where it had been smoldering. When he felt her knees weaken, he hugged her harder.

"That's right. It's okay. It's nothing to be ashamed of, baby. You want normal." He guided her to the chair he'd vacated. "There's a guy out there who'll hold your hand. There's a little girl out there. She's waiting for you. It'll be okay. It'll be okay." He knelt in front of her and rubbed her arms.

She slapped at his hands, letting outrage carry her words. "I don't want another man. I want *you*. I've killed for you. I've protected you. What the hell do you think you're doing? Do you honestly think these hands that kill can hold a child?" She held her fingers in front of her face.

"Yes. Absolutely. Don't you know, gorgeous? Mothers are some of the most vicious killers out there, if their kids are threatened. You just have more practice." He took her hands and kissed them.

"I've lost too much. I can't lose you. Don't make me. Please. I'll beg you if I have to." She watched his lips on her palms.

He shook his head and used her own words against her. "The hardest part of loving someone is not being with them when you want to be."

He stood, and she mirrored his motion, already shaking her head. "Don't say it."

Beckett ignored her; he knew what he had to do. He had to set beautiful Eve free to find that soft, touchable woman he'd seen her become with the little girl.

"I'm going to my brother's wedding. I'm his best man." He straightened his jacket.

"They'll arrest you. That's a wonderful present for him." She wiped tears off her face.

"Did you notice he can walk in the sun now, and I can't?" Beckett lifted an eyebrow.

"I can change that for you. We can get away — the money's there. Let's go. We'll go now." Eve grabbed his lapels.

He covered her hands. "And what happens when we get far away from here and your eyes start to glaze over again? What happens when a little girl loses her dog? Do you think I ever, ever want to see that pain in your eyes again? It was like I was shooting you myself." He looked down at their feet and back up at her again.

"Where would I get a kid for us, Eve? No one would let me adopt. Christ, *I* wouldn't let me adopt. You can get out of this free and clear. You *will* get out of this free and clear. It's my last order to you. Have a good fucking life. Promise? I'll beg you if I have to." He put his big hands on her cheeks.

Time ticked by as they stood at the edge. Beckett knew he was right. She wanted the kids. She wanted the normal — sticky waffle breakfasts and runaway dogs and a minivan that spilled Barbie dolls when the door opened. She wanted it so very much. He just needed her to accept that.

"I can't watch you get arrested." She finally dared to look in his eyes.

He nodded. "Then you can't come, can you, baby?"

She said nothing. Her breath was shaky.

"Know this: I love you so fucking much," Beckett said. "No other person has been to me what you are. No one else ever will be." He leaned down and gave her the sweetest, gentlest kiss.

He wanted her to know what she should expect from the next guy, what she should demand. And because he needed it once more, he tried to make her smile. "Though the first dude to give me the Prison Shocker will be a close second."

She shook her head and showed a ghost of a smile.

"I'm taking your bike 'cause you're going to need the minivan for all those kids." He winked and willed himself to smile at her.

Before he could change his mind, Beckett got on her bike. He fired it up and let it sit for a minute. After he'd committed her face, this moment, this heartbeat to memory, he obediently put on the helmet. Then he turned the bike and headed toward the road, intent on Poughkeepsie.

She watched as the dirt kicked up in a cloud. When it cleared, she couldn't see him anymore. She stayed until she couldn't hear him anymore.

Staying.

Not chasing.

Not stopping him.

She knew she could bring him back. She was more than capable, and yet her feet refused to move. It felt like the little arms that had encircled her neck still clung there.

Was it my Anna? Was her name just a coincidence?

Eve hated that she had these questions, and that the only man she wanted to talk to about them was David. *Have I just forsaken Beckett?*

Roots continued to form. Her murderous hands remembered how satisfying clicking the seatbelt around Emily's small body had been. It sounded just like releasing the safety on a gun. *Could motherhood be even a tiny possibility?*

Her inaction chose her future.

49

Will You Marry Me?

As he prepared for his wedding, Blake had arranged his shirt three times. It refused to be tucked into his pants in any normal way. He ripped it out and tried again as he heard someone's key in the lock of his apartment.

"Today's the big day!" Cole announced as he entered. When he found Blake in the bedroom, he started laughing. "Remember how many times I did my hair the day I married Kyle? I think that shirt is my hair for you today."

Blake sighed. "What? Could you not launch riddles at me? I can't think straight."

"I'd help you with your pants, but I think you'll manage." Cole sat on the edge of Blake's bed as Blake rolled his eyes.

The men skipped their traditional greeting. They'd dropped the ritual. This was their unspoken acknowledgment of Beckett's absence.

"Do you have the rings?" Blake finally righted his shirt and started on the tie.

"Yes, I do. Get used to hearing that today, by the way." Cole stood to retrieve the rings from his pocket. He was keeping them safe in a little satin bag. He emptied the contents into his hand.

Blake counted them out loud. "One, two."

Cole ribbed him again using his best cartoon voice. "Two! We have two rings! Ah-ha-ha!"

"Are you allowed to beat up the officiant before a wedding? I think we need to start that tradition today." Blake play-punched Cole in the stomach.

Light, funny, and slightly false, the boys tried to keep the giant, Beckett-sized hole in the room filled with their banter.

Cole grabbed Blake's jacket off the wooden hanger and held it open. Blake stood in front of the mirror, adjusting the tie again, then submitted to the jacket.

"Do you think I should smooth the hair? I mean, like, with a part or something?" Blake tried it out with his hands.

Cole tilted his head like a cocker spaniel. "Um. I'm going to go ahead with a *no*. You'll look like a newscaster." Cole made his voice deeper. "And today, in other news, Blake Hartt and his bride jammed up an entire train station with their love."

Blake smiled. "Some important people must really owe Kathy big. I'm still amazed we were able to pull this off."

Though she was a humble police station receptionist by day, Livia's dad's mysterious new girlfriend seemed to be hooked up beyond reason. She'd gotten the mayor of Poughkeepsie to allow a train platform wedding ceremony, although a train would make a noisy stop sometime during the blessed event.

After admiring his fully dressed self for a moment, Blake started for the door, pocketing his keys.

"Hey, we've got, like, hours to go before Livia shows up," Cole pointed out.

Blake looked at his shoes. "I don't want to be late. I don't mind the wait. I'm used to it."

Cole shrugged and followed his brother out the door. Blake consented to a ride in Cole's car only after Cole pointed out that the walk might dirty his tux. They arrived at the platform with two and a half hours to spare before the 7:30 p.m. ceremony. Blake assumed his position at the edge of the red paper aisle. His eyes tracked the scarlet trail to its beginning: the top of the stairs leading to the parking lot.

My Livia will come to me on this path.

At times the men made small talk or helped the wedding planner put the finishing touches on the silver-and-white decor. And they each lit what seemed like a million candles. Blake remained standing throughout the wait, sometimes gazing at the rippling Hudson River.

Today, when I count her smile, I get to keep it.

He asked Cole again to see the rings. The simple gold bands were old-fashioned looking and fairly thin, but Blake had bought them with money he'd earned at the piano bar.

As her wedding present, he'd composed a song for her on the piano at work, working at night after the bar closed. As long as he locked up, the owner didn't mind Blake's experiments. Livia had made only one of his Thursday night gigs. A study group ate up the rest of her free hours as she worked double to catch up on the material she'd missed while involved in Blake's drama. It had taken Blake a little while to come to terms with her course of study and planned career. But as he spent more time with Livia and talked to her about what she was learning, he came to feel confident that she saw him only as her soulmate and never as a potential patient. She wanted to help him and just happened to have an above-average knowledge of how to do so.

Blake had no piano today, but he hoped he'd have an opportunity to play her present for her soon. He'd written the music neatly on staff paper and folded it in his jacket pocket. He patted it now and smiled. He surveyed the scene and realized the guests had started to arrive.

Flickering candles climbed the stairs, and hundreds more trimmed the edges of the platform. White seats had been neatly arranged to hold the fifty or so guests for the occasion. Blake had a feeling the small check he'd given the wedding planner was not the only compensation she'd received for the wedding.

Kyle's old friend Lorraine, the night's DJ, was stunning yet understated in a silky gray dress as she arranged her iPod and speakers for the ceremony. Her big equipment was already set up at the park for the reception. Blake greeted the men and kissed ladies' hands as the guests continued to fill the platform. He nodded to the handful of police officers who arrived together, almost in formation.

"I'm asking my people to leave their firearms at home," Livia's dad had informed him the week before. "I think guns make Livia nervous after your...uh...incident."

Blake loved that John paid such close attention to his daughters. He'd not been the only one to register the flinch Livia still exhibited whenever she heard a sudden loud noise.

The sun sifted through the trees around the platform, and Blake stood proudly in its curtain of light. It would be retreating from him this time. He walked over to his old spot in the shade with victory in his step. He'd been trapped there for so long. He shook his head and returned to the sun's rays, amazed at how powerful that simple act made him feel.

By 7:28, all the guests had arrived, and there were three empty seats: one for Eve, who had yet to show up, another for John, who would have a seat after he gave his daughter away, and a third that would remain empty, save for the ball of soft white yarn with two silver knitting needles in it.

Lorraine had set an elegant tone with a subdued Verdi concerto. Blake heard the rumble of an engine and the cracking of gravel in the parking lot. *The limo. She's here.*

The steep staircase kept the guests' prying eyes from seeing the little family that had just arrived. As he waited, Blake glanced to his side, where his best man wasn't. Cole looked at the spot as well.

Then Kyle's smiling face appeared at the top of the stairs, and she gave Lorraine a thumbs-up. The dreamy music Livia had selected for the ceremony filled the air.

Kyle made walking down the steep stairs in high heels and a long silver gown look easy. She took care not to poke holes in the runner as she tiptoed her way to the dais. Cole received a kiss on the cheek and a wink.

As Blake leaned down to accept her hug she whispered, "Remember when you and Livia tried to hog the spotlight at my wedding? Just when you and Livia get to the good part, Cole and I are going to have porno sex right there."

She pointed discreetly at the spot to Blake's right, and he couldn't help but laugh. As the music switched from a cappella to a piano-filled marvel, Blake watched as all his hours of waiting paid off. At the top of the stairs, with her father holding her arm tightly, Livia appeared, looking demurely down at her feet.

She and John took one small step at a time. She was obviously much more concerned about tripping than Kyle had been. During her descent, Blake just looked. Her white gown fit her frame perfectly, and the strapless dress revealed the gentle, tempting curves of her shoulders. Her bouquet contained the paper-napkin roses he'd made for her, combined with baby's breath. A flowing train cascaded down the stairs behind Livia, and an even longer veil billowed in the gentle breeze like a blown wish.

Livia stopped to hold her small tiara on with her bouquet hand, and she finally looked at him. As always, her blazing beauty ignited him as she approached.

Me. She sees me.

She was only a few steps from the bottom when she smiled at him. Blake mouthed the number back to her.

"You're here," she whispered.

"Always," he said loud enough for everyone to hear.

She blushed. Her father helped her down the last few steps, and she returned her gaze to her feet. She looked down now because, Blake knew, she was trying not to cry. She didn't want to be a "blubbering mess," as she called it. Blake ducked his head lower to get a glimpse of her face. His beautiful love was just steps from him when Livia's father extended his hand. Blake shook it with a stern formality. This ritual was so important to him.

After transferring responsibility from one strong hand to another, John kissed Livia on the cheek. Blake could see he also wanted to hug her, but after a moment, he went to his chair without the gesture of comfort. John was also working not to make Livia cry.

Blake waited for her to look at him with a smile, but her shoes were still too captivating. He held a hand up to stop Cole from beginning the ceremony. He knelt on one knee, close to the hem of her dress, and looked up at her. She watched him as he kissed her hand.

"Beautiful, enchanting Livia, will you marry me today?"

Livia's disobedient tears emerged, gravity bathing his smiling face with their small, splashy wishes. She took her hand from his and covered her mouth. She nodded over and over as she cried.

Blake stood and gathered her. Livia dissolved into him, leaving the guests alternately tearing up or looking in other directions.

Blake tried to stroke her hair through the veil, but he was afraid he would pull it out. "Shhh. It's okay. I'm not that terrible, am I?"

Livia shook her head.

"I'm making you my wife right now, even if you cry through the whole damn thing." Blake switched to wiping her tears.

Kyle, the only other person standing close enough to whisper, leaned in to Livia's ear. "Quit being such a snot-flinging drama queen. Suck it up and marry him." She turned her attention to Blake. "Are you two going to be a while? Should Cole and I get started over there?" She pointed to her previously selected location.

Blake laughed and shook his head. Livia regained her composure.

Kyle held a tissue in front of her sister. "Don't ask me where I was keeping that."

Livia wiped her cheeks and eyes, then tucked the tissue into her bouquet instead of giving it back to her sister.

Years later, a little girl would pull that tissue out and ask her mother about it. "The Sobbing Bride" would become one of the girl's favorite tales. She would request it from her mother's point of view, then run to have her father tell his version.

But for now, the couple turned to Cole, who assumed a very regal tone. "Welcome, ladies and gentlemen, to a ceremony celebrating Blake Hartt and Livia McHugh. Today is not the start of their lives together. It will mark the day we all stood, clapped, and gave good wishes. But their fates were destined for each other long before they even met. True love, the kind that lasts forever, is very rare indeed. It takes compromise, continued growth, and trust."

Cole paused to look from Blake to Livia and back again. "Livia and Blake have a head start on all those things," he continued. "Time has tested them already, asking a fresh love to face terrifying and life-changing tasks. These two had to find and hold onto their love, even when it felt like all was lost."

Blake kept his eyes on Livia, though his body faced Cole. Livia would glance, smile, and look away, shaking her head while she tried not to cry. Lorraine left the Verdi on softly in the background, and Cole made sure to look at Kyle, surely remembering their own rocky path. The sun threw out glistening beams, making the platform golden.

The sound of a motorcycle in the parking lot caught everyone's attention.

Blake looked at Livia. "Eve's here."

He recognized the motor from her arrival at his apartment for their daily walks. Cole was about to continue when the engine cut out. The steps that approached were not quiet or delicate; instead they rang loud, widely spaced, and definitely masculine.

Cole and Blake raised their eyebrows at each other and looked to the top of the steps in tandem. Beckett appeared and stood for a moment, taking in the scene. Then he trotted down the steps.

Livia grabbed Blake's lapels. "Oh, God. No. They're going to arrest him."

Blake pulled her to him and kissed her forehead. "He knows that, love," he murmured. "He knows."

Beckett was halfway up the aisle with a huge grin when John stood and stepped in front of him. "Stop right there. Mr. Taylor. You're wanted for questioning in the murder of Chris Simmer."

Livia handed her bouquet to Kyle and picked up her gown. She stutter-stepped as quickly as she could in her heels until she was between Beckett and her father.

Beckett's gruff voice moved her veil as he spoke, "Happy wedding, Whitebread. But please, don't worry about this."

Livia shook her head at her father and turned to wrap her arms around Beckett. "I'm so glad you're here."

Beckett patted her back while keeping his gaze on her father.

"Livia, step aside," her father said. "Let me take care of this, and we can get back to the wedding. One of the boys can take him down to the station." He used his cop voice.

Livia put one hand on the center of Beckett's chest and the other on her father's, connecting the men's hearts through her own.

"Dad, please. I know this is an impossible thing to ask. I know you follow all the rules, and that's what I love best about you. But this man is important to Blake," she patted her hand gently on Beckett's chest.

John tightened his lips and shook his head.

"And I know you don't like him. And I know you *need* to question him. But I'm asking you, please, *please* do it after the wedding." She patted her father with her other hand.

Beckett removed her hand. "Go up there with my brother. Don't fight my battles for me, Livia."

Blake now stood next to John, ready to take Livia away from the confrontation. Cole came to stand on John's other side, his hands holding his Bible tightly, his mouth moving in a quiet prayer.

John bit his bottom lip. "Livia, the last thing I want to do is upset you. But Mr. Taylor here, he's a real slippery guy. I need to grab him while I can."

Livia made a fist and put it to her forehead. "Dad. Some people who should love me and should be here aren't. Like Mom."

Her father blinked.

"Beckett shouldn't love anyone, but he does, and he knows he shouldn't be here, but he is. I'm asking you, please, let him stay. I know I'm not being fair." Livia took her father's hand. "And if you really can't do it, if you really have to take Beckett now, I won't be mad. I'll understand. Sometimes the right thing can seem so wrong, like it does in this moment. But really, Beckett won't hurt anyone here. Not today. I bet he isn't even armed."

Beckett shook his head and opened his jacket for all to see.

John sighed. "Livia, even if I decide to let him stay, how can I ask that of the other guys?"

Livia turned to face the row of dignified police officers. "You can't, Dad, but I can. Would it be okay? Could you guys possibly let him be the best man?"

Finally, after some murmuring and grumbling, the officers nodded.

"Thank you so very much." Livia knew they must deeply respect her father to grant such a request.

John accepted Livia's exuberant hug. "Yup, all right. Better get up there and get married already. Time to let Blake have the pleasure of your nagging for the rest of *his* days," he said.

Gentle, tension-soothing laughter spread through the crowd, and John simply turned his back on Beckett and returned to his seat.

The brothers could not contain their enthusiasm. They wrapped their forearms together and pounded backs. Beckett and Blake each offered Livia the crook of an arm as they went back up the aisle.

"Baby, you didn't have to do that," Beckett whispered fiercely. "But thank you so fucking much. You look gorgeous today."

Livia kissed his cheek and let go of his arm so he could hug Kyle.

"Hey, Fairy Princess, I think you may be the hottest married chick alive right now," Beckett said.

Kyle hugged him and punched him in the arm at the same time. Cole resumed his place and opened the Bible, signaling the return of decorum.

"Let's start over. The sun still hangs by a thread in the sky for us. Please accept our humble thanks, Lord. The beauty you have wrapped around this loving couple tonight is the perfect backdrop." Cole gestured grandly at the spectacular show behind him.

The river was a silver mirror reflecting the rippling colors. The sun glowed red, as deep as love, as it headed for the horizon, and the clouds flaunted pinks and oranges.

Cole reached into his pocket and handed Beckett the bag with the rings. He held them gently in a cupped hand for a moment and smiled down at them. Then he put them in his pocket and held his head high.

"Blake and Livia have come before us today to declare their promise," Cole said. "They will fill their hearts with only each other and their love. It is our job as witnesses to support them and to send them positive thoughts when we think of this day and their life's journey together." Cole made a point to gaze at those seated before him. "The couple has prepared their own vows. Livia, would you like to go first?"

Livia nodded and unwrapped a pink page from the stem of her bouquet. She spoke softly, so only Blake could hear her. But the audience felt the moment by watching Blake's eyes as she spoke.

Livia read from the paper as if it were a letter. "Dear Blake Hartt, thank you. Thank you so much for thinking my smile was worth waiting for. Thank you for letting me see who you are inside. I found the sweetest spot in the world—it's wherever you are, surrounded by your arms. Please be my husband. I couldn't have it any other way. I promise to make you lose count. Love, Livia McHugh."

When she'd finished, Blake took the paper from her hands. He folded it and put it in his pocket, where it nestled side by side with his music. He kissed her ringed hand, and then her bare one. He had no paper, but he spoke clearly and unhesitatingly. There was a slight echo as his words bounced around the cement platform. He borrowed her letter format to respond.

"Dear Livia McHugh, I'll be your husband. I'll be nothing but yours for the rest of forever. A single, simple day with you is something I'll refuse to take for granted. You have been the reason my heart beats since the moment I saw you, long before your hands actually had to do the job for me. Sleep in my arms. Wake up by my side. My beautiful love, be my wife and make me the happiest man. And I will never, ever lose count. Love always, Blake Hartt."

Livia had to cover her mouth again, and her tears slipped over her fingers. She smiled after a moment and opened her mouth to speak, but no sound came out.

Finally Cole spoke. "Shall we exchange rings?" He nodded at Beckett, who let the rings fall into Cole's hands as if it were the most important job he'd ever done. Perhaps to him it was.

Livia removed her hand from Blake's to take his ring from Cole's palm. She kissed the ring and prepared to place it in its permanent home on his finger.

"Repeat after me," Cole instructed. "This ring is a token of my love. I marry you with this ring, with all that I have and all that I am."

Livia said her words and placed the ring. Her smile was huge. Blake counted again. Livia pulled off her engagement ring and held her now bare hand out to Blake.

Blake didn't give Cole a chance to repeat his script. He remembered each of Livia's words. "This ring is a token of my love," he said. "I marry you with this ring, with all that I have and all that I am."

He took the engagement ring from her right hand and slipped that on her left as well. Livia stepped into his arms and kissed him, her previous shyness overwhelmed by joy.

Cole laughed. "And you may keep kissing the bride. Ladies and gentlemen, I present to you, Mr. and Mrs. Blake Hartt."

He clapped, and the crowd stood to offer their congratulations. Blake whirled Livia into a dip and continued to kiss her, while Beckett whooped and Kyle whistled loudly. The train rumbled in behind the guests, the clattering wheels adding their noise to the standing ovation.

The unusual sight before them momentarily disoriented the passengers tumbling off the train. Blake and Livia came up for air, laughing and smiling at the crowd. Some commuters just powered up the red-covered stairs with nothing but a second glance. Most took a few steps forward and stood respectfully, taking in the romantic scene. The train had a schedule to keep and rumbled out of the station.

As the applause quieted down, a single loud voice came from the back of the crowd. "What'th the problem here? Let me through!"

An oily man with a horrible comb-over pushed his way through the spectators.

Livia and Blake's eyes widened. *Homeleth Humper!* she mouthed silently.

"Thith ith ridiculouth. Blocking a whole platform for thith carrying on? It'th dithguthing." He scanned the crowed with his beady eyes. When he finally spotted Blake and Livia, he was as shocked as they were. He opened his mouth to speak, but seemed to think better of it when he noticed a group of police officers rising to their feet.

John held out his badge. "Is there a problem, sir? We have a permit to be here."

A panicked, slippery look engulfed the man's face. "I wath talking on my phone, not to you people."

John looked the man up and down. "You *do* realize you're not actually holding a phone right now?"

The man looked at his empty hands. Then he took off running up the stairs, almost toppling a bank of candles. As he departed, Livia and Blake got down to the business of accepting congratulations from their guests.

"Hey, everyone, the reception is right across the way in Firefly Park," Kyle announced, taking it upon herself to direct traffic. "You can either walk or drive. The wedding party will be over right after pictures."

Beckett posed joyfully with his brothers as the photographer took shot after shot, maximizing the sun's final dramatic show and the candles' warm glow in the background. The wedding planner's assistants began dismantling the magical wedding setting.

After smiling for a family photo with his daughters, John announced, "All right. I talked to the boys. Beckett, you can stay for the reception." He nodded while he granted the reprieve. "Afterward, we'll bring you in for questioning."

John turned to leave, but Blake caught his attention. "Sir, thank you. It means the world to me that he's here."

"Yup. No problem, son." John stepped around the scurrying assistants, and rejoined Kathy to head for the park.

Blake pulled Livia to him. "How do you manage to be so brave every day?"

Livia put a hand on his smooth jaw. "I should ask you. Seeing you stand—here, of all places—in the sun to wait for me was amazing."

After they finished the pictures, Kyle made sure the bride and groom got a moment alone on the empty and now darkening train platform.

"We'll see you guys over there," she hollered over her shoulder, permission and a threat all rolled in one.

Blake ran his hands over Livia's bare shoulders. "Tonight, I'll make sure every part of you knows you got married."

Livia got on her tiptoes and nipped at his earlobe to show her appreciation.

"Can I give you my gift now?" Blake reached in his pocket.

"You gave me this already." Livia wiggled her ring finger.

He unfolded the music and held it open for her.

"You wrote me a song," she gasped. "I love it, though you know I can't read music." She kissed his lips and held the paper against her heart.

"Wait! Oh my gosh. Let me get your gift." She grabbed a gift bag Kyle had left by the steps. Just before she could hand it to him, she pulled it back. "But what if you hate it? It's either perfect or horrible. Now I'm worried."

Blake tilted his head and squinted his eyes. "It's perfect. I'm sure of it. Hand it over."

Livia looked sheepish as he moved the tissue paper out of the way. He unrolled the familiar-shaped cardboard and stared at the keyboard she had painstakingly drawn.

Livia tried to cover her worry with words. "I'm not sure if I should have replaced it. I mean, I know nothing could replace it. I tried to get the keys right. I went through like ten boxes and—"

Blake could move quickly when he wanted to, and she gasped as he kissed her mid-word. He finally stopped long enough to thank her. "Every time I think I couldn't love you a bit more, you stretch my heart again."

"So play it! Play my song. Please?" Livia sat down on the platform, right where she'd been standing.

Blake sat down as well, facing her. The moon now claimed the sky as hers, surfacing slowly over the trees. Blake tested her hand-drawn keys, and in his head he heard a full piano play his heart out loud for her.

Livia clapped when he was done. She put her hand behind his head and pulled his lips close. "I think I heard it," she whispered before kissing him.

Kyle's shrill voice interrupted their moment. "Figured you two would turn this into a scout meeting. Will you get your asses up here? People are waiting. I mean Beckett here has maybe a few hours before he's bent over a metal toilet getting it up the ass from a guy named Bubba. Do you want him to have fun now or not?"

The streetlight illuminated Beckett as he appeared next to Kyle. "Why would I be the bitch? I don't think that's a fair fucking assumption."

Kyle refused to look at him and crossed her arms. "Of course you'd be the bitch. You have dimples. Bitches have dimples. And I bet your ass is soft like two pillows. Bubba's going to love bouncing off of you."

Beckett stormed away, dragging Kyle with him. "I'll be the fucker," he told her. "Not the fuckee. The fucker."

"Fine, asshole, you're the fucker," Kyle's voice faded away as they returned to the party.

Livia touched Blake's chest. "We'd better go. Sounds like they need us up there. Are you ready?"

Blake stood, rolled up his piano, and tucked it back in the bag. "I'm totally ready."

He held out his hand to Livia and pulled her up easily. Hand in hand they walked over to their reception. Lorraine's music carried over the water, treating neighboring towns to the celebration as well. All the little trees around the picnic tables had been wrapped in white lights. The candles from the ceremony had been relit in the park, giving the evening a flickering, twinkling glow. The portable dancefloor could scarcely hold the happy crowd as Kyle and Beckett entertained with intricate dancing that looked almost like fighting. Between every song, however, Kyle took a time out to snuggle with Cole.

Soon John and Livia shared their dance, and John laughed out loud when Kyle horned in and made it a three-way love sandwich. After the dance, Beckett grabbed a champagne glass from a covered picnic table and stepped up onto it so everyone could see him.

"Hey! Listen up, everybody! I'm Beckett, and I'm the best man here. I do believe it's part of my job to give a speech."

Blake and Livia looked at each other, silently wishing for only clean words from their colorful, criminal groomsman. The crowd quieted, and Lorraine turned the dance music down.

"Blake, Cole, and I have been family for each other, because the ones we started with were for crap. Why they let me in, I still don't know. But because they did, I believed I was worth more than I would have otherwise." He nodded and gathered his thoughts for a moment.

"Blake's company made me want to hug trees and hear music. Cole's company made me want to try harder to be a better person. I never imagined that anyone could love either of these men enough for me to let them go."

A warm breeze blew as the giant man stopped to compose himself. The guests could almost smell the promise of summer.

"But I didn't know about the McHugh girls. Their love is fiercer than guns. More powerful than fistfuls of money. I can walk away because of them. Officer McHugh? I want to thank you again for letting me see this through. I know my peace of mind is far from your concern, but I appreciate it anyway."

Beckett held his glass up high. "To my brothers. They've finally gotten the lives they deserve."

The guests raised their glasses high, the clinking of the glass its own applause.

"Now, if I might have a little mood music?" Beckett continued. "I want to take this bride for a test ride on the dancefloor." He drained the rest of his glass and hopped down to find Livia.

She grabbed his hand as he passed. "Whitebread, you're edible. What a stunning lady you are. Blake's a lucky man." Beckett waggled his eyebrows at his brother as he spun, twirled, and dipped Livia out to the center of the dancefloor. Blake watched with a smile as other couples moved into the space around them and Lorraine filled the air with music again.

Having seen Beckett in action before, Livia just let his big hands show her body where to go. She concentrated on his face. His smile might fool others, but she saw that he was clinging desperately to the joy around him, as if he could somehow soak it in.

"Beckett, where's Eve?"

He hummed the song and twirled her around again, avoiding the question.

When he had her pressed to his chest, she tried again. "Are you going to tell me or what?"

Beckett sighed and looked into her face. "I left her, babycakes. She needs wings, not handcuffs."

He held Livia tighter, like she was a teddy bear.

She stopped moving her feet and hugged him around the neck. "You're not handcuffs. Don't you know that? She loves you. She does, I've seen it."

Beckett resumed dancing, dipping her again. "Look around, Whitebread. She's not here. She didn't try to stop me from coming. Her heart belongs to a dead man and a dream. I'm neither of those things." Beckett released her and clapped for the end of the song. He reached in his pocket and produced a crumpled envelope. "Here's my gift to you guys. I'm sure Blake won't want to accept it, but I'm hoping you'll convince him. For me."

Livia took the envelope and said thank you, trying to do something, anything that would make Beckett feel better.

"I better get over to your dad. I know he said later, but my job here is done." Beckett's voice was resigned.

"Beckett, would you do me a favor? For my wedding?" Livia asked suddenly.

He nodded. "You know I'll do whatever you ask."

She looked over her shoulder and back to his face. "In a minute I'm going to faint away from lack of food. When I wake up, I would appreciate it if you were miles away on Eve's bike."

"You're going to crack your fucking head trying to pull a stunt like that." He ran his hand through his hair. "And I gave your dad my word. I don't want him to think that was all a ploy."

"You said *anything*. Come on, big guy, give me what I want." She looked at him hopefully. "I'll explain it all to my dad later. I promise."

Beckett leaned down and kissed her cheek. "Fine. You take good care of my brother. Tell them both I said goodbye. I can't do it. I'm a pussy."

Livia turned her back on him, not wanting to seem upset. She gave him a two-minute head start, making sure she was far from Blake's fast arms and in full view of everyone. Livia went down as hard as she dared, her hands catching her despite her willing them not to.

But her ruse worked. She heard shocked gasps and quickly felt Blake's assessing hands. She could barely hear the motorcycle revving over the booming music. She waited until it faded before she opened her eyes. Ted appeared at Blake's side, looking concerned. After a quick evaluation he declared Livia fine. She made a point to tell those gathered she hadn't eaten all day.

Blake escorted her, like she was made of blown glass, over to the dessert table. He sat her down and carefully extracted a cupcake from the tower of confections that served as their wedding cake. After Blake broke tradition and fed only her, she made a miraculous recovery and survived to feed him as well. But when she saw her father watching them, shaking his head, she knew her act hadn't fooled him. However, he was still here, so it seemed he'd decided to let Beckett go — at least for now. Livia gave him a warm smile, so thankful he was her dad, and not strictly a police officer. She vowed to talk to him later — to clear Beckett's name of at least this offense.

Once Livia had thoroughly convinced Blake she was fine, he asked her formally to join him in the center of the floor. He took off his jacket and slipped it over her shoulders. Now, with her train bustled and her veil removed, she could settle deep into Blake's arms. Blake had picked the song for their first dance, and Livia laughed when she realized they'd selected music by the same artist, just different songs. She stopped laughing when she heard the lyrics. None present could miss the deeply felt meaning in the words.

The artist sang of dreams and a home. Blake moved slowly with Livia, and she could feel the lyrics vibrating in his chest as he sang softly with the music. Livia tilted her head so she could watch him mouth *home*. She loved the word on his lips and touched them with her fingertips. Blake stopped singing to kiss her hand. He took his gaze off of Livia to take in the guests surrounding the dancefloor. While the couple danced, the partygoers had lit floating lanterns. Blake and Livia were now surrounded by huge, glowing orbs.

With the last strains of the song's guitar, the group released the lanterns, which took flight like little hot-air balloons. As they climbed silently into the dark heavens, Livia spun and leaned her head against Blake's chest. He wrapped his arms around her, and together they watched the floating lights get smaller and smaller.

Livia took Blake to the gift table when the quiet show was over. She pulled Beckett's crumpled envelope from behind a box. "He gave me this, and he left. He told me to tell you goodbye."

Blake nodded and hesitated before taking the envelope. When he finally opened it, he found a simple account number and instructions in Eve's handwriting inside. Livia and Blake looked at each other in silence. Then Blake pulled another paper from the envelope: a reservation at a bed and breakfast in Rhinebeck. Blake nuzzled Livia's neck. "Now this I know what to do with. You've been my bride. I promise to spend all night making you my wife."

50

LOSE COUNT

Blake smiled, and Livia felt absolutely sure as he unlocked their room at the bed and breakfast. She waited, knowing what was next from her traditional husband. Blake stepped inside, set Livia's overnight bag on the floor, and flipped the light switch. He came out and smiled.

His eyes were a little glassy from the champagne Beckett had forced on him. She wondered if his lips still held a bit of bubbly. When she kissed him his perfect taste did have a hint of celebration left in it.

"May I escort you inside, Mrs. Hartt?"

Livia bit her lower lip and nodded.

Blake scooped her up.

To be carried was such a basic thing. And yet it felt...*Primal? Almost. Religious? Maybe.*

She focused on his deep, even breaths as he maneuvered through the doorway. Livia laughed a little at herself. She was grateful for the simple act of Blake's breathing.

Blake set her down gently and began exploring the room. Livia took his tux jacket off her shoulders and rested it on the back of a chair. After a moment he emerged from the bathroom with a wicked smile and proceeded to light candle after candle from the supply he'd located in a cabinet. Soon the room flickered with tiny flames everywhere and smelled of hot, pecan-scented wax.

She snapped off the overhead light. Blake hit play on her iPod, which he'd propped up on its speakers, and a slow, sexy song gave Livia tingles.

They stood facing one another, he in his tux, she in her white gown. The night was meant for them, for this. Shyness crept up the train of her dress and found its way to her cheeks. How she could be shy now, with him, was beyond her. Maybe because they were legally required to make love. Maybe because the look in his eyes was that of a hungry man.

"I want to change. Can you help me with this zipper?" she asked.

Blake spun her around, as if they were executing a dance step.

"Lift your hair." His breath tickled her ear.

She complied with her husband's wish and held her hair out of the way. He opened the zipper slowly. Livia held her breath as he traced the V her dress framed on her skin.

"Change if you must, but leave the heels on, please."

Livia wondered if all new brides had their knees refuse to bend after hearing their husband's lustful requests. Blake gently pulled the tiara from her hair and set it on the nightstand. Livia quickly grabbed her overnight bag, afraid he would distract her from changing. In the bathroom she traded her wedding dress for a cream-colored satin slip with spaghetti straps and hints of lace. She slid her heels back on and checked her hair once more.

She opened the bathroom door to see the room bathed in golden candlelight, pulsing like a beating heart. Blake sat on the bed, his tux tie undone along with the first few buttons of his shirt.

Blake stood when she stepped into the room. He held his hand out, and she gently put her hand and her trust in his. The scent of the candles and the look in his eyes were intoxicating.

He moved to stand behind her. "How many times did I watch you? So many. Wondering what you smelled like, right here." He lifted her hair and grazed his nose along the nape of her neck. "Exactly like fresh snow." Blake grabbed two fistfuls of her hair, letting his lips brush her ear.

"And how often did I wonder what you tasted like?" He used her hair to turn her head. He leaned down to sample her lips. "Vanilla and lust." He leaned down and ran his hands up her calves. "When you wore heels to the station? I couldn't think for hours about anything other than this curve, right here behind your knee."

She felt a chill of anticipation. He stood again, this time in front of her, and sculpted her shape against the satin of her nightgown.

"There isn't a single spot I'll miss tonight, my wife." Blake pulled her against him, tilting her head until he could kiss her again. His fingers and lips made her moan. He placed a hand on her stomach and the other behind her neck. "How many times can I make you come before you can't take it anymore?"

His green eyes smoldered, and his lips smirked. Livia felt her mouth go dry at the thought of his plans for her body.

"I think we might have one to count already." Livia gave him an embarrassed smile.

"Really? Just from talking? Imagine what'll happen when you feel my tongue inside you." Blake backed her up against the bed.

"Get on the bed, Livia. That lingerie is about to be a very pretty necklace." She sat and waited. Blake removed his tie. He kept his eyes on hers as he threaded the silky fabric around her wrists. "Is this okay?"

Livia smiled at his perpetual concern and nodded. He grabbed her around the waist and put her in the center of the bed, then stood and admired her.

"I love you so much, I think there are burn marks on my heart." Blake touched his chest.

"Do they hurt?" Livia wondered aloud with a wink.

"Only when I'm not holding you." Blake trailed his fingertips from her ankle to the top of her thigh.

"Hold me always then. I'm yours." Livia batted her lashes playfully until one of his hands gripped her gently bound wrists, and the other abandoned her leg to trace her jaw.

Blake kissed her lips until she finally fidgeted with anticipation.

"Wait. I do believe there's champagne, according to the receipt. Some for you?" Blake left her to open the mini-fridge.

Livia sat up and held out her clam-shaped hands. "How am I going to manage that? You've captured me."

She batted her lashes again. He stopped and looked at her, his hands full of champagne, flutes, and a glass bowl full of strawberries. Blake bit his tongue.

After a deep sigh he gave Livia a command. "Do not do that again. I'm trying to exercise some self-control here."

Livia pouted and batted her lashes some more.

He smiled and shook his head. "Damn it. You'll pay for that."

He put a champagne glass in her hands. Her job was to hold it still, he explained. Blake made an elaborate show of popping the cork and filling her glass. The gentle snaps of bubbles in the gold liquid tickled Livia's nose.

Blake stopped her from taking a sip. He dipped a deep red strawberry into the liquid instead. He tilted her head back gently with his fingertips and outlined her lips with the wet berry.

Livia parted her lips and tickled the tip of the strawberry with her tongue.

Blake knelt on the bed next to her, mesmerized.

"More champagne, please?" she asked, licking her lips.

Blake re-dipped the berry. She traced a circle around it again with her tongue and then scraped it gently with her teeth. He pulled the strawberry away and let it tumble to the floor. Their kiss tasted of champagne, berry, and victory.

"You ready?" He took the glass from her hands and set it on the nightstand.

"Yes." Livia shook her head so her hair tumbled around her shoulders.

He pulled her hands above her head by the tie. "Do you remember the pattern, Livia?"

"Blow…lick…bite." Livia wanted to say something cute, something funny, but he licked his lips and she forgot how to make any more words.

He moved the satin up over her hips, revealing her stomach. He seemed completely absorbed by the sight of her panting. He took his sweet time in removing her panties, sliding them carefully down her legs. She could feel his excitement as he crawled back up her body, pulling the hem of her slip to reveal even more of her with the movement.

He drew the fabric even higher until finally, her breasts were revealed for his eyes. Bare. To him, for him — she was bare.

His mouth took a journey it had been obviously plotting for quite some time. She kept track as he blew a gentle stream on her ear, down her neck, across one breast, circling her nipple slowly, and to the other breast. The other nipple received an up and down pattern. Then he traveled down the side of her ribs to the curve of her hip and slowly across her stomach to linger there.

She began to swear and pray at the same time when he skipped down to her knee. As if his breath could move matter, she opened her legs. He continued his travels to her ankle, then up her other leg until he had nowhere else to go. His five o'clock shadow scratched her inner thigh.

In me. Come in me. Have me.

Livia heard her thoughts echoing in the room and realized she'd said them out loud. His hands gripped her thighs, letting her know this was becoming impossible for him.

"Lick, Blake. That's next." Livia watched as he growled on his way to her ear.

"You're going to kill me. God, you smell so good." Blake let his clever tongue find its way on her skin.

The ear, the neck, the breasts, slow circles and up and down, the curve of her body, the thighs, the ankle. He stopped the relentless assault to take off his shirt. His chest was hard and tempting, with the scars from his move to save her carved forever on his skin.

Oh, God.

With that, finally, finally, his scratchy jaw and strong shoulders were where she needed him more than anything.

He paused until she locked eyes with him. "Count, Livia. Count out loud when you come for me."

Blake's tongue eased her need. Pure talent and muscle. She wanted his hands, she wanted his fingers. But he only gave her his mouth.

"Two, oh, three, God, oh, God."

Blake pulled himself up to nibble her ear with a look of sheer determination.

"Screw the biting. Just please, just more," she begged.

Livia realized her hands were free when she found them on his chest, tracing his trauma. His tie was nowhere in sight. Her flailing must have freed her.

He held himself above her, grinding his teeth as she ran her hands along his skin, finding his belt and zipper.

He cupped a handful of her breast, and she stilled, pressing into his hand.

"Biting is next," he said.

True to his word, Blake continued with her ear, then nibbled her neck.

By the time he was nibbling circles, she was counting again. "Four—your hands, use your hands."

Blake groaned again. He nibbled his way over to her side, his teeth becoming more insistent. One nip to her inner thigh and Livia arched her back. When Blake's face nestled between her legs again, he held true to his penchant for patterns: nibbling, testing, driving.

"Five...six...seven. I'm never going to stop..." She was almost panicked in her frenzy.

Blake stood and let his unbuttoned pants fall to the floor. When Livia saw him for all he was worth, she thanked God again. After all the teasing, after the panting and begging, they were here, in front of one another, starting their marriage. Livia stood on the bed and half bounced over to him, towering above his messy hair with her body once again covered by satin. He kicked off his shoes and socks, his eyes never leaving her. She tilted his face toward hers and took the straps off her shoulders, letting the glossy cloth slide to the floor.

"Make me lose count, Blake Hartt."

Livia let him lift her and guide her body onto him.

Joined. Inside. Together.

"I love you," they breathed.

His legs were powerful, his balance extraordinary, his sex, perfection. Inside Livia there was a spot made just for him. He laid her on the bed so he could find it again and again—so hard and so completely that she was useless by the time he finally gave in to his own release.

They laughed and cuddled in the wake of their ecstasy. Livia curled around the warmth of his skin, suddenly shivering from their exertion.

"Whoever said marriage is boring didn't marry you!" Livia kissed his cheek. "Thank you for that."

Blake kissed her forehead. "That was okay for you?"

"No, that made my orgasms have orgasms, so it was anything but okay." She smiled.

Blake propped himself up on an elbow to stroke her face. "My beautiful wife, welcome to forever."

Livia's eyes filled with grateful tears.

Blake brushed them away. "Now you cry? After I've made love to you?"

"It's just that you're the kindest person in the world. And you're here with me. I'll never stop feeling lucky." She burrowed her face into his warm hug. She felt his kiss on her hair.

"Livia, the luck belongs to me," he whispered. "The kindness belongs to you. One lifetime will never be enough for us."

ACKNOWLEDGMENTS

First, always and ever, to my son and daughter: You are air for me. I'm happier when I can see your faces. I love you both so very much.

Todd: This thing we've got? It's everything that matters. I'm very lucky you put up with me. I love you.

To Mom and Dad S: I can be anything because you were crazy enough to try everything. You taught me unconditional love, and I feel that lovely blanket of support from you every day.

To Mom and Dad D: You're in here. This book is the best I can do to let more people know how amazing you are.

Pam: Thanks for remembering my past, believing in my future, and being the only sister I could ever want. Wonder twins unite.

To my little nephew: You blow me away. Those are some wonderful parents you picked! I love you.

To the aunts and uncles: You've always been there, but to be here too? You guys know how to do love so very big.

To Kim, Jo, The Poughkeepsie Street Team, My Angels and Vixens, The Bookshelves Girls, UU group, and the readers that took a chance on reading a crazy story: You gave me so very much. Thank you!

Shannon: You I'm keeping. Your soul is gorgeous, funny, and endless. Your designs, time, edits, and late-night chats have kept me from tearing out my hair.

To Micha: For now and for back then, having you here has been wonderful.

Karen: To a friendship that stays strong through piles of years. Your voice is one I welcome in my ear. Your guidance and cheerleading make risks seem reasonable.

To the ladies at work who are reading this stuff: Let's all pretend we didn't read the romance scenes. Okay? And thank you so much for reading.

To the real John McHugh: If I'm not having a good time, it's my own goddamn fault. You're not here but you'll never be gone. Aaron and Bea: Wish you were here. Florence: The conversation we aren't having is so loud. Ted: What an honor to be your granddaughter.

To the Omnific staff and authors: What a fun ride. I'm proud to be on it with you. Elizabeth, thank you for treating my dream with such respect and care.

Jessica Royer Ocken: You do to my words what my heart wants to see. You read my mind, and you understand the characters, the commas, and the plot like a superhero. I'm so glad someone tricked you into working with me. ;)

ABOUT THE AUTHOR

Debra Anastasia is busy, just like every other mom. There's dinner, the dogs, the kids, and their homework. The laundry pile turns into a big, heaping monster. When the clothes finally make it into the washer, it gets unbalanced and puts on an elaborate show before it cuts out. This crazy job that never ends is her first love and her crowning achievement.

Her writing started a decent handful of years ago when along with the dogs, cat, kids, and husband, the voices of characters started whispering stories in Debra's ear. Insomnia was the gateway for the plots that wouldn't give up, wouldn't let go. In the shower, a twist would take hold and—dripping and frenzied—she'd find somewhere, anywhere to write it down.

Debra grew up in New York and got a bachelor's degree in political science at SUNY New Paltz. At the start of her marriage, she moved to southern Maryland with her husband. She still doesn't trust crabs and all their legs, though everyone else in her family thinks they're delicious. Her favorite hobbies include knitting, painting furniture and wall murals, and slapping clowns.

Earlier this year Omnific Publishing published her debut novel, *Crushed Seraphim*, and she's currently pounding out the sequel to angel Emma's adventures. You can visit her website at DebraAnastasia.com and find her on twitter @Debra_Anastasia .

check out these titles from
OMNIFIC PUBLISHING

◄ ┈ ►Contemporary Romance◄ ┈ ►

Boycotts & Barflies and *Trust in Advertising* by Victoria Michaels
Passion Fish by Alison Oburia and Jessica McQuinn
The Small Town Girl series: *Small Town Girl* & *Corporate Affair*
by Linda Cunningham
Stitches and Scars by Elizabeth A. Vincent
Take the Cake by Sandra Wright
Pieces of Us by Hannah Downing
The Way That You Play It by BJ Thornton
The Poughkeepsie Brotherhood series: *Poughkeepsie* & *Return to Poughkeepsie*
by Debra Anastasia
Cocktails & Dreams & *The Art of Appreciation* by Autumn Markus
Recaptured Dreams and *All-American Girl* and *Until Next Time* by Justine Dell
Once Upon a Second Chance by Marian Vere
The Englishman by Nina Lewis
16 Marsden Place by Rachel Brimble
Sleepers, Awake by Eden Barber
The Runaway Year by Shani Struthers
Hydraulic Level Five by Sarah Latchaw
Fix You by Beck Anderson
Just Once by Julianna Keyes
The WORDS series: *The Weight of Words* by Georgina Guthrie
Theatricks by Eleanor Gwyn-Jones
The Sacrificial Lamb by Elle Fiore

◄ ┈ ►New Adult◄ ┈ ►

Three Daves by Nicki Elson
Streamline by Jennifer Lane
Shades of Atlantis by Carol Oates
The Heart series: *Beside Your Heart* & *Disclosure of the Heart*
by Mary Whitney
Romancing the Bookworm by Kate Evangelista
Fighting Fate by Linda Kage
Flirting with Chaos by Kenya Wright

← ⟶ Young Adult ← ⟶

The Ember series: *Ember* & *Iridescent* by Carol Oates
Breaking Point by Jess Bowen
Life, Liberty, and Pursuit by Susan Kaye Quinn
The Embrace series: *Embrace* & *Hold Tight* by Cherie Colyer
Destiny's Fire by Trisha Wolfe
The Reaper series: *Reaping Me Softly* & *UnReap My Heart* by Kate Evangelista

← ⟶ Erotic Romance ← ⟶

The Keyhole series: *Becoming sage (book one)* by Kasi Alexander
The Keyhole series: *Saving sunni (book two)* by Kasi & Reggie Alexander
The Winemaker's Dinner: *Appetizers* & *Entrée* by Dr. Ivan Rusilko & Everly Drummond
The Winemaker's Dinner: *Dessert* by Dr. Ivan Rusilko

← ⟶ Paranormal Romance ← ⟶

The Light series: *Seers of Light, Whisper of Light,* & *Circle of Light*
by Jennifer DeLucy
The Hanaford Park series: *Eve of Samhain* & *Pleasures Untold* by Lisa Sanchez
Immortal Awakening by KC Randall
The Seraphim series: *Crushed Seraphim* & *Bittersweet Seraphim*
by Debra Anastasia
The Guardian's Wild Child by Feather Stone
Grave Refrain by Sarah M. Glover
Divinity by Patricia Leever
Blood Vine series: *Blood Vine* & *Blood Entangled* by Amber Belldene
Divine Temptation by Nicki Elson
Love in the Time of the Dead by Tera Shanley

← ⟶ Historical Romance ← ⟶

Cat O' Nine Tails by Patricia Leever
Burning Embers by Hannah Fielding
Good Ground by Tracy Winegar

Romantic Suspense

Whirlwind by Robin DeJarnett
The CONduct Series: *With Good Behavior* & *Bad Behavior* &
On Best Behavior by Jennifer Lane
Indivisible by Jessica McQuinn
Between the Lies by Alison Oburia

Anthologies

A Valentine Anthology including short stories by
Alice Clayton ("With a Double Oven"),
Jennifer DeLucy ("Magnus of Pfelt, Conquering Viking Lord"),
Nicki Elson ("I Don't Do Valentine's Day"),
Jessica McQuinn ("Better Than One Dead Rose and a Monkey Card"),
Victoria Michaels ("Home to Jackson"), and
Alison Oburia ("The Bridge")

Singles and Novellas

It's Only Kinky the First Time (Keyhole series) by Kasi Alexander
Learning the Ropes (Keyhole series) by Kasi & Reggie Alexander
The Winemaker's Dinner: RSVP by Dr. Ivan Rusilko
The Winemaker's Dinner: No Reservations by Everly Drummond
Big Guns by Jessica McQuinn
Concessions by Robin DeJarnett
Starstruck by Lisa Sanchez
New Flame by BJ Thornton
Shackled by Debra Anastasia
Swim Recruit by Jennifer Lane
Sway by Nicki Elson
Full Speed Ahead by Susan Kaye Quinn
The Second Sunrise by Hannah Downing
The Summer Prince by Carol Oates
Whatever it Takes by Sarah M. Glover
Clarity (A *Divinity* prequel single) by Patricia Leever
A Christmas Wish (A *Cocktails & Dreams* single) by Autumn Markus
Late Night with Andres by Debra Anastasia

coming soon from
OMNIFIC PUBLISHING

Client n° 5 by Joy Fulcher
Vice, Virtue & Video: Revealed (book 1) by Bianca Giovanni
Blood Reunited (Blood Vine series, book 3) by Amber Belldene
Keeping the Peace (The Small Town Girl series, book 3) by Linda Cunningham
St. Kate of the Cupcake: The Dangers of Lust and Baking by L.C. Fenton
The Plan by Qwen Salsbury
Legendary by LH Nicole
Kiss Me Goodnight by Michele Zurlo
Fatal by TA Brock
Blind Man's Bargain by Tracy Winegar

CPSIA information can be obtained at www.ICGtesting.com
Printed in the USA
BVOW04s011603121214

3774472BV00001B/52/P